J. Furniss Ogle

**Life and Missionary Travels of the Rev. J. Furniss Ogle**

J. Furniss Ogle

**Life and Missionary Travels of the Rev. J. Furniss Ogle**

ISBN/EAN: 9783337209070

Printed in Europe, USA, Canada, Australia, Japan

Cover: Foto ©Raphael Reischuk / pixelio.de

More available books at **www.hansebooks.com**

# LIFE

AND

# MISSIONARY TRAVELS

OF THE

## REV. J. FURNISS OGLE, M.A.,

FROM

### HIS LETTERS, SELECTED BY HIS SISTER,

AND EDITED BY

## REV. J. A. WYLIE, LL.D.

————

LONDON:

LONGMANS, GREEN, AND CO.

1873.

# PREFATORY NOTE.

THE preparation of a Memoir of the Rev. John Furniss Ogle was begun soon after his death, by his sister, Miss Jane Ogle. Her tender love and deep reverence for her brother would have greatly lightened her labours, but she had proceeded only a little way beyond selecting the letters that were to form the body of the biography when she too was called away. After Miss Ogle's decease the present writer was requested to undertake the task by the surviving brother, Dr William Ogle of Derby. After a good deal of hesitation, arising solely from mistrust of his fitness for the task, he consented. He can only say that he has found the study of Mr Ogle's character very profitable to himself, and he doubts not that, with the Divine blessing, the record of it here presented will be equally profitable to the reader.

NOTE.—The reader will please observe that Chap. II., pp. 5-9, giving the Pedigree of the Ogles, should be headed A.D. 1066-1823.

# CONTENTS.

## CHAPTER IX.

## CHAPTER X.

## CHAPTER XI.

## CHAPTER XII.

## CHAPTER XIII.

## CHAPTER XIII.*

## CHAPTER XIV.

## CHAPTER XV.

* NOTE.—This chapter should have been numbered XIV.

# CHAPTER I.

## INTRODUCTION.

### THE SOLDIERS OF THE SWORD AND THE SOLDIERS OF THE CROSS.

THE winter of 1865-6 was an unusually tempestuous one. Great storms swept the seas : oft-recurring wrecks strewed the shore, and frequent tales of calamity and disaster filled the columns of the daily papers. The first three and the last three months of 1865 were fatally marked in this respect. The registered number of shipwrecks during that period, as given in "The Times," was 766, involving the loss of not fewer than 1656 lives.

On one of the first days of December in that year, the French mail-steamer Borysthène, left the port of Marseilles for Oran. The voyage proved a stormy one, but now the steamer was off the coast of Algeria. It was Friday the 15th December ; the night was dark ; the wind and sea were high ; the captain looked anxiously for the light-house, which ought to have been visible, for, according to his reckoning, he was in the neighbourhood of Mersa-el-Keber. He sent a sailor aloft to search the darkness for the friendly beacon, but no light could he see. Alas! the captain had mistaken his course, and before the man could descend from the mast-head, and make him aware of his error, the vessel had struck on the rocks to the north of Ila Plane, and the waves sweeping over her, from thirty to forty of the passengers were washed overboard.

Among those who, on that night of darkness and tempest, found a grave in the sea, was the Rev. John Furniss Ogle, who was returning to Oran, Algeria, where he had been endeavouring to form a refuge for Spanish Protestants. It is the life of this man which we propose to write.

We do not think that we need begin our labours with an apology. The memoir which, in a dependence on help from above, we have undertaken to write, is that of a no ordinary man, and no ordinary missionary. Mr Ogle possessed a rare combination of excellences and gifts ; and his career, so suddenly cut short, in the manner we have described above, has about it points of great and peculiar interest. The narrative of his labours will be found, if we do not mistake, to stand apart among missionary biographies, having an attraction all its own, and that attraction springing out of itself, and not borrowed from any extrinsic source or art. To a degree not realized, so far as we are aware, in any other who ever went forth into heathendom, John Furniss Ogle combined the two characters of Christian traveller, and volunteer missionary.

Mr Ogle travelled and evangelized in many countries, European and African, and among diverse tribes of both eastern and western origin. The scene of his labours lay successively among his countrymen at home, among the natives of Patagonia, among Spaniards, Moors, Arabs, and Jews. Wherever he went, whether his tent was pitched on the *despoblados* of Spain, or among the sons of Ishmael on the plains of Algeria, whether he wandered by the Guadalquiver, or rested under the shadow of Mount Atlas, Mr Ogle was ever the English gentleman, urbane, kindly, trustful, generous, and magnanimous of spirit. He observed with the eye of a poet, he reflected with the depth of a philosopher, and he wrote with the elegance and taste of an accomplished scholar. His sketches of landscape are remarkably vivid and fresh. Artistic they truly are ; but they display a faculty of a higher order than art, and which is moral rather than æsthetic : an intense sympathy with nature, which puts a *soul* into his simplest touches, and gives them a power to go to the heart of the reader, so that he sees more than is on the page before him, and feels that he is the better for having beheld the scenes over which the traveller conducts him. But the traveller in Mr Ogle is ever subordinate to the missionary. No one can read a line of what he wrote, or accompany him a single step in his career without seeing that his motive-power was the love of Christ. And from that cardinal grace flowed in him every other ; entire devotedness, utter forgetfulness of self, a tender yearning over men in darkness, and unwearied efforts if by any means he might find an entrance for the light of God's Word into their understandings, and the love of the Saviour into their hearts. He in whom these graces dwelt was humble as a child ; but the natural endowments and gracious dispositions of the man could not be hid. They were around him and about him like a balmy air, and they left a line of light on the track over which he passed.

In ages to come, when the world's career shall be surveyed from a much more advanced stage than the present, the great pioneers of its march will be seen to have been not its warriors, not its statesmen, not its philosophers, but its missionaries. From the beginning the line of civilization has lain alongside that of the revelation of the plan of Redemption. Arts, knowledge and liberty have never preceded— they have always followed in the wake of supernatural truth. When the latter has stood still or gone back, decadence and extinction have overtaken the former. The one progressive power in the world is Christianity. Civilization apart from the gospel has no capacity of advance, no capacity even of endurance. Its career is a revolving cycle, emerging from barbarism and returning to barbarism. The world's wise men can have no golden age in their future : for the whole history of the race is just a demonstration of the utter inability of mere intellectual and political amelioration to rise above a certain point. Egypt, Greece, Rome, and in modern times, Italy and France are but successive demonstrations of this one fact. They made trial, one after the other, if haply they might reach a condition of stable civilization and of regulated and permanent liberty; but one after the other failed. They went on prosperously till they reached the fated line, but over it they found it impossible to pass; the laws which the Great Ruler has implanted in human society have fixed the "hitherto but no further" of mere intellectual and political progress, and from hence the night of barbarism has again closed in. The gospel is the only road by which the nations can advance to a stage from which they will never more fall back: and for this simple reason that the gospel is not only a force which propels and a law which restrains, it is above all a power which transforms; and being, moreover a scheme of individual and corporate life in perfect harmony with the government of the Eternal, it shuts out the possibility of collision with the Power that governs the universe. The gospel, then, alone is history, because it alone is progress. The wars and greatness of political empires will one day be forgotten like a nursery tale. Not so the labours of the missionary. The pen of inspiration in primitive times turned away from the conquests of the Roman arms to dwell on the footsteps of Paul, and record the victories of the first missionaries. It is not the "Acts," of emperors, but the "Acts of Apostles" which we have in the New Testament. Blessed are they who follow them in this great work. The missionary is not writing on the sand, where the returning tide will obliterate the impressions he makes, his labour is for all time. He is laying, under the great master-builder, the foundations of an empire which will fill the earth, and flourish in glory when all other empires have fallen.

On the pillars of that glorious edifice will his name be inscribed for ever. Stars, of apparently greater magnitude, will sink below the horizon: his will keep its place, and be seen shining across the ages. So hath the mouth of the Lord spoken. "And they that be wise shall shine as the brightness of the firmament; and they that turn many to righteousness as the stars for ever and ever" (Dan. xii. 3).

## CHAPTER II.

### THE OGLES.

#### A.D. 800-1700

THE family of OGLE is of historic interest, being one of the ancient families of Old England.

The town and manor of Ogle was granted to "Humphrey Ogle" by William the Conqueror "to hold as freely as he had possessed it in former times." This is recorded upon a monument in the south wall of Bothal Church, county Northumberland. Upon these lands a castle was built by permission of King Edward III., and the owner was called by writ of summons to Parliament as one of the Barons of England by Edward IV.

Very few vestiges of the ruins of the castle now remain, and the title has been for more than two centuries in abeyance.

The subject of the following memoir was lineally descended from that branch of this family, one of whom, in the troublous times of the sixteenth century, left Northumberland and became possessed of lands in the township of Flamborough in Yorkshire. A portion of these lands was inherited by John F. Ogle on his father's death (1850). By this possession he was able freely to devote the best years of his life to mission-

ary and other benevolent pursuits. It is to the memory of
these ancestors rather than to those whose names might be
traced back into the earliest records from which English history is drawn, that allusion is sometimes made in the following
letters. It was a favourite theory with him that the "emi-
gration" took place in order that, in a secluded village in his
own country, his ancestor might enjoy that freedom of conscience which, at a subsequent period, liberty-loving Englishmen
sought on a distant shore across the Atlantic. The true cause,
however, of the removal of a portion of the family from Northumberland to Yorkshire is now unknown. This much only
is certain, that they were God-fearing and benevolent men,
and that they left behind them examples which it is pleasant
to remember and which it will be well to follow.

An illustrative incident may be not unacceptable. It sheds
light on the Ogles as a race of sturdy philanthropists, who
took a hearty interest in the welfare of those they lived
amongst, and spared themselves in neither purse nor person
in order to promote it ; and it reveals noble traits in the
fishermen of Flamborough, who showed that they could appreciate sterling character, and were not content unless they
could express their gratitude by deeds as substantial as those
which had called it forth.

About a century and a half since a succession of unfavourable seasons had reduced to comparative poverty many of the
inhabitants of Flamborough, who were then, as now, chiefly
fishermen, or in some way dependent upon the sea for their
livelihood. The tithe levied upon all the fish that was caught
in the waters had long been a burden, and in the time of
scarcity its pressure was felt with peculiar severity. As the
legality of the impost was doubted by some, the question was
tried on behalf of the poor fishermen by Mr William Ogle,
who went to London and successfully carried the case through
the Courts. This triumph, doubtless, gave the man who had

won it a purer joy than if it had been gained for himself. But it was dashed with misfortune. The same messenger which brought to the inhabitants the news of their success in the courts of law, brought also the sad intelligence that their bene-factor had fallen ill of the fever called the black death, and lay at extremity. That intelligence was quickly followed by tidings yet more melancholy—even that Mr Ogle was dead. The grief of the fishermen may be imagined. There was not a family in Flamborough but felt they had lost a friend, and the mourning was universal. Mr Ogle had endeared himself to the people by many previous acts of kindness. But this last effort was a more important one. Its benefits would extend to the whole district, and not to those then living only but to their descendants after them. Family feeling is a distinguish-ing trait in these rough but honest and warm-hearted fisher-men, and it was resolved that the man who had died in their service should lie amongst them. Now came the contest who of these worthy people should have the honour of bringing home the precious remains. Their choice was soon made; and all acknowledged that it had fallen on the most adven-turous and skilful among them, and that the boat destined for this service, belonging to one named Cross, was the triggest and strongest of all the craft accustomed to ply in the stormy waters of Flamboro'-head. To London and back was a long voyage for a fishing-boat. The skiff, however, departed, and holding her southerly course, was soon lost to the eye. After the stated number of days she re-appeared in the offing, bearing bravely up toward Flamborough, and on board were the honoured remains she had gone to bring back; and so William Ogle, "the poor man's friend," was buried by the side of his fathers in the family vault beneath the south chan-cel aisle of the parish church. The whole town went into mourning for him, and a resolution was passed that when any of the family happened to reside in the place they should be

supplied with the best of their fish free of cost.  Miss Ogle
says, in her notes, that she had met with an aged fisherman
who was known as a descendant of one of the brave men who
sailed to London on this interesting errand.  The incident we
have just related has received mention in the parish register
books, where it may still be read.  Pleasant it is to record
such memories.  They are links between the present and the
past generations, for the descendants of these men at this day
line our sea-girt shores.  The influence of such reciprocal acts
of kindness is incalculable in strengthening the foundations of
the State, in conciliating interests which, though distinct,
are not antagonistic, and in uniting classes, which, though
separated as regards the place they occupy in the common
body, are not separated as regards the stake they have in
the common weal.  The base-stone and the keystone are
parted by the entire space occupied by the arch, but both are
equally parts of the arch, and the removal of either would be
ruinous to the fabric.

The region in the neighbourhood of Flamborough-head is
one of very peculiar interest.  It remained, there is reason to
believe, in possession of the ancient Britons after the whole of
England, besides a good part of Scotland, had been subdued
and occupied by the Romans.  The nature of the ground,
which is uneven, and was then covered with dense forests,
favoured the inhabitants, and enabled them to make a stand
before the victorious legions of Agricola and Claudius Cæsar.

In the times of the Ogles, Flamborough was a place of note.
Ancient charters attest its importance.  It has since fallen
behind in the race of progress.  It found powerful rivals in
the neighbouring towns of Bridlington and Hull.  The trading
vessels which visited that part of the coast turned away from
the storm-swept Head, and sought the more sheltered and
commodious harbours of the last-named towns.  Other causes
were adverse to its prosperity.  It is liable to be visited by

rude blasts, and its climate, chilled with eastern haars or drenching rains, is trying, especially in spring, to all but the hardiest constitutions. It is not surprising, therefore, that in process of time the Ogles ceased to live on their ancestral lands, and removed to parts of England lying farther south, and which offered greater attractions.

But when the subject of this memoir grew up, and learned something of the history and character of his ancestors, and the relations which had subsisted between them and the people of Flamborough, the desire began to arise in him to return to the place of his forefathers, and to spend his life as a minister of the gospel among its inhabitants. This idea, he was able in part to realize, although at the risk of bodily health and the sacrifice of many mental tastes. How this came about will appear in the sequel.

---

## CHAPTER III.

### CHILDHOOD AND EARLY YOUTH.

#### 1823-1842.

JOHN FURNISS OGLE was born February 1, 1823, in the rectory house of the parish of Skirbeck, near Boston, in Lincolnshire. He was the eldest son of the Rev. J. F. Ogle, curate in sole charge of that parish. His mother's maiden name was Frances Conington. She was a woman of refined mind, and of much intellectual vigour, which seems to have been inherited by her son. She died before he had attained the age of four years.

His father was distinguished as a man of great clearness of thought; a singularly judicious divine; and an earnest and laborious minister of the gospel. He belonged to that section of the clergy who combine a full acknowledgment of evangelical doctrine with a cordial appreciation of the ritual and the formularies of the Church of England.

He was an eminently conscientious man, reserved in the general expression of his feelings, but his children knew his deep and ever self-denying affection, while his character and conduct impressed them with that kind of feeling expressed by John in a letter written to his brother when he was at Cambridge. "Take no *human* example, not even our father's, as your pattern."

This reverential conviction of the consistency of his father's conduct, and of the Christian influence and principles which prevailed in his father's home was often alluded to by the son, and was cherished to the end of his life. The subject of our memoir owed much in early youth to the careful education and watchfulness of his paternal aunt Charlotte Ogle, who took charge of the four motherless children that were left with her deeply afflicted brother, on the death of his wife. This lady was assiduous in the religious and moral training of those thus committed to her, and by her care John's memory was early stored with considerable portions of Holy Scripture. His conscience also was informed as to his privileges and responsibilities as a member of Christ's visible Church, admitted by baptism, and a child of God by parental dedication, as were the infants of God's people of old.

The plan pursued by his aunt was to store his mind with the very words of the Bible. She did not prescribe large portions at a time; but whatever she did prescribe she insisted should be accurately got by heart, and by the repetition at intervals of the passages thus learned she made sure of their being retained in the memory. The value of such a training it is impossible to over-estimate. Wherever it is conscientiously followed, accompanied with prayer, it will result, in nine cases out of ten, in a manhood of piety, and an old age, should it be reached, of honour. The memory is the earliest mental power to be developed, and advantage ought to be taken of this, to store it with the Word of God. We thus lay up food for the understanding and conscience when these faculties begin to act. The first demands light and knowledge for its expansion, the last seeks principles and rules for its guidance; and here they are, collected and ready, in the storehouse of memory. The child so taught has a lamp within, which shines clearer every day; for as his knowledge and his conscience grow, so also does the light. The child whose unhappy lot it is to be deprived of the Bible in infancy, begins his path in darkness, misses the road probably at the very outset; false principles and evil habits grow stronger every day, and should he in after life come into contact with the light, he hates it, or if he embraces it, it is after a terrible conflict with the evil which he had adopted as good, and the false maxims which had been embraced as true. But, say some, "Bible truths learned in childhood will be common-place in the mind, and rejected in after life as the traditions of the nursery." On this principle all knowledge ought to be withheld, the knowledge of God Himself included. Experience has shown that this result does not follow: on the contrary, it shows that what will take place is just the opposite. The truth of the Bible eminently ministers to the soundness of the understanding, and the soundness of the understanding reacts on the Bible; for as that faculty expands, the majesty, beauty, and power of the Word of God are increasingly perceived and appreciated, and all life long there comes a deepening reverence for the Scriptures, to which is added a growing conviction of their truth. Terrible struggles with unbelief in after life is the penalty which those generally have to pay whose opening memory has not been furnished with the truths of the Word of God; they have no weapons when the day of battle comes to fight the enemy, no shield to parry his thrusts, and in too many cases they are vanquished in the conflict;

whereas those who have ready at hand the doctrines of the Bible wherewith to confront the sophistries of a " philosophy falsely so called," either escape these combats altogether, or, if not so fortunate, they triumph in the struggle, and come out of it more firmly persuaded than ever of the truth of God's Word.

Nor does the Bible in the heart dim the sunniness of youth. Religious training wrought no moroseness in the disposition of John Ogle.

On the contrary, the "joyousness of his youth" is mentioned as characteristic by those who knew him. His first tutor, the Rev. J. Sandars, thus writes to his sister respecting him :—" Your brother is well remembered by me as a boy of an amiable and cheerful disposition ; obedient and exemplary in the whole of his conduct. I never knew him have a quarrel with any of his school-mates. He was thoroughly without guile, and free from everything like deceit—as fond of play and innocent mirth as any boy, but neither rude nor boisterous. I cannot say that he was over-fond of books, being disposed to take things easily ; but you felt you could depend upon him both in word and action, and he was always the same.

" The law of kindness was his governing rule, and his conduct ever gave me the impression that he was a conscientious boy, and was under the influence of holy principles.

" Upon one occasion, towards the close of my connection with him, he disclosed to me his earnest desire to serve God, and to benefit others. He had been deeply affected by an address I had given to my pupils upon the necessity of youthful piety, and the impression made upon my own mind by his earnestness will never be effaced. . . . He was about to leave me for Rugby. His chief temptations were yet to come ; his principles to be sifted ; his character tested."

In 1838 he went to Rugby. There he manfully persevered in the daily habit of prayer and reading the Scriptures in spite of the annoyance which he received from some of his school companions. His abhorrence of bad language and of untruthfulness, or unfairness of any kind, drew down upon him much treatment that was hard to bear. Facts of this kind have been narrated by those who were his school-fellows, but he never alluded to them himself farther than in the slight manner of the letter subjoined. The letter, moreover, is a picture of Rugby School from the stand-point of a junior scholar newly arrived :—

"RUGBY, *October* 26, 1838.

" MY DEAR SISTER,—After a pleasant journey my cousin *
and myself arrived at Rugby, and were kindly received by Mr
and Mrs P. The next morning we underwent a short
examination to determine our place in the school. My cousin
was placed in the third form from the top, I in the seventh—
a form lower than I had anticipated. This was, I confess, a
disappointment, though I doubt not it was overruled for my
good by One who cannot err.

" I was at first a good deal ill-treated by my school-fellows
on account of my singularity (you understand me) ; this
has now, I trust, nearly ceased, and I hope it has not been
without a salutary effect. I find myself quite equal to the
duties of my form. There are about forty boys in it, and we
take places and are marked accordingly. Every month Dr.
Arnold examines us, and advances the highest and most
worthy to a higher class.

" Last examination I was second, but the Doctor thought it
advisable that I (as a new boy) should not be advanced so soon
—I rather think I shall be before the end of the half-year.
My cousin was first in his class, but the Doctor declined
advancing him for the same reason. We shall have a grand
examination in about three weeks, when all the half-year's
work will be examined, and whatever *extras* we choose to take
up. I have taken up four subjects, which will oblige me to
fag pretty hard if I wish to cut any figure in the examination.

" There are here about three hundred boys and eight mas-

* The late Professor Conington of Oxford.

ters. The 'sixth,' or first class, are heard by the Doctor, and are called 'præpostors.' They are about thirty in number, and are looked upon by us 'fags' as quite a set of superior beings. They exercise an almost absolute right over the affairs of the school in general, and are authorised to exact any piece of service from the fags, and, whenever they are seen out of the precincts of Rugby by any of the lower half of the school, they must be 'shirked'—*i.e.*, the individual must avoid the 'præpostor' by hiding himself or running away, on pain of a thrashing or a long punishment; and any one who intentionally strikes a 'præpostor' is expelled the school. I will only remark that this fagging is not nearly so disagreeable as I had anticipated. We are forced to keep goal for the players at football every half-holiday (unless some 'præpostor' will excuse us), which often occasions the delay of a letter. Gell* is the only 'præpostor' in our house ; he is always very kind to me, and seldom or never fags me. He also will always excuse me on half-holidays when it is in his power. I should like very much to form a closer intimacy with him, but I fear this is not practicable, on account of the great disparity in our ages and situations in the school.

"There is a neat chapel for the use of the school, where Dr. Arnold officiates. He reads prayers in the morning and preaches in the afternoon. His sermons are very beautiful, and exclusively adapted to his hearers. In short, I cannot conceive a person who should seem better fitted to fill his important station.

" I have a study with J. Conington ; it contains a few book-shelves, two tables, a sofa and chairs, and is decorated by engravings of our Saviour by Carlo Dolci, of the Last Supper by Lionardo da Vinci, a small Holy Family, and others. I trust you continue well, and are advancing in your studies, and especially that you may continue to grow in grace and in the knowledge of Jesus Christ, is the sincere prayer of your very affectionate brother,                    J. F. OGLE."

` The following letter, also, among others, shows his apprecia-

* The present Bishop of Madras.

tion of faithful Scriptural teaching, and that he thought others more helpful to him than the Doctor :—

"RUGBY, *March* 15, 1840.

"DEAR SISTER,—We are just come up from prayers, nine o'clock evening, at which, instead of the chapter which Mr Cotton * generally reads before prayer, he this evening read us a familiar discourse of his own composition, in which he proposed to treat of the common vices in a place like this ; and show their sin and consequent danger to our souls. I am sure it would have done you good to have heard the affectionate and earnest terms in which the opening address was couched—they were so plain, yet so touching. He expressed his concern for the existence of such vices, his fear lest this address should seem tedious ; and still he says that the great, nay, infinite importance of the subject must render this fear void, and drown it in duty and concern for the immortal soul. I think the strongest proof possible of the worth of so plain and earnest an exhortation is this. Just as we were leaving the hall where prayers are read, a boy who is addicted to most of the vices prevalent among us, whom I had observed to look unusually attentive, said to another—' Did you not like that which he read just now ?' in such a tone as left no doubt but that what had been read had entered in some degree into his heart. Who can tell but that God may out of us raise up some to glorify His name : well may we pray with our hearts as well as our lips, ' Thy kingdom come.'

" I will tell you of some of the events of this glorious day. Oh that my heart had been in a proper frame to have entered into the duties and exalted pleasures which it might have enjoyed. This afternoon we for once have heard a really good sermon, not from the Doctor, but from the master of our Form, Mr Anstey, who is a very nice man : it was from the Psalms—' I will walk before the Lord in the land of the living ;' and from this he took occasion to show how we might mix religion with our every day business and pleasures—how we might walk with God while the world would not perceive

* Afterward Bishop of Calcutta.

that we were doing any thing but what any one might do ;
he showed how the principle with which we performed any
action made it pleasing or offensive in God's sight.   I really
esteem and love Mr Cotton ; I think he does show a concern
for the spiritual as well as temporal welfare of his pupils, such
as you may almost in vain look for here.   I trust in God's
hands he will be made the instrument of good to some of us
careless sinners.

    This evening I have been reading ' Keith on Prophecy,'
and discussing religious topics with S—— and some others,
who are fond of discoursing on such subjects.   I beg, my
dear sister, you will remember me constantly in your prayers,
that I may increase in diligence and in every Christian grace.
I remain, my dear sister, yours very affectionately,

JOHN.

    In a letter written when he was at Cambridge, he thus
reviews his past life, and records his impression of the effect
for good or for evil of his school career :—

    " I was a piously-disposed child, of godly parents, had a
tender conscience, but was often frivolous, and disposed to the
gratification of my own will. . . . Soon after I had taken
upon me confirmation and sacramental vows, when I was
beginning to feel the power of religious truth in my heart, and
had so much ardour and love to the cause, that I felt I should
never again lose these impressions, I went to Rugby.   There
the teaching was of a very different kind to that to which I
had been accustomed.   The standard which had been given
to me, drawn from the Holy Scripture, as the rule of my life,
was far above that which I now heard preached as the highest
attainable by boys.   A sense of honour, without much religion
or morality, seemed to me to be the principle of the school,
and I began to believe those who told me, that the severe
persecutions which I for some time unflinchingly endured were
self-imposed tortures, and that my religion was fanaticism.
Thus I lost my anchor-hold of true faith in the power of the
Holy Spirit to teach me, and on the love of Christ to support
his servants. . . . and fell from one wickedness to another,

ever abhorring, and still falling into sin, till I gave way to a distrust of God, as if He were the cause of my growing unbelief."

The Christian character of Dr Arnold's teaching, and the high moral standard which he inculcated in a manner especially winning and attractive, is considered by his biographer to have been one great cause of his universally acknowledged success as the head master of one of our most influential public schools, and of his undoubted power in directing the minds of young men. Miss Ogle says in her notes—

"Whether the standard he proposed to their imitation was at all affected by his power of sympathy with his pupils, rather than simply drawn from the Word of God, and based upon the principle of love to Him, it would not be becoming in me to decide. This impression, however, seems to have been produced upon one, who was a thoughtful and attentive listener to his sermons, and who hoped to find in them teaching which would help to make him true to the highest aspirations of which he was conscious, and to preserve that enjoyment in his approaches to God as a reconciled Father in heaven, of which he had already had some experience."

From Rugby the subject of our memoir went for a year to the Rev. Thomas Scott of Wappenham, previous to entering upon a university career. It was his father's plan to spare no expense in the education of his sons rather than to make a pecuniary provision for them. He also wished to give time for decision as to the choice of a profession. In 1842 John Ogle went to Jesus College, Cambridge, where his father had held a fellowship.

# CHAPTER IV.

## LIFE AT CAMBRIDGE.

WE are now briefly to trace Mr Ogle's career at Cambridge, whither he removed, as we have said, in 1842. There is no more overmastering passion than the thirst for knowledge. It is a passion which it is even more hard to resist, and more difficult to appease than some more sordid desires. To accumulate riches, to grasp power, to achieve fame, has each its special fascination, and brings each its special enjoyment, but "to know" is to be "as God." Knowledge is part of that Divine image in which man was made; and the very constitution of his nature impels him to seek out and intermeddle with all mysteries. The desire lies dormant in the savage; it is scarce perceptible in many of the sons of toil, whose daily task of labour overbears the desire "to know;" but the passion once fairly aroused has an intensity and strength which hurries the man in whom it has been awakened onward without the power of pausing, regardless of health, of reason, and sometimes of life itself. This was the side on which the Tempter first approached man. The lure held out was knowledge. Other possessions are exterior to ourselves. Knowledge forms part of our very being, and so has a fascination unknown to other pursuits. The desire of knowledge prompted in the early ages to the study of unlawful arts, and the assumption of super-human powers. In our own day it ensnares and captivates many. In science we trace it in the many theories which set at defiance the first principles of the Inductive philosophy. And though we ought never to forget that knowledge is the glory of man, and that which gives stability to States, and that without it civilisation can neither advance nor be retained, yet the inordinate pursuit of knowledge for its own sake is a besetting sin, and an evil all the more seductive and dangerous that it appears so undeniably innocent, and so truly praiseworthy.

Athirst for knowledge, John Ogle now entered the gates of a renowned and venerable seat of learning. All that he saw and heard bore testimony to the excellency of knowledge. The reverence that waited on the dead, the honour shown to the living, the sumptuous halls, with their rich libraries, in which, as in a palace, dwelt the noblest thoughts of the noblest men of former ages. Their knowledge had exempted them from the common lot of men, for while others were dead, they lived on. It is still the old temptation " to be as gods, and to live for ever." John Ogle was not proof against this snare.

His letters and private diary written during his Cambridge career show that he felt a consuming desire to master all the learning and wisdom whose hoarded treasures were now opened to him. He wished to convey the whole at once into his mind, and he began to work as if this were possible. It is a common mistake. "The end of a University course," as Robertson has remarked, " is not merely the acquisition of knowledge, but chiefly the discipline of the mind." The intense desire for knowledge defeats itself, because it interferes with this discipline. Mr Ogle read much, but not steadily. He was too impatient to pursue the even course day by day and step by step. This spirit of impatience of control, and resistance to authoritative course of action was one of his faults—overruled for good in after life, but at this time and afterwards the source to himself of much sorrow, and of anxiety to his friends. Under the seducing plea of self-improvement he diverged from what seemed to be mere routine into more enticing pastures. His imagination beguiled him from the prescribed path of University study to topics which those studies suggested. He

devoured Carlyle, Mill, Browning, and other writers, even
those which are deservedly tabooed.    He had a circle of
clever students with whom he associated, and from them he
caught the idea that systematic study, or *plodding*, is a con-
temptible thing, an unfailing attribute of dulness, and that
the acquisition of University honours is, after all, an unsatisfactory and insufficient goal of a college life.    These opinions
he afterwards changed, expressing regret that he had ever
entertained them; but meanwhile they operated injuriously,
for he never, after his first successful examination in his
classes, aspired to college honours.  He was not idle, however.
He gave himself heart and soul to work, and his labours were
all the more absorbing and exhausting that they were so mul-
tifarious.    Concurrently with this irregularity in his course of
study, other irregularities of habit and acts of self-indulgence
too common among young men, took hold of him, not the less
to be noted as evil and pernicious that they were not breaches
of discipline such as could come within the cognizance of any
authority than that of an enlightened conscience.    His health
to some extent gave way.    He was subject to great nervous
prostration, which he never entirely lost, and to palpitation,
which made him at times feel certain that he was the subject
of serious and mortal disease of the heart.    In truth, the heart
was at fault, but not the fleshly organ, else he could not have
obtained even temporary relief from boating and out-door
exercise, which always restored him for the time.    It appears
to have been at this season of his life that Mr Ogle acquired
the power of intense mental effort and of physical endurance ;
acquisitions of the highest value, which he never afterwards
lost, although he had always to render an equivalent in the
mental and physical reaction which uniformly succeeded the
period of high-strung excitement and effort.

Reviewing his studies at Cambridge, we find Mr Ogle, in
1860, writing as follows :—

" I have been feverishly anxious to gain knowledge, by learning and by experiment, of many various branches of human pursuit ; not with the idea of perfecting myself in any one, but to acquire a large measure of capability and of power of comprehension. Conceiving wisdom to be the fruit of varied knowledge, rather than of a complete and perfect attainment in any one branch of study."

Mr Ogle's condition at Cambridge has been very touchingly described by his sister :—

" Of his religious life at Cambridge little that is satisfactory can be said. 'A Siberian winter' had fallen upon his soul. He did not join himself heartily to those who were known as decided in their religious opinions. His views upon the sanctity of the Sabbath, upon inspiration, and upon some other questions, were shaken ; he entered into metaphysical enquiry, and to anxious friends at home his mind seemed to be tossed upon the troublous ocean of human speculations, and reasonings on things divine ; in danger of losing his anchor-hold, and of drifting into a restless and miserable scepticism. It was the time of battle between the pride of intellect and the spirit of faith within him ; and though he came forth, not unscathed, out of the battlefield, yet his spiritual life, being sustained by Jesus, survived the agonizing conflict, while by it he was enabled in after years to help those who had fallen into the same temptation, and to sympathise in their sufferings and difficulties.

" He passed through that season described so forcibly by a modern biographer :—' It is an awful moment when the soul begins to find that the props on which it has blindly rested so long, are many of them rotten, and begins to suspect them all ; when it begins to feel the nothingness of many of the traditionary opinions which have been received with implicit confidence, and in that horrible insecurity begins also to doubt whether there be anything to believe at all. It is an awful hour —let him who has passed through it say how awful—when . . . the sky above this universe appears to be a dead expanse black with the void from which God himself has disappeared.'

" There is but one way by which a man may come forth from

this struggle victorious—by continuing in prayer to the unseen, unknown God—and by this way Mr Ogle was at length
led, and he came forth from that hour of agony his feet again
standing upon the Rock, many clouds still above him, but the
clear light shining also, which became more and more bright
unto the perfect day."

To a Christian friend who had written to endeavour to cheer
and to direct him to the Friend of sinners, he thus writes:—

" I scarcely dare reflect on such things, and beyond reading
the Sacred Word to the sick, and taking my class as usual in
the Sunday School, I do not do so.   .   .   .   I look up to the
nocturnal sky, and in the millioned distances which I traverse
by sight, I recognise the infinity of the Being who has made
me and them, and the distance between my heart and Him
seems greater than ever   .   .   .   What I have felt under
the silent influence which the ' roof fretted with golden fire '
exerts on our souls ! Is it not the voice of the Maker of all ?
When the instrument on which it falls is tuned to echoing
harmony, the language of the eighth Psalm is the sublime
response; but my heart is irresponsive.   .   .   .   The message
of mercy you preach is too good news for such as I ; it is sent
to those who are weary and heavy laden, who love God, and long
to become like Him, but my affections are set on this life
still.   Can it be that pardon and free, full salvation is *now*
offered to me ?   I seem rather to be described thus—' The
dead cannot praise Thee '—but you will pray for me, and in
answer to that prayer I may receive a blessing.

"The pride of my heart, and a dislike for the practical demands
of the religion I had come to know somewhat by experimental
acquaintance with its joys, this, and the subtleties of a vain
philosophy, led me almost to become an infidel.   I felt that I
had no *sure* grounds of faith, and acted as if I had none at all,
and now I cannot believe.   God seems to refuse to me the gift
of faith."

How affecting the following words to his sister, July 1846 :—

" There is sadly too little freedom in our social meetings,
and too much worldliness.   We reverse the petition of our

Saviour. We are taken in a sense 'out of the world,' but we carry with us its 'evil.' The enemy of souls now exercises full authority over my darkened spirit.

"I sigh, but cannot trust in Him whom I have neglected to follow after vanities. I have gone without preparation to the Lord's table, and now no preparation will give me comfort or confidence. There are, my beloved sister, those who shall knock when it is too late, some to whose call God will not listen, 'many who shall seek to enter in but shall not be able.'

"Watch you, and pray, and search your heart. 'To whom much is given of them will much be required.' God demands of all an undivided heart. Do not, as you love your soul, delay to examine yourself with all jealousy. I knew not the tempter's insidiousness, nor his power, well as I thought myself instructed. I followed not the good I knew, and I shunned not the evil which I did see. I am justly amenable to God's wrath—the fearful wrath of everlasting displeasure. I once feared lest death should overtake me before I had time to repent, I now fear that a spiritual death may anticipate the temporal.

"Pray for your most unhappy brother JOHN."

To a young friend at Cambridge :—

". . . I entreat you seriously to reflect upon the importance of eternity, the uncertainty of life, and the delusive nature of pleasure. I have tasted some of the highest gratifications, and have sipped the sweets in many cups of pleasure. I have delighted in knowledge and in studying many sciences, have read in almost all languages worth reading, so as to try from each source what pleasure and of what kind it could bestow, and I will not deny that the pursuit of knowledge was pleasant, that of amusement never satisfying. But in the hour of death the value of all joys and of all acquisitions is tested.

"Like the miser, you then feel that you have been toiling for that which you cannot retain. That moment discovers to you clearly a truth which reason's feeble glimmer failed to shew. What is the brightest ray of reason's lamp but a plausible theory which the breath of another world may dissipate?

"There is no wisdom in the pursuit of knowledge for its own sake ; as a means of enabling one to benefit others it is good, but the chief good is, to know how our present life will affect our future existence, and how to secure the highest good for that period. This is the province of God's revelation. . . . . What humility, self-denial, mortification of the evil propensities within our hearts this requires, I need not tell you, but you know the reward. . . . . My dear boy, prayer is the only means by which we can obtain a disposition to choose such a life, strength to embrace it, and grace to persevere unto the end. Ask first for the Holy Spirit to open your mind to *receive the Scriptures with implicit faith.* Then every promise will be your comfort, every command your clear guide, every warning your faithful monitor. This is the sword with which you are to vanquish Satan.

"Our Saviour shewed to us the example in His day of trial. It is plain on all important points, and where it is obscure we may look confidently for direction to Him who gave us the Word to be our guide, . . . and continue to act according to what you know.

"Happy is he that condemneth not himself in that thing which he alloweth. . . . Some of the snares by which Satan now entraps many souls I will name :—(1.) To compare our state with that of others to our own comfort. (2.) To persuade ourselves that the sin we now yield to can be repented of and forsaken hereafter. (3.) To forget that in ourselves there is nothing good ; that our prayers, our disposition towards what is right—anything good—is from the grace of God. If we neglect His grace—think ourselves safe—we fall. Oh how terrible such a fall ! I have thereby been led to seek peace in all manner of vanities, and the near prospect of death alone has aroused me from my delusions."

We have here a veritable picture of a child of light walking in darkness. The case is connected with no little difficulty, for one would scarce have looked for such a dispensation in one whose faith rested on an adequate basis of knowledge. When one becomes pious without much previous instruction, such a conflict is almost inevitable at some time or other. A belief largely traditional cannot go with one through life in the midst of doubts suggested by enlarging knowledge, or boldly propounded by infidelity. The hour of struggle must come, and that struggle will issue in faith being cast away altogether, or in its being rested on a foundation of fuller knowledge. An imperfect education in religious things, and specially the religious knowledge obtained from books (however excellent) rather than from the Bible itself, is, we are convinced, at the bottom of the majority of such cases. But in Mr Ogle's it was not so. From a child he had known the Holy Scriptures. The light had shone in through his understanding upon his soul. His beliefs were not based upon human tradition nor on his emotions; on the contrary, his emotions sprang out of his beliefs, and these rested on knowledge of the Word of God. And yet Mr Ogle had not gone far till both beliefs and emotions seemed to wither away and die. Why was this? Had he failed to receive that regeneration of heart which the Holy Spirit accomplishes by the instrumentality of the Word? We have no doubt as to the answer; nevertheless the question may be left to be answered, so far as deemed desirable, by each one for himself. It is enough to observe that this sore visitation was evidently designed for good and great ends. His heavenly Father meant it for correction, for Mr Ogle, as he himself tells us, had fallen from his first love, had become careless, had sinned against conscience, so in mercy God hid His face from him. But it came also as instruction. Mr Ogle had been sweetly drawn to the Saviour in his youth, without feeling the terrors of conviction. He was now made to taste " the pains of hell and the sorrows of death," that he might know from what a doom he had been rescued, and might the more prize his deliverance. And farther, he was taught that if he would make progress in the Christian life, he must cherish a spirit of simple, humble dependence on Christ, not only as his

Saviour from deserved wrath, but also as his deliverer from
the power of sin—a lesson which the young Christian is apt
to forget in the first outburst of his spiritual vitalities, and the
conscious joy and vigour which flow from their exercise.    But
specially this dispensation qualified Mr Ogle for public service
in the church and the world.    He came out of the struggle
with deepened views of his own weakness and Satan's subtlety,
and with better defined theological views.    The conflict taught
him more than he appears to have known before of the suffi-
ciency of Christ's death as an atonement, and the absolute
freeness of the gospel offer—indispensable qualifications in the
case of all who are to offer pardon to sinners.    Brought to the
very brink of despair, made to feel himself the chief of sinners,
he went forth into the world to tell men that in him they saw
"a brand plucked out of the burning," and to entreat them
to cast themselves on the same all-sufficient Saviour, whose
sovereignty and mercy had been so gloriously illustrated in
himself.    Much of the zeal of his after life, and the clear knowledge which shone in his teaching, may have come from these
hours of darkness.

The following extract from a letter to his sister seems to
confirm these views :—

"The omission of serious and strict self-examination and
renewal of repentance at certain seasons, which are the duty
of every Christian, was, I think, the way by which I became
self-deceived as to the state of my own heart, and finally fell
into alienation of mind from GOD. . . .    If you would avoid
such fearful risks as I have been running—such misery and
danger as I now experience—I beseech you, watch and pray.
Examine also yourself, not lightly, and as a dissembler with
God. . . . Pray for me ; indeed I need your prayers.    Oh !
if God would spare us all to live in sincere obedience to His
will ; in faith and in perfect charity, how happy should we, as
a family, be. . . .

" We should not waste time in sorrow and in self-reproach,

those will not atone for a single sin. . . . Come to Christ, who opens in His own sacrifice of Himself for sinners, a "fountain for sin and for all uncleanness ;" cleave to Him with a faith which shall never let go its hold, and in this continuance you are safe. But if you allow the allurements, the circumstances, or the requirements of the world in which you live to cause you to forget this great and only important relationship, through unbelief, you loosen your hold on Christ, and misery ensues. . . . I have given way to unbelief grievously, and have so often been a backslider, that I have the greatest cause to fear, and to cry, 'Lord, save me, I perish.' The *struggle in my own strength* is hopeless."

The Christian counsel of his father, sent to him at this season, is also worth preserving. They are words of counsel, tender and loving, such as an elder Christian still addresses to those who have to pass through similar trials and spiritual griefs.

" You seem to me to undervalue the proofs you possess of a love to Jesus, viz., an earnest desire to have Him as your Saviour, and to know and do His will. What can give rise to such desires ? They show your sense of need, your full assurance that He is ' the pearl of great price,' the ' chief among ten thousand and altogether lovely.' They show that you, like the *spouse*, are saying, ' Oh ! that I knew where I might find him,' and you ought to conclude that love only can excite such longing desires. But He sees it needful, some-times, to hide Himself from those for whom He has the greatest love, and to whom He intends, at the proper time, to manifest His glory in a most conspicuous manner. Tarry then the Lord's time ; read, and meditate much on His word, with prayer, and it will not be in vain. He has said, ' *Look* unto me and be saved ;' '*come* unto me *all* ye that are weary, and I *will* give you rest.' And, oh! think what He has done that He might make such gracious offers, and take away every obstacle to the full exercise of His loving-kindness to the very chief of sinners, and be not faithless but believing. . . . Stated times for prayer in concert are what many have agreed upon, and nothing can be more edifying and delightful to Christians,

when at a distance from each other, than to know that they
hold communion with their God at the same hours daily, and
then intercede for each other.  I would name seven A.M. as a
good time, and it would have other collateral benefits.  The
*time* once fixed, let it be strictly attended to, otherwise it will
interfere with other duties, and very probably soon be discontinued.  This is a day of constant interruption, so that I find
it very difficult . . ."

His father was pre-eminently a man of prayer, and he had
many other praying friends.  They waited long for the hoped-
for blessing, and in due time it came, so that they are enabled
to bid others " be of good courage ; "  " Wait on the Lord, yea
though He tarry, wait for Him, for He will surely come, He
will not tarry," and " Those that trust in Him shall not be
confounded."

Thus, the events of this period of his life, though, as already
stated, marvellously overruled, so as to be in some things
seemingly the necessary preparation for future usefulness, must
in all faithfulness be regarded chiefly with sorrow, as being a
time of spiritual declension, and are full of most solemn warning
to young men.   At the same time, the deliverance may well
encourage prayerful parents and friends who are mourning for
wanderers, and ready to fear the worst, having as it were but
one promise left—" Train up a child in the way that he should
go, and when he is old he will not depart from it."   But for
the ballast which by the grace of God had been laid in when
he was a child, and that there was a " man at the helm " guiding the frail bark by a way that it knew not, irremediable
shipwreck must have been the issue.   To God be the praise
for the deliverance !   Were John Ogle still living, none more
heartily than himself would say ' Amen.'

It is a very instructive fact that it was while trying to assist
others that Mr Ogle himself obtained deliverance from this
Doubting Castle.   He thus writes, March 5, 1846 :—

*March* 5, 1846.

" I must record the goodness and the long-suffering of God to-day. I have been to see some sick persons, and have been led in their company to be more earnest in prayer both for them and for myself. At our reading in the family also I was much affected by the passage in Bridge's CXIX Psalm, verse 126, and its fearful import to myself, yet I was able to pray that God would bless it to the regeneration and not the destruction of my soul ; and though I feel myself to be dead in sin, yet I do now hope for the same display of God's love in my soul as He shewed when He sent His own Son to die for sinners. He sent Him to those who had sinned against light and knowledge, and commanded the gospel to be proclaimed first 'at Jerusalem.' . . .

" Is God more hard to be entreated because our extremity is great ? Is the supply of His mercy, the gift of His pardoning grace, given on the condition of our being able to make a return ? Surely not. He says, ' Whosoever will let him come and take of the water of life freely.' 'He willeth not the death of the sinner, but rather that he should repent and be saved.' 'There is joy in heaven over one sinner that repenteth more than over ninety and nine just persons that need no repentance.' Let me then close with His free offer, and devote myself to His service willingly as an offering of love, not as recompence for God's favours, for His unlimited mercy. Let me not be like the nine lepers of Israel. . . . God has not, I feel humbly persuaded, forgotten His promises to pious parents, ' though their seed forget Him and break His laws, and He visit their offences with a rod, yet His lovingkindness He will not utterly take from them, nor suffer His truth to fail.' My father will yet have to rejoice and to thank God for ever for His mercy to me. Oh that I might be spared to serve God in this life, to engage in the glorious contest for God against Satan, secure in being in the army of the Lord, not ashamed to fight successfully under the banner, the standard which the Spirit lifts up. All praise be to God if I can but behold the land, and die with eyes of longing fixed upon the hills of Canaan, the land of His promise."

From this time his faith and peace of mind increased, though with occasional intermissions. A short voyage taken with a friend, who in his own yacht visited the coast of Spain and Portugal, was beneficial to his health, and proved to be the first link in the chain of providences by which he was eventually drawn to devote himself to the evangelization of the Spaniards in Algeria. He acquired a sufficient knowledge of the language to enable him to enjoy its scanty treasures of literature, and come home full of admiration of its best poem, and of pity for the condition of a noble and chivalrous, but an indolent because priest-trodden people.

The three following years were spent as a tutor. Although he now desired nothing so strongly as to spend his life in making known the gospel of the grace of God, he seems to have been diffident as to his fitness for the ministry. He had also many "schemes for improving education," and applied himself to their test in practice. At the same time he continued to spend much of his leisure among the sick poor, and whatever his own view of his unfitness may have been, he was pressed by at least one of the London clergy to take courage and to become his fellow labourer.

# CHAPTER V.

## LIFE AS A TUTOR—TOURS IN SCOTLAND.

Mr Ogle now removed to a tutorship in Scotland, where he remained three years. His residence was in Perthshire, and there he made frequent excursions into the Scottish Highlands, of which he has given, in letters to his sister, some fascinating sketches.

His conversion in early life, and his fuller consecration to

Christ by the season of spiritual darkness through which he passed when he came to manhood, did not destroy the idiosyncrasies of Mr Ogle, or change his constitutional tendencies and tastes. They purified and elevated, but did not extinguish them. His love of the beautiful, his sympathy with nature, his admiration of all that was noble and generous, his appreciation of literary and artistic excellence, and his turn for metaphysical disquisition, he still retained ; but all these faculties were sweetened and refined, and now they shone forth in him with a beauty unknown to them before. Grace consecrates and controls, but does not annihilate or lessen individuality. From this period Mr Ogle's character displays both more decision and more breadth. It is now that his many-sidedness begins to come out, and that many-sidedness was nothing but the working of a nature in harmony, and all the more so from the renovation it had undergone, with the universe—physical and mental—around him, as fashioned by the hand of Him on whom he leaned as his Saviour.

And so we now meet Mr Ogle in a new character—that of a painter, working with his pen. Wherever Mr Ogle journeyed, and however important and laborious the duties in which he was engaged, he carried with him an intense susceptibility to the beauty and grandeur of nature, and the solace he found therein, and the desire that others should sympathise with him in this permitted not his pen to rest. He must needs put on paper the scenes around him. His descriptions have a chaste but glowing beauty. His touches are marvellously vivid, and though few, they possess a magic which brings up the landscape in all the reality and truth of nature. As we accompany him to his mission fields, whether in Europe, in Africa, or in South America, we find, ever and anon, the plains and mountains of these regions of the globe rising before our eye in quiet but glowing light, and beguiling us into the belief that we have crossed the sea, and

are actually on the spot described.   It is a bit of the Scottish
Highlands which he now transfers to his canvass, but he discovers in this little picture the genius of a true artist.   We
are to see greater things of the same sort, and of higher excellence, before the volume closes.   From the place where he
was now residing, as tutor, he thus writes :—

### LOCH RANNOCH.

To his Father.

FASKALLY (PERTHSHIRE), 1849.

" .   .   .   I was on the Loch (Rannoch) this morning at
four o'clock.   The dark mountains sloping down to the water
of the lake, which was lit from one extremity to the other, a
distance of fifteen miles, by a bright path of sunlight ; the
snow-vested mountains behind me, in the west, lighted by the
first ray of the rising sun, seemed to be quite near, whereas
they are very distant, near to Ben Nevis, which is only visible
here from the highest summits.   .   .   .

" I wish I knew how I might best serve my generation.   I
hardly think I am fulfilling this, in my present occupation
teaching Latin and Greek, &c., to two boys, although one of
them will, if it please God, be laird of a considerable district,
and may become an influential person perhaps.   I feel myself
in danger of changing my opinions upon a question so important in reference to the ministry, that I dare not undertake
that office at present, and yet I cannot see it to be my duty
to prepare myself for any other profession.   .   .   .   I have
had a very kind and valuable letter from Professor Corrie,*
full of those lessons of Christian experience which are the
most valuable gifts of the older pilgrim to the younger in this
perplexing world.   .   .   ."

The depth of his poetic feeling, and the strength of his
descriptive powers come out more fully in the following letters
to his younger sister, which narrate a tour in the Scottish
Highlands, August 1849 :—

* Norrisian Professor of Divinity, now Master of Jesus College, Cambridge.

LOCH TUMMEL—THE GANNER—SCHIEHALLION.

FASKALLY, *August* 16*th*, 1849.

" My dear F——,

. . . " I have now to tell of scenes and scenery, enjoyed
in solitude among strangers.  I have been among the sublimer
scenes of Scotland.   On the 17th July, we started for our
visit to one of the shooting lodges of the Earl of M——,
grandson to the judge, and he of whom Cowper wrote, in the
verses beginning

> 'A nobler pile
> Than ever Roman saw.'

His valuable MSS. were burnt by a mob, to this he alludes—

> ' Ages yet to come shall mourn
> The burning of his own; (*i.e.* writings)
> The lawless herd with fury blind,
> Have done him cruel wrong.
> The flowers are gone, but still we find
> The honey on his tongue.'

The journey was through a beautiful country.   We ascended
through the woods of pine which girdle and fence the wild
hollows of Faskally ; drove through the birch trees which
droop gracefully on all the hills ; reached a higher road, and
had just time to admire the prospect seen on looking back
through the gorges which admit to, and give exit from our
garden among mountains.   While we stop to change horses, I
run through the low fir plantation which skirts the road, to
gain a platform of rock, and from it, such a prospect ! It seemed
a terrace tower formed to command the lowly valley.   Immediately below a tranquil lake.   The river flows from it to water
Faskally below me, 1000 feet.   The sides of the loch are of
sloping, heathery hills, uncultivated, the domain of the destined
grouse.   Further away in finer distance, are the Grampians
running along in a line almost unbroken—a rampart of precipices.   At the head of Loch Tummel towers Schiehallion, a
broad based pyramid vested in that dark blue colour which
seems borrowed from the thunder-cloud, or from the deep deep
sea.   It is the highest mountain—the beacon of the district—
and forms a beautiful feature in all our higher prospects here.

"Our road is taken through 9 or 10 miles of wild country, altogether abandoned to the black cock and moor game, and strewn as by Deucalion's hand with mighty stones. The river Tummel it is which still rushes over rocks into deep whirling eddies on toward the lake till we arrive at Tummel-bridge Inn, a comfortable looking house, and strange to say, threatened by opposition in an immediate neighbour of comely accommodations on the other side of the bridge. Passing this, the view through its graceful arch, and over it into the valley we have threaded, is very good, and shows the hills in their minor details diversified beautifully. Indeed, every turn of a road such as this, is to be noted, for the relative effects of the hills and vales, crags and slopes are ever changing, like the baseless fabric of a vision. I suppose there is nothing more beautiful in Great Britain than is this little Loch of Tummel as I see it here. Grasmere, with the Rotha's deep and quiet stream passing by may vie with it.

"And now we have a repetition of wild rock and moor, and toiling, tumbling flood like the former, and then one beautiful dark valley where the current is divided by a long islet of green pasture and dark pines, to rush dark and clear over the shelvy rocks, foaming white over alternating steps, to unite again and joyous plunge into a pool deep and still.

"The mountain torrent has often been written of in prose and verse : the truest emblem it is of this life of ours. To one of a reflective turn, of imagining power, unnumbered still are the fresh features in which it will be found to present a phase parallel to every passage of the most diversified life, from the tear-watered cradle to the wide ocean which 'swallows both at last.' The gay and happy world would see many a giddy hour of their own bright spring in the glass I am contemplating now, in the rushing flood sparkling and whirling as in pleasure's maddest maze, then stemmed a while by rocks of difficulty, compelled to take one turn in the dark waters of reflection, bitter and black as the peat mosses render on. Tummel, only to rush forth again, less impetuously now, and having left some floating trifles behind, and lost many a cherished treasure. Brighter days succeed, but its ever flowing stream passes under skies not so cloudless as at first, and through scenes not so wild and exciting, onward still. The calm lake—emblem of middle age—receives it. The watcher cannot now discern the current's course, but it is still flowing, and will emerge anew, perhaps, like the happy Tummel, to enter upon a course of prosperity and gratification, to visit scenes far more rich, and beauties vieing with its birth scene, to renew young pleasures with the young, and imagine the perpetual recurrence of a life of alternating enjoyments; but its course is rapidly moving onward now, nothing can stop the current; it is deeper too and broader. A short while and the bitter waters of the last afflictions mingle with it, the onward flow is checked, stopped, reversed; is it *really* a renewal of the lease of life to give a return to former haunts and pleasures? The *flow* is over, now comes the ebbing tide. The next flow and the ocean is reached—*telle est la vie.* The Christian wanderer too, in such scenes as this, will not neglect to take his account of them for pleasure and for instruction. But I must not weary you more with my reflections. Our journey resumed, and the fair features of an inland sea are before us, the mimic waves rolling their miniature crests upon the barrier sand. On the other side, the hills slope steeply to the water, and a watery but pellucid atmosphere. Sun upon us and clouds darkening the opposite hills, throw them into shade and give a good effect of distance. Schichallion begins to be seen from the western boundary, piercing the clouds with its spire-like pinnacle. One would fancy the bluff mountain had been touched with magic wand, and had developed into the fair proportions of the graceful cone. Were it not for the changing clouds varying the degrees and distribution of light and shade upon lake and hill, the aspect of a lake would be the most devoid of life in all nature. The still surface of white water, bounded sharply by the dark hills, tossed into forms as of living agitation, but frigid and motionless, combine to produce an effect on the mind, compared with which the boundless ocean breathes and lives even in a calm, and the desert is only desolate; the difference between the marble and the model, between the sleeper and the dead. But it is only for a

moment that the pall rests upon nature.  The black cloud
descends in a light-diffusing shower, the still surface is rippled
by the breeze, and ruffled by the raindrops; a web of watery
threads is dropt as from the heaven, and now, marvel of beauties!
a celestial shuttle flies across the woof, and the fairest scenes
of earth are over-arched by the bow of heaven, doubly precious
as the seal of covenanted deliverance.  Such was Loch Rannoch when I saw it.  We drove along the whole length of the
lake, and arrived in the evening at a sheltered spot at the
western end, embosomed in lofty hills, and sheltered close by
a fence of firs.  We have a rushing river close by.  It is called
the Ganner; but it is really parent of our own Tummel, and
great grandfather by the mother's side to the Tay.

"The ten days spent at Rannoch were passed in morning
work and afternoon enjoyment.  Fishing, rowing on the lake,
walking over the hills.  We had no fine weather, and very
little fair, but we got out every day, if it were only to get into
the rain or river.  We caught some of the monsters we had
been told of.  Three dozen of moderate trout repaid one of
my days in drenching rain, but I was always repaid by the wild
rocks and the rapid river.

### TOUR THROUGH THE HIGHLANDS OF RANNOCH.

#### THE LOST CHILD.

"On Wednesday, at 7 A.M., I set out for a walking tour,
and attended by a stout old Highlander, took the rocky road
by the Ganner side.  Nothing could be more beautiful than the
morning.  Every hill, from the distant peak of Schiehallion to
the snowy pyramids which guard the dread valley of Glencoe
before me, is clear and sunny.  The lake from which, as its
source, the Ganner flows, is soon reached (8 miles), and we sit a mo- .
ment to refresh ourselves with the delicious prospect afforded by
the cerulean waters, to hear tales of deer killing on the wooded
islands before me, or far away on the wild hills which bound
my prospect.  The Glenlyon hills are on the opposite side of
the loch.  It may be 30 miles to their summits, though these

appear to my eye, used to take in longer distance, to be but a step across the valley. Would I could for one moment take a giant stride to gain a prospect from those hill tops, and look into another valley different, but in general features similar! The same rock, and wood, and water, and azure sky. I should peer into Glen Lyon, the deepest and loveliest of glens; should descry the thousand deer of the Breadalbane, and scare the eagle and the osprey, as well as the tame ptarmigan and timid hare. Two miles more and I am at the shepherd's house, the only dwelling in this twenty miles. One hundred yards off you do not see it. There is a patch of cleared pasture—a 'bitty' garden, like the field of the sluggard in the fence, but some good potatoes, &c. At the black bothie door stands the good wife, bidding me welcome to a seat, and she gives me milk in copious bowls, and oat cakes like tables. Kebbuck too and butter are forthcoming. As soon as the darkness of the bothie will permit, I descry the inmates of the cabin. An infant, the ninth of the family, and a little maiden of eight years. About this last there hangs a tale. The shepherd was from home, and the child was lost. Neither appeared that night. On the father coming home, he and the brother searched on every side. On the third and fourth day, 150 men from Rannoch side, Glencoe, and Breadalbane, left, as they thought, not a spot unsearched within nine miles of the cottage. The fifth morning is come, and the mourning father takes his plaid and crook and his way to the hills; his eyes are on the rapid burn which flows down to his home, and he mingles a tear with its waters as he seems to see his child floating past on its bosom to her last bed in the lake below. 'Rough rocking to soundest slumbering eyes,' he says, as he turns from it. 'She must have gone that way!' The father is right; but she is safe! Creeping out from behind a big stone, he sees his lost little one, and scarce ten yards from the place on which he stands. At a bound he has cleared the burnie, and he has her in his arms before she can give utterance to the cry with which she meant to arrest him ere he turned away. She had seen on a previous day the men marching silent, and 'they looked so big and strange, she feared them and hid herself.' She had eaten a little bitty grass, and drank of the burnie. 'She looked,' he said, 'a little wild;' but the tears and kisses which may render the shepherd hut warm as the palaces of kings soon restored her, and now there is not a bonnier little lass beyond the head of Rannoch than the lost lassie of Loch Lydoch side.    I gave her a draught of milk from my bowl, a piece of my oat cake, and a little picture book from my pocket—its title, providentially, as I thought, 'The Lost Child'—and took leave of the hospitable shepherdess and of my guide.

## GLENCOE—THE MASSACRE—BEN-NEVIS.

" Refreshed and buoyant, I pursued my way alone.    Soft mosses, untracked by foot of man or animal, of mountaineer or of mountain goat, formed my roadway.

" I am to direct my course due west, to a lofty hill rising perpendicularly from the extremity of the moor.    I have to leap over a peat channel every tenth pace, but get on rapidly, rejoicing in the solitariness, yet shouting to the rock-echo verses made for the occasion, and having a chorus which suited my mood.    By and bye I found things less exhilarating, the mosses were become narrower and the bogs wider, while with my staff I could not find their bottom.    Not a house was to be seen ; the hill towered above me in horrid crags, resembling a yelling fountain which had become petrified as its streams burst upward.    A neat herd reassured me by saying I was in the right track, and but a short distance from King's House, Glencoe.    This inn is on the high road from Glasgow to Fort-William, the post-boys lounged and the waiter hugged his badge of office, the matron smiled, and the place was all activity, as if the savage fastnesses of the valley of Glencoe were become as busy as the marts of commerce or as the fashionable faubourg of a city.

" Taking my place upon the coach for Fort-William, I move more rapidly over the ground, though I should have been glad to linger in Fingal's birthplace—wild now as when the thousand streams rushed by his retreat into the roaring waters of Cona. A few heaps of ruins show where the Macdonalds of Glencoe were treacherously massacred as insurgents and rebels against William III. William does not seem to have been to blame for this disgraceful murder of peaceable men; but the Earl of Breadalbane and Lord Stair persuaded William that the Macdonalds were the only Highlanders who resisted his government, whereas their chieftain had, by great personal effort, testified his allegiance to him. Thirty-eight persons were massacred, and all the houses in the Glen were levelled with the ground.

" To all appearance this desolate glen remains as it was left after the work was done. I saw neither a dwelling nor a creature for ten miles, if I except the one *shieling* where our horses were changed, distant eight miles from King's hotel.

" But how shall I describe the wild grandeur of the drive! The precipitous mountains without trees, often without herbage, no feature but of sublimity. Their sides furrowed with watercourses. The road lying oftentimes over the banks of stones from thirty to forty feet high, which have been brought down from the summits by these torrents during winter. Here Ossian lived, it is said, and I shall read his poems again with fresh zest now that I have become acquainted with the solitudes which inspired his vigorous verse. Twenty-eight miles, chiefly through beautiful country, and by the shore of Lochs Leven and Linnhe, salt-water lochs, brought me to Fort-William, at the foot of Ben-Nevis, 4416 feet above the level of the sea. This mountain is a huge and uninteresting object, unshapely, and little distinguished among the high and rugged mountains around it. The only view I had of it, however, was that from the west, as we steamed out to sea by Loch Linnhe. The entrance of this loch is particularly fine, the rugged mountains of Appin on the south, the gloomy hills of Morven on the north contrasting with the cultivated slopes of the island of Lismore, and the towers of Oban amid the luxuriant forest trees which abound in its verdant precincts. The bay of Oban gives the soothing impression of sweet and absolute retirement, with its cottages on or near its glassy brink, and its church upon the hill. We did not land there.   The sea was calm, and the islands floated as it were ' en fleur d'eau ' at various distances.

" We crossed the Mull of Cantire by a canal into Loch Fyne, and had a beautiful voyage to Glasgow.   The banks of the Clyde are varied, not bold or mountainous, and ere we reached Glasgow I could have believed myself steaming along the unvisited and unattractive shores of my native Witham, rather than approaching a vast commercial and manufacturing city of 500,000 inhabitants.   We met neither a boat nor vessel of any kind, I think, from Dumbarton to Glasgow. The trade is by rail to Greenock, and thence to sea.   Glasgow was not the densely smoking city I had conceived it,—a forest of chimneys, and a mass of half-suffocated humanity.   I saw little of it, however, beyond the High Church and the University, the former a beautiful structure, in good repair, vieing with Selby church in size and beauty.

" I left Glasgow at 7 A.M. by steamer for Dumbarton."


### LOCH LOMOND—KILLIN—LOCH TAY—BEN MORE.

"  .  .  .  The morning was calm, and the sun just obscured by that lucid haze which admits the warmth while it shades from the scorching beam.   The lower end of Loch Lomond is not picturesque till the islands are reached, and then beautiful prospects of Ben Lomond and his rugged fraternity are obtained. Gleams of sunlight, passing showers, now the gorgeous blaze, and now the purpling shadows, embellished the scenery of the finest lake in Scotland.   I was all eye till the sight was almost wearied with seeing and admiring, then a brisk shower swept the lake, and the divertisement renewed the appetite afresh for another and finer prospect still of the mountain. From the lower end of the lake, and until Ben Lomond has been passed about five miles, the mountain itself is not seen in its grandeur : indeed, its appearance would at first disappoint most persons ; but, as the lake narrows towards the head, the mountains become wilder and more precipitous, and successive elevations at advancing heights throw its towering summit into finer distance.   The great height is then perceived ; and

when, as I saw it, a purple shading darkens the summit, while
the mountains nearer are brought out by sunlight into strong
relief, the effect is quite beyond pen or pencil to describe.  A
young lady was trying to sketch ; she was armed at all points;
but not an outline could she transfix or transfer, so rapid were
the changes ; and I suspect she felt how impossible it is to
give in outline any conception of these scenes to which atmospheric colouring gives so palpable a charm.   Arrived at the
.extreme end of the loch, at the narrow mouth where runs the
burn which feeds the lake, we left the steamer for a coach,
and exchanged the loch and its mountains for the tumbling
burnie of Glen Falloch, scarcely less picturesque in its way,
and with mountains equally grand—one in particular (Ben
Ean) gilded by sunlight so as to combine very striking effects
of purple and gold.   This mountain is seen for many miles at
the end of the long deep valley.   The name of the glen is
soon changed, for it receives the waters of another stream
which form a small picturesque loch, Dochart by name.   On
an island stands an old castle, one of the retreats of the de-.
liverer of Scotland, Robert the Bruce.   Our road passes close
by the majestic Ben More, and soon we arrive at Killin, the
grave of Fingal, at the head of Loch Tay.   Killin is a romantic
village between two rivers.   The furious Dochart rushes over
a thousand steps of stone to unite its waters with the broadly
meandering Loch Tay.   On one side you look up to Ben
More, the finest shaped mountain I have seen ; on the other
rises Ben Lawers, huge and high.   Before you the brother
streams unite to fall together into the noble lake.   At Killin
is a beautiful inn.   Several families appeared to be staying
there.   A very pleasant halting-place it must be.   There are
boats for those who like the lake ; for others there are the ruins
of the old mansion of the Breadalbane lords, whose territories
stretch from hence one hundred miles north-west, and embrace
all the country round.   An ancient wall pierced for arrows, a
few fine trees, are all that remain to indicate the site.   I
rested a few hours, walked up the hill for a prospect, eat a
basin of porridge, and left carrying my plaid and a large
botanic tin box.   The road I took commences at a wild glen

deeply cleft through the mountains. The sun scarcely visits
its bottom, the eagle hovers over its narrow chasm, and forms
her eyrie in the overhanging rocks. It is named Glen Ogle.
You will find it in the maps west of Loch Tay. I had not
time to explore its recesses ; my road lies in the pleasanter
neighbourhood of the serene lake, and the lofty Ben Lawers
looking down on us from the further, the north side. I
walked leisurely along in admiration of the setting sun and
wreathing clouds which shrouded the tops of Ben Lawers and
bedarkened my own footsteps. My road was good and well
defined by the side of the lake. A few trees intervene between
me and the placid waters. I have ten miles at least before
me, and it is past 10 P.M. I must take up my lodging in a
whisky-shop or by the fire of a cottage, and here is one. Man
and wife both answer the inquiry made at their open door as
to the road and distance to Kenmore. I do not much fancy
their cabin. Half a mile further I spread my plaid under a
bank, and, folded in it from head to foot, seek repose. Here
I had comfortably slept had not an envious mouse beneath my
head roused and fidgeted me. I got up and walked a while.
The moon is full, and sheds on me a dazzling beam through
the parted clouds and shows me the lake and the mountains.
I move on and find a couch on a broad stone, but this is hard
and adds to my weariness. My night is ultimately spent
between sleeping and waking under shelter of a cart shed. At
3 A.M. I am on my journey, and witness the preparations for
the sun's *levee* on another glorious morning. One mountain
in the distance becomes finely illuminated, and Ben More behind me is seen clear and noble ; but the sun does not appear
till it is high in the sky. At 6 A.M. I reach a small village,
and make bold to enter a cleanly cottage, where, I am told,
they keep cows, and ask to be allowed to share their meal.
The family bid me welcome, and I am witness of the mysteries
of porridge preparation. In honour to the hungry stranger it
was cooked in a cauldron nearly three feet in diameter, and
served in old china punch bowls of a gallon each. I ply
heartily at my Benjamin, and at least diminish the weight of
the bowl. Porridge is eaten, dipping every scalding spoon-

ful into cold milk, and is very pleasant, especially after a
night on Tayside. I then pay the costs and sally forth renewed to my walk. I diverged two miles to visit a very
beautiful fall, Acharn. A stream shoots over a precipice of
200 feet, and discharges its water thence by a deep wooded
dell into the lake. The fall is into a steep basin, feathered
with the most lovely wood. You obtain with difficulty a view
of the falls. I gazed on them for a long time, and they will
ever live in my memory. I brought away a dozen cuttings of
honeysuckle which are flourishing here. At Kenmore I remained during Saturday morning, and proceeded, after a view
of Taymouth Castle, to Aberfeldy, where another fall, or succession of falls, more rocky and varied, but in beauty not equal
to Acharn. I was fortunate in finding a returning carriage to
Pitlochry, and walked into my study to find all well and happy.

Soon thereafter there came another tour. It was undertaken, we may say, to realize a principle. It led Mr Ogle
across the Grampians to Braemar that he might have the opportunity of worshipping in Crathie Church with the Queen,
and of feeling that the peasant and the monarch of an empire
on which the sun never sets, stand on the same level in the
presence of the King Eternal.

### Spittal of Glenshee—Braemar—Crathie Church— The Queen.

FASKALLY, *September* 1849.

" MY DEAR JANE,—I have it again in my power to entertain
you, it may be, with the particulars of a tour upon which I
set my mind the first hour I knew that I should be within
thirty miles of our Queen's ' Highland Home.' To see her in
her chosen retreat, to realise by being personally present in
the village church the equality of all in the presence of the
Almighty, the kindred needs and enjoyments which our
Christian Sovereign acknowledges by meeting with her subjects in their village church, and in no wise distinguished

from them, to be instructed and to worship as they. The lesson she thus gives of enlightened liberality and toleration is a subordinate, but not an unimportant one. By attending the services of a church professing the same faith, and appealing to the same standard, though not preserving the same offices and orders, Her Majesty teaches us to recognise in it a living member of the great visible body of Christ's Holy Catholic Church. The incidents of travel are more numerous, and will occupy more of my description than the end of it. I went not to see the Queen and her Court, but to realise what I have described. A double holiday coming in the regular course of our arrangements gave me that wished for opportunity. I got a pony from the inn at the village, and started on a beautiful Saturday morning at nine, September 8. My road lay in a direction north east over the lower hills, the features of a wide undulating waste covered with scattered crags and huge stones, with frontier hills, the eminences of the range of which the waste is part would gain nothing of definiteness from description. I will therefore pass over the first twelve miles, and not delay at the hospitable farm-house to which I was directed by Mr B—— for refreshment, but enter on the second stage, a rude track along a valley crossing at considerable altitude to another range of hills. The starting of the grouse, the luxuriance of the heather, the sunny steeps, the ever-varying aspect of the mountain tops, whether as viewed from different points, on different sides, or ranged in ever-changing groupings, the recognition of some well known summit of my old friends; majestic Ben-More, that darkens Glen Ogle with a perpetual shade; Ben-Lawers, whereon hung the canopy of cloud which screened me from the moonbeams in my heather couch; and Tay-side, or *Ben-y-wracky* and *Ben-y-Gloe*, our own mountains here; *Schiehallion*, too, the graceful pyramid once arched by the rainbow on Loch Rannoch; all these and more delights cheered my lone pacing (for I was leading my horse all the way). A ridge is before me, and is soon surmounted. I look down from a height of 1000 feet at least into a deep hollow glen, perhaps four miles across; the bottom is green in fresh pastures and corn fields;

half a-dozen houses, very white and slated neatly, are visible. A bridge leads a winding road through the glen across the river, and this last shews me a curiously serpentine course when I trace it a few miles up a ravine ; a multitude of windings, is no unimportant feature of the very striking prospect which I first enjoyed of the *Spittal of Glenshee.* I must not omit to mention that the mountains are of greater heights on all other sides, and run steep down, as this on which I am, into the valley. There are four considerable exits, one to the south, by which the Queen came from Perth ; one to N.E.N., by which I am to travel on her northward track ; to the N.N.W., and to the west are other ravines. After a rude sketch of this very striking view, and taking the bearings of the mountains on all sides, I descended leisurely. My pony is a climber and safe-footed, wherever I myself can hold upright. We soon made our way to the inn in the glen, where I got excellent tea, bread, oat-cake and preserves, feed my pony, and start in an hour for Braemar. I may mention that the inn is precisely like that at the entrance to Glencoe, and the hills very similar, though not so wild. The geology is different, and for the rugged steeps and abrupt precipices, we have here vast rounded and protuberant mountains swollen and smooth, grassy, heath-clad where not too steep; the tops steep, and evenly pyramidal, and apparently of grey sand, furrowed by torrents. It is the quartz and limestone series of the primitive rocks. I raised my cap, and whirled it to greet the fluttering ribbands and faded foliage on a light arch, which spans the bridge, erected as a welcome to our mountain-loving Queen. My pony, O horror! responds by a start, and breaks into the lamest trot any luckless traveller ever bestrode. It is only a shoe loose. A nail or two enables the beast to travel, but I dare ride no more, and so I have fifteen mountain miles to trudge, bridle on my neck, dragging my locomotive up the hills. It is slow work, and I am not five miles away before darkness is visible. At least "seven miles more before you're over the hill, and it's three good miles to Castletown after that."

"Shall I meet with a house if I should lose my way, or my beast here break down, or anything ?"

" There's never a shieling till you're ouer the holl."

"Some comfort," says I.   "Could you give me a shed for my horse, or a shake-down for myself?"

" We've just got in a traveller, and there isn't a byre for his beast neither."

I saw his pony grazing with the saddle on, so there was no disputing it.  I essayed the "holl" under the starlight.  Straight before me is Cairnwal ; to my right, numerous heights, Glassmuir and his broad brethren.   My road has been tried ever since the Romans, in Agricola's time, or ere that, first taught the Celtic barbarians that " wisdom is better than weapons of war."   My wisdom in other countries, and less happy times, would have been to " keep my tongue still, and stir my stumps," but there can be no danger where my Queen has travelled a mile ahead of her guardsmen so lately, and so as soon as I was out of hearing of the cannie Scotchman, I taught the echoes all the tunes I knew to whistle, and most of the songs of which I could recollect snatches, and when tired of bawling, I recalled to mind some of the incidents of the Christian Pilgrim, and bethought me too of " the Cottar's Saturday Night."   At last I got over the hill, and descended into a valley, long and steep, widening in front, a roaring stream made music for my marching, and the silver sheen of the rapids and ripplings, under the soft ray of a lovely moon, made the mountain river appear like a bright serpentine attendant, as gay, and not less welcome than when our first mother fondled the beauteous folds of the fell deceiver in Eden.   Braemar is an Eden, though of a grimmer aspect than the Euphrates Paradise, where

> ' Eden stretched her line
> From Auran *eastward to the Royal towers*
> Of great Seleucia, built by Grecian Kings ;
> .    .    .    .    .    like that
> Southward through {Eden \ went a river large ;'
>                   {Braemar}

and if its 'crisped brooks' roll not 'on orient pearl and sands of gold,' the rest of the beautiful description, (Milton's Paradise Lost, Book iv.) 'under pendant shades,' 'lawns or level downs, and flocks grazing the tender herb,' ' umbrageous grots, and caves of cool recess,' may well apply to the murmuring curren of the swift flowing Dee sweeping through Braemar, laving the walls of Balmoral and the grounds of Abergeldie, and so to the Northern Ocean at Aberdeen. I arrived late at the Fife Arms, a comfortable inn at the Castle town, found a little difficulty in rousing the inmates, fortunately none in procuring a good bedroom. Next morning I heard the unwonted sound of two eight o'clock bells, one deep-toned, and the other an iron clinker, such as too often offends the English ear in the Highlands. The deep sound was the *ear-alluring* call of the Romish chapel, which attracts half the inhabitants. The morning was wet, and so I was almost despairing of being able to walk the nine miles to church at Crathie, where her Majesty attends. I learnt in the inn, that a Rev. Mr M'Rae from Castle Town had hired a gig to go to preach at Crathie. I instantly penned a note, representing myself an University man from England, and asked to share his expense. I called with the note, and was kindly received and permitted. The good clergyman proved to be of the Free Church, and I got a broad hint that sight-seeing on Sabbath days was not part of the religion of the Free Church or their adherents. I excused myself by asking the Preacher whether, with his practice in the pulpit, and still more in the pulpit preparation, he could at once *realise* the equality of all ranks before the Omnipotent Ruler of men, and as fellow heirs of the promises of the Christian Covenant? if he should find her Majesty one of his own congregation that morning? And I believe I succeeded in impressing him favourably with my motive for indulging the proverbial sight-seeing inclinations of Englishmen. It is, I do feel, a valuable exercise in *practice* to have thus tested one's theories, to have worshipped with little distraction oneself among others apparently simple, reverent, earnest Christians who forget their Queen in the words and worship of their common Maker. There was no crowd ; the church was well filled, and contained no doubt more better dressed persons than usual, but I observed nothing peculiar in the aspect or behaviour of the majority. The Church is a plain edifice situate 20 feet above the road on the hill-side : below is the Dee, and opposite, on the level

side, stands Balmoral Castle, embowered in trees, and under
the steep protection of hills richly furred with heather, behind
the cloud-concealed summits of Lochnagar (3700 feet high).
I watched the party issuing from the Castle ; the Queen rode
(for the rain was falling) in a covered yellow Barouche, preceded at some distance by four in Highland garb walking,
and one outrider.   I therefore stood, cap in hand, and waited
the approach of her carriage, and as she raised her happy
unanxious countenance on the first view of the Church-yard
and the Congregation, (not standing, but moving from her
into Church and mostly seated already,) I assured myself
that it was my Queen ; I cannot tell you how she was dressed,
but that the Prince and she were like English folk, nor
did I enquire who were with them.   I have since learned
that the historian of the revolution Sir A. Alison, Lord J.
Russell, and several Dukes, &c., were in her train."

The following is a bit of forest painting, at once delicious
and delicate.   It has all the minuteness, but none of the
hardness of the pre-Raphaelite School :—

THE WOODS ON THE APPROACH OF WINTER.

To his Sister.

*October* 19th.

"   .   .   .   POOR D——.—I hope he was prepared for
his sudden call.   I remember sitting by his side and
talking with him and thinking him a serious reflecting
man.   How many, alas ! let reflection be the whole of their
religion !   .   .   .   On the subject of retrospect.   Had
my hopes for you been realised you would now be looking back upon a varied, busy, fatiguing week of travel among
the hills and braes of Scotland.   You would have had beautiful weather, brilliant frosty mornings like a premature
Christmas, Summer at noon, and Autumn sunsets.   You
would have witnessed the most sudden changes in foliage you
ever saw.   At first the hills would have presented their
summer vesture of unvarying verdure, as the frosts succeeded

one another you would have noticed the birch first betraying its delicacy of constitution and displaying that of its form, you would have detected the taper birch and pines by their faded gold, contrasting the more by their proximity to the dark Scotch fir, the ash by its leafless boughs, a presentiment of Winter,—notes of his ravage borne on every breeze. I have never seen more beauty and variety than is now around me.   How lovely is the evenly wooded hill I am looking upon.   Every tree is outlined distinctly in contrast with others in different stages of their wintry change : here and there a birch, with bright golden yellow, or an aspen with ruddy brown ; a silver willow, contrasting with a dark spruce ; a line of elm and birch marking the course of the high road. I need not weary you with description of the fantastic forms thrown into relief by the fading hues of lilac, rowan, lime, &c., or by the constant laurel, yew, or juniper.   Were it not for the melancholy inseparable from faded beauty and foregone delights, the thought that

> " Age, youth, and infancy will soon be this,
>     A sere and yellow leaf, that rustling strews
>     The wintry path, where grief delights to muse."

Were it not for these mementos of lapse and decay, I might judge this the fittest season for enjoying the beauties of scenery like this, gifted at all seasons eminently with the attributes of picturesqueness, and even of grandeur.   We must leave the sublime to the Alps and the Pyrenees.   But for that loveliness which delights with colouring, enchants with novelty, entrances with variety, presents ever individual objects of beauty, and groups them into combinations still more striking of concentrated and accumulative graces, I believe we need not go further from home than to the hills and valleys of Perthshire ; the stony parentage of the Tummel and the Tay.

We now enter upon other scenes.   Early in 1850, Mr Ogle was summoned to his father's death-bed.

D

"During this last illness," writes Miss Ogle, "many weighty words fell from his father's lips. He died of apoplexy; but for some weeks he was withdrawn from the world, as it were, only so far as not to be fully conscious of people and things about him. The effect of this was, that the ordinary tenor of his thoughts was more apparent. In health he was reserved, a man of few words, and of much thought. Now, he thought aloud, and his earnest prayers for his children, for his people, his reflections upon passages of Scripture, and the disclosure of his innermost feelings, was most touching, and produced upon his son a deep and abiding impression. The immediate result seems to have been to make him hesitate no longer as to his duty to enter the ministry. For this office he had been educated, and had in fact been preparing himself whilst engaged in tuition. Writing to his father from Stepney Grammar School, where, for a short time, he was second master, he says :—

"A clerical friend has asked me to become his curate. My parish would comprise a district which has been much neglected, containing 6000 inhabitants, and would be a mile distant. I fear I could not undertake the work, for I can now knock myself up among the poor near my present home in a single afternoon, as I have already found to be the case."

The Scottish reader may wish here to put a question : "We have traced," will he say, "Mr Ogle to Rugby, thence to the University, and thence to a tutorship in Scotland; but at what point does his theological curriculum come in ?" The simple fact is, that in this, as in many other instances among devoted ministers in England, the deficiency was made up in other ways. Mr Ogle received a theological training which falls to the lot of few. From his earliest years it was his happiness to enjoy the instructions of a pious, evangelical, and judicious father. He had, moreover, passed through a period of mental distress, which made him look narrowly at the foundations of Christianity, and study the Bible with reference to his own heart and his own soul's salvation. He had, besides, taught the doctrines of the gospel in the Sabbath school, and applied them at the bedsides of the sick and the dying. Hence the clear views and accurate knowledge of the scheme of salvation to which he attained, as shown in his after labours and letters. He was taught of God, whose providence had placed him in situations fitted to train him specially as a preacher of the gospel; and so, when he began to teach, he was a workman not needing to be ashamed, rightly dividing the word of truth, and giving unto every one his portion of meat in due season.

Mr Ogle was admitted into orders as curate at Burton-on-Trent in the spring of 1850. The story of his life there will be best told in his own words. The spirit of self-humiliation, exhibited in the following extracts, is not uncommon in those who have grace to aspire to a high standard, and who feel how far short they have come of it. But this is the spring of spiritual, as of all other kinds of progress.

Writing to his sister, May 27, 1850, Mr Ogle says :—

" I will not excite your sympathies by detailing the struggles I have gone through before taking this step of entering the ministry of the gospel. I have one only hope, that Jesus has taken my sins upon Himself, and that He will make use of His most unworthy minister, to spread His kingdom among men, and to advance His glory. I have many fears, but I feel strong when I trust simply on Jesus. You must, my dear sister, be very much in prayer for me; that GOD will give His word free course among my people.

" I have three cottage lectures during the week in different parts of Burton ; for these I write notes in preparing my subjects, and deliver the lectures extempore. I have also a meeting for the instruction of the young, and a Sunday school teachers' meeting—these, with the services upon Sunday, I find rather hard work at present.

" I hope I shall gain strength to pray the prayers as I read them, and to preach from the heart. How terrible to be using with the lips words to which the heart responds not."

After a short sojourn of three months, Mr Ogle left Burton-on-Trent for the incumbency of Flamborough. Of these three months, he thus writes :—

" The events of those three months at Burton will never be forgotten by me. They were days of much depression and anxiety and sorrow. I felt upon me a responsibility I knew not how to meet ; a burden too heavy for me to bear. The energies of both mind and body were exhausted by self-reflection and in the contemplation of the greatness of my work. I saw vice in many of its grosser forms, and worldliness in its gigantic proportions, hurrying on to destruction a large population of all ranks of society—fellow-heirs of immortality occupied with the dross and empty pursuits of a perishing world. I longed to discover, but found no remedy. I remember well that I had contemplated the work of the parochial minister with much expectation and pleasure, but realities soon undeceive. The path of the future decked in the bright colours with which anticipation invests it, is far other than that which the sombre tints of reality reveal, and I carried away from my first curacy many a sad memory, many a conviction of individual unfaithfulness and of general neglect of duty.

" Not only do we deceive ourselves, however, by false expectations, it is also true that hindrances often arise of which no foresight could premonish.

" Satan, who marks the youthful warrior's taking up the armour wherewith to assail his hitherto quiet realm in the hearts of mankind, prepares a fierce defence and meets them in every effort with assaults never felt before, and puts forth his utmost violence to destroy them, or, at least, to mar their work.

" The craft, the power, the virulence displayed by a multitude of agencies—in other men, in the world in general, in his own heart, all this and more, that it were vain to try to tell—conspire to beat down the arm that is upraised against his enemy. Blessed be God, feeble man is not alone in this conflict, still he is oftentimes, as it were, taken by surprise at the strangeness, and by the nature of the conflict, and his enemy gains some advantages over him, and casts him down if he cannot conquer. Thus it was with me. I left Burton feeling as if I had not done any work there which would be productive of permanent good. If I warned any sinner, or reclaimed any wanderer from the fold; if I consoled any feeble ones and helped their faith in Jesus; if I instructed any wayfarers and directed them towards Zion; if I helped any to maintain their stand against evil, or encouraged any to persevere; to the Lord be all the praise.

" It is true that from a place to which I came as a stranger, I went out leaving behind many with whom I was closely bound in the alliance of Christian fellowship, whose sympathy and prayers have followed me to this hour. This is a reward immeasurably beyond the desert of my labour. I accept it from God, not as merit, but from His grace."

The following brief but philosophic remarks on Germany derive additional interest from events which have happened since they were written. They are addressed to Miss Ogle, who was making a short tour in that country in 1850 :—

" . . . . I shall think with great pleasure of you as you stem the tide of Rhenus, and whirl along past the renowned cities of the country of all others the most interesting, from the vicissitudes it has created rather than caused. There has ever been a great restless current in the mind of Germany, ever flowing in one direction, like her mighty river. The overthrow of established empires, whether of paganism and luxurious tyranny, as when, under Alaric, Genseric, Odoacer, or Attila, the empire of the West was prostrated and trodden under foot; or, as when a thousand years after, Luther, the fearless, Melancthon, the mild evangelist, Zwingle, the ele-

quent priest of Zurich, led a nobler and more resistless host ;
commenced a new warfare, which is still raging ;—the spiritual
combat of intellect and of the conscience against ignorance and
bigotry.

"Enquire after Rongé and Czersky. It was like a son of
Germany, that speech of his against Bishop Arnold of Trèves :
'Christ shed His blood for His flock, He left His coat to His
foes.'

"I would you were well versed in the history of Germany,
for, though it be the history of man wilful and wicked, it
contains episodes of energetic opposition to the great rolling
river of evil. Strong swimmers were Tell and Hofer, as well
as Zwinglius and Calvin, who, in another age,

> ' Fighting hard against the stream,
> Saw distant gates of Eden gleam—
> And did not dream it was a dream.'

Let us love their lands with love brought from out the storied
past : the venerated past, which has reserved to us so much
of good and so little of evil, that we think of it as dimmed by
a golden halo, and name it 'good' and 'old.' Goethe is one
who, if I mistake not, for I know but little of his writings,
deserves to be mentioned in the roll of German spirit-stirrers,
truth-defenders. Dim may have been his sight, and dim is
our own ; that he wished to see clearly is his praise and our example. Scorn luxury and sloth, and court toil and energy, and
forget not your loving brother, John."

# CHAPTER VI.

## LIFE AT FLAMBOROUGH.

In the autumn of the year 1850, Mr Ogle received from Walter Strickland, Esq., the patron, the incumbency of Flamborough, and removed at once to that village, the home of so many of his ancestors, full of sanguine hope and of fervent desire of good towards a people in whose welfare he had been early accustomed to take an interest. It was his father's habit to visit Flamborough every year. He, as a youth, during occasional visits to an aged relative, who spent part of each year in the old family house there, had established a Sunday school before such institutions were common, and he continued throughout his life to inspect the scholars yearly, and distribute among them rewards of books, which he chose with great care. Tenants were likewise visited, and friendly relations kept up every year. Partly by reason of the seclusion of their village, partly owing to their own occupation as fishing folk, they remained destitute of many of those advantages which, by the spread of education and the increased facilities of travel, have changed the character of most of our English towns and villages for better or for worse. With a generous desire to make the land of his fathers participate in the good things which hitherto had lain beyond their reach, the son now addressed himself to the improvement of the people doubly linked to him, not only by the mere chivalrous tie of ancient interests, but by the sacred responsibilities of a resident clergyman. The people too—the more ancient ones especially—were pleased that a man whose fore-elders they knew so well should come to live among them.

These sentiments, perhaps, prevented the necessary consideration as to the suitability of the climate to his health, and
of the sphere of labour to his mental acquirements. Many of
his best judging friends considered that the sensitiveness of
his disposition, his refined and cultivated tastes and acquirements rendered him unsuited for the post ; and this was found
to be the case, so that after five years of much self-denying,
although not of the usual routine kind of labour, he felt himself
obliged to resign the incumbency. Yet if a memory which is
embalmed in the hearts of a people still, after the lapse of
sixteen years, is cherished with love and veneration, be any
test of a clergyman's work, then may it be said that Mr Ogle's
labours in Flamborough were not in vain. His example, as a
kind, holy, and a Christian loving man of God, is not forgotten at Flamborough. His evident anxiety to lead sinners
to the Saviour, his generosity to all in distress, his pleasure in
all that was for the good and healthful recreation of the children, his tears over the impenitent, all have made an impression upon a rough, it may be, but a generous-minded people,
which will, we hope, help forward all future labourers, and
prove to have been good seed which shall bear fruit in due
time. If the utility of his life at Flamborough be also judged
by those kind of efforts by which a clergyman's activity and
usefulness are sometimes tested, we have to record how he
gave lectures for the instruction of his people upon general
subjects, illustrating them by the valuable diagrams published
by the Working Men's Union in London, and by other equally
attractive means. He also built an infant school and presented it to the parish. The numbers in the national school
greatly increased, and a night school was established. He
taught the children singing, using the tonic sol-fa system of
Mr Curwen, and encouraged devotional and congregational
psalmody. In these and in many other ways did he heartily

endeavour to promote the advancement as well as the spiritual interests of his people.

After the first spring, when he was ill for some time, he felt convinced that his stay could not be long, but this persuasion made him the more anxious to improve the parsonage, and to have in the parish other substantial benefits which could be enjoyed when he was gone. It must however be confessed that in the pulpit he was not at this time successful. His sermons were not of that kind which are suitable for the instruction of a congregation little given to book-learning. He generally preached extempore, but he always wrote out at least one sermon each week, whether he was engaged in parish work or in the more varied occupations of his later life as a missionary, pioneer, and colonist. The advice of his father upon this point has been preserved—" Choose your text early in the week ; think frequently upon it ; look out all the parallel passages ; better still, write them out, and note their connection. Consider the simple meaning of the words, and make sure that you rightly understand and can explain them ; study the context, then consult the writings of biblical students, and of those who possessed much of the Spirit of God." His Father's sermons are remembered to this day, and are spoken of as models of useful and judicious Scriptural teaching. With such instruction enforced by example, the son, though not thus methodical, was an earnest student of Scripture, and appealed " to the law and to the testimony " in proof of what he offered to his hearers. In the pulpit, however, he generally found that his thoughts overpowered him, and he frequently " burst the fetters," and used to think that he was most successful when he neglected his notes altogether. He seldom could finish one of these discourses without being overcome with emotion. Like St Paul, he would say of his own ministrations, " warning every man . . . with tears." This, though "due to nervousness," proceeded from the depth of his convictions respecting his subject. He thought, to quote the words of an eminent Christian evangelist, that "a preacher should feel and should strive to make his hearers feel." He felt that in every congregation there are many persons who are asleep upon the brink of a precipice, and that the duty of the preacher is to do what he can to awaken them that Christ may give them light.

The following letters are descriptive of his life at Flamborough:—

" . . . I have to report a sad calamity. My house was broken into on Thursday last, and all my plate, except two or three spoons and forks, were stolen. I am thankful, however, to say that £100, which I had that day received, was not discovered, and desire to submit with cheerful acquiescence to the greater loss. The unfrequency of robberies ought to remind us to be thankful that there are so many honest men; nor should this occurrence make us apprehensive of the few who are thieves. 'Lay not up for yourselves treasures on earth, . . . but lay up treasure in heaven,' is the warning appropriate.

"We are doing all in our power to discover the offenders. . . . I do not feel disturbed about the matter, but I am grieved. . . . There is danger under such circumstances of giving way to a spirit of retaliation, rather than to seek to restrain crime, which is the christian view with which we should seek justice. I am grateful for much sympathy and help which this event has elicited, thus my losses become a gain.

" . . . I am so tied by my work in the Parish National School just now (he was sole schoolmaster during the temporary absence of the usual teacher), that I cannot trouble myself much about personal matters; indeed I look upon it as a providential circumstance that I have not time just now for anything but my school work. . . ."

In the spring of the year he suffered from the effect of the east wind which is peculiarly trying on the north-eastern coast. He was obliged to get a curate to take his parish duties for some weeks, and was advised to go to a more sheltered climate.

" Wearisome days and nights are appointed to me ; all, however, is ordered by a providence that cannot err in wisdom, or fail in love. . . . I scarcely like to leave my parish, though I can do nothing here. . . . ' Closing with Christ ' is the Scotch expression : this is the chief thing in religion, to know Christ, to lean on His merits, His finished work, to love Him supremely. I seem to be able to make the nearest approach to communion with Him in sick rooms among my people. . . .

" I have applied for leave of absence for a year, but in the spirit of one who knows not what may be on the morrow."

A short tour in Ireland was beneficial to his health, and he afterwards took charge, for three months, of a small parish in Herefordshire, whither his sisters accompanied him.

To his brother, who had been at death's door from fever caught as a medical student, he writes—

*March*

". . . I trust through God's mercy you are now so far recovered as to be able to read a letter. I pray God, that as we have suffered together, we may together rejoice. Oh may we renew the dedication of our hearts to Him to be cleansed and to be renewed. I feel the need of both. Let us pray for one another for special gifts. . . . I have, I believe, experienced seasons of special grace at times when I felt no doubt that a christian friend was in prayer for me, and this kind of answer to prayer is what we may look for.

" I am still ill, but am much better than when I last wrote. Oh may I live for God's glory ; growing in faith, and joy, and love, with hope firm as an anchor. What firmness, what strength is implied in that expression—Do you ' lay hold on the hope set before us.' I am too apt to go back ; ' laying again the foundation, when I ought to be building on that which is, I trust, laid on Jesus. . . .' "

" I am still an invalid, and I fear am likely to continue so from the state of the atmosphere ; but I go about my work though feeling very unwell.  Being in Hull, whither I have come to procure books for a Sunday school treat, I have consulted Dr S———, he says I ought to leave my parish for, at least, four months, and go to a warmer climate.  I am quite cast down at times when I think upon my life ; that which was to me once so marvellous in the excitement attendant on an opening future, all unknown, but certainly full of wonder and of mystery—now, not for me to take any part in !"

".  .  .  I suppose J——— has told you of our excursion to Llanthony Abbey, a fine ruin in early English style of architecture, situate in a narrow valley between lofty hills ; also of our climbing the Vow church hill to hold an extemporised missionary meeting, in a fancy building resembling an heathen temple.  [Mr Weeks, the late Bishop of Sierra Leone, was with us.]  I desire to realise more the faith which alone can animate a missionary, or sustain a minister anywhere, which shall conquer sin and the world, and accomplish a victory over every corruption.  Oh let us pray more for this."

" I have found employment in finishing my 'Notes on Hebrews' and in reading up astronomy, having had sixteen volumes lent to me from the library at Hereford, a most thoroughly interesting study."

To this study he was induced by a recent purchase of an achromatic telescope, and the knowledge he at this time acquired, was useful to him during future voyages, not at this time at all contemplated.

The 'Notes on Hebrews' refers to the share he took in an edition of 'the New Testament in Greek, with English

Notes and Prefaces,' edited by his friend Mr Macmichael, head-master of the Ripon Grammar School.

The custom prevalent among the farmers in Hereford-shire of giving all the farm labourers a supper upon the Sunday evening, afforded Mr Ogle an opportunity, of which several permitted him to avail himself, to meet the young men and others, and in a friendly and familiar manner, to give them religious instruction. Their ignorance respecting the histories and teaching of the Bible was lamentable, but the interest they often displayed in listening to their temporary pastor, was very encouraging.

HIS HEALTH RESTORED, HE RETURNED TO HIS OWN PARISH.

The following letter introduces us to a variety of matters, confirmations, discussions respecting the Church, &c. :—

FLAMBOROUGH, *June* 27, 1854.

" My dear Sister,—

" I had an interesting day on Saturday ; thirty-three of my parishoners came to renew their vows in the presence of the people of God. And I had very great satisfaction in their behaviour at the time. I wish I could say that, since that time, the same comfort has been mine. I have little hope that it is more than a morning cloud. After confirmation, at which good Bishop Spencer (ex-Bishop of Madras) officiated, I gave dinner to more than thirty, and, afterwards, tea to the same in the tent. The evening was spent, partly in reading to them, partly in their play, partly in instruction, and con-cluded with singing and prayer.

" Mrs B—— and Mrs R—— managed all nicely, and the Sabbath was not disturbed by any disorder, as is too often the case after Saturday entertainments. I had, however, only ten of them at church on Sunday, to hear a sermon which I preached on the glorious prospects which open before the young Christian on his first entrance on the spiritual warfare. I feel, however, that what labour I did bestow on my candidates

for confirmation was not thrown away, but the contrary. I
believe that my class was honourably excepted from the rest
by their superior attention and seriousness.

"Yesterday I took a holiday. Mr F——, and a friend
from Cambridge, came to spend the day. We went to the
rocks, and on the water. Alternate showers (and thunder
showers), and the bright clear shining which succeeded, the
exquisite beauty of cloud, and sea, and shore, the varied incidents of a boat excursion, combined to render the day one of no
common enjoyment. We went nearly to Speeton under the
magnificent white cliffs which, beetling, overhung the boisterous
restless sea, the feathered tenants of the rocks in clouds outfly-
ing. We sailed at a very brisk pace : sometimes 'twas all we
could do to balance the wind, when gusts came down the gullies
in the cliffs, or the sharp shower swept the sea. Once we shipped
a large quantity of water, the side of the boat going under
and filling the boat up to our knees in a second. Our
fishermen appeared not at all disconcerted, and said it was of
frequent occurrence. As it was otherwise very fine weather,
and the accident resulted from a hitch in the rope preventing
the sudden slackening of the sail, we thought less of it than
we should have done ; but had you been with us, I should
have felt that the carelessness of one man had wantonly imperilled us. We had a luncheon on the rocks at Bempton.
While there, two men appeared above and pursued their perilous
occupation over our heads, climbing with double rope and bas-
ket backward slung, to search for the eggs of sea birds scarcely
hid upon the ledges of the cliffs. I was watching to see that
nothing came down from them to us, as well as to observe
their venturous game. Presently a huge stone, dislodged by
the climbers, took a side direction in its fall, bounded on a
slant of grass half way down the cliff, and flew off at an angle
towards us. I darted from my place, and the same instant
the stone came down between me and my companion, knocking off a savage piece of rock from the place where my elbow
had leaned a second before. Mr B—— said, ' Well, I never
saw a nearer escape for a man's life than that."

"I replied, 'It is indeed a cause of thankfulness to the Almighty, who has preserved us both.'"

"I hope I felt what I said. Of course we quickly resorted to a shelter. He was a very pleasant companion—a fine young man every way—and I hope he will have profited somewhat from the strong Protestantism with which I met his miserable Romeward-verging theology. I have learnt another lesson of the insidious under-working which threatens our faith. This youth, son of a good clergyman, I am told, confessed that if sacramental grace and hope in Purgatory were taken from him, he should have neither faith nor religion! The Bible he could not understand, and thought it taught all opinions alike, because, forsooth, all men pretend to have its authority for their opinions. He appeared to have some seriousness, and a foundation of good in him, and professed abhorrence of many things which, such as he, would have excused when I knew Cambridge. I wish I could do some good there. Alas, there is much evil to counteract. I have heard of two instances of women (ladies), one advocating the *Church* against the Evangelists, as if the Church was aught but a name, and its members to be found as well in one class of men as another; for the Lord has His own people who are His Church. But where is there any encouragement to the notion that the true Church is to be found *en masse* in great assemblies? Few among the wise, or learned, or rich, or powerful are called. We must rather look into 'the lone sequestered vale of life,' 'hid,' 'poor,' 'despised,' 'outcast of all,' 'persecuted,' 'slain.' 'Which of the prophets have they not persecuted' to the death, and it shall be so to the end. So the Saviour taught. The Church of Christ, then, is only seen, as I conceive, in the victory of suffering, in the pre-eminence of its reproach and oppression furnishing notable world-known examples of extreme endurance and of patience. This is their glory, not to be great or successful, but to suffer. This is the true, the only true Church of Christ. To be supported by authority, is all anomalous; to have rule, all exceptional, not impossible, not unpromised, but not to be expected now.

"The other woman was a Mormon, and heaped texts of Scrip-

ture on her opponent till he was stupified, to prove that the
almighty, invisible God, has a body and passions of a man?
When women rule thus, a state is sick indeed.   I hope you
will learn a good lesson to be modest and diffident, and to say
little, but that little for the truth.   Make good use of your
opportunities for cultivating faculties which now or never
must be developed.   Suppose we should have to end our
days as exiles, how we shall need to know how to do everything, and how to live happy and content on the recollection
of the past, and expectation of the future ; neither finding
luxury nor wealth ; no worship will be attainable then,
but the benevolent heart, the contented, cheerful disposition,
the delight which is in doing good, sympathy and affection,
vivacity and solid acquisitions, will be invaluable.   Then, oh
let us pray for oneness of mind, and devotedness to the
Saviour ; a sense of need, and assurance of His all-sufficiency
and all gracious willingness to save.

   " This will be a pillar of strength, though kingdoms fall and
the earth be moved.   I hope I shall learn by these tokens of
His loving-kindness and gracious preservation to trust Him
ever, and to expect in greater and more imminent danger to
be ' covered in the shadow of His hand,' to hide myself in
the exhaustlessness of His mercy,—the ocean of His love,—as
the sea-bird, when she sees the flash of firearms, seeks her
shelter under the waves."

   One who knew Mr Ogle, although only in his mature years,
said of him that he much resembled Henry Kirke White.
There were not a few points of resemblance between the two.
Both were great readers from the same cause, avariciousness of
knowledge.   The mental and material organisation of both
appears to have been very much alike.   Apart from that
renovation of nature which they underwent, both instinctively
shrunk from what was low and vile, and were irresistibly drawn
to what was pure and lofty.   A yearning for the sympathy
of their fellows, combined with the solitariness and pensiveness
of genius, characterised both.   The elements of a poetic tem-

perament as really existed in the case of Mr Ogle as in that
of Kirke White. It is seen more especially in his power of
idealising all he saw, and in those touches which come upon
us like flashes of beauty. Had he given himself to writing
verse he would probably have achieved no mean place as a poet.
As it is he has left a few small poems, some of them frag-
ments, but all of them, we venture to say, instinct with true
poetic fire. They have a simplicity, a sweetness, and an ease
of versification which remind us of the poet of Nottingham.
The following piece accords well with the conversation just
detailed.

### THE SHADOW OF CHURCH.

" From earliest youth to life's decline,
The shadow of the Church was mine—

\*　\*　\*　\*　\*　\*

" Thy presence makes the floweret fair,
And the green grass grow greener there;
Fools only, who despise or dread
The church's shadow on their bed.

" A thousand thoughts thou bring'st to me,
A thousand things I learn from thee—
Memorials of a Presence high
And monitors of Destiny ;

" A shadow from the noonday glow ;
The Rock whence healing waters flow ;
The ark where rests the peaceful Dove—
An emblem of our home above.

" When fears distract, and pleasures flee,
From every foe a sanctuary,
Thy sombre beauty pictureth
The hopeful, awful shade of death.

" Awful when island, temple, tower,
And rock and mountain own its power ;
Hopeful when in the brighter day
All earthly shadows fled away."

E

The building referred to is no doubt the beautiful parish church of Boston, Lincolnshire, of which his father was the vicar. The old vicarage on the north side was necessarily shadowed by the church.

The following little drama was composed by him with the view of arousing in his youthful parishioners a sound independent Protestant spirit, combining amusement with the intellectual efforts required in the school. It reminds us of the dramatic poems written and acted at the time of the Reformation, both in Scotland and France. Sir David Lyndsay, at the court of James V., and Margaret of Valois, at the court of Francis I., strove in this way to expose the ambition, luxury, and idolatry of Rome, and to pave the way for the introduction of a better system. He was to be alone at Christmas ; his sisters, who frequently stayed with him, were from home, yet the good old festivities must not be omitted. He would make a feast for the children, and prepare gifts more enduring for their parents, and the children should help him to amuse themselves. It was a sudden resolve. The whole affair,—the little feast, its conception, and its accomplishment, did not occupy more than a week, and this when he was out of health, suffering so much from palpitation (solitude ?), that he was in London with his brother the doctor. When lying awake at night, the idea was conceived. The experiment was successful. Children who were not usually ready in learning by heart learnt these almost impromptu verses and recited them with the greatest pleasure.

The patterns for the dresses, as well as all the banners and decorations, were made by the pastor himself, who never seemed to be better pleased than when he was making arrangements to give gratification to others, and especially to the young. Afterwards in distant lands, and here as ever, religion and instruction mingled their wholesome influences with all that was cheerful and hospitable and kind.

## A SERIOUS ALLEGORICAL PERSONATION

### IN ILLUSTRATION OF

## THE EPIPHANY.

*All nations bringing their tribute to the Christian land.*

MASTER OF THE FEAST   .   .   . (The Pastor.)

GUESTS   .   .   .   .   . (Children of National Schools.)

*Verses, &c., recited by Children of the first class.*

PROCESSION FROM ROME.

CARDINAL.   *Train borne by six Priests, followed by six attired as Jesuits. Twelve Nuns.*

MASTER.   (*To Spectators.*)

"My friends, a pompous pageant here we see:

(*To Cardinals, &c.*)

Stand, Sirs, and say from whence, and who are ye?"

CARDINAL.   "From Rome we come, the nations' Queen,
     The Pope our Lord has ever been:
     In right of him we claim to be
     Foremost at this Epiphany."

*Cardinal is dressed in broad black hat with gold tassels,
     cloak of scarlet flannel with white cross on back.
. Priests in surplices, black crosses behind the back, black caps.
     Banner, " Mystery, &c."
Nuns in black hoods and white dresses, bearing lighted tapers.*

REPLY.   (*To Romish Procession.*)

"Your name is Babylon the Great,
     Your mystery is all a cheat."

(*To Spectators.*)

"We're honest Protestants we hope,
     And serve our gracious Queen, and not the Usurper, Pope."

(*To Cardinals and Priests.*)

"The blood of saints deep dyes your clothes,
     And marks you for their deadly foes:
     Christ's Image and His Grace you lack,
     And put His Cross behind your back.
     To use few words and plain is best,
     Know then, with us, Rome finds no rest;
     With apes like you we're summary,
     We'll not abide your mummery;

But take your gaudy robes that they
A useful part may come to play.
This hat will fit our postman's head,
And our good wives shall wear your red."

*(Disrobing the Priests and dispersing them.)*

HERALD, *with flourish of trumpets, bearing a flag with star.*

" A royal company admission wait "—
" Declare forthwith thine errand and estate."

THREE SAGES *in red, blue, and white, with crowns and stars,
    singing—*

" From far off lands we come to bring
Earth's richest treasures to her King,—
Gold, spice, and precious gifts have we,
To honour Christ's nativity."

*Answer—*

" Since such ye are, at least ye seem to be,
Right welcome to our Festival are ye."

*(They bear a cake ornamented on a tray with scarlet cloth.)*

EIGHT CHINESE. (*White coats and pantaloons, red caps
    or hats—lanthorns, yellow banner with red characters,
    bearing on a tray ornamented chests of tea.*)

" Hither advances a fantastic band,
Methinks you greet us from some distant land."

*Reply—*

" From China's land, and famed Assam,
Half o'er the world these treasures came;
Our offerings, too, with songs we raise
To celebrate our Saviour's praise."

TWELVE TURKS, GREEKS, AND ARABIANS, *in blue cloaks, red
    caps, white dresses, and red and white turbans; in red
    cloaks and white turbans, bearing coffee, oranges, fruit,
    &c. Banner of Mahomet, and copy of Ilion Ghoral
    inscription, crescents, &c.*

" Say whence do ye, so richly laden come?
What are your nations? what land call ye home?"

*Reply—*

" From Turkey's spicy shores we come,
And blest Arabia is our home.
These grateful offerings receive,
To grace your feast this Holy Eve."

*(They ring a bell, and chant Muezzim.)*

" But what is this, we pray you tell,
  This crescent bright, and sound of bell?"

*Answer—*

" This is the chant we Moslems sing
  To Mahomet our Prophet King."

*Reply—*

" Not Mahomet's followers nor Mormons we :
  Our Prophet, Christ alone, and King, shall be ;
  But if with us you'll join His praise to sing,
  We'll welcome you, and take whate'er you bring."

TWENTY-FOUR JEWS *from Assyria, Nestorians, now Christians supposed the lost tribes.*

ADDRESS—WELCOME TO ISRAEL RESTORED.

" A goodly host, see, as a cloud they come,
  Like doves unto their windows hastening home.
  Fair as the moon, bright as the morning sun,
  Doth from the purple East his golden journey run.
  An army terrible in its array,
  A bannered host, most beautiful are they ;
  Our spirits are appalled as we view—
  Pray, Sirs, inform us, whence are ye, and who ?"

*Answer—*

" From fair Assyria we, Israel's lost seed,
  Out of long bondage, we through Christ are freed,
  And now, with grace and supplication, we
  Would claim our part in this festivity."

" What are the broidered robes ye wear?
  What standard is it that ye bear ?
  Why as a host with banner tall,
  Grace ye our simple Festival ?"

JEWISH MAIDENS' REPLY.

" Our robes with righteousness inscribed are,
  And Judah's Zion is our standard fair :
  No other banner but the truth we raise,
  Through which we conquer by our Saviour's grace."

*Reply—*

" We welcome you as Israel restored,
  None are so honoured as those once abhorred,
  Judah's true sons, acknowledging their Lord."

*Re-enter the expelled Boys dressed as fishermen with implements.*

" Whence come ye, late and last ? I ween
  Ye once before our face have been ;
  But useful symbols now you bring to view,
  And you have changed your scarlet for true blue."

*Reply—*

　　　" We once were slaves to Master Pope,
　　　　But we know better now, we hope,
　　　　For we have learnt, thank God, and you,
　　　　To render honour where 'tis due."

### Song—God Save the Queen.

　　　" We fishermen of Flamborough, known of old,
　　　　Are honest and respectful, but we're bold ;
　　　　We answered all your questions, and we too,
　　　　Would in our turn enquire, Sir, whence come you ? "

*Answer—*

　　　" Your question is a bold one, as you say,
　　　　But to a true man will not cause dismay ;
　　　　My purpose is a right one, and to you
　　　　Who ask me a fair question, I make answer true.
　　　　I am your brother, and I hope to prove
　　　　I ever bear for you a brother's love.
　　　　Still, I must not withhold there is another,
　　　　Whose kindness sticketh closer than a brother.
　　　　I am Christ's servant, and by Him I'm sent
　　　　To be a pastor, for a season lent ;—
　　　　And if you would His benefits partake,
　　　　You will receive me, for my Master's sake.
　　　　I preach His gospel, and I hope to find,
　　　　In you a willing ear, and an obedient mind,—
　　　　For though your sins I must not shrink to show,
　　　　I'll point to whence the healing waters flow.
　　　　Like you a stranger, and a pilgrim, I,
　　　　From sin, and Satan, and from hell we fly,
　　　　From dark Destruction's City we are come,
　　　　And both shall find at last
　　　　　　　In Paradise a home."

*Chorus—*

　　　" Oh, that will be joyful,
　　　　When we meet to part no more ! ' "

　　　　*After all had partaken of tea, cakes, &c., the contents of
　　　　the chests of tea, the calico and flannel robes, &c., were
　　　　distributed to the poor.*

This trifling incident was very characteristic of the man.
Solitary and depressed, he sought relief by doing something to
make others happy. The suggestion of the season was followed.
Difficulties supplied but a stimulus to exertion. He never

succeeded when things were ready to hand. He rarely failed when success would seem to others impossible. His brother informs me that his own feeling about him used continually to be, " Give him money and means, he is sure to come to grief ; let him be in a strange land without sixpence in his pocket, and he will accomplish all he purposes, and, moreover, be seemingly unconscious of having done any thing remarkable." This will be seen abundantly in his foreign travels.

We cannot dismiss the above scene without remarking that it is altogether different in principle from those " Passion Plays " which are so common in southern Germany, and of which we had a sad specimen on a large scale at Oberammergau last autumn. The " Passion Play " brings the " Crucifixion " upon the stage in successive tableaux, and gives a dramatic representation of all its events and persons, not even excepting our Lord himself. It will be pleaded by some that this is simply a device for conveying some knowledge of revealed truth into the minds of an ignorant population. But it is to be borne in mind that these representations are presented to those from whom the Bible is withheld ; that they are, in fact, a substitute for the Word of God ; that they are accompanied by no instruction as regards the true nature of the sufferings represented, and the end for which they were endured ; that they degrade the work of redemption to the level of a mere historical event, which may be dramatised and acted on the stage ; and that, taken in connection with all the concomitants of these exhibitions, they tend to profane and desecrate Christ and his redemption in the minds of men. But in the above " Impersonation " we have neither divine persons nor supernatural doctrines represented (which two points of distinction make an essential difference), but simply a future event which stands predicted on the page of inspiration, the submission of the nations of the earth to the gospel, and which may therefore be lawfully represented, as was done here by the fishermen of Flamborough.

# CHAPTER VII.

## HIS VISIT TO ORKNEY AND SHETLAND.

MR. OGLE's spiritual ideal was very high, and what he had read of the attainments of others, impelled him ever to strive to reach the standard he had set up for himself. But he came short of what he hoped and desired, and the consciousness of this engendered in him a feeling of sadness. The question he would be ever putting to himself was, " Are these shortcomings and deficiencies consistent with the possession of the Christian life ?" This depression, amounting at times to almost hopelessness, was especially frequent during the early years of his ministerial life. Physical causes contributed to this despondency : a want of vigorous health, too close attention to study, sleepless nights and late morning hours were the signs and the causes of this state. He was again strongly urged to go from home for a season. Travel always braced both his bodily and mental frame. His great sensitiveness, which made him liable to depression, had this compensatory quality, that it gave him a keen enjoyment of the happy points of life, and of all the fitness and beauty which abounded in the world around him ; and therefore no sooner was he again under the blue sky, or gazing on the shore or the mountains, than his sadness would depart, the tide of health would flow, his joyousness of spirit would burst out, and even his hopes as a Christian would revive and flourish anew. He now directed his steps to Orkney and Shetland, and his quick eye and ready pen gathered up and treasured in his letters the novel features of these northern regions. His sketches from the *Ultima Thule* are characteristically fresh and truthful. What another man would, perchance, have turned away from as simply a land of heathery moors and naked rocks, becomes under his pen a land of no little interest and beauty.

SHETLAND.

" . . . I was quite unprepared to find the Shetland isles so large, and so distant from the north of Scotland. The largest island, in which Lerwick is situate, is sixty miles in length and twenty-five in breadth. It is intersected by ranges of hills; the valleys open to the sea, so that in travelling due north or south you have a hill every two miles. Each hill forms a promontory, and every valley a bog. The hills are generally about 800 feet in height. The aspect of the island from the sea is not inviting. It appears to be uncultivated, houses are few, peat bogs like those in Ireland are numerous, Shetland ponies in droves, black lambs timidly starting with arched necks and scrambling over the hills; the snipe and the plover, the raven and the buzzenel, the hawk and eagle, are indigenous; there are no hares or grouse or partridges, and few cattle; I do not recollect to have seen either a swallow or a sparrow, or to have heard any songster but the lark. Alpine plants are abundant—I have not made any collection; ferns are few, vegetation stunted, trees absent. I visited the extreme north island, and the extreme north of it. It has an historic name, 'Harold's Wick,' in Unst. Wick signifies bog, and Harold is the cognomen of a Dane (perhaps the English Harold). From the summit of a Jhoog (hill) I gave to the listening zephyr three cheers for Queen Victoria, uttered a prayer for her prosperity, and sang 'God save the Queen;' gathered a wild flower, broke off a fragment of the summit, and, after one cheer more, descended southward. This was the turning-point of my travel. I had stood on the extreme northern rock looking over the Arctic, the limit of Her Most Gracious Majesty's possession in direction of the North Pole. It is rare to reach a limit of such an empire as God has given her.

## A SHETLAND MANSE.

At the foot of the hill I rested at a hospitable home —Dr. Lawrence Edmeston's. I had heard of him, and as the historian of Shetland I approached him with the respect,

mixed with confidence, which a reputation for literature and
for science inspires in any breast that is elevated by kindred
pursuits.   I found the doctor seated by his fire, his barefooted
offspring having the liberty of the house.   Over his mantle-
shelf, on which stores of books are piled, hang fire-arms of
antique construction, and a few curious skins, &c., are about
in the room.   He received me with some dignity, not unmixed
with coldness, I thought ; and it must be confessed that my
travel-worn attire afforded the excuse.   Imagine your brother in
a ' paletot' much the worse for wear, with a hat on his head commonly called " Prince Albert's sou'-wester ;" on his shoulder a
gun, and his knapsack tied with a piece of rope upon his back.
Such was the Rev. M. A. Cantab, who introduced himself to the
most eminent man residing in the far north of our isles.   After
a few minutes' converse, in which I sought information respecting a mine of cromate of iron I had seen on the hill, he asked
me to take ' bread,' and, after a frugal repast, took me to see
his garden.   Thinking of my own home at Flamborough, I could
listen with the interest which similar experience gives to his
detail of struggles against a stormy climate, and against still
stronger local prejudice, while he pointed to his success in
rearing a few trees.   They looked prosperous considering the
latitude, 61 deg. N., and the prevailing easterly or northerly
gales.   I now asked his permission to write a few lines from a
situation so interesting, and I wrote a letter to the children
of my national school at Flamborough.   Mrs E. and the children
were then introduced, and we became good friends.   To the
children I gave some little books, and read to them the letter
which I had just penned.   I was pressed to stay and dine, to
which I willingly agreed, having a desire to enjoy longer a
conversation which exhibited the man of thoughtful, reflective
habit, with an intellect enlarged by study at home and by
travel abroad, and a character matured by the experience of
sixty years, many of which had been spent in rustication on
his paternal soil.   He drew from me the narration of my
travels, my life's struggles, and many incidents in our family
history.   I found several points in which the past traditions of
his family resembled our own—e.g., their migration from the

seat of an ancient race about the same period as our ancestors
left Northumberland for Flamborough; a preference for an obscure
quietude apart from gaiety and from luxury, living among their
adopted people and winning their affection and respect; and
the contrast between the difficulties which I had fancied almost
forbade my entrance into the good man's house, and the cor-
diality to which it had given place, made the pleasure I was
deriving from my visit the more enjoyed. My host seemed to
participate in this pleasure. He thanked me courteously for
the frankness with which I had cast myself upon his hospitality,
having no other introduction than that afforded by a conscious
bond of mutual tastes and occupations. Meanwhile the sun
was stretching out the shadows, and a superlative evening
invited me to commence a journey already too long delayed,
but mine host again detained me by the remark—'I discover
in you, sir, many kindred sentiments and inclinations, perhaps
you would be willing to listen while I read to you a few
thoughts I have recently set down;' and then from his note-
book he read a clear and beautifully expressed essay upon the
causes which render family distinction [the worthy records of
our father's lives] the most prizable of all birthrights. The
next extract was still more interesting and valuable, embody-
ing a nice distinction and definition of a difficult point in
theology. The style reminded me of our own good father's
best words, while the benevolent pleasure with which my entertainment and instruction was sought recalled him frequently to
my memory during that happy visit. Finally the good doctor
accompanied me for a mile, as far as to the foot of the hill,
pointed out the road, and saying, 'Now, Mr Ogle, whenever
you or any of your friends come into this country, you must
promise me to make ' Balta Sound' your home; and let me
know that God's providence has brought you safely to your
own. I say to you, as we say in Shetland, 'Happy to have
met, sorry to have parted, hoping to meet again. God bless
you.' 'Good bye, dear doctor,' was all I could say, and I
turned me to the hill. As I reached the summit, I paused to
mark the form of the dear, kind Doctor Edmeston, as with
head a little depressed, as if meditating—praying, per-

haps—he slowly hied him home. I took a careful sketch of
his country—the hills, the deep sea with its islands ; then of
the house, the kirk and manse. I did not feel as if I were
taking a long farewell, for I must not forego the pleasure of
another visit to these interesting islands, where truth and piety,
simplicity and hospitality, taking leave of the bad world, have
lingered ere they returned to heaven !

### A SHETLAND FISHERMAN'S COT.

" I spent two hours in wandering amid the finest of wild
scenery; rock, and wide stretching upland, or boundless ocean
lay before me. I had turned from the road indicated as the
easier path, to follow a wild glen, sure of its leading me to
the shore. At nightfall my sporting propensities were strongly
excited by flocks of wild ducks and of plover, flitting to and
fro, to find a resting-place for the night. None, however, came
within shot till it was too dark to take aim, though at dusk
my imitative cry brought them around me, and I could hear
their wings close to my ear.

" I soon found myself at a loss as to my route—a high wall
on one side, a forbidding looking hill to the left, and a lake to
the right, seemed to have shut me in. Climbing the wall I
then discovered a fisherman's cot at some little distance, and
thither repaired for shelter. The humble home, with its
bright fire, presented an appearance of cheerful industry prevailing, and the pleasant and honest-looking faces of the family
within, induced me to ask if they had room to give me a
lodging for the night. ' Oh, yea, we have room for ye. Ye'll
get a good bed here, if ye pleeze.'

" ' Will I get anything to eat ? '

" ' Oh, yea, ye'll get what ye pleeze.'

" ' I'll stay the night with ye then.'

" The peat-fire was quickly fanned into a blaze, and the
family bade me welcome, giving me the seat of honour. I
chose, however, a wooden chair, and asked for eggs, meal,
milk, sugar, butter, and a frying-pan, made an omelet, cooked
and enjoyed it greatly.

" I then administered advice to the father of the family,

who was suffering from a whitlow; found with pleasure that I had entered into the house of a truly Christian family; and after reading with them from the Scriptures and prayer, we retired to our several dormitories.

"My bed was in the second room, used as a store or shop, a cupboard door being opened, behold a bed—good feather bed, with neat counterpane, &c., complete. The cupboard above also soon had its occupant, and the rest of the family were similarly accommodated in the adjoining apartment. Thus the whole household seemed to surround and to shield the guest. Humans above and around, and quadrupeds below, a little hive of somnolent life—all probably but the centre one somnolent—for I slept not, as you can perhaps imagine; nevertheless I was well pleased to have escaped the wet blanket of fog which filled the valley.

## SCENERY OF THE ISLANDS.

"At four o'clock next morning I turned out, and could have sailed in Ariel's boat upon the cloud-lake stretched below. I tried, but in vain, to find a wild-fowl for our breakfast; I saw the sun rise clear, and the cloud disperse; breakfasted upon porridge and milk, and repaired to the beach, accompanied by two of the fisherman's sons. They rowed me across the sound, a distance of two miles. It was a deep, clear, rapid stream of salt water, the high road of the herring and the mackerel, and fitted in its clear transparency to exhibit their lustrous forms. The lobster and the crab rest undisturbed in caves and coverts amid the forests of algæ, which resemble tropical palms and jungle, as seen covering the rocks below. The cormorant and the diver sport upon the waters; ducks sail like a wind-wafted fleet in regular array; the screaming gull soars aloft; the active tern skims the water like a swallow, with plumage changed to Arctic whiteness, and used to dip his feet in the wave instead of the pool; the shore bird, between the elements amphibious, with webbed feet paddles in the margin washed by the constant ripple, his beak inserted in the sound, his plumage glistening in the sunbeam. The borders of the stream are not tame mud-banks or marshes broad; but

granite barriers of sheer rock dipping down as far as they rise
above in cloud-piercing pinnacles. The acquainted oarsman
finds out a creek wherein to thrust his skiff, and we land on
the rock-strewn beach, thence to the hill. Views, wild at
hand and wide afar, and stretching over the isle-studded ocean
to north, to east, to west, all various, all the same. In detail
various, in aspect all alike.

" This description represents my journey across the second
island of the group on which I had landed.

" Thursday was diversified by interesting conversations with
the islanders, the distribution of tracts, reading passages of
Scripture, and gifts of pictures to children.

" I noticed as I ascended one of the hills a little fair-haired
girl seated upon a green bank, about a quarter of a mile distant ; near to her played a highland collie. She was
whirling a shawl round and watching it float in the free air.
I approached her within five yards unobserved, and stood a
minute right before her. Her eye then caught sight and contracted suddenly. She uttered no cry, but, ' Oh, my Lord !'
in a faint musical voice, then seated still, she put a hand
over her bended head, and in that posture seemed disposed to
stay, her face directed towards me, covered with her hand.
I spoke, she looked up, pale, and as if recovering from a strange
surprise. ' I was frighted,' she said, and then suddenly seemed
to forego her fright, answered questions and asked them with
a quick, timid inquisitiveness. I showed her pictures. I had
brought some very pretty cards with Scripture subjects painted
in gay good colouring, with sweet verses below. ' Oh, what a
lovely thing !' she said. ' I'll give it ye, if ye like it.' ' Yes.'
Then, getting up, she said, dropping a curtsey, ' Thank ye,
sir.' No boisterous joy nor ecstasy exhibited, no rudeness or
familiarity. A simple child, that gently draws its breath and
feels its life in every limb.

" Such are the pictures of life and manners, such the scenery
of nature, one meets with in these isles remote. Long have I
searched for simplicity, and seem to have overtaken it here—
myself alone artificial. . . ."

On his return southward he took Orkney in his way, travelled over its islands, paid a visit to Wick, and there saw what all who have seen it acknowledge to be a very impressive sight—the fleet of fishing boats sailing out to sea.

"The sight of a thousand boats getting out to sea, the activity in the harbour, the fleet stretching away, and blackening the ocean to the horizon, and the sun sinking into his watery bed, hissing hot, repaid me for the fatigue of the journey. I also got some good specimens of asterolepis and other fossils characteristic of the region, so well described by Hugh Miller in his 'Footprints of the Creator,' which volume I took from your bookshelves in anticipation of my visit, judging, no doubt, rightly, that to have been on the spot described would benefit the book, as well as give it increased value to its owner—just as a cask of London Madeira gains a smack of the climate by being carried in a ship's bottom to the West Indies and back! The simile is the more appropriate since your book lay in my portmanteau till the occasion for using it is past.

I have been from home twenty-nine days—have travelled seven hundred miles by sea, and an equal number on land, and have enjoyed better health of late, than I have had for years past—thus, I hope, I have laid in a stock of health and of preparation for better work at home.

### A LESSON HARD TO LEARN.

#### TO A YOUNG FRIEND ON GOING TO LONDON.

". . . If I mistake not, you have begun your religious life with a wrong idea—a resolution to serve God, whereas you ought to have begun in a conviction that you cannot serve Him. It is this conviction which opens the heart to Jesus. When we are feeling ourselves to be helpless, blind, empty of all good, powerless and sinful, then He comes as the all-sufficient Saviour, the Strength, the Light, and the Comforter, in short, the fullness of the Godhead.

"Alas, how hard a lesson this to learn, our corruption and misery! That there is in many a preponderance of what is good, and right, and true, is their great hinderance to a saving faith in Jesus, for it seems to them to be possible by conforming themselves to the good examples set before them, by engaging in works of charity—excited thereto perhaps, by living among, and acquiring the habits of those who are truly converted to God—to work the work of God. Whereas the ' work ' of coming to Christ and believing on Him, realizing our need of His help, and following His example, remains to such as unknown as ever. Seek then for a personal love springing from faith in the Lord Jesus, a warm feeling of lively gratitude to Him as your known friend, as one who can sympathize fully, and who will grant to you a spiritual knowledge of Himself, ' manifest Himself' to you. Seek to advance His cause in the world when your heart beats warmly towards Him ' for whom you live every hour,' communion with whom will be the joy of your eternity.

"Is this possible ? Yes, I believe it is so, and that nothing short of this is meant by the expressions, ' that I may know Christ.' ' Being one with Him.' ' Setting our affections upon things above.'"

## CHAPTER VIII.

### VIEWS ON CHURCH REFORM.—RITUALISM, &c.

WE come now to speak of Mr. Ogle's views on more important matters. It was impossible for him to live in the times he did, without having his attention earnestly turned to the state of the Church of England, and coming to decided opinions on those great questions which have of late been so much discussed within her. Mr. Ogle was a loyal son of the Church of England. He cherished for that Church not only affection but veneration ; and we are bound to add that the *ideal* he had ever before his mind, was the Church of England as historically exemplified in her reformers and martyrs, and doctrinally exhibited in her thirty-nine articles. These articles he would have been willing to subscribe with Cranmer's pen, and to maintain with Cranmer's stake. But his relation to the Church of England of the present hour requires a little more explanation. His views on the general question are briefly, but clearly, stated in the following extract from a paper in which he appears to be reviewing the conclusions to which his anxious study of Church matters was leading him.

" I love the Church of England! I love the idea of a national establishment, with efficient agents, enjoying a sound scriptural constitution, maintaining evangelical doctrine, providing spiritual instruction and consolation, visiting men in every hour of difficulty and distress, to guide and to aid ; able to direct the wandering, and to support the weak, and reclaim the erring. The friend of the parent, the instructor of youth, &c.

" Church subjection has its hardships, but we may challenge the world to show us a system without these defects, and we can show in our own a provision made for the application of a remedy for each as it arises, if only there be a disposition to avail ourselves of it."

But there were things in the Church of England as he found her, which conflicted rudely with the idea set forth above. These occasioned to Mr Ogle many anxious hours in his study at Flamborough. He could take nothing on the authority of man. He must sift everything to its foundations, and be convinced on solid grounds. We have seen how he had to pass through the fires of doubt and unbelief at Cambridge, and only after coming to deeper and larger views of the gospel, did he enter into possession of solid peace. A similar, though not so severe a struggle awaited him now as a clergyman. The church of England puts into the hands of all her ministers the book of Common Prayer as their guide, subject always to Holy Scripture, in the instruction of their people. Mr. Ogle shared the admiration common to all the members of the Church of England for the Liturgy, so largely drawn from the

F

fountains of inspiration, and blending the massy grandeur of the awakened Saxon intellect of the sixteenth century, with the simplicity and sublimity of the Hebrew prophets, and making it perhaps the noblest book of devotion ever compiled by man. But there were parts of the Liturgy at which he always stumbled ; those to wit, which taught, or appeared to teach baptismal regeneration and apostolical succession. Neither of these dogmas did Mr. Ogle believe in the least. He was among the earliest to welcome the Society formed for the further revision of the Prayer Book, and to contribute to its funds. He clearly foresaw the use which would be made by the Rome-ward party when more definitely formed, of certain expressions in the Liturgy, and therefore most earnestly desired their removal. He understood and loved the gospel too well to attribute either to the sacrament, or to " him who administered it," any mystic virtue or power to regenerate, and he saw with a corresponding dismay and grief, the return of symbolism, rightly judging the progress of ritualism to be the measure of the decadence of the Church of England, and of the return of the nation to the darkness and bondage of popery. Such an issue he could not but deplore, as a Christian, and as a patriot ; as a Christian because the souls of men were thereby imperilled, and as a patriot because liberty was being undermined. But we shall best bring out his views and feelings on these all-important questions, by selections from his letters, written at different times. Soon after leaving Cambridge, 1847 ; he writes to a friend :—

" You seemed to think that Baptism is the only means for the bestowal of renewing grace, and that other means of grace, such as prayer, the sacrament of the Supper, are for sanctification of the believer. Now as such a belief would quite shut the door of mercy against me, and against thousands of persons who feel that they have not only sinned after baptism, but have lived, from a feeling of unbelief or from despondency, in a state of habitual neglect towards the grace then conferred, so that it kept them not from daily and hourly offences condemned by their own consciences, I cannot admit this limitation of God's offered mercy to sinners.  It must appear to any one who thoughtfully considers the subject, that to preach the doctrine I have named would be to preach a doctrine which is not only against the constant tendency of the word of God—full as it is of offers of mercy to backsliders who have broken the covenant, if they will 'return unto' the Lord—but would also make the ministry of the Gospel useless except as a confirming means of grace to steadfast believers ; that repentance could, to a professedly Christian congregation, be no more preached ; and that those who have been baptised have been by their parents placed in the fearful condition of a liability to apostacy, invested when unconscious infants with a responsibility for the fulfilment of which no adequate provision has been made ! No, my friend, I do not find in the word of God that to baptism is assigned the change of character, of state *within* a man ; it introduces us into a 'state of salvation,' a state of entrance into that covenant with God through Christ, by which He promises His Holy Spirit to those who use the means which He has appointed for obtaining that heavenly gift. Study the Bible with earnest prayer, and you will, upon this and upon all essential points, be led to form right conclusions."

He writes on Symbolism in 1855 :—

".   .   .   I had time to look over the church at N——. It is a magnificent example of modern decoration and restoration.   Everything has been brought back except the mass-book and the priests, if indeed I ought to make the last exception, for there are many who are the ministers of a false religion closely approximating to Rome.   Gilded mystic symbols are conspicuous, a chancel screened off, &c., &c.   Five thousand people are to be there to-morrow to celebrate the re-opening, to witness a procession—a hundred clergymen, with the bishop at their head, in sacerdotal vestments !  England bowing its head to the advancing idol, and no one lifting up his hand to heaven to avert the evil.   Streets filling with soldiery, and churches with Popery, are striking facts, significant of some great changes soon.    Let us be armed and vigilant.

"I did not like the festival at St. Paul's in London at all; the impression it left upon my mind is, that religion is becoming more and more an imposing ceremonial rather than an act of hearty, simple worship.    God is honoured by the worship of an humble heart, not by the wealth and pomp of men, exhibited in mystic symbols and a gorgeously imposing display, appealing to the eye and ear of man.

"A traveller describing the religious worship of Thibet, exclaims against their pomp and superstitions as an offence to Heaven. 'Sixteen priests,' says he, 'preceded by the high priest, or Grand Llama of Lassa, walked in a solemn procession from one to another of their temples, dressed in robes of white silk ornamented with gold, and bearing the symbols of their superstition, the people gazing with an expression of idle curiosity, or with blind reverence for the Divine principle supposed to be manifested only in the persons of the sacred Llamas.'

"What, I ask, is the difference between these spectacles, processions, &c., in England and in Tartary?    What? save that Llamaism is obsolete, and enforced as a yoke upon 400,000,000, while the superstition of England is a voluntary return to a long-abhorred and exploded perversion of Christianity.    It is indeed time that something be done to put a stop to the advance of the flood of superstition which will otherwise soon overwhelm us.    To support the languishing vitality of public worship by external additions is to kindle the blaze of a strange fire, and to extinguish the smouldering sparks of the true. Let true Christians beware, keep from outward compliances, lest they become tinctured with the spirit of error.    There is danger to all.    The seed of all this superstition is within our Church, in the confused notions which prevail respecting sacramental grace and apostolical succession, and these are growing and overgrowing Christian doctrine—the faith once delivered to the saints.    If I had not a personal sense of unworthiness and of unfitness, I must leave Flamborough for the sake of protesting against the apathy in our church.    .    .    May I be guided safely into all truth, out of all error in practice and in doctrine, through Jesus Christ!"

These convictions deepened every year which he passed as a parish minister, and he conscientiously resolved, since he could not cordially teach what he believed was included in the " assent and consent to *every thing contained* in the book of Common Prayer," to resign his living and to devote himself to evangelistic efforts wherever and however God should direct. He saw all the dangers, personal and social, which usually attend the formation of sects and parties, and refused the advances which were made to him, that he should take charge of a " Free Church of England " church.   " No," said he, " I belong to the Church of England.   I admire her so much that I cannot endure the defects which I see, and will not endorse or participate in them by eating her bread, neither will I rest till I have used every means which are proper in a humble individual to get her purified ; but I will not act against her in any way."   A few extracts from letters written at various subsequent periods will exhibit the progress of his judgment upon this subject.

*December 14th,* 1863.

" Luther and others could not at once get free from the entanglements of long years.   They slowly attained the place at which at length, as we think, they halted.   The Church of England reformers went a step, nay, many steps further. But the Church of England, like all human things, was left incomplete.   However, there remained room for protest and for striving after higher perfection.   Then came the Laudites, and invented ' subscription ' and tests, and then heartburnings began, and the Nonconformists came out, two thousand at a time, and the lights of truth burned brightly from their pulpits.   Witness the clear silver shining of pure evangelism from Baxter, Henry, Howe, &c. &c.   To the teaching of these men I believe we owe the truth proclaimed by Scott and Newton and Cecil.   These last, however, held that their forerunners acted unwisely in leaving the Church of England, and here lies the question still.   Surely we might decide it, and taking wings of faith overleap the feeble barriers of expediency and love of dignity and human help. . . . . The Gospel of Christ is able to do all now that it did when first the apostles went forth without purse and scrip and shoes. I allow that such faith is hard to find. The old Nonconformists possessed it. Their light was bright, their teaching was distinct, their faith was strong. It seems to me that God has placed his Church (*i.e.*, his genuine disciples) always in this position in the world, that faith tried as by fire may ever appear to His praise. . . . . How difficult it is to hold the true course in a tossing sea! I dare not, however, take B— N— as a pilot, nor B—, nor N— H—, nor S— as my leaders. Each seems to me inferior to Bickersteth, and Goode, and Champneys, and a host of others in the establishment.

"There can be no doubt that very many, if not all evangelical clergymen do repudiate the doctrine of baptismal regeneration (as it is called), and that they are offended in their consciences by the countenance given to it in certain expressions in the Prayer Book, yet they have decided to uphold the Prayer Book because of supposed dangers from innovations. Here is one passage of Scripture which seems to touch the subject and to justify their conclusion. 'Let both grow together until the harvest, lest while ye gather out the tares ye root up also the wheat with them.' And my controversy on this topic would altogether cease if the *existence* of tares or even *the possible existence* of tares were ingenuously conceded. It is when I am compelled to subscribe *ex animo*, &c., to all and everything contained in the said book that my conscience refuses, and I say, 'There are, in my opinion, points of positive objection, and also points of doubt and hesitation, both inconsiderable in proportion to the mass of sound doctrine, but which do not allow me to make the declarations and subscriptions required by clergymen in the unreserved and absolute manner demanded. That all men do not see with me that differences of opinion upon important subjects, necessitate withdrawal from communion, is strange but not inexplicable. To adjust the balance so as to decide between two evils is a very difficult process. For myself I say : Do I find any part of the services I am obliged to use in conducting the worship of God contrary to the dictates of my conscience ?  If so, then I must refuse to conform thereto, and must take the consequences.  That I must therefore relinquish many privileges, a position of advantage, &c. &c., but duty, plain duty, compels, whatever be the sacrifice.

" I allow all the force of the arguments in favour of an established church.  I see, perhaps, more plainly than many who hold to it—for I have made it the subject of some study —its great usefulness, as a power of doing good ; the nation's duty respecting religion ; and yet I contend that a clearly discerning Christian mind would reject with decision and abhorrence the doctrine which so many deduce from the words in the baptismal service, " we yield thee hearty thanks, most merciful Father, that it hath pleased thee to regenerate this infant—since it is one of the most dangerous and fatal errors which Satan has yet introduced into the Church.

" In our own day and Church the effects of this error have given rise to the daily increasing Puseyite abominations which have incontestably opened the ready road to Rome. We must, at all risks, refuse to sanction these, and take the consequences of our refusal in cheerful confidence.   ' Duty is ours, events are God's.'

" One thing comforts me, viz., That as churches approach purity the points of error they still retain will be more and more transcendental, if I may use the term, less palpable and obvious to ordinary men, less gross and glaring, belonging to the higher subjective portions of Christian doctrine, consequently only appreciated by a certain class of mind and a certain rank of attainment.   Still, from those who do clearly apprehend the error and its antagonistic truth a protest is imperatively, as I think, demanded.   When I look at the spread of Popery in the Church of England I cannot but attribute it to the retention of those expressions which are used to sanction these errors, and thus I take a serious estimate of their dangerous tendency and of the duty of protesting against them."

Again :—

*December, 8th,* 1864.

"I am still in full communion with the Church of England in doctrine, and agree in all necessary points with a succession of the best and greatest of her eminent divines; above all, with the Reformers, so that I have no conscientious hesitation as to retaining my connection with her; but I have scruples as to certain acts which, as a *parochial minister*, I could not avoid."

He, therefore, in the subsequent years of his life, although gladly accepting ministerial work when in England, always declined to receive remuneration for his services, or to accept any permanent appointment as a clergyman—conscientiously abstaining from 'eating the bread' intended for those who are consistent labourers under the guidance and subject to all the rules of the national church.

---

## CHAPTER IX.

### RESOLVES ON BECOMING A MISSIONARY.

It was put, we have seen, before Mr Ogle whether he would be the founder of a "Free Church of England." He weighed the matter calmly and prayerfully, and his answer was in the negative. He could not work for a Disruption in the Church of England. In this resolve, we happen to know, he coincided in judgment with one whose opinion was of great weight in these matters—we refer to the late Hugh Miller. We have more than once heard Mr Miller, referring to a possible disruption in the Church of England, say that it would work in the reverse way to that of the Scottish Disruption. In Scotland, he said, the people, feeling the question their own, came out with their ministers; but in England, in the event of a disruption, the clergy only would come out, and the people, too little interested in religious matters, would remain in the Establishment, and fall under the teaching solely of Ritualistic and Armenian clergymen. The Disruption greatly strengthened the Evangelical and Protestant interests in Scotland, but having regard to the different circumstances of the two countries, Hugh Miller thought that a Disruption in England would greatly weaken these interests.

We may add another consideration unfavourable to the success of a religious movement in England, of the same sort with that which has been followed by such marked and beneficial effects in Scotland. There is no common ground on which the several bodies which leave the Establishment may take up their position and form a united Church. The different denominations in England do not approximate. Each body has its own constitution and standards, and therefore, though outside the Establishment, they continue apart. In Scotland it is not so. All the bodies which have left the Establishment have the same constitution, the same standards, and the same doctrine ; and these are the constitution and standards and creed of the Established Church. The process of separation which has been going on in Scotland for a century and a half is in reality a process of re-union. The Scottish Church is being reformed outside the limits of the Establishment, and by the end of the century, we venture to affirm that the old National Church of Scotland will be reconstructed and be as entire and unbroken as at the beginning of last century, with more liberty than perhaps it ever enjoyed, and a tenfold greater amount of religious life.

From his earliest years the thoughts of Mr Ogle had been directed, at intervals, to missionary labour in a foreign field. He felt deeply his responsibility in connection with the heathen. Was he not a man, and could anything that appertained to the interests, happiness, and destinies of his fellow-men be foreign to him ? It mattered not what their colour or their tongue might be, or in what part of the world they might dwell, they were wanderers from heaven, they were without God and without hope, and they could return to their Father by only one way; and of that way they were ignorant. He would go and tell them of the Cross. Its light had scattered the darkness upon his own soul; its love had slain the hostility of his own heart; and was it not able also to dispel the gloom that shrouded them, and, showing them the face of a reconciled God in Christ, bring them in penitence and joy to His feet? Mr Ogle was in this respect like Justin Martyr, who declares again and again in his "Apology" that he would hold himself guilty of the ignorance of the Pagans if he did not do all in his power to make known to them the gospel of salvation. With Mr Ogle's system of theology there was combined a very active piety, which enabled him with great self-denial and moral heroism to carry into practice what he held and taught as a theory. In this he resembled another early father of the Church, Pantænus to wit, the founder of the famous school of the catechists in Alexandria, who vacated his chair of divinity in that city that he might carry the gospel to the barbarous tribes of the East.

It was this year that Mr Ogle became acquainted with the secretary of the Patagonian Missionary Society. The touching narrative of the martyr-like death of Captain Gardiner, which had temporarily arrested the operations of the mission, had deeply stirred his spirit. His interest was awakened, his sympathies drawn out for those poor Patagonians "perishing for lack of knowledge," and he began to hear in this the voice of God. The more he pondered, the more he felt himself drawn to this field of service; and now he was revolving the question with himself in what capacity and to what extent was it the will of God that he should embark in this enterprise.

The plan of the Patagonian mission, as originally sketched, was so far a novel one. Its projectors aimed at combining *colonising operations* with *missionary efforts*. Their main object, no doubt, was to plant the gospel in Patagonia, but they wished to present Christianity to the Patagonians, first of all, under the form of a *life* rather than a *doctrine*. They would show the natives the Christian life of England. They would introduce into those remote and savage abodes English husbandry, English arts, English education, and thus exhibit a specimen of that social, industrial, and intellectual life which Christianity ever brings after it. Not that they would neglect their proper work as missionaries, but having regard to the difficulty of savages in apprehending abstract truths, and the readier access which knowledge sometimes finds by the eye than by the ear, they resolved on combining the colonist with the evangelist. The manifest blessings of civilization might draw, they hoped, some, at least, to value and embrace the infinitely higher yet less manifest blessings of salvation. We think that the plan has substantial wisdom in it, and that, although the gospel is the great civilizer, it may be that in our great missionary associations, it has been shown too completely dissociated from the practical and worldly benefits that ever come in its wake.

At all events the plan of the mission strongly approved itself to Mr Ogle's mind. He became so much interested in it as to give £500 towards the building of the mission ship, which was to bear the name of "Allan Gardiner," the man whose life, with that of many others, was sacrificed in leading the first enterprise. Though Mr Ogle declined the offer subsequently made to him to take charge of the expedition, yet from this time he kept the thought of accompanying those who were to go out continually before his mind. He felt the gravity of the point. He had looked at the matter on all its sides. He clung to Flamborough and its people, but his health was not equal to its stern climate, and, however reluctantly, he had been forced to the resolution of leaving it. But that did not necessarily imply that he should leave home and kindred. His tastes, habits, and scholarly acquisitions seemed peculiarly to fit him for home

work. These so far from being aids might be actual hindrances
in the rougher fields abroad. But he had conscientious
difficulties in the way of accepting another parish in England.
The nature of these difficulties have already indicated themselves in his correspondence. He had the offer of a Free Church
of England chapel in one of the colonies. Or, should he prefer
remaining at home, he had literary work in connection with a
home-revival pressed upon him, for which he was more than
ordinarily qualified; or he might resume his former favourite
occupation, the instruction and training of youth. But he did
not see that Providence called him to any of these spheres of
work. He longed to preach among the heathen the unsearchable riches of Christ. The years he had passed at Flamborough
had, although he knew it not at the time, been years of preparation for the work on which he was now about to enter.
They had added to his stock of spiritual experiences : they had
improved his gifts for dealing with men about the matters of
their eternal salvation : they had taught him the need, in
addressing the ignorant and the careless, of a full reliance upon
the Holy Spirit, who alone can make the word as "a two-edged
sword, quick and powerful," and so, riper in graces, fuller of the
Spirit, more zealous, and more humble than when he entered
on his home work, Mr Ogle took the decisive step to which
God in His providence appeared to be hedging him in. In
coming to this decision, it may be truly said that he conferred
not with flesh and blood. And so we now see him, with a
calmness and a cheerfulness in which we behold grace signally
triumphing over all the tenderness of an affectionate nature,
proceeding to make arrangements for his departure from his
native land.

His decision is announced in a letter to his sister as follows:—

"April 10.

" . . . . My offer to the South American Missionary

Society to accompany their missionary as a volunteer is accepted. . . . I do regard the command to 'go into all the world,' &c., as specially belonging to me, and I feel no fear that I shall have a greater measure of success as a minister in obeying it than would have followed me in any other sphere of labour.

"I feel, however, how greatly faith is needed in following such a path : every hour we must walk by faith not by sight, but this is the great advantage of the position ; at least I fancy that the necessity may be more realised in an enterprise like ours. So to live is always our duty, but often a difficult one from our intercourse with men who 'walk by sight.' . . . I trust that my faith, so feeble now, may be strengthened and upheld by the power and grace of God. . . . The stupendous fact that the whole continent of South America is without a missionary proves how little Christian enterprise has yet accomplished."

His sister thus writes of him with special reference to the determination to which he had come :—"He was in many respects fitted for the life of a pioneer missionary. He possessed a body capable of enduring much occasional hardship, and a spirit not easily daunted or turned aside by danger. His gentleness of disposition, and his power of attracting and bestowing love, won for him the kind reception which ever awaited him, whether among the wandering Arabs of the African desert, or among the still less civilized Patagonian Indians. They all acknowledged in him a friend, and it was thus his happiness to be quickly loved by all with whom he came in contact. Many a half hour's conversation has been closed with tears, and a most affectionate parting on both sides, although it was perchance their first and last intercourse on earth.

"When among the Arabs of Algeria, an incident occurred illustrative of the impression which Mr Ogle's manners and appearance were fitted to make upon the people of the countries where he sojourned preaching the gospel. An Arab who had returned from Paris, and who had occasion to be in the company of Mr Ogle, appeared surprised and astonished at a phenomenon which he could not explain, but with characteristic gravity and reserve he remained for a while silent. At last he said abruptly to one of his companions, ' What can have induced a man like that to leave England to come and be kind to the Arabs in their poor and dirty tents ?' He knew not that the spirit of the gospel can make the most refined and cultured sit down beside their degraded brother man, recognising in him one of a race for whom Christ died, the heir of an endless existence, to be passed in moral and intellectual progress, and an ever-expanding felicity, if, through the truth, he should be brought under the renewing and sanctifying influences of the Holy Spirit."

To his brother, a physician, he thus writes :—

"April 3, 1856.

". . . . We shall go out fourteen or fifteen in number, and shall have no medical aid. Will you think of what is likely to be of service, therefore, in that department.

"I do hope I may be permitted to go and do work when out. It seems to my mind (as Captain ————, R.N., expressed it) a shame and a reproach to all the Christians in England that nations of savages such as those to whom we propose to minister still exist in the world !

"I believe that Christians will be, and that they have often been, driven by God and scattered over the earth by various afflictive circumstances, because they go not from motives of loving obedience to fulfil our Lord's plain commands, that we should visit and evangelise the dark places of the earth. . . .

"If my own anticipations of an early death be fulfilled, I shall die no sooner than if I had remained at home, and perhaps I may be permitted to accomplish some good first. . . . As a minister in England, I find my conscience violated and my life useless."

Some verses, written about this time, and most probably suggested by the eloquent and touching address of Dr Duff, delivered in Edinburgh just before that great missionary's return to India, describe the thoughts which were cheering Mr Ogle's own mind in the prospect of his departure for Patagonia.

## THE MISSIONARY'S FAREWELL.

Fare thee well, Scotland! thou land of my fathers,
    Eldest born isle of the Emerald sea;
Fair though thine hills are, and snow-white thy mountains,
    These shall not lure back my spirit to thee.

Fare thee well cradle and grave of the martyr,
    Home of the hero and church of the saint;
Clouds of thy witnesses urge my departure—
    Arm me with courage, forbid me to faint.

List to their hymning that burdens the breezes,
    Solemn and sweet in the voice of the past,
So the soft melody echoing pleases,
    Wafted o'er waters or borne on the blast.

Sons of the Covenant, ' church of the First-born,'
    Beckon me forth from the shores of my birth;
Pilgrims and sojourners, e'rst ye were earth-born,
    Now ye no more seek a city on earth.

Here ye no more have a place of abiding,
    Here ye no more have a city of rest;
In the bright promises firmly confiding—
    Strangers from henceforth, and exiles confest.

Glorious confessors! I follow your leading,
    Though to yon Orient you bid me depart,
Little the Torrid or terrible heeding—
    Firm is my purpose, resolved is my heart.

Finally farewell! the thought shall not grieve me,
    Land in affection the fairest and best:
India! thou land of adoption, receive me,
    Scene of my labours and place of my rest.

Broadly and swiftly thy rivers are rolling,
    Crowds of adorers are kissing the wave;

Would they know Him who, the waters controlling,
  Stooped to invite them, and suffered to save.

Then would their rivers be streams of salvation,
  Then should their hills and their valleys rejoice;
Kingdoms should own Him, and every nation
  Joyfully list to the sound of His voice.

See on the summits of old Himalaya,
  Glorious the feet of the heralds of peace;
List to the heaven-lifted accents of prayer
  Mingling with fragrance in every breeze.

Lightly they value the metal Potosian,
  Not e'en Golconda brings offerings meet;
Gems of the mountain and treasures of ocean
  Forth in profusion are poured at His feet.

Soon shall the city whose walls are salvation
  Rise o'er the top of delectable hills;
Valleys shall echo with loud acclamation,
  Peace every province with righteousness fills.

Sceptre of David and Israel's banner
  Over earth's loftiest battlements rise;
Children of Zion, rejoice with Hosannas,
  Join Hallelujahs with those of the skies.

                                    1855.

Before his departure, Mr Ogle visited many of the towns of England, addressing meetings, and trying to extend the interest of the Christian community in the Patagonian mission. He preached a sermon on missions at Cambridge, which was published by request. All being ready, he sailed from Plymouth June 4, 1856, in the company of the other members of the mission, as a volunteer to labour in the field at his own charges.

# CHAPTER X.

## THE VOYAGE OUT.

Mr Ogle, in letters to his sister, has given us a very animated description of his voyage. He permits us, in a sense, to go with him, and to share in all the excitements of his journey. The arrangements of the ship, and the occupations with which her passengers beguiled the tedious months, are told in a way that gives us a very interesting, as well as a near view of life at sea. He chronicles, too, the changes of the sky, now smiling in beauty, now darkening in tempest; and the wonders of the great deep, calm as a mirror this hour, with the ship's image or the constellations of heaven reflected from its surface, and the next, lifting up its waves in storm " and making a mighty noise." Nor does he hide from us his own hopes and fears as he journies over the world of waters to his adopted country,—all forming an unconscious portraiture of a child-like character, delighting in the happiness of those around him, and ever devising methods of promoting it ; full of sympathy with all that is beautiful and sublime in the material universe, but with a soul yearning for higher delights and panting for the salvation of the heathen world.

A small steamer carried Mr Ogle and the companions of his voyage to the ' Hydaspes,' which was lying out in Plymouth Bay. As they steamed to their ship the sun was setting in a cloudless sky ; Mount Edgecombe lay in the shadow of eve, and the spires of Plymouth, retreating into the distance, were disappearing from their view in the haze of night. On stepping aboard the ' Hydaspes' Mr Ogle and a fellow voyager

G

retired to the cabin, where they joined in fervent prayer,
thanking the Almighty Orderer of events for this prosperous
commencement of their voyage.   His next thoughts were of
the anxious friends on shore, from whom he had just parted
in mingled sorrow and joy, and who, he knew, were watching
their decreasing size and vanishing form as they went out into
the night.   How naturally does the following incident,
detailed in a letter to his sister, return to his recollection at
this moment.   "I remember," says he, "a poor woman
coming up to Flambro' Head to see a ship pass in which her
daughter was sailing for America.   She watched a speck on
the waters till it disappeared, and then waving her hand,
returned to the village."   The ship in which Mr Ogle sails
has vanished from the eye of his watching friends, but his
graphic pen enables us to follow her all the way, till at last
she arrives safe on the Patagonian shore.   His first letter is
dated June 3d, 1856.

### THE VOYAGE.

'HYDASPES,' *at Sea, Lat.* 39.24, *Long.* 13.55.

"MY DEAR SISTER,—

"We have been a week at sea; have had uninterruptedly
fine weather, and almost a constant fair wind, gentle breezes
just heaving the sea, and ruffling the surface; a steady progress about seven miles an hour, and with all sails set.   You
would watch us out of the anchorage, and into the night, as
we left Plymouth.   Were all the voyage as hitherto, I could
not wish you better than to be with us.   We had only two
days' sea-sickness: 1st, spent on deck in vain efforts to keep
up our spirits; the 2nd, in bed by many, myself among
the number.   I had proved on former occasions the value of
this principle: towards evening I rose, and have never been
ill since.

"But you wish to know who *we* are, and *where* we are,
and *what* we are doing.   *We*, then, are the Rev. George

Pakenham Despard, wife and family; Frank and Tom, orphans: their ruddy and plump faces speak for our healthy and happy condition; Miss ————, the governess; and Miss ————, a protegée voyageress, whose father is in the Falklands; Allen Gardiner,* Esq.; Mr R. Turpin, and myself. Thirteen persons in all."

## A DAY ON BOARD.

*June 16th-23rd.*

" The best notion of our life will be formed from a sketch of a day on board. The original is before me—the cool, bright morning, the sunny noon, the warm afternoon, the dusky eve, the brilliant moonlit sea, succeed each other with exact uniformity on this happy voyage; the wind blowing perpetually in a favourable direction, right aft, and the deep blue waters, crisped all over and crested with white, have formed a scene so uniform, that we might fancy days at sea a perpetual summer of the most delightful weather, bright, breezy, beautiful. The bleating of sheep and the lowing of kine, the familiar sounds of home wake us in the morning with an impression of pastoral felicities; the cackling loquacity of chickens, ducks, &c., with the shrill clamour of swine, suggests associations of rural life which the heaving of our habitation scarcely dissipates. Just enough of motion to assure us of progress, not sufficient to disturb the most absorbed student. Beyond the first thirty-six hours, not a symptom of illness has been manifested; appetites are the sharpest, and a life perpetually al-fresco keens every sense and faculty and capacity of enjoyment. An orderly ship, large enough for every one in his place, without infringement on that of others; no inconvenience night or day; ports open, keeping us cool; an awning screening the scorching ray. We live *sub umbra et super ripas*, lying down by the flowing waters and in a perpetual shade. Our occupations commence with the light, and continue till the sunset, then meditative evening calms the soul and fits us for repose. At six A.M. the busy sound of running to and fro and dashing water tells our room is getting ready: our myrmidons are washing decks. We rise and

* Son of Capt. Gardiner.

hasten forth to breathe the vaporous air, and inhale the
breath of morning—here, as on shore, seeming fraught with
additionally freshening influences.    We prepare for the day's
work.    The pastor cons the passage to be read and ex-
pounded, and meditates his prayer; the instructor prepares
his lesson, and the pupils their tasks ; all assemble to breakfast at half past eight, with sharp apprehensions and appetites.
Each contributes a verse, self-selected, to the common instruction ; and the meal despatched, and the tin receptacles of
tea and coffee disburdened, and the new loaves, and fresh-
laid eggs, and new drawn milk consumed, we go on deck to
prayers and Scripture exercises : the last precede, and occupy
about an hour.    The children, with their instructress, learning verses and hymns, and reading ; the others pursuing
their own studies, Greek, Hebrew, and the various versions
with which their missionary labours will need their acquaintance.    At ten the ship assembles, Captain Tod always
setting the example of attendance with his Bible in hand.
His mates follow his good example, and many of the hands
constantly present themselves.    In the morning many cannot
be spared from labour, or are ekeing out the abridged
slumbers of their nightly watches ; but evening worship is
always a full muster.    Thus the faces of all become familiar,
and no disagreeable familiarity does it prove to be.    The happy
sail-maker, the thoughtful carpenter, and the merry cook ; Dick
a true tar, who has been at the siege and capture of Sebastopol, and says, ' No mortal knows how it was took ; it was
a clear gift ; ' and the active, obliging, cleanly steward, are
known to us all.    The rest are younger, mere lads to look at
the most of them, but active, and apparently steady lads.
    At ten, then, a chapter or a few verses is read and com-
mented on by the chief of the Mission, who also offers an
extempore prayer ; to thank God for remarkably favourable
winds and pleasant weather, to implore a blessing on our
enterprises, to ask for continued peace and increasing religion
at home, and the diffusion of Gospel light abroad, are, as it
were, a recurring expression of sentiments universally prevalent and appropriate.    At half past ten, the second in the

Mission staff conducts a class in Spanish; the catechist and three of the children form the audience, with the two missionaries. At eleven, Hebrew, under the instruction of the chief, takes place, and continues till eight bells announce that the sun has been caught by the vigilant eye of the captain, and he proclaims it high noon : then activity of other kinds succeeds—the men, and all below the poop, to dinner, and those above, to reading, and play, and music, and a variety of ingenious and agreeable occupations. Tom is warbling in a corner; Frank chiseling with his new tool-box; Emily and her friend, the lady passenger, with one or two others, are singing; little Packy is mounting a mast, and will soon come down upon deck with a hole in his cranium which nature intended not. I suspect two or three of the party at letters home to be ready for the first ship; the rest are taking up Nautical Astronomy in the shape of the sextants, which have just been laid down by the captain and mate, or are busied with their own concerns.

"One P.M. brings a call to dinner—a plentiful, but not luxurious table. Fresh meat killed on board, potatoes and preserved meats, fruit tarts and puddings, remind us as much of family arrangements in happy, plenteous England, as possible. Lime-juice instead of wine, supposed to be taken to counteract the scurvy, and a frame-work of wood for the benefit of the crockery above, tell us we are at sea. At two, school again, the Spanish and Hebrew as before. At four, dismissal sounds, and again the swinging and climbing, and playing at touch, and reading and writing, and playing on the concertina and flute, the dulcet glasses, and the shriller fife. Harmoniums buzzing, or emulating the music of the shrouds, combine or succeed each other in the most agreeable confusion—a perfect Babel of harmonics. At five, tea, as breakfast, but with preserved fruits instead of, and in compensation for, the plenitude of salt substantials previously supplied. Till seven, each takes his several way as inclination or duty calls, save that at half past six a voluntary singing class is held by the missionary No. 2, who also conducts evening worship at seven, much as the morning, sav-

that the New Testament forms the subject of illustration and instruction.

"Twilight succeeds to day more rapidly and more early than in our own land, and the dominion of night is fairly established before eight o'clock. These darkening hours are the most active of the day: the young limbs reflect that the day is fast departing; and yet no weariness can claim repose, and they redouble their efforts to make up for want of space and exercise circumscribed. The boys below on the main deck are performing gymnasium in the shrouds, or dancing in the vicinity of the fore-mast.

"'Hands aft the main sheet,' 'lower your flying-jib,' 'down with your main-top-sails,' 'lower on your hailyards,' shouts the captain from the poop, holding a little one in either hand: there is a voice far off, 'Lower it is, sir.' 'Haul-ye-hoy, now haul ye again, ye-haul-ye-hoy,' sung out by the fore-man of the watch, the rest pulling in time. 'Belay,' cries the captain;' 'belay it is, sir.' 'Make fast your main-sheet;' 'fast it is, sir,' and then all goes on as before till the lessen-ing light compels the juvenile revelries to cease, and the elder members of the party are left to their own perambulations and their quiet thoughts. Presently the sextants come out again, and a *Lunar* is taken for the longitude. The log is hove and the rate ascertained. At supper, the distance passed in the day, the latitudes traversed—generally two and a half degrees in the twenty-four hours—are the topics of converse and the news of the ship. Before eleven all is still save the shrouds which rattle, and the sails that flap, and the water that rushes on divided by our prow, and the tramping of the watch on deck, and the whistling of the look-out man on the forecastle head. Such is life at sea."

## SCENERY OF THE TROPICS.

MONDAY, *June 23d.*

"We have entered that charmed circle which one has been accustomed from one's earliest years to think of as *the Tropics;* have overtaken the sun, and have him now from henceforth behind us, on the opposite side to that we have ever seen him ; we look north at noon and south at night ; have flying-fish, and grampus, and sharks as our only visitors. The re-splendent heaven of the tropics, and new constellations ; and the ocean, more splendid than the sky, filled with fire, now spangling its surface in golden dust, now illuminating its depths with flashes and flakes of fire numerous as the snow-flakes in a winter storm, and bright enough to enable me to read the smallest print from their light alone. The first sight of this beautiful phenomenon fairly overstepped my previous knowledge. I had conceived of a sea whose waves were sprinkled with bright particles, and whose every ripple showed sparks and scintillations of phosphorescent light ; but to see, as I did two nights ago, flocks and shoals of floating moats and masses, from the size of a crown-piece to that of a hat, distinctly floating and whirling as the eddies treaded in the wake of our vessel, was altogether unexpected. For hours I watched them, wondering whether they were material or gaseous, organic or amorphous, animal or inanimate, and now can scarce make up my mind. They did not mingle nor separate : far as the eye could trace the course we had tra-versed, a crowd of bright, luminous spots waited on our track like denizens of the deep waking up to life at sight of a stranger, and dancing for the pleasure of having seen him passing by ; like a swarm of fire-flies in the forests of the tropic isles, lighting up the impenetrable shades : those deep in mazes of the weed, these sportively playing on the surface, and down into the depths of the sea. The old sailors saw nothing to wonder at : it was very common, they said ; but we have only seen it once (in lat. 17, off the African coast). One would think a stream of newly melted ore were flowing ever out of the Gulf of Guinea, or that the Niger or the Gambia were pouring their auriferous waters to mingle with the currents, and to swell the treasures of the deep."

## A SQUALL.

*June* 30*th.*

" The last day of our first month. Since writing the last we have had changes, from fair to foul, from a steady breeze and unclouded sunshine, all the way from England till Thursday last, to wind a-head and a pouring rain. This change is the only novelty, and has reduced us here as in England to talk constantly of the weather. I am now surrounded by as black and changeable-looking a sky as the old country boasts, where summer airs grow cool, and evening draws in too soon by an hour in a night of tempest. It was Thursday, at noon : we were sitting as usual under the awning, and rejoicing in a little alleviation of the tropical heat, the vertical sun being under a cloud, and I was making out the similar latitudes throughout the globe, a geographical amusement in which I find much pleasure. It was that of Madras, of South America—the North coast, and nearly of Sierra Leone on the other side, one place about midway between the shoulders of the two continents, eight degrees north of the equator. The captain came to the weather side and looked out anxiously, then gave his orders in a sharp tone : ' The first cap-full of wind,—a squall is coming ! All hands on deck and get sail off the ship ! ' We hurried below to make all snug in the berths, which fine weather had somewhat lumbered with moveables. Meanwhile, the vane sways to and fro and flickers like an expiring flame, the ship rolls, and her sails flap back against the waists, and then fill again. There is a dark cloud coming up fast, with a light, hazy horizon against which the black waves show a fantastic outline. A whited line of water advances. ' Make quick, my men : ' a rush of wind causes a whistle in the shrouds, and heavy drops of rain fall at intervals. The grey rain curtain is approaching, the foam is plainly seen ; and now the gallant ship leans over, and the ripple of water is heard ; she heads and majestically rises again ; and now she is cleaving the ocean, leaving a foam-covered pathway, and dashing the spray from her bows like a sea-horse that paws the deep. What a change in half an hour ! rain pouring in torrents, the ship laid over and scudding before the blast, sails yet unsecured flapping heavily, all hands as busy as sailors alone can be. ' Now start the waggon a-hoy ! ' ' Now give her a filip, a heave, oh ! ' Or if a main-brace or cordage were the point d'appui, a longer strain: 'Haul the bowline, the bonny bonny bowline; haul the bowline, the bowline, oh.'"

"However, the excitement was but short; though a squall, decidedly it was not a hurricane; and though followed by two days' bad weather (if anything God sends be bad), it has cleared at length for half a day, and now we have had a second half without a shower; but the worst is that we have made no progress, scarcely fifty miles since Thursday, and it is now Monday afternoon. Our last day's work was four miles backwards, and we have wind nearly a-head still. How different from the first part of our voyage, in which we made 150 miles a-day, and 1200 miles a-week. At this rate we shall get home again; but this, though not to be wished, is to be expected for a season. We have run through the proper limits of the Trade winds, and are in the zone of variables—and variable, indeed, we find them; only never fair for us. On Saturday we had a tropical rain in torrents; the sailors stript their upper garments, and stood under the streams that came down wherever a sail, or a shielding, formed a watershed, and seemed to enjoy the changes from sun to shower as much as the ducks and swine and the various animals, who, unacquainted with geography, no doubt, wondered what sort of summer they would have before it was the hottest day."

## THE SOUTHERN HEMISPHERE.

*Monday, July 7.*

"The line is crossed—to cut short the long story I was beginning (not so long as the reality though). After two more days of variable winds and unproductive voyaging, we had a clear sky and a brisk breeze; though not a fair wind, we got a tolerable run, and away we started across the Atlantic. We were off the bend of Africa, and very near Sierra Leone (long the only bright spot in the benighted land of Ham), and are now rapidly nearing South America and the mouth of the Amazon. Our approach to the *Line* was very anxiously looked for. The children, I believe, thought there must be some sort of materiality in what is so often named, described,

crossed, and marked down in maps, and which plays so important a part in all geographical exercises."

## CROSSING THE LINE.

" That No. 1 of the great circles of the globe should be a
mere cipher!    The children find a difficulty in conceiving that
so much fuss can be about nothing, and hence the questions,
' When shall we see the Line ?' ' where is it, Captain ?' to
which the Captain answered, ' I'll wake you when the ship's
keel grates upon it.'   ' Oh, then, we shall not see it, it will
be dark ?'    ' No, you'll not see it, but you'll hear it,' says the
Captain, and true enough we did hear it, for the rushing water
keeps up a constant rustle as we traverse the zone of ocean
which constitutes *the Line*.    We did hear it, for voices raised
aloft in songs of praise and prayer and joyous shouts told us
the Line was being crossed, and bid us ' praise God from whom
all blessings flow,' and borne on the breeze of night, were the
words of Heber's Hymn,—

> ' Salvation, oh, salvation !
>     The joyful sound proclaim,
> Till each remotest nation
>     Has learned Messiah's name.
> Waft, waft, ye winds His story,
>     And you ye mountains roll,
> Till like a sea of glory,
>     It spreads from pole to pole.'

The men responded to our cheers, and coming forward to the
poop sung ' God save the Queen,' and then we all joined in
the evening hymn and parted in mutual good-will.    The
ceremonies of the latitude were dispensed with, out of deference to the ladies and children.    And now how shall I give
you an idea of what the south world really is—only by describing the world you know already ; but the brightness of its
weather, and the most beautiful of its aspects sea and sky,
clouds and stars, more bright and beautiful than ever.    A
warmer sun, not without a cooling breeze, those light fanning
airs, that like the cool zephyr of summertide, bring health and

freshness. No wonder I write of it, for I am in the midst of its enjoyment. The long cool night succeeding a sultry day brings me such pleasurable sensations as cannot be described. I have the heart-ache though to think of England and her sins. . . ."

### SOUTH AMERICA SIGHTED.

*July* 14.

" On Saturday at sunset we had a faint view of the coast of South America ; the great headland of Cape St Roque. This was a cheering incident in our voyage, and especially as it is our first introduction to our adopted country.—Your affectionate brother, J. F. OGLE."

*Continued, July* 21, 1856.

" There is not much in a voyage to interest, except [to me] the novel position, and the ever present elements, air and water, the heavens and the ocean, both vast and grand and variable, but there is not much of incident connected with them. They supply food for contemplation, and one can gaze on either with untiring attention, and watch the changing aspect, and the beautiful forms of cloud or wave, and admire their simple grandeur ; but there is little to say which has not been said, nor to think that has not been thought. The world is hackneyed and worn out ; we go into remotest regions and the most deserted, and find just what we have been taught to expect ; what the last voyager most elaborately saves us the trouble of describing."

### A DOLPHIN.

" The cry of this morning, for instance, ' a dolphin,' excited no surprise, and we just quickened our steps for fear the poor animal should have the trouble of dying in beautiful agony for nought, and without a spectator. The thing has so often been done and described, that I was quite glad to find that the innocent monster had slipped off the hook and enjoyed his native element with all the zest of a reprieved criminal. Poor dolphins ! they deserve not their frequent fate unless it be for their

merciless persecution of the flying fish, whose aerial evolutions
are mostly stimulated by their dread of these foes.    We often
watch them ; they abound in tropical seas, and leap from out
of the wave, which we dash from our bows, in shoals.    They
look very like water-wagtails (*mota cilla*), for your learned
ear), just dip up and down skimming the water in similar
flight.    They fly against the wind, and vibrate the wings
rapidly sometimes, but generally the flight is steady, like that
of a great dragon fly.    They are dark bodied and transparent
winged ; one flew on deck, which measured four inches in the
wing and five from snout to tail.    The body was like a sprat
in form.  This was a large specimen.  We often see from twenty
to thirty at a time.    These, by day, and the spangles phosphorescent at night, prove great attractions to our young companions."

## WINTER OF THE TROPICS.

" We have been lately experiencing the *wintry* passage of the
region of perpetual summer, with squalls instead of hail storms
and night dews for frost.    The wind blows from the cold
quarter, S.W., and is soft and balmy, reminding us what a
furnace heat we might have had to pass through in these
regions.    Thus by a most gracious and merciful Providence,
dear F——'s tenderest anxieties for her brother are anticipated.    I often think of the passage of Scripture given to us
at parting at Plymouth (Isaiah xliii. 2,) as applicable to our
experience.    Once only, on Sunday, after preaching in the
latitude of Sierra Leone, and near the African coast, have I
been overpowered so as to feel ill from the heat ; but when the
night-dew fell and cooled the air, I lay on deck wrapped in a
blanket, and in a few hours was well again.    I should compare
the weather to that of a very fine and sultry summer in England ; but as we have had chill, and even cold days occasionally,
rain has been frequent and clouds never wholly absent, we are
bound to call it winter for the tropics, and have been nearly a
month in traversing these tedious parallels.    It is called the
zone of ' variables.'    We have found the light shifting winds
untrue to the name only in one particular—invariably unfavour-

able to our progress. For several days we had perpetual squalls of wind and rain, perpetual shifting of sails and 'tacking,' the wind blowing all round the compass in an hour. These were not disagreeable when we came to understand them. The gathering cloud was always visible for a quarter of an hour before it came, the under surface low and black, a dark shadow on the sea, and inky streaks upon the face of day, a line of white water and toppling crests, then mighty heavings, and down comes the rain. At the first warning we clothe ourselves in coat of mail and helmet of [water] proof, and then enjoy the shower together with the sailors and the ducks; these last vociferously manifest their satisfaction in the luxurious prospect of a pool."

### CAPE ST ROQUE.

" We spent four days off Cape St Roque with adverse winds; our consolation was that we thus early in the voyage should see South America, our destined sphere of labour. Every spot in it has charms; for it may, we hope it shall, receive seed from our hands, and produce a good harvest. We were glad then to sight the very first possible point of the vast continent, to be held in the attraction of its mighty waters; the current formed by the backwater of the mighty Amazon held us for days spell-bound in our course."

*July* 28.

" Another week has passed. Why tell you my troubles, the perplexities and questionings I have had during its course? God has mercifully given me in Allan Gardiner, who shares my cabin, a most congenial comrade. We have sweet intercourse together respecting things of deepest import."

### SCENERY OF THE NIGHT.

" I am getting acquainted with the appearance of the ocean, and the heavens in rough weather, and also with the management of the ship. The sun sets to us now at 6 o'clock P.M. (longitude 30° W., latitude 16° S.); half-an-hour afterwards it is dark, but *such* darkness! A sky flushed with bright orange colours, in which purple clouds are floating: the horizon a

bank of clouds of most fantastic outline ; above, great masses
like mountains moored in mid-air, with their snowy summits
in relief against a sky of perfect azure, the perfection of tender
and delicate tinting.   No rubies or carmines, as with you, but
neutral tints of softest shades and blended lines, like rainbow
colours, distinct yet not abrupt, passing from deep orange and
pale amber into sapphire, and so to the blue vault.   The
exquisiteness of this blue after sunset is something quite
unknown to Europe.   The Italian sky is not like this, nor the
clear atmosphere of the Alpine region ; an early winter day in
Scotland, when the air is clear and still, and the clouds rest
upon the mountains in downy folds, most resembles it of anything that I can recall to memory.

" Then the night, when those blue fields sparkle with gems,
and star after star comes out till all is [fretted ?] over with
golden fires, every orb is distinguishable, and no *flickering*
interrupts their light.   Twinkling there is, but it is like the
more ardent glow of steel at white heat, which comes in flushes
of greater brightness, not as of a feeble ray occasionally cut off.

" I spend much time looking at the stars.  .The Quadrant
given to me by R—— S—— is my principal amusement, and
I have measured all the distances of the stars of first and
second magnitude, and hundreds of others, trying my calculations with the ship's officers, whose better instruments often
give but a mile difference from my estimates.   I intend to make
a map of the stars, dividing the sky into regions (reg. celestes)
as a more natural division, and am now ready to begin."

*August* 18.

" A fortnight of stormy weather has caused a long pause
in the journal for my friends at home.   An extract from my
daily journal would resemble a tiresome quotation from the
ship's log.   Hydaspes sailing to S.W., between latitudes 24°
and 25°, in continual heavy weather, with cross winds, &c.

" On the 5th, birds—hitherto quite absent, save now and
then a petrel skimming the waves and dipping like a swallow
—arrive.   The most numerous are about the size of a pigeon,
and are beautifully mottled with white.   The head is black,
breast white, wings black and white.   On the water they have

a lively, gentle look, much like a pigeon, and are graceful in their form and motions. The sailors call them 'Cape pigeons.' With them came a black bird with sharp wings, like a grouse in size and general appearance, the irides of the eye white and the beak hooked; these are familiarly known as Cape hens."

> The winds are all hushed o'er the bosom of Ocean,
> Save the breath of a zephyr, which fanneth the sail;
> The surface is heaving as if with emotion,
> So passion subsides like the yesterday's gale.
> The nautilus gaily her canvass is spreading,
> With rainbow-like beauty adorning the brine,
> The flying-fish leaping and flutt'ring and scudding,
> And gambolling porpoises, snouted like swine.

### THOUGHTS ON NEARING PATAGONIA.

*August 1st.*—Steady breeze. This month we shall be (D.V.) at Stanley. It is time to prepare for work in earnest. Let me do it by searching and trying my ways, by true repentance and humiliation before God, by spiritualizing my views and seeking singleness of aim; by cementing unity and concord; forbearing and forgiving, yielding and sacrificing, being diligent in every good work; not to purchase God's favour or a freedom from his chastening, but that this may be unnecessary, otherwise it would be an act of grace, and given to fit me for usefulness in His service. Probably this is the eleventh hour of the world; a short twilight hour, and then the Son of Man cometh and calleth His servants, takes account of their work, receives of the fruit of the vineyard, and gives them their wages, beginning from the last unto the first. Let me, therefore, put away the works of darkness, and put on the armour of light; gird up the loins of my mind, not self-confident, but redeeming the time.

*2nd.*—Lethargic; self-indulgent; thoughts occupied with the future, and how to secure myself from discomfort, and perhaps neglect. What is my object in taking this missionary voyage? Is it bodily comfort? worldly advantage? honour from men? pleasure? These are husks. Oh Lord, give me faith to overcome the world, and to work by love.

## A STORM.

*Aug.* 6.—"Ten o'clock P.M.—All sail shortened; heavy lurches; all things rolling; boxes break loose, plates, dishes, cups, knives, chests, etc., crash and clatter; the water dashes to and fro over the deck; the wind whistles, and the ropes and sails resound; billows break against our bulwarks; waves thump against our sides, and a momentary expectation of something worse seizes the mind. The still night is disturbed by unwonted sounds: the captain cries, 'All hands on deck.' The singing is become sighing; and the concert of voices resembles a wail or lament rather than as it is wont to be a merry concert of workers at a pleasant toil.

"In the morning we find the wind blowing furiously, sea covered with foam, storm clouds and storm birds and storm sails and storm threatenings everywhere; and we hold on by a rope to the weather side in pelting rain and dashing spray. Still there is no sense of danger, and scarcely a diminution of our comforts. On deck the ship appears to ride upon the waves easily and securely. She lies over very much, though there are only two small sails set. A broadside billow lays her lee bulwark under water, and you feel it is no more in proportion than what every boat suffers in every stiff breeze, and not more dangerous to the big ship than that to them. A nut-shell may be swamped in a tea-cup, and the ark be safe in an universal Deluge.

"Our ship, I trust, resembles the Ark in many ways—in the protection of a special Providence, in its pious purpose, and its God-fearing freight."

12*th.*—Heavy gale. Spent the day chiefly in the cabin writing out Chilian vocabulary, reading "Borrow's Bible in Spain," "Marshall on Sanctification."

*Thursday,* 19*th.*—Very much vexed; complained to A—— G——. He spoke of imitation of Christ. He is right and I am wrong. Our time of prayer and reading (Rev. viii.) spoiled by similar discourse; the things of the kingdom made to give way to the paltry matters of an hour. Prayer for submission to God's will, to be allowed to have a share in doing Christ's work on earth. Felt the workings of unbelief at prayer. Oh for light, understanding what the will of the Lord is."

" 20*th*.—Provisions begin to run short; animals are fed on biscuit purchased from the ship. Conversation with D—— about Keppel ; fear I vexed him ; I wishing to know, as a member of the mission, what preparations have been made, and to supplement deficiencies. I have a strong suspicion from what I have observed that we shall find no preparation nor provision made for us at Stanley. Read Revelation ix. with A. G. Observed the fearful plagues denounced, and the mercy implied in the mention of sins which might have been repented of and judgment averted. Prayed for knowledge of the Divine will, for simplicity of purpose, unity and concord. Played the harmonium for an hour after tea with comfort. On deck till twelve o'clock ; read Wilberforce's Practical View. A fine night wind blowing nearly a gale. Sea not high."

" 21*st*.—A large hawk seen ' blown off land.' Rio Negro, Patagonia, on our lee ! Distressing apprehensions that I shall never see the shore. Wrote sermon, ' Looking unto Jesus.' "

" 23*d*.—Very cold. Birds are now numerous. We are now in the latitude of Patagonia. We have thought, read, dreamed, about Patagonia—barren and forbidding ?—but the more room then on which to plant our affections, to fix and build up our hopes, if recusant, tempting us to pursue and exciting emulation to attain. How shall we gain over those obdurate hearts, how win them ? how subdue that tyrant, treacherous, cruel nature ? Is the gospel able to do this ? The simple message of salvation by Jesus Christ, is it efficacious or not ? The answer to this question seems just now dependent on the issue of our experiment in Patagonia. How great, how thrilling an interest, does this thought give to a journey thither.

" We look into the western haze, and in the dark cloud we seem to descry the shadow of that dark land going up to quench the sun's ray. In the loom of evening we seem to see their dusky forms, distinct, then evanescent. They sullen sit, they gaze upon the deep, they burnish up their wooden

H

spears. Poor Patagonia! 'A book overboard,' a Bible.
Perhaps it may float to the Patagonian shore: alas, valueless
to them! Reminded of Coleridge's illustration of the effects
of ignorance. A savage finds a Bible. He has skill enough
to discover some order and token of design in it. It is not
chance which has collected these slips of paper, similar in use
and in appearance. No fortuitous blotching is this marked
page. He arranges the marks into twenty-four classes;
observes the forms, and re-arranges these in divisions, as one or
other predominates. Again he classifies the words according
to the similarity of the letters which compose them. What
is his gain at last? So we in classifying nature."

"*Thursday 28th.*—At four o'clock A.M., almost calm. At
six, wind blowing freshly; sea rises during the day. At two
o'clock P.M., wind blows 'a gale.' At six P.M., heavy seas
strike and break over the poop; a storm. One degree of
latitude only remains to us to traverse."

"*Friday.*—A fearful storm is on us; we seem to be at the
mercy of the waves; but we are in the merciful hands of the
Ruler of the universe. God visited my heart in the night
season. He bids me search out the secret corruptions, and
enquire respecting all His dispensations, 'Is there not a
cause?' It is that we may be purified from our worldliness;
renewed to more spiritual affections, taught to place all our
desires upon things above; that we may be led to feel our
dependence upon Him, exercise faith, render obedience, have
greater reverence, love, and gratitude.

"At two o'clock P.M. went on deck. Sea running very
high, but the wind has abated. The grey dove and the Cape
pigeon seen. To-morrow we shall cast anchor."

"*Saturday 30th.*—'Land.' The Falklands seen. It is
the north coast of Berkley sound.

"At four o'clock we came in sight of the entrance to
Stanley harbour. Schooner seen; she carries a blue flag with
white centre, 'tis the olive branch on a white shield, which
distinguishes the '*Allan Gardiner.*' Then, up go her numbers
—no other schooner has a number; certainly no Stanley
schooner. 'Tis she! she stands towards us, we show our

name, and are answered by a challenge on the other side; a ship bound round the 'Horn,' her red gig boat on her quarter shows her an old acquaintance of the guano trade. The schooner approaches; her short top masts and her sails, her boat in davits and her smart appearance assure us that our conjecture is right; we tack and stand in for the entrance of the harbour. A boat approaches from the schooner. It is Capt. Snow who hails us, waving his cap in great excitement. I give him a hand, he comes on board and greets us with enthusiastic ardour. We feel a thrill of pleasure gushing to the very eyelids; little Harriet scarce restrains her tears. After a multitude of explanations, ' how long we were thought to be in coming; how anxiously waited for; how kind the governor of Stanley; how natural the anxieties of Mr Dean; how adverse some to the mission settlement; how desirous others of a location at Stanley; yet how felicitous the choice of Keppel; how dear bread stuffs; how plentiful the geese and the rabbits, &c., &c.'

" There is time now to look around; piebald porpoises; the offing is fine; the mount low, seen edgewise; Mount William and the Saddle on the other side of the harbour. 'The Seal rocks;' the 'Lighthouse,' scene of wrecks innumerable; the glowing, clear, but chilly sunset; the '*Allan Gardiner.*'

" We go down into the cabin to tea, and resume the interesting themes of conversation; 'the visit to Koolya and how Jemmy Button, (the islander who had, in his childhood, been brought to England,) looked, and acted, and spoke; the Banner cove natives.'

" Then more serious intelligence—no provisions are procurable at Stanley save at ruinous prices, bread sixpence per pound, coals vary from thirty-four to sixty shillings a ton, very disheartening trade, heavy gales, wars in South America make ships very rare. Have been gales for three weeks, so heavy on Thursday all concluded we had been lost in it.

" As this our voyage, such is the Christian's life. At first by tender solicitude of others, guarded, freighted, commissioned, and committed to the ocean with prayer and provision. The first part of the voyage is swift, and smooth; sunshiny and placid; plenteous and mirthful; midway, clouds arise and tears flow; the burden and heat of the day are beginning to be felt, the contest with others; and then the way grows weary and seems long; progress is no longer rapid, bright sunsets occur now and then, and days of storm, and of calm alternating; colder the world becomes, days are darker and shorter, but we are approaching the end. Fierce gales arise threatening to end the voyage abruptly—the haven not reached—the violence baffling skill; the blackness of heaven above, the weakness of this frail tenement, the sighs and struggles of the disordered frame; every weakest point most tried; the changed aspect of things once delighted in. Little progress made towards the haven, yet an imperceptible advance is made. The canvass which was wont to speed her rent asunder, stripped off, the comeliness gone, treasures parted with for life; surely the last storm will conduct us into port. No, a placid close follows, calm though perhaps beclouded. The land is seen as through a mist over the waters, 'tis hailed with pleasure, unknown but sunlit, and promising; we drop our anchor and wait for a few Sabbath hours, yet another storm, a final struggle against nature; the anchor holds, we quit our ship, and are received with joy; and then shall go up to the heavenly city where await us greetings from friends who have gone before us, the kingly welcome, and the prepared home.

"*Sunday* 31.—At anchor in Port William, a narrow inlet, half closed to seaward by projecting rocks and islets, white sand beach ahead. The entrance to Stanley harbour not discernible. A barren, bleak scene, and rugged hills around, drifting clouds and a lashing sea; a violent storm of wind, snow, and sleet, came on, and prevented our going up to Stanley. Had service in the saloon at 10 a.m., and again in the afternoon; preached from one of my father's sermons on the text, "Eye hath not seen nor ear heard," &c., 1 Cor. ii. 9.; felt the charm of rest and comparative stability after being three months at sea.

"*Stanley, September* 9.—The first sight of the Falklands

was very beautiful ; fine ranges of rugged hills, though bleak and desolate, snow-clad and with driving storms of sleet, yet beautiful. . . . We have been here a week, receiving every attention from all classes. I dine to-day with the Governor, to meet Commander Robert Otway ; he is kind, friendly, and cordial to me. How abundant the mercies of God ! He has sent me here to find good friends. May I not abuse the bounty, but live to His glory ; especially may I be enabled to promote this great work for the advancement of Christ's kingdom upon earth. Oh how much need have I to be wise as a serpent, and harmless as a dove. But 'it is well,' and it will be well."

## CHAPTER XI.

### PATAGONIA—FALKLAND ISLANDS.

THE Falkland islands are about two hundred in number, but only two of these are of considerable size.

They are situated in the South Atlantic to the S.E. of South America, and lie between the parallels of 51° and 53° S., latitude ; they extend from near 57° to 62° W. longitude, The two larger islands are called East, and West Falkland. Between these lies Falkland Sound. The islands belong to Great Britain ; upon East Falkland is the government colony of Stanley. To the north of West Falkland lies the little island of Keppel, on which is the colony founded by the Patagonian, now the South American Missionary Society.

The islands were first discovered by Captain John Davis in 1592. "In the relation of Davis' voyage is the following simple but distinct account of this discovery;" Aug. 14, 1592. "We were driven in among certain isles never before discovered by any known relation, lying fifty leagues or better from the (Patagonian) shore ; east and northerly from the

Strait of Magellan." The Falkland islands, so named in 1689 in honour of Viscount Falkland, are eighty leagues distant from the Straits of Magellan.

Commodore Byron was sent in 1765 to survey and take possession of the islands in the name of his Majesty King George III., and in consequence of his favourable report, their colonisation was determined upon. Spain however laid claim to the islands as belonging to her American possessions, by virtue of the famous papal bull, by which it will be remembered that the Pope bestowed a large portion of the world known and unknown upon his favourite prince, Charles II. and his heirs, to be claimed and taken possession of at their leisure! The Spanish government placed a small garrison at the eastern extremity of the Archipelago but subsequently withdrew it. England never gave up her prior claim, but did not think the islands of sufficient importance to do more than to maintain her protest.

The Falklands remained uninhabited for some time; their excellent harbours, however, became the resort of sealers, and subsequently of the merchant vessels of all nations, whose crews slaughtered great numbers of the wild cattle, besides pigs and horses. The crews of the merchant ships also killed seals indiscriminately and wantonly, at all seasons, so that eventually the British government, finding that other nations were sending protection to their ships, determined to assert the rights of the British flag, and from that time, writes Admiral Fitzroy, " Those unhappy islands have been more ostensibly British, though but little has been yet done to draw forth the resources and demonstrate the advantages which they unquestionably possess.

" The climate of the West Falkland is said to be milder than that of the Eastern large island. Wind is the principal evil : a region more exposed to storms both in summer and winter, it would be difficult to mention.

"Fruit does not ripen upon the islands, and it is very doubtful whether corn can be cultivated. There are no trees, but a useful kind of brushwood grows in the valleys; this is used for lighting the peat which is very abundant and of good quality. The country is covered with a long brownish-looking grass, Tussac, at the roots of which there are sweet tender shoots much liked by the cattle.

"Cranberries, of which the wild geese are very fond, are to be found in some parts, and a small plant popularly called the 'tea-plant' grows like a heath in many parts of the Falklands as well as in Tierra del Fuego. The leaves of this plant are frequently used instead of 'tea,' and the infusion made from them is very similar in taste to that made in our English homes. Good water is plentiful everywhere."

Such is the description given by Captain Fitzroy of the islands.

The mission ship "Allan Gardiner," was already in those waters, and the mission party expected her Captain to be prepared to take them to their island home (Keppel) at once. It was the place from which to make excursions to the coast for the purpose of evangelising the natives, and bringing any who were willing to the mission colony at Keppel.

Mr Despard, the head of the mission party, had been the Secretary of the Society at home, and was therefore well acquainted with all the arrangements which had been made. Many difficulties however beset his path on his arrival at Stanley, owing to the disordered state of the Society's affairs there, which need not here be related. Though differing from him as to the best method of employing the men and the means which were at his command, as well as on some other particulars, Mr Ogle always gave him the full meed of 'praise, due to a man of honest purpose, and who used to the best of his judgment the means which appeared to him calculated to extricate himself from a situation of much anxiety. Mr Ogle appreciated also fully the situation, as respects

the Society, and with the frankness, generosity, and disinterest-
edness which were prominent features of his character, he offered
not only advice, but substantial assistance.  He at once proposed, since the mission ship was to be employed for a time
in collecting supplies, and the season was that in which alone
voyages to the islands, the scene of their proposed mission,
could be attempted, to become responsible for the hire of
another vessel in which he would be employed with Mr
Gardiner in visits to the heathen, while Mr Despard was
engaged in the ' Allan Gardiner' as he thought best.  This pro-
position was misunderstood.  The two men were very different
in temperament and in character.  In one respect they were
one, in love to their Lord and to His cause, and their very
dissimilarities, therefore, although they caused temporary
estrangement, and to one at least personal inconvenience, were,
we believe, overruled for good.  The wisdom of the acts of the
one to whom power to direct had been confided, must of course
be judged by their results, and the other may well be content
to be judged by the same criterion.  It was thought that Mr
Ogle desired to escape the hardships inseparable from the
course resolved on, and was inconstant in his purposes,
whereas he was only desirous to be engaged in the vanguard
of the battle.  The proposed period of absolute inaction
offered to him on Keppel island was, he knew, as unfitted
to his mental ardour as the occupation of cutting turf and
building the walls of the mission house was to his physical
powers.  The subsequent sad fate of one of the members of
the mission staff seems to have justified the decision.

Our readers see how the matter stands.  The ocean has
been crossed, and the party is now on the scene of their
missionary labours.  But it would seem that no preparation
whatever had been made for their arrival, and the mission
party were thus suddenly brought face to face with difficulties
which none of them appear to have foreseen.  Had they been

amply supplied with funds, or had there been friends on the islands prepared heartily to aid them, the initial difficulties might have been got over; but unhappily, money, provisions, and friends were all lacking. In this perplexity what was to be done? Provisions were exorbitantly high, and it seems to have occurred to Mr Despard that he had nothing for it but to set out on a cruise in the "Allan Gardiner" and collect food for the mission staff. Meanwhile the members of that staff were to be conveyed to Keppel Island, which had been fixed on as the head quarters of their operations, and were to be employed in erecting habitations for their future occupancy. This implied great manual labour; they would have to dig turf, build walls, and do whatever else was necessary in rearing a little village of huts for themselves. All this had to be done on an island where there were no inhabitants, and where no shelter or accommodation could be had on shore. They would be exposed to the storms and lashing rains of a climate as variable to the full as that of England. The missionaries must have dwellings, and seeing they were not got ready, as perhaps they ought to have been, before their arrival, they must be got ready now; but it was questionable whether such a task was suitable for Mr Ogle, and whether it did not imply an amount of exposure and physical endurance which might, with his constitution, have proved fatal to him. There were men on the mission staff habituated to those labours, or to similar ones; Mr Ogle's energies might be turned to better account than in being occupied in these duties. He had come out as a volunteer: he was labouring at his own proper charges, and this gave him certainly some amount of discretion—larger than he appears to have claimed—as to how he could best promote the interests of the mission. If it was necessary that the mission ship should cruise about collecting supplies, (and how otherwise were the missionaries to subsist)? we do not see that Mr Ogle could do better than accompany her, and so have an opportunity of visiting the islands, meeting the natives, acquiring their language, and, in short, acquainting himself with the characteristics, physical and moral, of the mission field. This was an indispensable preparation for future labour. The sooner it was acquired the better ; and the time devoted to it would be more profitably spent certainly than in uncongenial toil, for how long no one could say, for it was uncertain when Mr Despard might finish his cruises, and be able to revisit the party imprisoned meanwhile on the island of Keppel.

A few brief extracts from Mr Ogle's journal and letters will enable the reader to trace the progress of the affair, and also to judge of the spirit manifested by Mr Ogle under these disappointments and crosses.

"*September* 10*th.*—Letter from Mr D. asking if I will go to Keppel in the ' Allan Gardiner' and remain there, &c. Reply, ' Far be it from me to hinder the work I have so much at heart. I will go—at the same time I must add that I shall be very much disappointed if I am not to accompany the ' A. G.' on all and every of her expeditions to the natives, for this purpose I came out.' ' Whence come these divisions if not from our sins, and for them ?'

" No doubt this is a sifting trial for all, would that I may be refined thereby. I am oftentimes tempted to feel very much irritated .... but I remember ' it is the Lord.' He sees my sinfulness, and takes this method of bringing me to repentance. This thought does not extenuate the misconduct of others, but it enjoins submission on me. I pray that a happy issue may be brought about without any injury having accrued to the Lord's work, or any hindrance been given to those who are engaged in it."

Subsequently we find him recording :—

" ' The ' Victoria ' is hired for £80 to carry the party to Keppel and to remain there six days. They are to sail on Thursday morning. I shall remain at Stanley, waiting for an opportunity to get to the poor savages whose good I came here to seek.

" God has given me many friends here in the wilderness. Captain Snow refused to give up the ' Allan Gardiner' to Mr Despard, he says he has not received either instructions or intelligence of our intended arrival. He has no money and cannot find a crew willing to go to the coast. This is a long history and not so easy of solution as my own. I have had no communications with Snow, however, of late, having my own troubles. He offered to acknowledge me as the Society's agent, but I positively refused to have anything to do in the matter, telling him frankly that he ought to give up the ship to Mr Despard, and I have not seen him since. Poor fellow, he seems driven to desperation by the state of affairs— nevertheless he had his duty to perform."

Finding that the party were going to Keppel in another ship, and that the ' Allan Gardiner' was to be employed in collecting supplies both of provisions and funds, Mr Ogle offered to *hire her* for the strictly missionary purpose for which she was built. This offer gave rise to the article which appeared in the society's report under the head of " Rev. J. F. Ogle, and Captain Snow." It was a hastily written attempt to account for a state of things which with their very imperfect knowledge of the facts which had transpired, the committee could not at all understand. His own feelings and conduct when that interpretation of his generous offer became known to him will appear in subsequent letters of date June 1857.

This is the place to give Mr Ogle's first impressions of the infant settlement in which he now found himself. His mind was singularly observant, and his pen ever ready. The town and harbour of Stanley, with the society of the little place, are vividly sketched in the two letters that follow.

## STANLEY, ITS SCENERY AND SOCIETY.

THE GOVERNMENT HOUSE, STANLEY.
*September* 23d 1856.

TO THE REV. H. BARNES,—

. . . . " Leisure and comfort have come to me again after long tossing on the horns of uncertainty as to where ?—and what ?—the place to live in, and the thing to do ?  On the unstable equilibrium of expectation—on the wings of change —from temperate to tropic, and again to chill and wintry weather — from old, yet ardent England, to the slumbering regions of the sunny south—and near the antarctic, to old and irritable England again.  Stanley is another Bridlington and yet it is very different.  A newly inhabited and uncouth village, a small society—few poor, many pretenders to be rich ; some really nice people.  I have been here only since the 1st inst., so small a place is seen in an hour and seen through in another.

" There is the governor, his secretary, and the colonial magistrate, the chaplain, the doctor, Captain P., a colonist and land owner, the Falkland Island Company's manager, and the merchant ; then come employées, artizans, pensioners, guachos, a few old soldiers, the military body guard, and fortress men ; and sailors and sealers, of course—*quid mihi inter omnes* [blank in letter] the position of a pilgrim, a stranger, shall I say truth, an exile ?—Yes, it is so.  The sunny side is turned to me just now . . . the governor, &c., are very kind to your poor friend Ogle, who sought not their friendship, but on whom it was generously forced even without an introduction. The former would have me take up my abode at his house— I made a faint struggle and—as ever—yielded, so that I have been here ten days but I retain my lodgings in Stanley and return to them in a day or two.  I am no longer what I came to be, the coadjutor of the principal of our mission.  I was obliged to separate, reluctant as fore-looking, but not so as retrospective."

A further description of his early impression of Stanley is given in a letter written a few weeks after the date of the above.

STANLEY, EAST FALKLAND,
*September 9th to November 15th* 1856.

Thermometer at 2 P.M. 59°.          Thermometer 56° 9 A.M.
                                  „          49° 6 P.M.

" MY DEAR BROTHER,—The notice board (our only news-paper) announces 'a mail on the 19th inst.' I will therefore occupy my leisure in writing. A life of inactivity in business but of activity of thought must result in a vast accumulation at the end of a few weeks, of uncommunicated matter. I feel this just now and scarcely know where to begin. Whether (1) to give information respecting this (to me) new scene and society, or to relate my intervening history since the last letter, or to write of the events (not unimportant) which have occurred to *the mission party;* or to anticipate the future by revealing my plans and pourtraying prospects; or to reply to yours of August 8th, received October 19th; or, &c. &c. These heads will be more than sufficient for my present opportunity.

" I will sketch Stanley, and this means the Falkland Colony, for there is no other settlement upon those islands, and but one hamlet of three or four houses; the farm and buildings of the Falkland Island Company are situated upon the other side of this island. Keppel colony is not yet a reality but a project.

" Stanley is an assemblage of cottage residences on the southern side of the inner harbour of Port William. Captain Fitzroy's 'Voyage of the Beagle, 1830,' will give you some information respecting the country and Captain Sir J. Ross in his 'Voyage to Antarctic Seas, 1842,' more of Stanley itself, but the origin of the present place is subsequent to both these dates—the latter book is well worth reading. I could fill many sheets with the extracts I have made from it, all bearing on what is around me. The book is defective in arrangement, and incomplete as a history of the island, but it contains a descriptive narrative, and notices of natural history of great interest. Darwin's narrative of a journey round the world (Murray) will supplement it and give the observations of an intelligent writer and an able naturalist.

" The gray green bank, 100 feet in height, which encloses

the harbour, is the limit of enclosure, and of civilisation in
the Falklands. The rocks on either side are perpendicular
where they crop out, and they form, on the hill top, lines of
obelisk-like stones and slabs of granite rock, seen from some
distance, they are similar to rude fences made in a clay slate
country. This rugged line runs parallel to the harbour on
both sides along the very summit of the hill and resembles
strictly a rough fence of slabs of stone of huge dimensions and
great thickness set nearly erect, very little addition of art
would convert them into a stockade of masonry, proof against
a battery. From the water the harbour presents an appearance of almost complete circumvallation. The sloping bank
is a tolerably steep declivity, formed of peaty soil covered
with tufts of wiry grass, and here and there are patches of
heather-like shrubs (*Empretrum rubrum*),—you may see it
at Kew. The peat is in many places eight feet thick, and
very solid; it is used for firing (I send you my sketch).
Looking inland, along the valley which runs up from the
harbour, the view is varied and agreeable in outline. The
absence of any dominating height is a disadvantage, but there
are blue hills of two hundred feet, within the range, which
diversify the landscape if they do not suggest sublimity—
what is generally unenclosed reminding me of parts of Scotland
in its general appearance, scanty herbage, &c.

"The town of Stanley consists of a collection of small houses
of one storey in height, built of wood and covered in with the
same. Even the governor's house is similarly built, a square
of such houses. The buildings extend about a mile along the
south side of a fine inland arm of the sea in which is the
harbour I have before named. We found, on our arrival,
every article of food enormously expensive; for instance, bread
is 6d. per lb., potatoes 3d., eggs 4d. each.

"A simple pudding made of rice with eggs and a little
butter cost me half a crown. You may be sure I did not ask
for that kind of pudding again.

"I am in lodgings in a neat little house, which is in appearance like a road-side inn in England—the Star at Flambro'
—but the rooms have uncarpeted floors, are unceiled above,

and have only batten doors, altogether inferior to any fisher-men's cottages at Flambro'. For two of these rooms I pay two pounds a-week. The weather is like March weather in England, yet I am sitting with the doors open, sunshine comes in at both door and window; before me is the water at a few yards' distance. The 'Hydaspes' (in which the party came out) lying off shore, a Hamburg brig which has come in for repairs, the 'Syren,' H.M.S. from Monte Video on special service, the mail schooner, the 'Allan Gardiner,' the governor's yacht, and several smaller craft are in sight. You may imagine the scene from what you saw when at Bute.

"Treeless are the hills here, and the hoar rock and the swarthy peat stacks present the only contrasts.

"There is an air of activity and an appearance of prosperity about this little settlement just now. The governor promotes lectures and a library, visits the schools, etc., and exercises hospitality. He has just interrupted me by a visit, and kindly presses me to come to his house to take up my abode when I lose Allan Gardiner, my true Christian friend and guest, who is going with the schooner to Keppel. I remain at Stanley, and shall try to be doing some good here. If I could have helped them (the mission party) by being with them at Keppel I would have gone there, but under present circumstances I should only add to the burdens. There is every reason against my going to Keppel. . . .

"The governor has offered me a free passage in one of her Majesty's ships, but I have declined this, for I do not wish to return home without having done something in the work for which I came out."

Though remaining at Stanley Mr Ogle was not, and could not be idle. He preached before the governor and towns-people, and expresses himself in his journal as having found no little enlargement and success in ministering to them. He gave a good deal of time, moreover, to visiting the ships that chanced to put in at Stanley harbour. The crews bound on such distant voyages have few opportunities of hearing the gospel, or of receiving religious instruction, and

not a few in these ships did Mr Ogle find who stood in
need of direction and comfort, and to whom he appears to
have been useful in leading some to the Saviour who had
never known Him before, and in helping on others in the
way of Life.

He used to sail out in his "boat to meet them," weather
permitting, taking Bibles, etc., for those on board. Many
records of these visits are found in his journals, for these
opportunities of occasional work for the good of souls were
thankfully embraced while he was waiting for the ardently
longed-for time when he should find a ship to take him to
that field of labour for which he left his home in England.

One or two extracts may suffice :

"*Dec.* 14*th.*—Held a thanksgiving service on board the
'Cuba.' This brig arrived yesterday having on board sixteen
men who were saved from the wreck of the 'Lord George
Bentick.' They had been five days in an open boat in
boisterous weather without an oar, or a sail, or rudder, or
compass, or food, or water. The 'Lord George Bentick'
foundered at sea, when her captain and four men were lost.
The poor fellows who were taken up by the 'Cuba' were in
the last stage of exhaustion. Mr W., the first mate, is a
well-disposed man ; we have prayed and sung hymns together
and read God's word. To his prayers when in the boat the
poor sailors attribute their marvellous preservation; when he
was getting exhausted they would wake him up from sleep to
pray ; but, alas ! all seem to have forgotten God in their
prosperity. I pray God that my visit to them may be for
their good.

"I was able to spare some clothes for the poor fellows.
J.'s ample and judicious providings have met all my requirements ; but, as I gave my only extra coat to W——s, your
unexpected present of a greatcoat proves most opportune.

"There is here a small Spanish population who are already
much attached to me and say, 'All the Spaniards, men and
women, are your friends, Sir, the little children "especial-

mente." '  A poor man died on Sunday whom I had been leading to Jesus in my poor way.  I had the satisfaction of hearing him say, ' Creo en Jesu Crito.'  He used to utter a very feeling ' Amen' to my prayers.  This man I had met with at Hope Place (the Spanish settlement), and there spoke to him about his soul, and gave him a good tract.  He was then ill, and is come here to die among his friends."

The difficulties in the way of visiting the coast of Patagonia and acquiring the preliminary knowledge necessary to fit him for afterwards successfully evangelising in those parts, were such as Mr Ogle could not foresee before leaving England. He found them, now that he was upon the spot, all but insuperable.  Few trading vessels made their appearance at the Falklands ; and the captains of such ships as did occasionally visit these islands were unwilling to take on board any but their regular crews.  Many considerations made them so, and in especial the necessity of being able to exercise complete control over all in the ships.  Mr Ogle offered fifty pounds for a passage to Tierra del Fuego, but in vain. While waiting at Stanley for an opportunity of being carried across to his selected mission field, he made occasional excursions among the Falklands.  The incidents of these journeys, and the scenery amid which they were performed, are well sketched off in his letters.

HOPE PLACE, ON FALKLAND SOUND, *Sept.* 25, 1856.

" MY DEAR SISTER,—This is the evening of my first day of real life in the wild, unless last night, spent in my little tent on the open hill, claims precedence.

" To learn my whereabouts, you must go to the map of the Falkland Isles, and trace the Eastern Island across from Stanley in a direction due west, and there on the Sound is my present sojourn.  I want to bring you to the spot, or the scene to you : Three low, barrack-like houses, built and furnished wholly out of the wreck of ships on this ' foul weather shore,' a few yards from the strand; before us a range of snow mountains, and behind another, nearer and more picturesque in outline; under these, an intervening 'Camp,' as all the grassy open country is called; not another habitation visible; no signs of culture; wild cattle, wild hills, away, away, till you reach Northern, Southern, Eastern, or Western Sea.

" The island opposite, the West Falkland, here about ten miles distant, is wholly without inhabitants.

" On the East Falkland there are a few servants and herdsmen of the Falkland Island Company, and the population at Stanley.    I am half-way between the two.

" It is about nine o'clock p.m.    The room I write in has a table, a box, two chairs, a bed on the floor, a clock; has two small windows, and an unceiled roof over head, but it is weather-tight and whitewashed; it is the Saloon of the Falkland Island Company's manager's house !

" The manager is in the next room, writing also, and I came as his friend.    A cup of tea, made from the tea you gave me, in a caldero, or Spanish hot-water jug, biscuit from Plymouth —(it was a good thought my buying those two barrels of biscuit; it is very coarse, but 5d. per pound was offered for it before I left Stanley)—and your little ginger-cakes constitute my repast; and I write, while tea cools, by the light of a composite candle.

" The manager is a tall, strong man, and wears a suit of leather for riding across the wild; he, with his Guacho, who is a Spaniard, and myself, have been sole companions.    We travel fifty miles a day—ten hours' hard riding—for a country of bog, and mountain stones, and hussocks of balsam-bog, as big as little haycocks, all over, is hard riding, even at a slow pace; down come horse and all, inevitably, two or three times, but you stick to the saddle, and flounder up again, and so on. Then a wild bull comes running across towards you, looking this way and that—stands—charges the dog; the dog takes to flight, and comes to the horses for protection.    The horsemen disperse in various flight, and the bull singles his object and tears after.    There is safety in flight, however, unless you get bemired, or on soft ground, where the bull's broad hoofs can play better than the small round pasterns of the steed. But the bull has come up to the baggage-horses—two, carrying tent, provisions, &c.—the guacho is off, and at a distance. 'The bull will kill the horses,' cries my friend, and it seems inevitable, he is within five yards, and furious. I am in breathless suspense, and I know there is no help but One—help not unsought, nor sought in vain. The horses do not run, that would be fatal to them with their loads, and in such a country; they seem not to heed him, and after a moment's deliberation close to them, he turns round, and head in air and tail uplifted, dashes past them towards us. 'Now, what shall I do, Mr H——?' I exclaim; 'I will do just what you tell me, for I know neither the country nor the nature of the animal' (he is not fifty yards off). 'Keep on hard ground,' says H.; 'Keep up, I will follow you,' I reply. 'Very well,' he says, 'keep up the hill.' We ride together as quickly as our horses can go over the ground, then turn again, and ride zigzag, not directly away, but across the bull's path. 'More nimbly,' cries H., 'and we shall do.' The bull slackens his speed, and we increase ours as getting further off and higher up the hill. Still he appears to be meditating his rush, which must bring him upon us. I do not look at him, but at H. and at the ground I am riding, I have enough to do; mentally I pray the while. 'Now, then, we are safe,' says H., drawing rein; 'we are on hard ground.' I look, and see the monarch looking too, but in his old place; he means to come yet, think I. I ask for an explanation, and am told that on hard ground these horses, knowing well what awaits them if the bull overtakes them, will go of their own accord faster than he, and the rider just lets them do as they please, knowing their instinct. Or if the horse is very hard pressed, then the rider must throw himself off into a quagmire, and the horse will stand and kick, directing his strokes so well towards the eyes of the beast, as *generally* to deter him from close approach, even if the man has not been able to quit the saddle. But as H. says, 'You *must* leave it to your horse to take care of himself and you too.' I was truly thankful not to be tried,

at least in this early stage of my experience, and I was so
weary with twenty miles of such riding as to be little fit for a
trial of horsemanship.    The Lord delivered me, and I will
praise Him.    This incident did me great good ; it nerved me,
and made me feel well able to go on ; it awakened those
sentiments of devotion, which a pleasurable excursion is apt to
damp, and it gave me confidence in my companion, who was
really afraid, but not weakly so—perfect master of his faculties,
and aware of every circumstance likely to occur.    I think his
anxiety was on my account, because I did *not* know them.    I
found him apparently placing more confidence in me afterwards, and we kept out of the way of bulls as far as we could,
but it was impossible to do so altogether, they are so numerous.
We encountered two others very near, and escaped them only
by timely flight, besides several which have attacked our
dogs, or run across our path at a moderate distance, but no
determined foe like the first.    I wish I could tell you half, or
a hundredth part, of what occurred in our very interesting,
and, taken altogether, our very delightful journey hither, and
may I never forget God's many mercies.

"Yesterday, at six a.m., we met for the expedition.    First
start a false one ; the horses got away (all the country is
open, even in Stanley itself), and one shook off its load, and
kicked the articles one by one over the field.    It was ludi-
crous, though at our expense, to see the tent roll lumbering
into the mire, and cast like a football by the retreating hoof
into long distance.    Then the beef for dinner fell, then the
Molitos—these are saddle-bags of ticking, lighter and more
used here than leather—mine were merely thrown off.    Mr
H.'s, entangled in the hide-thong, fell on the heels of the
horse, and were kicked and kicked again, till the animal was
exhausted with vain endeavours.    How paint-box and brushes,
and the toilet furniture, and sundries fared I know not ; but
as these things often happen, Mr H. said very little, but went
home for a fresh horse, this being quite useless after such a
beginning.    Start again, and this time all right till we reached
the rough road, and saw the state of the country ; this is the
first ride that has been undertaken since winter, and Mr H.

says he never saw it so bad. We breakfasted at eight, some miles out, under a rock. Before dinner, came the bull meeting; and having lost time, we stopped not again till we came to a place where to pitch our tent for the night. The last two miles of our fifty were misery to me, and I fell behind, quite unable to keep the pace. H. could not stop, owing to rain coming on, and a probability of thick weather, in which we could not search for a suitable place. I lost sight of them : however, having observed their track, I held on, and soon saw them again. The guacho (guide) turned back, and was good-natured. I had prudently secured his good-feeling early, by giving him one of my knives, and it was well-bestowed. This won the fellow, and I became a favourite. It was exactly the thing for him— a long clasp knife, with 'Espagne' on the blade. I bought two dozen of them in Lincoln on purpose. When I reached the wind-sheltered dell that H. had chosen, he, perceiving how weary I was, begged me to lie down, which I did, spreading a water-proof sheet under me. In twenty minutes I was refreshed, the tent was pitched, fire lit, coffee made, beef roasting, and horses grazing—quite a picture !

" ' Now,' said H., ' make your bed, for in twenty minutes it will be dark, and we cannot do it.' I had nothing to do but to spread the aforesaid red sheet—a most capital thing, light, warm, and quite waterproof—and then assemble various coats for covering. H. got a quantity of heather by way of mat-tress, and provided for covering as I did. After a hearty meal taken outside in the warmth of the fire, made of a resinous gum shrub like heather, which blazed beautifully, we sat talking some time, being in no hurry to rise ; but at length finding the air blew chill, we retreated into our little tent, which was just large enough to hold us one on either side ; and here we burnt a wax taper, and remained talking till nine o'clock. Not a breath of wind disturbed us.

" To-day has been bright, sunny, warm, clear, the country beautiful ; ranges of mountains always in sight—birds of all sorts in abundance—the land (or camp) dry—the wet ground being, where many disadvantages prove to be, the nearest to Stanley.

"At eleven, we met a troop from the camp, bringing fresh bread, butter, and eggs—a repast worthy of a prince. . . . . I have abundant reason to think that my journey will not be without real good. I come as a clergyman and a missionary, and as such the people receive me with warmth. Most of them are Spaniards, the rest English, Irish, and Scotch. . . . I found thirty men, with families. Among them were Spaniards, Patagonians, Guarani, and Canary Islanders; I preached on the Sabbath to a mixed congregation (Spanish people on one side, and English, Scotch, and Irish on the other), partly in Spanish, but chiefly in my own tongue. The people seemed very much pleased, and I hope benefitted.

"I christened a Spanish woman's babe. The mother of the infant was distressed because I could not re-marry her to her husband. They had had no minister there, so could not previously be married, except by rites of their own, which they are very careful to perform. She wanted me to marry her by proxy, as her husband's work obliged him to be absent; but I said I had no service for this kind of wedlock! and, besides, her husband was not only absent, but knew nothing of the matter. I hope this visit is a token for good; the words I did say, which this poor young woman could understand, pointed to the Saviour of sinners, and told her that he gave himself that whosoever believeth should not perish, but should have everlasting life; and I left her a Spanish gospel with the humble hope that God may bless this feeble effort in which I am but the instrument.

"As this is an agricultural establishment I was much interested in it, you may be sure. Everything is done on horseback in these farming settlements. The men are splendid riders, and have an air on their fine horses that would astonish you, for they look black, unsociable savages when on the ground. That Sunday night was most interesting to me. My quarters were in a low house on the coast. There, in a kitchen, half full of firewood, and without furniture, except a quarter of beef hanging from the roof, ninety pounds weight, which they said would last two men four days, lay a Patagonian by the fire, his broad features and immense shoulders half covered by his cloak.   Two or three others came in, and roasted meat, and made their evening meal.   I took a beautiful tract, on the exceeding love of Jesus in dying for poor sinners, and sitting on a log by the fire, I read it aloud.   Presently the poor Patagonian uncovered his face, and lay awake, looking fixedly at me.   I did not address him, but went on reading the Spanish tract aloud. Thus I preached the Gospel for the first time to a native of the tribe we came to seek.   The next day I rode with this man, and talked with him as well as I could in Spanish—told him I came to preach to his countrymen, which he said was good, and that it was good to know God, who is the Creator, the Preserver, and Saviour of all men.   He took more plea-sure however I fear, in his fine horse—which is his only possession of value—and wanted to know what sort of horses we have in England."

STANLEY, November 15.

" I find little in my journal to interest you.   The narrow limits of the settlement preclude any great events.   A little community of four hundred persons can have little beyond personal matters to chronicle. . . . I do not remember to have heard the name of Jesus from any lips in conversation since I entered the colony ; social intercourse never verges on the things pertaining to the kingdom which shall soon—how soon !—be exalted above the kingdoms, and all nations shall flow unto it.

" May I be preparing for that glorious event, though driven into a corner, at the end of the earth.   Many are the precious promises which reach me and are specially applicable to my case.   Why repine at inactivity and poverty ?   Have I not been preaching for years that the Lord is coming out of His place to visit the inhabitants of the earth for their iniquity, and that the duty of the true Christian is to wait often in silence and in sorrow for the revelation of power from on high ? Providence has given me many friends—has made all men friendly to me."

From another letter.

"What an event a ship is here, you can have little conception. There have been many since we arrived. This morning as I rose from breakfast, I saw a fine barque with colours flying, pass the window. I threw open the door, and shouted as if the house were on fire, ' Goss, Goss ! (my landlord's name is Goss) what is the ship ?' Goss comes running, ' It is a ship in distress from Swansea with emigrants.' I cannot but grieve that it is nothing in my way, for I am looking and longing for an opportunity to reach the Patagonian coast, and get to the poor savages whose welfare I came to seek.

"That I might be with 'Jemmy Button'* in four days is a thought which keeps me anchored in the port of Stanley; sometimes it stimulates me to think of desperate means to lessen the distance. What! within four days of a prospect of evangelisation to tribes uninvited by Gospel sounds from ages, in dark fetters of heathenism. A few hundred pounds even to *make the* ATTEMPT were nothing. A sin to spare it, and sit idly. There is a ship that would take me to-morrow for £150, and a good one too. Jemmy may die, and then the Fuegians are sealed up again. There is no other key to open that dark door. I could weep for the misery of my captivity. I can but pray. Merchants prosper and go hither and thither everywhere. The Christian missionary alone is unable to go on his errand of mercy. But I hope I shall find the way opened if I wait a little longer. God has been very gracious to me hitherto."

Although the ship was not one that could further his wishes by carrying him to his mission-ground proper, yet he found work on board, and was useful to her distressed and destitute crew. He hoped by waiting a little longer to find the opportunity he

* Jemmy Button is the name of one of the natives who were brought to England many years ago, and he retains the knowledge of the English language, with a great respect for the English people.

so ardently longed for. And in this hope he drops the desponding tone which characterises the first part of his letter, and proceeds to give directions respecting the arrangements to be made to supply his wants and enable him to meet the large demands for board, and the short voyages in prospect. The letter continues :

" That I may be able to get about on these islands I have bought a pony and a horse. The former is the counterpart of ' Jerry,' but the horse, an awkward animal, to carry the tent, &c. I find my little tent (Edrington's) and my camping apparatus very good, but the camp kettle is too heavy for a country where there are no roads. The ground is either boggy or very stony, and very hard to travel. The prevailing wind (westerly) appears to check vegetation. It often occurs to me, however, that this climate is not worse than that of England, has more fine days but less warmth. Where drainage and cultivation is practised we shall see a change in the country for the better.

" I have been out for two days with the governor and Mrs M. I slept in my tent ; made a bed of heather, and slept as comfortably as in any house ; nor did the air when the tent door was open appear cold. I have been busy collecting plants, shells, &c., to send to you. There is a pretty plant, a creeper, which covers the ground under grassy banks, and bears a beautiful orange berry. It is poisonous. I hope you will be able to cultivate it ; one root would soon cover a large space. I have sent some hundreds of plants, and I wish them to be sent to public institutions, Kew, &c. I think they will live and grow, though a year will have been lost to them, for they will have no summer this season. Every joint of the creeper bears a berry, and the elegant form of the plant excites admiration. The collection of shells consists of all the common and some rather rare varieties.

" The ' keyhole limpet' is a characteristic shell, and is valued as such. The seal-skins are only common ones. Our natural curiosities are penguins and seals. I have not yet seen either except in captivity. This is the season for the

former : the penguins inhabit rocky places just as the sea birds
do at Flamborough, but there is not one of these 'rookeries,'
as they are here named, within my distance, and as I have not a
boat I cannot approach them.    I much fear I may not receive
any money from you till May.    If I anticipate my income,
and send you drafts, I shall have to pay twenty per cent.,
which, except, as now, in a case of necessity I have no wish
to do.    I cannot stir till I receive money, but I am not
unhappy ; God has been, and is, very gracious to me, and
though I never leave my present abode, I may have sweet
intercourse with a Father reconciled through Jesus.    I often
look at my sermon preached at Cambridge (which was printed
by request) and rejoice to find the precious Gospel repeated
again and again in its pages—the joint testimony of our
dear Father and myself to truths which we love and live by.
I pray that it may be useful—if any soul which is seeking
light, any honest heart feeling after the way of salvation,
should read that sermon, they will bless God for it.    It is
my prayer that it may be at least to one soul a savour of
life. . . . .

    " Capt. O. offered me a free passage as his guest to Rio
Janeiro to enable me to return home, but, though I felt the
temptation great, I have declined.    If I can I shall get to
Monte Video in December or January, visit the Rio Negro
Patagonians, and, if recommended to do so by M. Lafone, go
up one of the great rivers which discharge into the estuary of
the Plate.    I have collected a great deal of information
respecting these countries, and conceive of them as beautiful,
fertile, and tolerably accessible.    There is an old book by
Robertson and a new one by Charles Mansfield on those
countries.    Sir W. Parrish is, however, the chief authority,
but his book is as dry as a 'Hortus siccus.'

    " On Friday last I started at six o'clock A.M. to ride with
—— round the enclosure.    The morning was wintry cold.
We got out to the hill when rain began to fall ; we rode on,
however, and found, as is generally the case, that out of the
line of Stanley foul weather changes to fine.    Stanley is
situated in the mouth of a funnel of hills, down which the

west wind drives a constant current charged with vapour to the sea. Though cold the day was pleasant. We had the cattle of about four miles square to drive. Cattle when approached run in an opposite direction, and will seldom allow you to come within 'shot:' thus a wide country may be driven by a few men on horseback. While H. turned back to ride after some cattle seen in our rear, I dismounted to rest, but could not regain my seat. My horse, a spirited animal, was alarmed by my plaid, which was blown into his face, reared and struck at me, caught the plaid and went off with it round his heels, and though I caught him again by the long thong which is used to tie horses to a bush while feeding, I could not remount him. However, though I thus lost the sport with the cattle, I did not the less enjoy a long tramp over the country, every part of which is interesting while novel. Two hundred and fifty cattle were driven on that day, and brought into a corral by three men—the corral is an enclosure built of stones. There they were examined, and some had their horns cut off.

"The method of dealing with the troublesome bulls is curious. A rider approaches and throws the lasso over the horns of the unruly animal; he tries to run off, but is soon brought up by the rider to the crupper; the lasso is then tied. His next attempt is to rush on the horse, but the horse is too quick for him, and keeps the lasso tight till he brings his antagonist down upon his knees. Sometimes a bull will bound into the air like a mad cat tugging at the lasso; the vigilant horse never suffers him, however, to gain an inch of ground. If he tries to run in a circle, the horse rushes round also. This goes on till the infuriated animal is wearied out, when he suffers himself to be dragged to the ground, and then the men rush in and despatch.

"I must return, after this digression, to my own affairs, and mention what I shall require to be sent out for next winter. If I get to the natives I shall require flannels and blankets, blue beads, and fish hooks of all sizes, &c., &c.

"I thought to have taken a cottage here, but have rented a small garden as it will be an amusement to dig there, and I

shall remain in this house where I can tell of Jesus, and where
I do hope will be found one of God's own people, an aged man
long a wanderer from the fold."

To his sister,—

*January*, 1857.

" During the past season of Christmas I have thought constantly of you.   It is one of my main comforts that I have
praying friends at home.   This often sustains my spirit in
seasons of despondency, how much more, as you remind me,
the thought of our great intercessor above.   Tribulation is
the lot of the individual believer, and the frequent condition
of the Church of Christ on earth—the glories of this future
kingdom—the character of the early missionaries (the apostles)
these are my subjects of thought.   I have preached frequently
to the sailors here, my topics, those affecting practical piety.
I grieve to confess that I do not appear to myself to make
progress therein.   That you may be preserved from the
deadening influences of worldly society is my prayer for you.
It is easy to fall into a *habit* of religion while the heart is
unmoved.   The dust in the ' house of the interpreter ' as seen
by Christian there, lies long undisturbed : when trouble or
sickness come, and the atmosphere is agitated, if death should
suddenly open the door, nay, if the slumberer himself awake
and stir, what clouds, what confusion ensue !   (Send me a
Pilgrim's Progress, a Spanish translation if possible, by your
next opportunity).   Oh, to be ready for Christ's appearing.
I find myself tempted here to succumb to my condition, to
repose in the lap of such comfort as this kind nurse of English
outcasts offers to her foster sons ; but, no—I regret this—I
must be a protester in many things.   I long to find evangelical
piety, ' fearing God and keeping His commandments.'   I
must be an enemy of Rome if I am a servant of Christ ; can
I then be friendly with Romanists ?   I fear not, but in so small
a community I do not wish unnecessarily to be unfriendly.

" The news from England is cheering, especially the Denison
case."

At what time the following fragment was written there is

nothing to show. We insert it here as congenial with the mood of mind in which, as his letters testify, the writer then was.

## A FRAGMENT.

"A solace in sorrow, or, light at eventide."—ZECH. xiv. 7.

THOUGH morn should break in darksome hour,
Though noon o'ercast and tempest lower,
Though not one hour of all be bright,
" At even-time it shall be light."

Though life's short conrse be early run,
Though cloud throughout should veil the suu,
Though sickness, sorrow, death, affright,
" At even-time it shall be light."

Thus with the world the day began,
One radiant hour alone for man,
Soon fallen, dishonoured, disesteemed,
For him no mid-day glory beamed.

To toil from morn to eve consigned,
Poor, miserable, wretched, blind,
Groping at mid-day as in night,
Yet shall thine " even-time be light."   ·

Thus Israel's history appears
A vale of Baca—place of tears,
Egypt, the desert drear and wide,
Nor Canaan seen till eventide.

And such in after years their course,
For, Canaan gained, no rest affords,
But Gideon's faith and Barak's might
Meet Philistine and Moabite.

Such thy career, Manoah's son,
Though toils be borne, and battles won,
Foiled by thy wife, long years in chains,
The sport of Philistine remains.

Long years remain, bereft of sight,
Of God forsaken, shorn of might,
Yet gains in death a victory more
Than in long years of strength before.

So ———

# CHAPTER XII.

### VISIT TO PATAGONIA AND ASCENT OF THE RIO NEGRO.

WE left Mr Ogle anxiously waiting for an opportunity of being carried across to the South American continent, there to begin his work among the natives of Patagonia. Not a ship entered the harbour of Stanley which he did not eagerly scrutinize, if haply it were bound to the coast he so much longed to visit. There were many disappointments in store for him. Week passed after week, and still no suitable vessel arrived. The detention at Stanley, however, was neither unpleasant nor unprofitable in other respects. Mr Ogle found many opportunities of preaching the gospel to a mixed population of Britons, Spaniards, and Indians, who stood nearly as much in need of having the message of salvation proclaimed to them as the Patagonians themselves. He was busy, moreover, arranging for his voyage, acquiring information respecting the country and the people, and otherwise preparing for the fitting opportunity when it should arrive. His Excellency the Governor of the colony showed him much kindness, making him welcome at all times to his table. This, with excursions into the interior of the island with obliging companions, lightened the period of his waiting. But his heart was not at rest. He longed to be on the scene of his labours. And besides, he found that he could not maintain spirituality of mind while mixing in worldly company, and would rather forego all advantages on earth than compromise a principle or weaken a religious habit.

Besides, Mr Ogle saw things at Stanley which the duty he owed to God and His gospel compelled him to protest against. We refer to concessions which had been made to certain Roman Catholics in Stanley. No man ever lived who was less the

bigot than Mr Ogle,   Even with regard to those from whom
he differed on the most important points he ever cultivated a
spirit of self-renunciation, and deported himself with humility
and meekness.   Nevertheless there was in him a boldness and
wisdom, ever exercised in love for souls and zeal for the glory
of God, in resisting evil which was not inconsistent with true
liberality, and which he regarded as an essential part of the
Christian character.   The higher the style of Christianity the
more surely would that quality, he believed, be found associated
with it ; as, for instance, in the example of the Lord Jesus :
and also in that of Paul, of Luther, and others.   Good part of
his life was passed in intercourse with the members of other
churches, the Roman among the rest, but he laid it down as a
principle that in this interchange of mutual kindnesses due
from all men to each other, there was to be a frank and dis-
passionate expression of opinion on vital matters, as occasion
called for, and if this could not be had, the acquaintance must
be relinquished as a thing which fettered freedom and hindered
sincerity.

The exact circumstances referred to, and which occasioned
some distress to Mr Ogle during the latter days of his stay at
Stanley, we learn from a letter to a friend, from which the
following is an extract :—

"I left Stanley in a sad cloud.   A Romish priest had
obtained from the governor the loan of the old Protestant
church for the mass, and it was going on with great éclat ;
many Protestants were attending.   I was thinking to request
the governor to give me the same building, but did not do so,
though I gave him many hints of my desire; and lo! he gives
it to my enemies.   Ah, dear friend, this is what we shall see
in England ; compromise weakening our hands in the church,
the enemy gaining ground till he comes in like a flood, and no
man to stand in the breach."

The opportunity for which he had so long and prayerfully

waited came at last. An American brigantine one day cast anchor in the waters of Stanley, and to his delight Mr Ogle found, on making inquiry, that the ship was bound to the Patagonian coast. He arranged with the captain and set sail. He had the satisfaction of thinking that he should be, by some weeks at least, the first preacher to the Patagonians. We shall permit him to tell, in his own words, the incidents of his voyage.

"I am in a nice little ship, a brigantine of New York. The voyage has been so far very pleasant; and though we have but one cabin for eating and sleeping in, we get on nicely. We are in all five adults and two children, beside the writer. Except that I sometimes smoke a cigar, I am very little altered by my rougher life. I pursue all my avocations, reading and writing, without interruption now that sea sickness is over. For four days I suffered severely. We had very fine weather for a week, but head winds; then a change. The wind blew a gale, the ship labouring and leaking from the strain; the main-stay sail is blown to ribbands, captain swears, and men are sullen. Heavy squals come on with rain, and sea running very high, but it moderates, and the sails are set again. Clear skies, a steady breeze, blue water, curled and crisped with the wind, show that we are at a distance from the ' Foul weather islands.'

" Thursday, at noon, we sight the coast for which we are bound, but do not arrive in port till Sunday, having had contrary winds, and a river to enter which has a bar over which we can pass only at high water. The coast of Patagonia, under which we anchored on Saturday, is a long even cliff of sandstone rock, the lines of stratification in it are visible till lost in the distance ; a green hill points out the entrance of the river, and hills rise to the north. The cliff extends to the Straits of Magellan."

## First Impressions of Patagonia.

" In the afternoon I accompanied the mate of the ship down the river in the boat. The heat had opened her seams so much that two out of the three persons in the boat were obliged to be hard at work baling water. I found this very trying work for the first hour, then I had to pull to cross the tide waves on the bar. The pilot of the river has a cottage near the fort, but not a creature was to be seen on shore. It was sunset, and we were now four miles from the ship. We deliberated whether to go on shore or to return. The wind now prevented all possibility of the vessel's entry into the river that night, otherwise we were to have piloted her by signal lights. We thought of the Indians and of our leaky boat and returned across the bar to the ship, which we reached in safety.

"The next day, Sunday, the captain weighed anchor, to my discomfort, for I believe nothing is lost by trusting in God and keeping His commandments, and my opinion was soon confirmed, for we were bumping on the sandbank, and it was a time of great anxiety to all on board. I prayed silently that if it were the will of God we might not suffer, though our sin deserved it, and in a few moments more we were safely over the bar and in the river. The pilot boat came out too late, we were surprised to hear all voices in it English. The pilot is from Philadelphia, U.S. In personal appearance he is a brawny man, six feet two inches in height, like a Scotch Highlander in appearance, frank and good natured, but a man of firm resolve and good courage. We had a pleasant sail up the river. Delighted to see green trees again : they were the first I had seen since leaving England. Wild fowl are here in abundance, swans with black heads and white bodies, ducks, plovers, gulls, kites, vultures, &c. The familiar swallow flits in clouds, pigeons in flocks. These remind me of home, but the town is altogether foreign. The religion is Roman Catholic, and I much fear there will be little encouragement given to a preacher of the gospel.

"I spent the evening pleasantly reading to the sailors on deck. The day had been hot; at night I lay down in the open air, hoping for a good night. About one o'clock, however, the wind blew so violently that I was driven to my berth. It has been raining hard, and the air is now cool. The country is much parched by drought. The harvest has just been gathered. In fear of the Indians it is housed almost before ripe, but the heat renders this safer than it would be so to do in England. I do not see any wheat stalks, all is cut short and stowed away in barns, as was done in Palestine. Were this a truly Christian country it would be a delightful land, but cursed with sin, all the inhabitants are in poverty, and under oppression and fear. I shall go on shore to see if I can do anything here. May God give me the faith and patience of those who, 'not mindful of the country whence they came out,' sought a country, even a heavenly, and for whom GOD hath provided a 'city which hath foundations.' May I, 'a pilgrim and a stranger confessed,' be led only by providence, and have no home nor treasure here below. I very much wish for a ship of my own, where I might have those about me who fear God, for I am weary of living as I now do among blasphemers, and apart from any Christian intercourse. Our Captain has been knocking about in these waters for forty years, oftentimes in great dangers, shipwrecked four or five times, and yet he does not fear God nor reverence religion.

"He is very civil to me, and I live comfortably enough in most respects, but I do not find it helpful in my real work— that of the Mission—to be in such a position, and if I do not see my way to some place where I can prosecute my object, I shall return to England in the course of the year."

A few days after this was written the great desire of his heart seemed as if it would be granted, and he had an opportunity of speaking to a few Indians of the things concerning their eternal welfare. In a letter to a relative, dated March 9th 1857, he gives a retrospective view of the place and of the work which he had been permitted to commence there.

## Town of Rio Negro.

"Rio Negro is a settlement of Spaniards on the banks of the river of that name. The people, a mixed population, black, copper coloured, and white in complexion. The first are negroes, once slaves of the Spaniards, the second named are Patagonian Indians, the rest Spaniards, and a few English.

"The appearance of the town is singular. It is built on the steep bank of the river in a deep bend, so that every house is visible from it, one over the roof next below, and the fort crowns the ridge. The houses are of mud-brick, grey, and sombre looking. Fences and defences of rough, unequal sticks give the place an untidy and a foreign aspect. The absence of windows and of chimneys, and the general style of building remind one also of distance from home. The weather is very warm. Yesterday was sultry, thermometer in the cabin 86°. Hundreds of inhabitants were on the shore, under the branching willows, gazing at our little vessel on our arrival.

"The majority are dark coloured folk, their dress a shawl of dark blue, or of red, hanging down over the back nearly to the feet. Some had white trousers, others merely a piece of scarlet cloth tied round the waist, a round hat or a roll of linen cloth on the head, completes their picturesque costume. The women are dressed nearly as in England, prints of light colours appear to be their favourite material. They wear a shawl on the head instead of a bonnet. Fruits of all kinds known in England grow here. Apples, pears, plums, peaches, nectarines, apricots, grapes, melons are ripe at this season, or will soon be so. Horses seem to be the principle stock of the place, they resemble our coach horses in England, and are good for riding. The inroads of the Indians, and the requirements of the Buenos Ayrean government have greatly diminished their number. The first man we saw on arriving brought word that there had been an attack in July last. More than a thousand Patagonians, some mounted, some on foot, attacked the fort, and were only repulsed after a desperate struggle, in which forty of the Indians were slain. Their bodies lie about the place at the present time. The Indians are expected shortly to return in still greater numbers. The fort consists of a low tower, apparently little protected beyond a stockade or fence of sticks. These attacks of Indians are much feared by the inhabitants."

## TOWN OF CARMEN.

" The north bank of the river is a steep, rounded hill, about seventy feet high. I am told that Carmen stands upon the side of this high bank, which extends for many miles. It contains about one hundred houses, such as they are, its edifices being only the next remove from mud huts. They are built of unbaked bricks, consist but of one storey, and have roofs formed of rough poles covered with thatch or with mud, but from a little distance the appearance of the place is picturesque, owing to its elevation. The only pretension to architectural ornament is the fort, with its tower about thirty feet high, built of stone and brick with a red cupola. The bugle and fife frequently remind us that a garrison is near. They perform their part well. The soldiers are said to be ruffians and robbers, and the whole place bears a very bad name.

" The present state of this country is said to be anything but secure. The Indians come down two to three thousand strong, burn houses and crops, steal cattle, and kill all they can. The pilot's house was attacked on the 27th of July by a large number of these depredators, who were only repulsed by the most desperate resistance ; one hundred and fifty are said to have fallen.

" Their fires are visible to us every night, and an attack is daily expected. I do not feel any fear of them, and so far as I have seen and heard, the Patagonian Indians are more likely to receive the message of salvation kindly than the Spaniards, who have a perverted gospel. The Patagonians are more kindly disposed and generous in disposition than the Spaniards. You can scarcely imagine a more ill-looking set of people than these are. They carry huge knives, worn in a sheath, in a girdle, and upon any quarrel use them. I saw one of these encounters, and expected to see blood shed, if not life taken, but some bystanders interfered."

## PRODUCTIONS OF THE REGION.

"Below the town of Carmen there is a broad level of rich land, on which are houses and gardens. The west bank of the river is steep, and is covered with bushes, as is the country so far as I have seen it, to the north. When walking, the appearance is most singular. You seem to walk in a miniature forest, your head overtops all the trees. I found about twelve different kinds of shrubs, of these seven were armed with thorns, and very fierce thorns they were.

"Figs, apples, sugar-cane, &c., grow wild, but not in these thorny plains. Lions, tigers, jaguar, fox, porcupine, tortoises, armadillo, are the animals. Quails, snipes, partridges, plovers, abound; beautiful doves and parrots are said to be in the country. Bats are frequent, rabbits and hares in certain localities. The number of birds of prey strikes me greatly. Vultures are always soaring overhead. Hawks are seen in flocks, and owls are numerous. I have been out twice with my gun and shot a partridge, a black rail, a hawk, a fox, two plovers, and a dove. I cannot, however, give myself to natural history collections, having another object; but sometimes it serves a useful purpose. The natives are very suspicious of strangers, but can understand a person going out to shoot birds, &c. There are few Indians in this neighbourhood. The tribes which generally infest the country in hordes have been driven away. This is a country where every luxury might be enjoyed. Sheep and horses and cattle abound. The ground is fertile and the heavens propitious. All fruits ripen freely, yet there is not heat to destroy verdure. Man alone is the curse of the land. Well! it makes one long for the better portion. . . . . May we both be striving together in prayer, as you said at our parting interview, with one spirit striving together for the faith of the gospel, in nothing terrified by our adversaries."

Mr Ogle ascended the river with the view of exploring the territory, and in the hope of meeting with opportunities for proclaiming the gospel. The navigation was a difficult and dangerous one. In the river were hidden perils, and on shore

were the wild beast and the wilder Indian. The small craft
in which he was embarked was leaky, and otherwise uncom-
fortable, and the hardships he encountered in consequence
were great indeed ; but all were borne with a singular
patience and cheerfulness. By the good hand of God he did
not suffer in health on the voyage.

*February 9th* 1857.

"I am now in the damp and dirty hold of a small river
craft, where I have slept upon sacks laid upon the wet floor.
The rain pouring in above, and the river running in below, but
I do not suffer much, for the leakage does not come up to the
level of my couch, and the black and red coverlid keeps off
the dripping and the rain, though the hatch is open beside me.
I have slept in peace and in safety, and feel refreshed after a
breakfast of farina and of broth from the pot in which ostrich
flesh has been cooked, with tea and sugar from Brazil. My
present companion is an Irish lad. We sit and eat together
as comrades over our fire of sticks, made in a box of sand.
How did I come here ? you will ask.

" The son of an Englishman, named Harris (the same mentioned by Captain Fitzroy), offered to take me up the river
Rio Negro from El Carmen. We have had a rough and
dangerous voyage, violent and heavy rain, a strong current
against us, and numerous shoals, islands, and 'snags,' rendering
navigation at all times difficult. These snags are trees which
have been washed down, and are lying in the river ; the
branches sometimes visible, sometimes a few feet below the
water. When we arrived at our destination, a leaking hut
was all the protection the shore afforded. I was there most of
yesterday in the rain. It is a room from twelve to thirteen
feet square, with a large open chimney, clay walls and floor,
wattled roof, leaking almost everywhere ; pools of water on the
floor, a few logs for seats, benches made of wattled osiers served
for bedsteads, cow-hides for coverlids, no blanket or sheets.
A hide serves also for the door of the hut. The inmates
numbered ten, being English, Spanish, negroes, and a Patagonian Indian."

## An Adventure.

"At night I thought it would be preferable to be on board
the cutter so went in the steeping rain, wading through mud
and water for a hundred yards to the boat. While pulling
back a rowlock broke, and just as we reached the cutter
we lost a scull. I had leapt on board. Jack with the one oar
drifted down the current. I watched him anxiously, and soon
perceived that he had no chance of its recovery. The current
was becoming too uncertain to permit him to follow the oar,
and the night too dark to see twenty yards beyond him. I
saw him carried across the river, and no more. I was alone
on board, a roaring current running, some hundred yards from
the river's bank, and a quarter of a mile from the hut, without
a boat; but poor Jack! Well, I watched for half an hour.
At length he returned, without the oar of course; he had been
on shore, and had hauled his boat till opposite to the cutter,
and so came back. Many dangers attend our present circumstances—the currents, the apprehended flood; but an attack
from the Indians is most dreaded, for we are near their territory.
Tigers also often come down the river on the drifting trees which
the floods bring down. These trees drift at the rate of five or
six miles an hour, will sometimes penetrate the bow of a vessel,
as she lies at anchor, or will so encumber her that she gets
adrift and entangled with them. No danger has happened to
us, and though I expect to be here some days, owing to the
rain, and to be left alone, as my friend will return to El Carmen
by land, yet I am not alone, and I feel no anxiety. I had
rather be here in quiet than with the blaspheming A——— and
his crew; and the object for which I came thither is to get into
intercourse with foreigners, and to gain them for Christ. I
would gladly become all things to all men, as to externals, for
this purpose. To the Spaniards, as a Spaniard, as far as I can
rightfully, but to blasphemers, fornicators, thieves, not as they!
I have one great advantage when with such here. I cannot
understand much of what they say, while they can understand
me. I speak little, but that little is always friendly, and sometimes useful, I hope, and though I mourn over my uselessness,

and the little I know how to do among them, yet a word may prove to have been spoken in season."

He therefore went on shore during the day, and returned to the ship at night.

" 9th.—I visited the Salina or Salt Lake which is described by Darwin. It is an expanse of water, with a shore of salt, not of sand. Large crystals of gypsum and of saltpetre are scattered around, and I observed the huge mounds of salt which were ready for shipment. The commandante of the fort was there. He took me to the fort in his boat. We had much conversation. He gave me maté (the beverage of the country, resembling our tea). He has two boys who are deaf and dumb; both are active and intelligent. I sent the alphabet which is given in 'Charlotte Elizabeth's Happy Mute' to the father, but it was in one of the letters which I was told had fallen into the hands of the Roman Catholic priest of Pueblo, the contents of which he removed.

" During this time, from Saturday to Thursday, I visited every point of interest which was within reach, including the main object of my visit to this place, viz., the Indian encampment. When in the Indian hut I wrote a few lines to you, descriptive of themselves, and read it to them in Spanish before we parted. They appeared to understand the passages from the New Testament in Spanish which I read to them, and when I took leave of them, it was with many mutually kind expressions. I feel sure that they will tell their people of my visit with pleasure, and that they understand that English Missionaries wish to be really their friends. They evidently distinguish me from the Spaniards, with whom they are perpetually at war."

This visit is referred to more at length in his diary.

" *March 9th.*—We are still in the Rio Negro River, the wind being contrary. A fortnight ago we got out to sea for our return to Stanley, but were driven back by a severe storm, in which we lost our foremast. I have not been able to get on shore lately; this is very grievous to me, but 'it is well.' If I had £400 to spend, I would purchase a small vessel for myself. Oh, for an overcoming faith! I have almost determined to return to Carmen, if God spare me, but having broken a small blood vessel during the last voyage, [this was during the storm, in efforts to assist in the ship, for with him prayer was always accompanied by energetic effort,] I am doubtful as to this matter of remaining here, and I can scarcely bear to be separated longer from a place from which I have communication with friends at home. I have not heard anything since October the 9th.

"May I be kept continually prayerful as well as prudent. . . . . Why should the merchant and the man of the world be enterprising and the Christian be timid and distrustful? Still, though I can look back with little satisfaction on this visit to Carmen, the time has been well spent in amassing a great deal of information, and as to its missionary capabilities I feel that it has been thoroughly surveyed. It possesses many advantages for a permanent establishment: it is near the work; we should have the Patagonian Indians for neighbours; and, in comparison with the Falklands or Terra del Fuego, it is paradise. There is a fine climate and fertile soil. With a better style of cultivation the necessaries of life would be abundant. . . . . Now dear sisters twain, I must conclude my descriptive narrative. This letter will reach you in May, when I shall be in winter at the Falklands. It is summer with me now here. I shall take the first opportunity to go from Stanley either to Valparaiso and the river of Coquianbo or to Monte Video, and make a point of returning to Rio Negro before September. After the sowing is over the Indians go to the plains. It would be useless to come here, therefore, after their spring has commenced."

## THE TOLDO OF A PATAGONIAN.

"I am now where I have long wished to be, sitting among Patagonian Indians, eating and drinking the food common to them, sitting upon a log of wood, under a roof of skins, before a fire. A man and two women are here; they are precisely like the representations given in Captain Fitzroy's book. Ostriches are feeding at the door, they are quite tame. The old woman prepares maté. The younger woman offers it to me. The man is very intelligent, and speaks Spanish, so that I can make myself understood. I told them of Captain Gardiner, and preached Christ to them. They, and others who heard the word, manifested evident pleasure and much tenderness of feeling."

We add the following sketches, which will complete the picture which Mr Ogle gives of the aspect of Patagonia, the manners and customs of its inhabitants, and the moral and social condition of the country, which, in the luxuriance of its soil, forms so melancholy a contrast to the spiritual condition of its people.

" What a change from Stanley, Rio Negro, and the Falkland Islands ! Here one sees signs of semi-tropical fertility and luxuriance. New birds, new fashions, new faces, a strange, yet pleasing land ; a town rudely built, surmounted by a ruder fortress, having a grey and desolate aspect, but (as I found it afterwards) enlivened by constant activity. Men of various races—the Spaniard, lean and sallow, with dark eyes, riding a steed of symmetry and mettle; the Patagonian, with independent air and bronzed complexion, with features cast in a coarse but not unhandsome mould, mounted as his lord ; the African drudge, hewing wood and drawing water, mounted too. A gag pouch or kerchief sets off the person, displays taste, and diverts the eye from the squalor and poverty which in most cases may be also observed; the unfrequent Englishman, stout, sturdy, and good humoured, here, as everywhere. Such is El Carmen, its streets deep in never consolidated but often shifted sand, its neighbourhood an upland of slight elevation, covered, as far as eye can reach, with stunted bushes, verdant and not unpleasing. Below, the river winding in a long sweep, under the hill, and following its outline to the east and to the west into the blue distance. An ample, level tract of land separates the parallel elevations on the north and south, and invites the agriculturist by promise of teeming harvests as of ancient Nile, fertilized, as is that region, by annual overflow ; but men are not ! South America, in its untrodden tracts of fabulous fertility on the borders of its great rivers in the north, has riches so vast that the southern land, said to be chill and desert, has neither name nor notice. I have good reason, however, to believe that there are four considerable rivers, exceedingly eligible as means of communication with the interior of this land, and irrigating districts of very great extent and fertility. These are the Rio Colorado, Rio Negro, Rio Chupat, and the Santa Cruz; and the country—far from being that sterile and uninhabitable region which it has so often been described—is one capable of supporting a large population. But the Patagonian Indians—hereditary nomads —are masters of all the territory south of the River Plata, and threaten Buenos Ayres itself. This is one cause of the desolation of the country.

"Excursions of the Patagonian Indians are a source of continual distress to the colonists, and the narratives of their exploits form the subject of constant conversation.

"The Spanish settlement at Bahia Blanca, on the Rio Colorado, consisted in 1856 of a governor and a company of fifty horsemen, and a small number of inhabitants. These latter are occupied in the traffic of the port, which is somewhat difficult of access, but is of importance since it is the outlet of a large agricultural district, which furnishes hides, ostrich feathers, and dried fruits. Early in this year the commandante, who with his soldiers were at some little distance from the town, were surrounded by a multitude of the Patagonian Indians, and are said to have been cut off to a man. In August of the same year they made a descent upon the colony on the Rio Negro, intending to carry off the cattle from all the estancias (farms), which lie from three to four miles apart, upon the banks of the river. The fort at the mouth of the river is in charge of the pilot and his crew, and is furnished with one gun besides a good supply of smaller firearms, while in front are two small pieces of cannon, but without fence or embrasure. The guacho in charge of the cattle belonging to the fort, which number about 300 head and 150 horses, gave notice of the approach of Indians. The cattle were driven into the *corral*, a fenced enclosure in front of the house, but before this had been effected, Indians appeared on every part of the range of hills which are to the north of the river about three miles distance; down the horsemen came in vast numbers, they dismounted at a short distance from the fort, and advanced naked, armed with their lances to attack the place. An embassy preceded the main body, their errand was to offer to take the cattle and the big gun as compensation for sparing the lives of the inhabitants. The pilot, who was in command, hesitated, he had but five men, but he returned answer that he would not give up the gun; onwards, therefore, came the yelling crowd, a volley of musketry received them, and the gun sent a booming shot, to the consternation of the assailants. The chiefs now led on the attack, and so pressed the besieged that they retreated behind their walls, the door-ways, windows, and roof, which is flat, and has a low parapet wall. They defended themselves with desperate valour, many of their foes were stretched upon the shingle; the Indians withdrew to consult together; another shot from the big gun killed several members of the conclave and dispersed the rest. The Indians remounted their horses, and, driving before them the cattle and horses of the settlement, returned to their camp. About twenty horses and fifty cattle alone remained to console the pilot's gallant heart. A noble horse, a few lances, and a pile of skulls and bones remain to this day trophies' of the victory. I bought the horse, but was obliged to forego my purchase as the captain refused to take him on board for me. He was a fine animal, dark bay, with white forehead and pasterns, like the big mare I had for W——'s farm at Flambro', but lighter in limb, and finer in head."

These tragedies did not discourage, but only seemed to kindle anew the ardour of Mr Ogle's desire to try the effect of the Gospel upon man in his wildest mood.

"There is not a town to the south of El Carmen on this continent, consequently all the Indians of the south come here to trade. Just now they are, as I have said, at war with the Spaniards, and are almost masters of the situation, for they come in great numbers, carry off cattle and horses, and go back to their plains, leaving the Spaniards only their houses and poverty. They are but revenging old oppressions, and being at this time in the ascendant, no Spaniard dares to leave the town beyond a few miles, nor can they occupy their farms in the neighbourhood. This state of things is not in my favour. I have seen but few Indians, but have visited those who are resident, and who can understand the Spanish language.

" I have spent a long time in their toldos (cabins), and have preached the gospel to them, and given them presents, and I feel sure that they understand that an Englishman has come out to do them good. A very great degree of friendship is the result of these visits, and they will tell their Indian friends, who will receive me favourably when I come again, as I hope to do as soon as I can make the needful arrangements. I could give you very interesting accounts of these poor people, of the pleasure with which they regarded my visits. I have not seen any men of extraordinary stature. The tallest I have seen were not much beyond six feet. The pictures in Captain Fitzroy's book, 'Voyages of the *Adventure* and *Beagle*,' are precise resemblances of them. The booths in which they dwell, the dress they wear, and their features, are there accurately given.

" I spent the morning, a few days ago, with an Indian of another tribe from those described by Captain Fitzroy. He is the tallest and strongest man here. His brother was shot by the Spaniards, and was a giant in strength. They had put him in the stocks, his head being bolted down, he lifted stocks and posts out of the ground, and stood up with them. They condemned him to carry them thus round the fort, which feat of strength he accomplished, but afterwards he became violent and obtained firearms, so he was shot. His brother is not a dangerous man, but he is a sad drunkard. The Spaniards encourage this vice among the Indians; thus they get an advantage over them."

## VISIT TO AN INDIAN ENCAMPMENT.

"The other day I went out to a small encampment of

natives, about twenty-five miles from Carmen.   We ascended
the river in a boat, then took horses, myself and a Spaniard
who offered to conduct me; we rode to the extent of cultivated
country, entered the forest, and in its deep recesses found the
toldos pitched in a cleared space, a few acres in extent.
Ostriches were feeding, the weapons and implements of Indian
life arranged around, and the inhabitants seated under a
stretched hide in the shade.   We dismounted, went and sat
down on logs near to the Indians, and entered into conversation with them.   My guide explained our visit a little, and
then I spoke, told them I came from England to see them and
to do them good; that I succeeded others of my countrymen,
who had perished in attempting the same, and I hoped to
succeed.   They invited me to enter the toldo, a booth made
from ox-hides stretched over poles of wood, in the same way as
gipsies make their waggon-covers serve for tents, but these are
larger, about five feet high, eight or ten wide, by twenty long.
The entrance is at a corner; opposite, the beds of the family
are arranged; in front of them, the fire.   We seat ourselves
on logs around the natives; *maté*, a decoction of the leaves
and stems of a plant grown in Brazil, is prepared in a little
gourd-skin teapot, and it is imbibed from a tube inserted in
the pot: each drinks in turn.   Sugar, and sometimes milk, is
put into the pot with water; this is the common hospitality
offered everywhere, at great houses and small.   I like it very
well; it is something like green tea, aromatic and bitter, but
not disagreeable; when not strong, and well sweetened, it is
very pleasant.   Add to the infusion the constant desire for
fluids which hot weather creates, and you will cease to wonder
at my taste.

" My hosts were highly pleased when I showed them several
useful articles of English manufacture, a repeater watch, a
pocket compass, telescope, lucifer-match box, etc., and tried to
explain them, and not without success.   I told them that our
fathers were as they, and that religion made the difference
between us.   Then, taking my Testament, I read in Spanish
several passages, illustrative of the character of the Christian
religion, and concluded with some of the most plain of the in-

vitations to come to Christ by faith, and of salvation through His blood and righteousness. They were very attentive, and evidently felt the word. I sat some time with the family, and wrote part of a letter to my brother in this toldo, telling the natives that I was writing to friends in England, who feared that the Indians would kill and eat me; and that I was writing from their house to say that we were in friendly intercourse, and that they received nothing from me, but had invited me to eat and drink with them. Now I must not leave you under the impression that these were the *wild* Indians. No; these were of the same race, but they have separated from them, in appearance at least, and they live in friendship with the Spaniards, acting as a mediating party. All that I said to them will be repeated to the wild Indians, and it will tend to dispose them favourably towards us. I have since sent them a considerable present, and some copies of the Gospels in Spanish, and I hope this happy beginning may be the commencement of a new kind of intercourse."

## ROMISH PRIESTS.

"No one has obstructed my peaceful work here but the Roman Catholic priest. He got possession of a number of gospels and some tracts which I had sent to various persons; he also opened letters and took out the contents. This unwarrantable and illegal proceeding will not, however, I fear, be punished. Though toleration is the law of the country, the Roman Catholic is the religion of the State, and the people have such confidence in the priest that they allow him to do what he pleases. We, in England, put no restraint as to religion on any man; the priest of any religion under heaven may teach and practice his own in any of our towns or cities, and all men are at liberty whether they will reject or follow his creed. If I return to settle at El Carmen, the commandante must give me this liberty, no man being permitted, as heretofore, without rebuke, to steal my books, or to open my letters. It is a bad creed that warrants such infractions of the first principles of justice, and which requires such aids in retaining its hold upon an unenslaved people.   The religion of Jesus Christ needs no defender but its own force of truth, by which it goes home to the heart of the hearer.   It speaks peace to the guilty conscience through faith in the blood of Jesus, and tells of a promise of a heart renewed, and of holiness to be implanted by His Spirit's work within.   This Christ bids us seek by prayer, saying, 'Ask and ye shall have,' etc.

"Though Satan strive to maintain his sway, the kingdom of Christ is sure to prevail till it overtops the mountains and subdues all nations.   'Not by might, nor by power, but by my spirit, saith the Lord of Hosts.'   This is my comfort in the battle we must fight against principalities and powers, Satan may seem to triumph, but the triumph of the kingdom of Christ is the reality.   Great successes are wrought by feeble instrumentality, and real advancement is being made to a total and a supreme dominion."

## CHAPTER XIII.

### RETURN VOYAGE TO STANLEY.

HAVING explored the country of North Patagonia so far as the means at his disposal enabled him to do so, Mr Ogle resolved, March 1857, on returning for a while to Stanley.   His short visit had prepared the way for a permanent settlement on the mainland where he meant to carry on the work of evangelization.   He had made himself acquainted with the capabilities of the country, the tribes that occupy it, their language and dialects, their spiritual needs, the facilities of the region as a missionary centre, and he had even broken ground in it by announcing the "good tidings" in the toldos of the Indians; and though he now left it, it was with the fully formed purpose of returning soon, and of beginning permanent work there.   He thus records his views and feelings :

## RETROSPECT.

" I now look back on my visit, and review its employments and incidents. How much cause have I for gratitude ! No Indian has harmed me, no Spaniard stabbed me, no wild beast injured a hair of my head ; the heat has not hurt me, the lightning scathed me not. I leave behind a people very friendly to me, and desirous of my return. I have preached the gospel to many, and left nearly all my Spanish testaments, gospels, and tracts, in hands where they will not be thrown away. If I have not opened my mouth in public, it was not for shame, nor from fear, but from a conviction that it would do little good, and a hope that seed scattered here and there might be guided by the Great Husbandman to soil suited for its development. I have not professed myself a missionary so much as a traveller having a missionary object. I believe the result has been that opposition has been disarmed, and prejudice dispelled. I now know better the state of things here. I find the people are by no means bigotted.

" I intend to return to this place (D.V.) as a favourable centre of operation,* and I think for this I have made a good beginning ; I have reason to think most of the influential families are favourable to me, and that I shall have no difficulty in settling here in peace. My mission would be to the Indians, and I should leave Spaniards very much. I have improved my acquaintance with colloquial Spanish, and got assistance in respect to the Indian language. I find that dialect of which I translated the grammar and dictionary is understood by nearly all the Indians I saw. It is the language of the largest and most powerful of the five tribes who inhabit Patagonia—the Chillenos. A few months here would enable me to speak it, and, what is still more important, I could procure some tracts and portions of Holy Scripture in the language. I have gathered a good deal of information on the nature of this country, its soil, the quality of the land, and productiveness in various

* This is now a station of the ' Patagonian,' which has grown into the ' South American ' Missionary Society.

L

crops, the price of all kinds of produce, the resources and capabilities of this river as a site of colonization, and I am very favourably impressed with its suitableness for that end, more than any other in South America. It is more temperate in climate than the Plata or its tributaries, *a fortiori*, than the Amazon, Orinoco, or Rio Grande of the Brazils. It is more convenient for trade than the Chupat, or Santa Cruz, which are southern streams suitable for European occupation, in an extent of fertile land, and the proximity of guano. Here we have a considerable river, as large as any in England, navigable for 200 to 300 miles at least, probably for 1000 miles for small craft. On one side is a level plain, from seven to ten miles wide, excellent land, supporting vast herds of cattle and horses, and producing, with the rudest cultivation, large quantities of grain. Fruit, &c., of every kind, from the sugar-cane and tobacco to the currant and strawberry, grow almost spontaneously, and trees of all sorts. Game is abundant on the hills, and there is unlimited grazing for cattle beyond the bounds of the level, the whole of which appears to be adapted for the plough, and would repay the husbandman amply.

"The great drawback, I am told, is 'the Indians;' these are now masters of the country. Land cannot be occupied more than twenty leagues up the river because of them, nor cattle pastured more than three leagues from the river. The inhabitants do not build, nor improve, nor plant, nor accumulate stock, for the same reason. Indians may appear any hour, day or night. Burnt houses and cornfields, cattle stolen, everything devastated, tell the tale of their deeds ; I am hourly reminded of this. We are comparatively safe in the river, as the Patagonians are horsemen, and will not swim, except forced to do so ; but our neighbours on shore are on the look-out continually for Indians. I slept ashore three nights since. Every dog that broke watch, my companion, a resident here, rose and went out to see if Indians had disturbed the sentinel. If a deer is seen running scared on the hill, it is expected the Indians are near ; if a man and horse are seen, all eyes endeavour to detect some token of his lineage, nor rest till satisfied that he is of Christian blood."

The result of this visit to Patagonia, together with all the information which was deemed likely to be useful to the Patagonian Missionary Society, was communicated to the Committee. As to the impression left upon the inhabitants of the place, one fact only need be mentioned, namely, that a messenger was sent over to Stanley a few months after Mr Ogle's departure to invite and, if necessary, try to induce him to return to them. When the expense of the means of transit is taken into consideration, and the great difficulty which from other causes is often experienced in obtaining a passage in any of the few vessels which keep up the communication between Rio Negro and the Falklands, the value of this testimony to the kind feeling which he had been able to establish between himself and them, may be better understood. Mr Ogle was very ill at the time when the deputation arrived, and was unable to yield to the entreaties urged, but it was no small comfort to him to be permitted, ere he left that part of the world, to see the dawn of light appearing, and to be assured of the willingness on the part of these neglected and consequently careless and ignorant people to welcome an instructor, and to prepare for his reception.

After being detained a whole week by contrary winds, the ship in which Mr Ogle was embarked, crossed the bar, and stood out to sea. There is only one half hour during the day in which a ship can pass the bar at the mouth of the Rio Negro, and a favourable wind having at last sprung up, the opportunity was seized, and the ship got clear of the river. In the afternoon of the same day, a gale set in, which, growing speedily to a storm, placed the ship and all in her in great peril.

## A Storm and Deliverance.

" In the afternoon," says Mr Ogle, " it blew a gale; suddenly our foremast gave way, and in its fall broke the fore-topmast

also at the point to which all the rigging forward is fastened.
You cannot conceive a more complete state of helplessness
than that to which we were reduced in a few minutes.   The
after-mast would not hold a sail, for it had lost its support,
the foremast was stripped and the broken mast-head hanging
from the splinters and swinging dangerously in the increasing
gale.   The night was coming on; however the sea had not
got up, or we should have been in the greatest danger.   As it
was, we lay in the trough of the sea, rolling heavily, the top
part of our mainmast whipping like a fishing-rod.   It was
necessary for the men to go aloft to cut adrift the ropes which
held the broken spar.   This was at the peril of their lives, as
every rope was slack, and they were thrown off as the ship
rolled, and could save themselves only by the most violent
efforts.   The officer who performed this arduous task was ill
for two days after, from the effect of the strain.   Another
sailor was thrown off the rope, and held on by his hands.
Most painful of all was the fearfully profane language of those
who were on board.   Nevertheless by the mercy of God the
humble prayer of his servant was heard; and may we not
also hope that the blasphemers were spared to give them space
for repentance and the enjoyment of pardoning grace.

"After this we had fine weather, and sped before the
breeze till Tuesday the 16th March, when the wind moderated,
and the Jason Islands, off the West Falklands, were in sight.
This voyage of five days has passed as a dream.   Our voyage
to Patagonia had been eleven days, and when on shore there,
the country was so different from the Falklands in condition
and in climate, one felt as if the distance must be formidable.
We have now, as it were, flown across the expanse of waters,
and have been wafted from summer into winter in less than a
week.

"*Wednesday.*—We are sailing through a maze of islands,
the scene varying every half-hour, as we rapidly pass the head-
lands and outlying islands of the west; bluff promontories, bold,
precipitous rocks, rounded hills, distant mountains, solitary
islets, finely feathered with tussac down to the water's edge;
isolated rocks, breasting the waves, and reverberating the roar

of waters from their pillared fronts and caverned sides; deep
creeks and harbours secure, and again exposed shores, on which
breaks the unappeasable rage of billows from the ocean or from
the straits, through which they rush with impetuous velocity,
in whirling, eddying, tumbling tides."

## Three Days in a Cove.

"Onward we rushed, a headland rounded, we descried 'a
sail,' a tall three-masted vessel, secure under the lee of lofty
land. Our captain suspected it friendly, and altered his course.
The stars and stripes hoisted by us were answered by the kindred
ensign at their mizzen, and we soon came to anchor in a cove,
and manned a boat to visit the stranger. She was equally
anxious to make our acquaintance, and a fleet whale-boat came
alongside in half-an-hour. We all then went on shore. The
island was one of the uninhabited Western Islands, and we
found fertility and luxuriant vegetation, till then undeemed to
be within the possibility of the Falklands. Three cheerful and
sunny days were spent in our snug cove. From morning dawn
to evening grey I was on the island exploring; occasionally I
persecuted the wild geese. We found these excellent eating.
Three times a-day a roasted goose, fat and fine, smoked upon
the cabin table. Three times a-day the forward-board was
furnished with three lusty chickens of the main; six hungry
sailors discussed the fare, and it was said that the cook, often
finding empty dishes, always kept a fourth for the good of the
galley. The whaler had thirty men on board, and took twenty
per diem. This bird is not so large as the native of our geese-
fens at home, but weighs, on an average, about six pounds. I
brought five one morning as my contribution to the common
stock, and found them as much as I could carry, the distance
being three miles over the hills."

## A Penguin Rookery.

"The most remarkable feature of the island is a penguin
rookery. When seen from the sea it resembles a tract thickly

strewn with stones, such as the hills on the Falklands everywhere present. The birds sit or stand by thousands, motionless, in close array, rank above rank on the cliffs, and raise a
deafening clamour as the traveller approaches. They will not
move unless driven off, and then their motion is most absurd;
they hop with a flexure of the back, like a man jumping in a
sack; frequently they tumble over each other and shuffle up
again. The collecting of penguins' eggs is a source of great
emolument to the inhabitants of the Falklands; guano is also
taken, but the ruthless purveyors to the needs of experimental
and artificial systems of agriculture, have not been content to
take these supplies, they spare not the birds; piles of decaying
carcases, left upon the spot, testify to a destructive rapacity
not satisfied with the limitation imposed by their ability
to carry off their spoil. The survivors, however, cover in
myriads the steep declivities of a considerable hill. Below is
a luxuriant garden of tussac, exceeding difficult to traverse,
except by leaping from crown to crown, and this is not always
easy; from top to top you leap and scramble, but the long
strands entangle you, and conceal pitfalls which will make the
traveller acquainted with the world below, where his luckless
legs will be beset by beaks innumerable; for the female
penguin claims the tussac bower as her peculiar province, and
resents intrusion with clamour and resistance. A mile of this
sort of travelling is no bad preparation for a wild-goose chase,
with the prospect of securing a wild-goose dinner! Such was
New Island.

"My chief interest in exploring these islands is in reference
to the missionary settlement, I take great interest in it, and
shall perhaps keep up my connection with it.

"The view from the heights, of the sea and its numerous
islands, with their varied west line, was beautiful. It reminded me strongly of the scenery of the Orkney Islands, but
there appears to be more fertility here. These islands appear
to me to be very superior to the neighbourhood of Stanley.
That island is barren and gray, these bright and green. I
have reason to think that the common saying at Stanley is
true, viz., 'that the least habitable part of the Falkland Islands

has been selected for the colony and Government settlement.'

"The outlines here are most varied, and the rocks grand; there, all is tame and monotonous, the absence of features of interest concurring with the want of everything desirable. The colony is located upon the side of a hill, in the mouth of a funnel, through which all the fogs and mists of the islands discharge themselves, and the wind roars with almost uninterrupted blast. Here, and on all the west islands, though there is wind enough to be sure, yet it is a fine healthy breeze, there is a clear sky and a fertile land."

## East Falkland, and Arrival at Stanley.

"*March* 21*st.*—We sailed early, though the sky was lowering, with a favourable wind, and had a rapid and delightful run till we anchored for the night in a bay off the East Falkland, where we were detained till the 23d by the weather.

"*Thursday.*—We have sailed through intricate passages among these islands, having had fine weather. East Falkland is as flat and dull as West is bold and beautiful. The poor horses were hoisted to-day from the hold and dropped into the sea to swim on shore; all reached it, but three of them died on the beach, the rest shook their heads and trotted off to 'pastures new.'

"*March* 28*th.*—Arrived safely at Stanley, Goss came for me in his boat, and I have resumed my old quarters in his house. I see much to be thankful for, and much to be hopeful of—my health has been good here. I have enjoyed uninterrupted health with the one exception, when at sea, from the rupture of a blood-vessel. I am surrounded by kind friends, all the inhabitants of Stanley welcome me cordially, and only complain that I will not visit them, except the chaplain, whom I have offended by opening a room for a Sunday-school and an evening lecture and prayer-meeting, making it plain that I greatly differ from his views of doctrine. Still we speak—are in no uncharitable state of mind towards each other I hope. I have my amusements also—in a boat and horses. These

last I rarely use, for I can seldom get at them, for horses range
at will when turned out.   My pony is very fat and frisky.   I
lend him to the ladies, and he carries them with the airs and
fleetness of an Arab.   In the open camp, he leads the troop of
horses, snuffing the wind, and is really a beautiful creature.
The other day he carried me twenty-five miles, over spongy
ground, in four hours and a-half, we crossed five road-tracks and
many streams, awkward from the boggy nature of the ground;
one slip only occurred, he sank up to the girths in a bog, but with
neck and nose saved himself from entire submersion.   I maintained my seat, and he floundered out in safety.   When we
arrived at home he was set free, as is usual here, and has not
since been heard of.   How he fares in this wintry weather I
know not, probably some broad rock shelters him, and the
summer fat supports a little privation.

    "My little room, twelve feet square, is more comfortable.
While I was in Patagonia, Mr Jacob Napoleon Goss bought a
carpet and put up a ceiling and book-shelves for his lodger.
The lodger added a sofa, a chiffoncer, and an easy chair;
purchases made at some of the recent sales.   Everybody is
leaving Stanley, and so those left behind get some advantages.
Opposite to me is Mr Gardiner's cheerful face.   A Fuegian
dog, bought from the natives last week by my friend, lies upon
a guanaco skin at my feet.   I do not mind the peat fires now.
Outside is a hurricane which sends rain in at the window,
but a box of Patagonian plants, brought from the Rio Negro,
receives the superfluous moisture.   And now you have an idea of
my surroundings."


### THE STATE OF THE CHURCH OF ENGLAND.

*May 8th*, 1857.

    "The appointment of Buchanan as President of the United
States, and of two good men to bishoprics in England,
together with the Bishop of Exeter's letter, interest me very
much.   I cannot but wonder that there should be no action of
one or other party in the Church of England.   It is obvious
that both cannot, and ought not, to remain in it" (alluding to

the Tractarian, now known as the Ritualistic, and the Evangelical parties). "I have my fears (for the Church), but in the absence of light, I may hope, and I will pray for faithfulness, and piety, and resolution, even to suffer for the truth's sake, and that the present state of compromise may be ended. I believe the time of suffering to be very near, for I seem to see signs unmistakeable of the near approach of Christ's kingdom; and that blessed event shall not be consummated without a previous great apostacy, and a fierce struggle. Prophecy seems to bid us look for a time of darkness and of distress among the saints, and in the world. It is, I hope, preparative to this state that I am not permitted to set my affections upon those worldly advantages which I once fondly cherished, and to which, had I been permitted to retain them, I should have become very closely attached; but the disquiet of my conscience in relation to my duty" (in the indiscriminate use of the burial service) "poisoned all, and made my residence in England a bitterness and a vexation. May your heart, my dear sister, be lifted up above this world, and may you have your enjoyments and your happiness so connected with things above, that vicissitudes may not affect your peace. Tribulation may come, like an unexpected flood, but we have peace in Christ. I do not look for a continuance of our present prosperity and state of security. England, as a land of light and of power for good, has not fulfilled her mission; she is set upon her idols—ambition, vanity, luxury, wealth. She has given power to Christ's enemy—anti-Christ—and her ruin is decreed. I have been reading Bickersteth on the prophecies and on the Jewish question, enjoying his simple, scriptural, and spiritual writing, and striving to rise to his ardent faith and great expectations of the coming glory of Christ on earth. He often expresses my common train of thought, 'The Church of England is so inwardly divided that a schism seems inevitable.'"

## AFFAIRS AT STANLEY.

*June 16th*, 1857.

" MY DEAR SISTER,—The past week has been eventful, and I must begin at once to write my weekly contribution to the next letter home.  First let me acknowledge particularly the valuable unexpected supplies you sent me by Captain Prevost, found on my arrival from Patagonia—the Crimean sheep-skin cloak, the box of groceries from ' Young's,' in which he had opportunely enclosed several missionary periodicals.  Among these I found the journal of my dear friend, Andrew Frost, who is in India, and a very important notice of a project for the removal of the Papal seat from Rome to Jerusalem.

" The *Allen Gardiner* arrived here on the 14th of last month from the coast, bringing Mr Despard, Gardiner, and Dr Ellis.   They had left Banner Cove on the 10th, a proof how readily communication might be maintained between the islands and the coast, weather permitting.   Gardiner came again to be my guest, and Ellis comes frequently.   I begged them to make my rooms their home while on shore.   I can do this comfortably, as Goss (my landlord) is a reasonable man, and in consideration of my abiding in his house, allows me to use it as my own on these occasions." . . . .

## THE MISSION PARTY AT KEPPEL.

"So much monotony as there is in a residence in these *weary winter* islands, which summer does not even turn green, makes it quite excusable to look for a little solace in the meeting of social parties.  I do not rejoice in dancing and song singing, but if I get to Keppel I shall try to make a social fireside for the members of the mission party.  Poor fellows !  There have been three catechists, with Mr Ellis (the surgeon) and Mr Gardiner sometimes, on that desolate islet for more than a year.  They have seen *two* ships; the last seemed as a terrible apparition to their morbid imaginations, so dejected and down-hearted had they become. . . . . People here very naturally ask, ' What are four catechists and a surgeon doing at Keppel? They had better be scaling,' and I think so too!" . . . .

At this time Mr Ogle, having been unsuccessful in the offer which he again made of his services to "accompany the mission party in their ship, for the strictly missionary work of visiting, or of instructing the natives," reconsidered the circumstances in which he found himself. He took counsel with his friend Mr Gardiner, with whom he had ever been able to maintain a cordial Christian friendship. Mr Gardiner, on his part, desired to establish a branch mission at Banner Cove, and he proposed to Mr Ogle that they should together have a vessel in which from thence they might visit the neighbouring islands. The inhabitants appeared to be friendly, and he shared in Mr Ogle's desire to devote his voluntary labour more exclusively to the work of evangelisation than circumstances permitted those to do who were engaged in bringing Keppel island into a state suitable for the mission-colony.

The following "fragment" shows the spirit in which Mr Ogle was prepared to set forth :

### A FRAGMENT.

*"June 26th,* 1857.

" Into the silent land,
     Who shall lead thither ?
Who ? with a gentle hand,
     Thither ! oh thither !
Into the silent land."

"The die is cast; the resolve is taken; 'into the silent land!' not the land of eternal silence (*D.V.*), but like that in its dark shroud of ignorance, of poverty, of obscurity,—Fuegia a land of storm and desolation,—I see it nigh; I feel its cold breath; I seem to see its flitting forms, shadows more than men. They beckon, they implore—'come to the silent land.' 'From the uttermost parts of the earth have I heard songs.' This shall be ! Oh that it may be true of the silent land—

' Who in life's battle firm doth stand
     Shall bear Hope's tender blossoms
Into the silent land.'

"A long conflict of doubts and fears, of allurements on one side, of threatened evils on the other, results in the resolution which I have taken, 'Into the silent land.'

"'Forward,' said the voice of God by Moses to Israel on the brink of the Red Sea, which bounded and barred out the wilderness. The voice of external providence seemed to say, 'Return to Egypt and submit to Pharaoh,' but the still small voice of God speaking to the heart within pointed to the cloud, and by His prophet uttered the direction, 'Forward.'

"Who shall lead us thither? [to Fuegia] Shall sentiment and sympathy taking the form of some disconsolate daughter of the lost tribes * allure us by the bonds of a compassion for her people's woes? No! When danger nears and thickens around, fear casteth out love; her human eye is glazed by terror. She cannot lead us thither.

"Shall the kindred impulses of brotherhood to a race forlorn, yet akin to us as being members of one universal family, lead us? Will not a nearer view persuade us *they* are not our kindred? or if so by blood, by some dire curse excluded from the claims of brotherhood?

"Shall lower aims conduct us? Such are the presiding genii of this world's enterprises. The phantoms of Gain and of Glory lure men on through flood and fire; they heed no hardships, they dread no shape of death. True; but not thither. There the keen eye of avarice detects no glitter of the idol gold. Ambition's blind imagination cannot shape upon that rigid outline the legend word 'Excelsior.' What has civilization's utmost effort achieved on yonder island [on which the Government colony of Stanley is situated] in a quarter of a century? A sickly settlement, swallowing the substance of its inhabitants; and this land [Terra del Fuego] is ruder, rougher, more a wilderness; witness its wretched races, their misery excluding hope, preventing pity."

And again, he writes:

"Let my brother do with my property as he judges best,

* This alludes probably to the supposition which has been suggested by some that the lost tribes would be found in those unknown and inclement countries.

only let him try to help me here. If a settlement at the Rio Negro be practicable for me, I should wish to begin in such a way as would be likely to be of permanent utility. I am very much set upon the work for which I was sent out, and shall not lightly leave it.

"I do refer all things to God in prayer; and though the cloud over my path is very dark, I see a gleam of light sometimes. Pray for me: if I have God's favour, not his frown, all things which occur will be to my own good as well as for that of others. As to my difficulties, my own spirit needed chastening; and perhaps if I had gone to Keppel I might have realised, still more than I have done here, the condition of a stranger and an exile. Still I could not look forward to the prospect of the absence of any employment for months together, with nothing but salt provisions, which always make me ill. I used to live frequently when on board the 'Hydaspes' on biscuit and coffee. I am sure, if the benevolent purveyors for the Crimean heroes knew the case of the poor fellows at Keppel, they would send not only 'comforters,' but other comforts by the ship-load. Remember, if you send such commodities for me, I hope you will do it on a scale commensurate with *their* wants. It is true that there are cattle in abundance upon these islands, but the owners will not part with a single hoof to them."

By the same mail he wrote to an aged Christian lady, an intimate friend of his own family, who had taken great interest in the Patagonian mission; but to her, for fear of injuring the cause, he says not a word about his disappointment.

STANLEY, July 1857.

. . . "From the country to which you and other Christians in England have sent us, that we may act for you in preaching the glad tidings of the gospel of Jesus Christ, I again write. I presume you will regard with the feelings of a mother in Israel the efforts of young soldiers in the army of our Joshua, and think that the news of their progress will encourage and stimulate your prayers for them. This is what I desire to

know, that for me personally, and for my work, pious Christians
are praying ; and I have the happiness to know it. Oftentimes when weary and somewhat cast down, a refreshment, as
from heaven, comes to my relief, and I recollect that it is the
time at which some Christian friends in England have promised
to pray for me.

"As in the church in the wilderness, the famished host was
led by a hand unseen, and guided by a supernatural light,—
living 'not by bread only, but by every word of God,'—so now
our dependence is on prayer. Jesus intercedes, and by His
intercession judgments are deferred, vengeance is averted, and
gifts bestowed—chief gift of all, the Spirit to help our infirmities.
It is not so much your prayers as an individual Christian that
are of value, as it is that they are those of a member of the
body of Christ, sympathizing with the Head ; as such, our
prayer hath favour with God. I have visited Patagonia ; an
initiatory and exploratory visit. I do not know that any
European missionary has preceded me there. Yet I think it a
most important station for our work. To El Carmen, the most
southerly town in the South American continent, the Patagonian
Indians have for a century past been accustomed to resort for
purposes of trade, and although that trade is at present interrupted by the occurrence of war between the Spaniards and the
Indians, resulting in mutual recriminations and much slaughter,
yet there is a prospect of peace, and that a treaty will soon be
concluded between them, which will restore peaceful intercourse.
I have conversed with many Indians who are settled in the
town of El Carmen and in its neighbourhood, and find them
well disposed, as far as I could judge, to receive instruction.

"These live in huts, such as those of our gipsies, made of cow-
hides stretched on poles, placed in a clear space in the centre
of a forest. Ostriches were feeding around the door, as turkeys
do with you. Their food, the large grasshopper, so abundant
here, is very similar to the cicada of Spain. Like that insect,
it infests in myriads the parched grass and the stubbles in
autumn ; groves of trees are vocal with its ceaseless chirp ; it
is not easily seen, but flies in clouds before the horseman or
the foot passenger. The 'voice of the cicada' is synonymous

with 'day.' One can understand the allusion in Ecclesiastes, how, from the impaired faculty of attention in age, the constant din of busy day, though in a measure so modified as in the concert of insignificant insects, becomes 'a burden.' I was continually reminded of Scripture imagery and incident, as I had been when in Spain, and some other countries where the climate corresponds to that of Judea. It is not a little singular that the inartificial mode of life we read of in the Scriptures and in anti-Christian classics should still obtain in so large a part of the world; that invention and improvement should be confined to so small a portion, and that portion the least remunerative to its outlay. The hard stimulus of necessity appears to be the only successful incentive to man's industry.

"I told them of the interest the report of their uninstructed condition excited in England, that an officer of the British navy had devoted his life to seek their welfare, and had perished in the prosecution of his benevolent enterprise, that his only son had determined to follow his father's footsteps, and was actually in the South country at this time, and that I am but a member of the same mission. They had heard of Queen Victoria, the benevolent, and appeared to be delighted when I told them that she is the patroness of the missionaries. As there were not any Indians belonging to the hostile tribes within two hundred miles of El Carmen, I could not obtain an interview with any of these."

This plan was, however, abandoned at the wish of the superintendent of the mission. Mr Gardiner returned in the *Allen Gardiner* to Keppel island, and writes thence to his friend :—

*September 30th*, 1857.

. . . . "What a pity our scheme about the 'Perseverance' came to nothing. It is a real grief to me not to be associated with you in the work. To think that after coming out from England together, and having so often taken sweet counsel together, we should be now so unhappily sundered, and between us a strait which I cannot pass! Still we cannot tell what may be in the future. Perhaps brighter days will come. Tell

me your plans, as if by any possible vicissitudes we should meet
again, it would, indeed, be a comfort."

Mr Ogle remained at Stanley, "being," as he says, " unfitted for the labour of digging peat and hewing stone.  I could
only do about one fourth of the work of one strong man, and
then the risk to my health would probably more than
counterbalance any advantage gained to the mission by
my toil.    At Stanley I have a small house, which I
use for a Sunday school and lecture room, and for an
evening service on the Sundays.    The children go to church
with their parents in the morning."    At Stanley also he had
the sick, whom he visited.    Writing of an aged sufferer, he
says, "I hope I see in him an heir of glory.    Indeed, I often
think that I was sent here to gather this long lost wanderer
into the fold of Jesus Christ."

Yet he ever looked upon Stanley as a place from which he
might find an opportunity of getting into the work for which
he left his parish in England, and not as a permanent residence.
The sad state of Monte Video, at that time afflicted with yellow
fever, so severely that "all business was suspended, fifty persons
dying daily from the scourge, strongly tempted" him to visit
it.    He waited upon God in prayer, asking that circumstances
might favour the plan, "if He see me to be a fit instrument
to work for Him there ; without this I could not go, as my
affairs now stand."

His independent conduct, however, drew forth some severe
comments from the Society at home which appeared in their
little organ the "Voice of Pity;" but his mind though
pained was not soured.    On receiving the intimation of it in
June 1857, he thus writes to his sister.

"I was accused of being too calculating and considerate.
Reflecting on what the misfortunes of the past ought to teach
us (alluding to Captain Gardiner's sad fate from failure of
supplies), upon the necessity that still exists for careful economy,

prudent caution, the source whence we derive our supplies, etc.; wise and precautionary provisions, foresight, as far as man can carry it, seemed to me to be necessary, as well as a confidence in His aid who admits us to be fellow-workers with Him. But the state of things connected with the mission, found on our arrival at Stanley, and the arrangements I observed, led me to anticipate a repetition of errors and mismanagement, of disappointment, and of ultimate failure. Was there not reason in my asking for information as to the provision made as to Keppel? Conscious of a desire to support our chief in the circumstances of difficulty in which he was placed (though as managing secretary of the Society at home, these should not have been unknown to him), and anxious to show myself ready to suffer for the cause, and to share with my companions, I decided to abide the risk I perceived, otherwise I had tendered my resignation at once. But eventually Providence, in what afterwards occurred, led to the course which I have adopted. . . . . Still I hoped that by remaining quietly at Stanley, I should not injure the mission, and I willingly take the opprobrium, glad that the Society has not suffered. . . . I cannot but acknowledge that abundant cause existed [in me] why the great Head of the work should reject me as a co-operator with Himself, and regarding the errors of instruments as permitted to work out His end, I took the chastisement, as I still do, as the act of a gracious God, correcting and not destroying, 'for our profit, that we may be partakers of his holiness.' When that end shall be answered, I shall, I doubt not, be permitted to have a share, however humble, in this glorious work. There are various points of view from which every course of conduct may be regarded. I have tried to view this matter dispassionately, and in a Christian manner, and I acquit Mr —— of *intentional* wrong. But I have changed my view respecting him as a prudent and judicious manager of a mixed enterprise like ours, in which a Christian object, a work eminently of faith, is sought to be carried out by means and agencies of ordinary Providence.

"In such, the knowledge, the experience, the skill, the

M

diligence, the caution of the manager, must be distinguished, or success cannot reasonably be hoped for.

"I felt that I did not myself possess these qualities adequately, and therefore declined the offer made to me at first to take charge of the mission.

"However gratifying it might be to me to publish a meek and temperate vindication of my conduct, which might procure an acknowledgement of error, I think such a course less accordant with the strictly Christian profession I have made in entering upon this work than silence is. 'Avenge not yourselves, but rather give place unto wrath,' and if I copy in this respect the example of my Master, reviled, I shall not revile in return, but commit my vindication to Him who judgeth righteously. If I am fairly judged, my sacrifice for the Society's cause will be set off against my sins against it, and if I am thought to have acted under 'hallucination,' it will be deemed the aberration of a well-intentioned spirit.

"Through the grace of God, I trust I am not losing ground in the Christian race, and though I am fallen into the vicinity of Doubting Castle, I shall not, I trust, be immured in the dungeons of Giant Despair. How beautiful is this allegoric portrait drawn by the prisoner of Bedford Jail ! . . . You will think much of your absent brother, and when you receive this solution of his present circumstances, and this assurance that he is cheerful and contented, happy and hopeful, you will yourself be all these on his account.

"I have good hope for the mission itself, Mr —— evidently increases in spirituality of view. We were widely different in opinions upon what are deemed my extreme views. His recent sermons have shown me that he is unconsciously approaching to my point of view. When a minister comes to look at himself and at the Church, and into the doctrines of man's sinfulness and of God's grace, from the position of a missionary, whether it be to the dark inhabitants of England, or to those of South America, his views expand, and he sees all the work to be God's, and comes to value, at its proper estimate, all human systems as mere instruments."

As to his feelings regarding the Committee at home, he writes :—

"I shall always be glad to find that the cause prospers in the hands to which I committed my own share in the undertaking. I shall communicate information to the Committee, point out openings, warn against dangers, and actively contribute to their success in every way that occurs to me, and look forward with a confident expectation that all will be overruled for the furtherance of the great object—the spread of the kingdom of the Redeemer among the benighted inhabitants of this part of the world."

The Society, has now entered upon a new career, having adopted a new name, "The South American Missionary Society." By enlarging its sphere of labour, and by giving attention to the more simple and ordinary work of the mission scheme, it has provided fields of labour sufficient to employ the energies of educated labourers; and they, being placed in countries where, supposing them to be capable of maintaining amicable relations with the inhabitants, will no longer be exposed to the fear of starvation nor to the mental strain of want of suitable occupation when left for months together upon a small and almost uninhabited island, which proved so fatal in poor Mr Ellis' case. The mental depression produced upon the minds of some of those self-sacrificing and noble men at Keppel was similar to that well known to be the effect of solitary confinement. All this is happily past; and though the faithful narration of disappointments and of disasters is important for future guidance, it should not prejudice any against those who were, to the best of their power, working out a great and an untried problem. Those who suffered from their own mistakes or from those of others have suffered nobly, convinced of the goodness of their cause, of the love of the Master whom they served, of the sincerity of their companions, *and* of the imperfection and evil which remain to be "crucified" in the hearts even of the most

advanced Christians ; they suffered in silence.    Each, as far as
we have records to guide us, must be said to have endeavoured,
so far as they were able to do so, to further the great cause of
a mission of peace to the neglected inhabitants of the south,
for which they had left their home and their country.    A
commencement has been now made, and " if pious Christians
at home aid them by their prayerful efforts," there is good
hope that a mission, which has cost many tears, will be consummated in joy.    (See Appendix A.)

    This trying period may be fitly concluded by an extract
from a letter received from the Secretary of the Patagonian
Missionary Society, a little more than a year after his return
to England.

CLIFTON, August 9th, 1858.

    . . . . " That principle of Christian charity which 'thinketh
no evil—while at the same time it suffereth long and is kind,'
—is, I am persuaded, active in your heart.    For, however
right we may think Mr ——, it is nevertheless most true
that you, in differing from him, had much to bear.    Our trials
cannot be measured by the calm judgments of outstanding
witnesses.    And to you there can be no doubt that the experience of circumstances, connected with our mission abroad, and
the expression of opinion at home, has been *hard* to bear.
But your conduct is a striking testimony to the triumph of
Christian principle ; and I do sincerely hope we may all gain
something by observing your example of love."

    Soon after these occurrences, Mr Ogle began to feel symptoms
of serious illness.    We have already mentioned that he burst
a small blood-vessel, in the tempestuous return voyage to
Stanley.    This made exertion for the present dangerous.    His
illness increased.    His health, taken in connection with the
wild and inhospitable region in which the mission was to be
discharged, forced him to contemplate returning home.    Unwilling he was to entertain this conclusion, but at last he felt
that he had no alternative but to do so.    The voyage, which was
made early in 1858, was beneficial to his health, but some

months elapsed before his strength was sufficiently restored to enable him to think of regular work. His time was mostly passed with his brother and sisters who resided in London, and he could not be in the capital without having his attention awakened to the state of the godless masses around him, and asking himself what he could do to help to remedy it.

With returning health he longed to be engaged again in the great work of the Gospel. Preaching in theatres had not then been attempted nor proposed ; but the thought occurred to his mind, and he was only prevented by personal circumstances from trying the experiment of hiring the Victoria Theatre in Lambeth for this purpose. Alone, he found himself "unable to undertake it," and, at that time, he feared "that his Christian character and ability would not be trusted."

Before, however, embarking in other labours, Mr Ogle, for the re-invigoration of his health, resolved on a tour in the Highlands of Scotland. He passed north to Oban, and on returning southwards he halted at Edinburgh. In that city he met with some Christian friends who were planning measures for the evangelization of Spain. Everything bearing on the emancipation of that country from the crushing yoke it has so long borne had a deep interest for him. A voyage which he made to Spain in 1846 had first kindled his interest in this people ; and during his residence at Stanley, and his voyage to El Carmen, he had met many of that nation, and this intercourse had increased his knowledge of their tongue and deepened his interest in their welfare. He therefore gladly acceded to the wish of the "Edinburgh Spanish Evangelization Society," that he should visit the province of Oran in Algeria, and report upon the state of the Spanish Protestants there, and enquire into the openings for the proclamation of the Gospel to their fellow-countrymen. In pursuance of this arrangement, Mr Ogle proceeded to Algeria, and we are now to accompany him thither.

# CHAPTER XIII.

## ALGERIA.

### MARSEILLES TO ORAN—INCIDENTS OF JOURNEY.

In the latter end of October 1858, Mr Ogle set out for Algeria. Passing through France and embarking at Marseilles he came, after a prosperous voyage, to Oran on the 15th November. The incidents of the journey, so far as our traveller deemed them worth narrating, will appear in the letters that follow. Meanwhile a glance at the past history of the country will be interesting.

The name Algiers, suggests the recollection of piratical outrages, and of the indescribable horrors of the Moorish penal system, to which all foreigners who intruded into the territory of the *Dey of Algiers*, were wont to be subjected. The coast of Africa seemed like a den of lions, and of fiercer savages. Our vessels were wont to keep clear of, and out of sight of, the abhorred and dreaded shore.* One never reads of a traveller who visited the territory. The only name familiar to our ears from Fez to Alexandria was Carthage, a city that has, for near 2000 years, ceased to have a place or an inhabitant.

The City of Tunis is not far from the site of ancient

---

* Previous to Lord Exmouth's appearance in the Bay of Algiers in 1816, a yearly tribute, amounting to 858,610 francs, was paid by certain European nations to purchase exemption from the piratical attacks of the Algerines. These fierce pirates, who swept the South Coasts of the Mediterranean and the shores of the Adriatic, used to land their prisoners, and to deposit their booty upon the narrow ledges within the caves and grottoes which are washed by these seas. The *grotto des Schiavi* (of the slaves) is one of those which derives a mournful interest from well authenticated facts respecting the cruelties practised by these marauders. By the bombardment of Algiers by the English fleet, under Lord Exmouth, many christian captives were liberated—and piracy was greatly suppressed.

Carthage, but this city was utterly demolished by the Romans.
The ruins of Carthage are as complete a type of desolation as
are those of Thebes, or even of Babylon. Beyond Tunis we
have a faint. impression of the situation of Tangiers, and of
Tripoli. Algiers was, certainly, familiar as a household word,
but 'twas as a name of dread ; and who knew anything of
Constantine, and Bona, and Djideti ; of Nesila, and Milianah,
of Bistray and Bledah, of Mostaganem and Mascara ; of Flem-
cere, ' one of the most curious and beautiful Moorish cities
in Algeria,' and Oran ? Yet all these names now represent
towns of importance, crowded by a mixed population of Arab,
Moor, Turk, Christian, and Jew. Fair cities to behold, and
pleasant to visit, they have goodly houses and luxuriant
gardens ; abounding (as did Palestine of old) with corn and
wine, with oil-olive and honey. Hither come the swallow and
the nightingale to find a winter home, when northern winters
drive them from our shores. Flowers bloom and fruit ripens
in mid-winter here, and even the winter months equal the
fairest of the year in our own land. Why then had we so
little knowledge of so fair a territory ? so near to us in comparison with many more frequented lands. It is but six days
journey from any part of our island. Why ? Because we
cared not to investigate, and few were found to tell us what they
had learned ; again, because prejudice had fixed upon the
northern shore of Africa as upon other portions of that long
doomed land, an epithet of aversion ; and we turned from it
as if it were still a region to be shunned. The knowledge
that our polite and enterprising neighbour France, had taken
some part of the coast under her protection scarcely relieved
our apprehensions. We thought rather that all that subsists
of hereditary enmity in France, must of necessity develope
itself in the congenial soil of the Barbary Moor, and the pirate
Algerine ! This also is a mistake. Nowhere is the Frenchman so little obnoxiously French, as in Algeria ; he has taken

root there deeply, and has become a vigorous plant, with more
genial qualities than on the colder soil of Europe, and he
becomes your friend (though you are an Englishman), if you
approach him frankly and sincerely. His wants are here
supplied, and with little cost or trouble : in ease and abundance he expands and lives, like the land of his adoption, in
perpetual sunshine.

About 40,000 Spaniards, at least, are to be found in
Algeria. It is a French colony, and all the inhabitants professedly enjoy liberty of conscience and of worship.

There are many large and flourishing towns along the
sea coast. Oran, the capital of the province of that name, is
one of them. It is distant about three hundred miles from the
city of Algiers.

The province of Oran is near to the kingdom of Morocco.
Thither the brave chief Abd-el-Kader, 1842, fled for refuge,
when driven by the French from the province of Algiers ; and
from thence he passed over to Morocco to persuade the
emperor to espouse his failing cause against their common foe.
The city of Oran contains about 35,000 inhabitants. These
and the various nationalities, which crowd its busy thoroughfares, are described in the letters that follow. The 'religious
liberty,' which is enjoyed in Algeria, consists mainly in the
permission, granted by a licence from government, to the
members of the different religious communities to meet for
the celebration of their worship. They are thus placed under
strict government supervision, and the pasteurs know that
they are liable to be deprived of their licence at its pleasure.
The effect of this system is often most lamentable. It crushes
all religious zeal and activity in all but the most self-denying, and in time produces an universal deadness as to the
importance of the subject. Such was the state of religious
feeling found by Mr Ogle on his arrival. As he went on his
way to this new and unpromising field of labour, he

scattered around him the good seed. The following are instances :—

" In the rail-carriage en route to Dijon, I had many willing auditors to whom I told of the Bible; how we value it in England, and have it freely circulated everywhere, etc. A peasant begged to buy a New Testament: he said, that ' his wife kept a school, and he wanted the book " pour les enfans." ' I wrote some texts in it for him, and read from its sacred pages to all there."

## A Fellow Pilgrim.

" At Lyons, where I arrived, as at Paris, after dark, on a bitterly cold night, I was again detained. However in the streets I addressed words of grace to my fellow-men, and found, at least, three persons willing to receive the blessed words of peace. An old woman, who supplied me with a cup of hot coffee, at a street corner, from a little stall, in the icy atmosphere, I found to be a Christian indeed : and a few minutes' conversation with her were to me, and, I trust, also to herself, as rivers of refreshment in a desert land. Poor Protestants in France have few friends or neighbours like minded. Hatred and persecution, often avowed, and, if otherwise, always secret, make their journey sad, and their lives bitter. What is it not worth to them to meet with a fellow-pilgrim, if only for a momentary exchange of a few words of affectionate greeting, ere he is gone ? They are no longer alone in the world ; sympathy, that dear necessity of our nature, has been exercised, and the time when the sweet society of kindred spirits gathered from every nation, and language, and tongue, and people, shall be for ever constituted, seems to be near and certain."

## Voyage to Oran.

" . . . . The voyage from Marseilles to Oran was pleasant, the sea calm, and weather fine ; by day beautiful, by night placid, and rapid throughout. Spain was touched at Alicante,

where some of the passengers disembarked. I stayed there
three hours, and left I hope, some good behind. Alicante is
a small town with a port and a castle. It is desolate looking,
owing to the whiteness of the soil and rock, and the absence of
vegetation. . . It appears to be a very poor place, but all
Spanish towns have this appearance. How strange that riches
instead of improving should bring poverty over a land!
It has been so with Spain. The gold of the Indies has
impoverished the whole of Spain. It may be so with a land
in spiritual things also. If the riches of its spiritual treasury
be not expended and distributed according to God's will, He
will take them from that land, and leave barrenness.

" We reached Algeria by night, and lay to in heavy rain till
daylight. Then the port of Oran (distant five miles) was seen.
We soon disembarked, but 'twas only to remain for some
hours waiting for our luggage, etc. Clad in waterproof from
top to toe, I sat upon my boxes, a sort of pattern voyager, and
did not mind the delay ; independent of all circumstances I
had made many friends during the voyage ; the boat had been
crowded with French soldiers.

TOWN AND SCENERY OF ORAN.—(*November* 1858).

" . . . . How shall I commence to speak of this place, and
of my work ?   Before me, from my window, I have the most
charming picture I ever beheld. I must give you a rough
sketch.

" The hotel in which I write is in the centre of the city.
From my room I look over the flat roofs of the houses to the
citadel, which crowns a rock 500 feet in height. A traveller
who has just come in, to whom I have shown my sketch,
approves it, and remarks the houses in Oran are like those in
Jerusalem, but whiter and cleaner looking. The citadel is in
the centre of my picture, the hill precipitous and rocky, in
colour rusty red, with a grateful relief of vegetation (prickly
pear chiefly). Below, in the town, you see the chestnut with
rich rounded foliage, the fig-tree and the myrtle, the palm, and
other trees, some, as the laburnum, in flower, all looking

brilliant in that sunshine which you see only on Mediterranean shores, that bright azure, cloudless, against which the white citadel stands clear. The house-tops, for the most part used for various purposes of utility and enjoyment, form a sort of plateau, upon which the world is moving apart from the busy scene of the streets. Then the climate! how I wish dear F. could come to breathe the air, like oil to the enfeebled organs of respiration. The weather has been delightful ever since I arrived, like our brightest summer days in England, but without too much heat, gentle breezes from the sea. The days are short, but brilliant from morn to eve. Verdure is luxuriant. The summer heat acts upon vegetation as a winter elsewhere in checking growth, and now the plants revive and bloom as with us in spring; the genial rain which falls at night produces an effect marvellous in its rapidity, beauty, and energy of growth.

"The scene has changed! It is just twelve hours since I commenced this letter—how altered all. From a palace to a prison? No, thank God, not a prison, but like one in loneliness, in obscurity. I see nothing from my windows now but blank walls and barred windows; but this change is as voluntary as my exile. It is self-selected, God's providence has directed my way. . . I have a compact suite of four rooms, all clean and tranquil, close to my work, close to the sea, but having no view, thus I shall not be tempted by these lovely nights to sit at the open window looking homeward over the Mediterranean—the blue Mediterranean, and its bold rocky shores.

## ALGERIA IN SPRING.—(*March* 9.)

"Except that the days are short, you would think it May. The country is covered with flowers, the marigold predominating. There are two kinds, the pale yellow and deep orange. There is a purple flower also, which grows in patches and quite covers the ground; so that there is a close resemblance to the beautiful and gay parterres of the Crystal Palace garden without their formality. Since the rains of

February we have had unchanging fine weather, nights always clear, days ever sunny.

" Oran is a large town, capital shops, everything you can wish, and cheap.    It is very picturesque, and has great variety.    It is like three towns in one, each different in every respect, indeed, belonging to, and inhabited by, different nations.    Oran has the charm of having open country within a mile on every side ; so that the choice of occupation or amusement is very great.    The regulations are admirable ; you have no difficulty, no danger, no restraint.    The only tax is a dog tax.    If the sales were not on Sunday I could pro-vide myself with everything for very little cost.    There are two lakes near, one of salt water very extensive.    The sea bounds the prospect in one direction, mountains limit it in every other.    Herds of cattle, droves of camels, goats, pigs, sheep, horses, give life to the scene, and Arabs picturesque in costume.    The last time I crossed the plain a very large encampment of Bedouins was visible, low brown huts like cobwebs stretched on the ground.    I met also 100 camels, several of them with the picturesque furniture one sees in pictures, and standing precisely in the conventional posture. I have not mounted one ; generally their furniture is so dirty-looking, that one has a repugnance, and the squalid ragged figures who have the charge of them are not inviting.    It is very difficult to realise that one is in Africa, and that these are real Arabs on their own soil ; that Englishmen can settle and occupy such a country without molestation speaks volumes in its commendation.

*Shrove Tuesday*—The Carnival.—It was kept in Oran with great spirit.    Hundreds of masks were abroad, and all sorts of absurd costumes making sport, practical jokes, mock bulls, as for a fight, led through the streets, &c., &c.

## COSTUMES IN THE STREETS OF ORAN.

" You may see in the streets of Oran any day nearly twenty different costumes.    There is the European, the French pea-sant, five different dresses of French soldiers, of which the

Zouave with shaven forehead and red skull cap, with long blue tassel, blue jacket over red shirt or vest, which is tied below the knee, white gaiters, and a green turban, when on duty, is the most curious; you would think him to be a native of Morocco, or of Algiers, of India, or of any place rather than of gay and lightsome France, yet he is oftentimes a true Frenchman, though many of them are half or wholly Arabs. There are three Arab costumes, the red, the black, and the white; the red burnous shows the Arab of Oran, the black the Nomad or Bedouin. The women are enveloped in a white dress, wear white shoes, and look like sheeted ghosts, one eye only peeps out at a triangular aperture. The Turk has several costumes, as he is a Turk of Syria, of Constantinople, or of Malta. Of Spanish, there are two dresses; of Italy, two; of Jewish, three or four. The Jews are very conspicuous, they employ much colour, and with good effect. On Christmas day I went with ten or twelve Jews, who waited for the Jewish missionary, at the door of the Protestant temple, dressed in their gayest clothes,—it was their Sabbath. We had for three hours close controversy respecting the Messiah. They were unable to prove that Jesus is not 'Messiah,' and could not refute the arguments in favour of His being so ; but they appear to be determined not to receive His gospel. I encourage Jews as well as Spaniards and Arabs, to come to meet me, and then I show them the truths of the Bible in Arabic, Hebrew, &c., and try to direct their attention, not to controversy, but to practical subjects. My argument on Christmas day was this : There is promise in the Prophets that Christ shall come, and that the Jews shall be restored. We both [Jew and Christian] look for these events. What is the *character* of those to whom He shall appear with joy? The penitent, the 'contrite and humble in heart,' 'the mourners in Zion.' Are we such ? This is the best controversy. It is the Lord's controversy."

## THE JEWS.

" The Jews say that they were driven from Spain when the sign of the Cross supplanted that of the Crescent in that

Peninsula : that they were received with joy, and had all
the privileges which they formerly enjoyed in Spain awarded
to them by the Moslems in Algeria.

" Under the Turkish rule, however, they had to suffer
again both cruelties and degradations, though they were for
the sake of commerce permitted to exercise their wonted trade.
They were the sole bankers in Algiers, and were very necessary to a people who lived upon piracy and required a separate
class of persons to act as a means of communication between
themselves and the lawful traders of other nations. Under
the French rule they possess the same privileges as are common to their fellow subjects."

## THE MOORS.

" They execute the most delicate embroidery in white and
coloured floss silk, sitting with naked feet, surrounded by
heaps of the raw material lying about them in the narrow
street at their doors.

" Each nation appears to have its own quarter of the city
where they reside, though the streets are often thronged with
people of every race."

## THE FRENCH CAMP IN ALGERIA.

In Algeria there are often 100,000 soldiers. The open
country is used as a camp, where the military hosts can
be conveniently and unostentatiously marshalled preparatory
to their embarkation for foreign service. The "army of Italy"
was here assembled and finally equipped in 1859.

In Mr Ogle's letters, under date 1863, we find reference
made to the "army of Mexico," which, like that of "Italy,"
was prepared in Algeria, out of sight of the world, till it was
ready to go forth on its path of conquest. Good part of the
vast army which in 1870 was launched against Germany was
brought from hence also. This appears to have been the
main use which the emperor made of the colony of Algeria ;

it was a vast recruiting and drilling ground; a terrible menace while in the hands of France to the civilization of the world. This is a curious history to have to record in the latter end of the nineteenth century. As the devastating tempest is born on the summit of mountains, or in the silent heights of the firmament, so the solitudes of the African continent were the birth-place of the armed hordes of the French empire; there were they disciplined and equipped, and thence sent forth to ravage a world which had been kept ignorant of their existence till they suddenly burst upon it, as bursts the tempest upon the earth.

## Breaking Ground.

"All simple as my life here has been—for I do not seek after great things—each day brings its opportunities. To-day, for example, I have a cold, and the weather prevents my getting out to make special efforts. Is it a lost day? I trust not, for I have been able to add to the friendly sentiments entertained towards me by the members of six neighbouring households with whom I have commenced an acquaintance with a view to their eternal interests. In three of their houses there is now a New Testament; one in Italian, and two in Spanish. The rest have not reached that stage yet. I must hope that the ground is ready, and then sow the seed."

An indiscriminate distribution of Bibles, or even of tracts, to those who neither desired to possess them for use nor knew their value, was ever avoided by him. But he diligently sought to excite the desire, and having made his work the subject of much prayer, he watched the answer, and hopefully and gratefully recorded it as from God's grace. His faith, as to the answer God gives to faithful prayer, was simple, strong, and childlike. He expected the fulfilment of the promise, "Ask and ye shall have." To return to the narrative of "the day's blessings."

## A Zouave.

"I have been recognised by a French soldier, whom I did not recollect. He accosted me when a few yards from my house. He was one of the fierce-looking fellows who form the Zouaves of the French army; but I found he was one to whom I had given a tract with the words 'Read this and lend it to a comrade till the end of the world,' written by me upon the cover. He said 'he had obeyed my directions, and the book was being read by many.' I took him home, and gave him two more tracts similarly inscribed. Thus the bread which was cast upon the waters, when on board the steamer from Marseilles, has been found; and more has been scattered. While God grants me such encouragement, I hope to remain in this dark land, where the mere fact of a Christian, living as such, cannot be without its good effect. I hope that every penny I spend here serves to advance my Master's kingdom, and to dissipate the prejudice that exists against those who hold a different and a better faith than that which here prevails. If I can maintain a frank and cheerful spirit in my daily walk, I shall do something to commend the gospel I teach to those who now regard it as a fable, and dread it as a heresy.

"Some missionaries, I think, frustrate their object by their mode of work. They think to gain a country by a single stroke (or more frequently perhaps others expect this result from them), whereas they are strangers to the habits, the manners, the language, the religion of the people they visit, and they have a host of other difficulties to contend with besides these named. Generally, they accomplish little until, by force of circumstances, they have become residents among the people, their conduct and manners have been seen and approved, and they are therefore looked upon with less distrust.

"I do not always commence among strangers by direct missionary effort; that is to say, by introducing religious conversation. By ordinary acts of kindness and courtesy, and a free and easy manner, the French soldiers have become my friends. Now, a French soldier, as a rule, hates the Englishman. He desires a quarrel with England; relying on the numerical strength and military character of his nation he expects to triumph. It is therefore no small matter of rejoicing to me, that I have now fifty friends among the military of various ranks, and I know that my fifty friends will, as they go through the province, make many more for me, more I mean, who will take my books, and will listen while I tell them of things good for their soul's health."

After about a month's residence in the country he writes :—

" I wear the dress of the country—a loose coat, with a scarlet scarf round my waist; a straw hat, which is several feet in height; and ride to and fro into the country, sometimes upon a saddle, sometimes upon a sack, giving everybody, high and low, a recognition as I pass along, and am still surprised how the plan is successful in eliciting both kindness and respect from all.

" I know there are a straight-laced sort, who would be very shocked to hear of my going so far in my friendly intercourse with these poor fellows, especially when it extends to an exchange of cigars, but in my circumstances, I think this way of procedure is not so unlike His who 'eat and drank with publicans and sinners,' as might at first sight appear. I am very conscious that I do not thus act from a feeling of enjoyment. I do not understand their patois, and make all the talk myself therefore. I never touch their drink, and take the cigar only by necessity, for I hate smoking, and only force myself to it for companionship. I have long tried the different ways of getting friendly intercourse with men of all classes, for their good, and at present this succeeds. If, instead of ' passing by ' my neighbour, I can please him without doing any harm; if I can a little influence him for good, excite right feelings, check wrong, and ease the burden, I am not useless."

## CHAPTER XIV.

### ALGERIA—COMMENCEMENT OF MISSIONARY WORK.

ON arriving in Algeria, Mr Ogle found a state of things which led him to contemplate a prolonged stay in that country. Nearer home it was yet very unlike England. Its history and its cities, the manners of its inhabitants and the character of its productions, all of which vividly recalled the past, were precisely such as would have a powerful charm for a man constituted as was Mr Ogle. Its climate suited him; how different from the bleak and storm-swept Falklands! But what weighed most of all with him was that it appeared to present numerous openings for the gospel. He felt that the hand of God had led him hither, and in this conjunction of favourable circumstances he heard His voice bidding him remain and labour here. Accordingly, after he had discharged the special service on which he had been missioned by the Edinburgh Spanish Evangelization Society, instead of returning home, he resolved on a permanent residence in Algeria, and proceeded to make arrangements for regular missionary labour. He began household visitation in Oran, and by and bye he extended his visits to the villages in the neighbourhood. Day by day he won upon the natives by his kindliness, and by the mutual interchange of acts of friendship, in which he ever took care to leave them his debtors. Thus he went on sowing the seed in casual meetings and familiar conversations; he expected the results to be slow in developing themselves. The incubus of centuries, he knew, was not to be removed in an hour. He sowed with the husbandman's faith, diligence, and patience; trusting that the harvest would come in its season.

Writing to the Society about this time, he begged of them only one thing, to be allowed to work in connection with them, but without pecuniary aid, and without being bound down by precise instructions. The position of a voluntary agent, it seemed to him, was not inconsistent with that of a close connection with a Society established for missionary purposes. What he wanted was their prayers, their advice, their help sometimes, and their interest in his work at all times. To direct that work would, he believed, be all but impossible for them, and might, were they to attempt it, render it useless. He did not wish to compromise either the Society or himself, and to shut out all risk of this he recommended that the Society should avow the footing on which he stood, viz., that he did not act, save on his own responsibility, and at his own charges.

The following account of his labours occurs in a letter of date December 1858:—

" You would like me to give you some account of my work in detail. It consists of daily visits to different houses in the Spanish streets of Oran, for the purpose of conversation upon *the* great subject with individuals. Till Tuesday last, I had not been one mile from the city. I could occupy myself for months without passing beyond its ancient gateways. But I have now visited some of the neighbouring villages, riding thirty miles yesterday. It is, however, not very safe, I find, to proceed thus far. The priests have such a hold on the minds of the people, my work would be at once stopped if they perceived it. Take an instance from my experience yesterday. I had conversed with one or two persons, and had read a beautiful and appropriate Spanish tract to a poor and sick woman in one of the cottages, by which she seemed much comforted. The villagers gathered in angry groups in the street, and when I came out of the cottage were ready to stone me. Why was this ? A strict system of espionage is carried on, and I am already closely watched. An aged matron *eccle-*

*siastique* had followed me in a carriage from Oran, and remained in the village all the time I was there, departing when I left."

This is sufficient to explain the behaviour of the people, for human nature when not perverted by a fanatical faith, and enflamed by its priests, is everywhere the same, and ever appreciates kindly words and true sympathy with suffering and sorrow.

In another letter of the same date he says :—

" The weather is almost cold, and the days are very short. A fire in my room makes it look like Christmas. The wind howls in October fashion; it is a northerly storm. When I was in the streets I could with difficulty keep my face to the wind at the exposed corners. The sea is white with foam ; and I am reminded of a certain August gale we had at Bridlington Quay which did so much damage. Last Thursday, however, when —— and —— dined with me we had lamb and green peas, the common fare here at Christmas."

That the climate of Algeria has its changes as well as that of our own country, and is not without those quick alternations from warmth and sunshine to frost, which are so trying to the constitution, should be known to all who would choose it as a place of winter residence for the invalid. Many passages in letters of different dates plainly indicate this. Take an instance :

" *February 24th*, 1859.

" Rose at dawn and worked in my garden. Found the ground frozen, and a white hoar-frost upon the grass. The sun rose in a ruddy orange-coloured horizon without a cloud. . . . . When I returned to my house to feed my horse, &c., I found him in a great rage, and without food. He is a charger, and a good model of the passage in Job xxxix. 19–25. White in colour, and fiery in temper. At mid-day, it is too hot for me to ride fast to save the post, and I am stiff from my morning's work."

The following letter to his brother contains some details of Mr Ogle's home arrangements, and of the manner in which he felt his way among the Arabs :—

December 23d, 1858.

## COUNTRY HOUSE.

" Of the past week six days were passed in Oran, one in the country. The consul, Mr M—— , has offered me a house of his, a cottage four miles from Oran. There is no land save a small garden, twenty feet square ; but there is waste near, so I can cultivate, if I please. I think I shall accept it, as it will not cost me £10 to make the house comfortable, and I can keep a horse almost without more expense, and there will be something for my old man to do. I shall now have a room in Oran at 10f. a month. This plan is adopted by all the missionaries, of whom there are three now in Oran. There is no English clergyman here, but two French and two German pasteurs. I have little work to record as yet ; it is better to remain, however, at Oran, especially as I have opportunities of evangelising every day. Not a day but brings its work, new oftentimes, and interesting and hopeful. Yesterday, for example, I went out at half-past seven to market."

## ARAB VISITORS.

" On my return I overtook two tall Arabs, their white dresses showing superior circumstances. I accosted them in Spanish, spoke of England and Algeria ; the reason of the disproportion, in natural advantages, and actual condition, etc. Religion, if good, is a remedy ; if bad, a poison. Spoke of the Bible and Koran ; that the latter acknowledges the former. Bible much more ancient—compare them and you will say Bible is far better,—invited them to come to my house,—they would ' come immediately.' I was thankful, and conducted them ; they were pleased with my nice looking room, and the respect I showed them. I gave coffee, bread, raisins ; they partook, but not without pressing ; they occupied themselves with the Arabic Bible to the neglect of the coffee. I showed them

Isa. xxi. 13, etc., Numbers xxiv. 18. They read with attention and pleasure; they promised to come again.

"I am learning Arabic, and already can read. it a little. An English missionary from Gibraltar dined with me yesterday, and gave me the pleasure of speaking in my own tongue; at other times I speak French and Spanish uninterruptedly. Send me books for children, and as many Arabic and Jewish tracts and Bibles as you can get for me. I am helpless at present, because I have none left. How glad would our Missionary Societies be of many an opportunity of distributing the Word, which I am forced to forego on this account. Of additional Spanish books I want the Pilgrim's Progress, Andree Dunn, Manuel Biblico, etc.

"I wish I could show you the beautiful Oran, with its castle-crowned hill every day growing more green; the blue expanse of Mediterranean waters; the plain covered with verdure and marks of cultivation; the forest beyond, and the knots of dwarf palm trees and low shrubs. An invalid could live here better than in Madeira, it is 4° warmer, and one-third of the distance from England,

"I wish I could tell you how pretty the flowers are, how picturesque the costume, how blue the sea, how azure the sky, how bold the coast, how bright the air, how balmy, how lovely the night; whether, as last week, a soft flood of moonlight bathes the scene, or, as now, the stars look down, as if there were no obstructing vapours, right down from the clear heaven. Oh! when will the Sun of Righteousness arise to give to these realms of night the vivifying ray of day divine? Alas! Heber's hymn comes often to thought, 'Every prospect pleases, only man is vile.'"

## MOHAMMEDAN WATCHWORD.

"An Arab, who was near me, cried out angrily, 'God is great, Mahomet is his prophet.' I went up to him and said, 'Look into my book, and I will show you the original of your watchword.' In the passage, Job xxxvi. 26, the Hebrew and Arabic words are the same—'Allah is great, and we know him not.' I said to him, ' Mahomet took his motto from here, where it was written 4000 years ago.' He was struck with silence ; his manner completely changed, and he followed me, pressing me with questions, and begging for my Bible. I could not sell it to him, for I have at present not another in Arabic. I conversed with other Arabs, but having seen me friendly with the Jews they will hardly associate again with me ! This is the case with all the races here. If I go to the French immediately after having conversed with Spaniards, to Jews after Arabs, or vice versa, I am no longer regarded as really friendly to the former. What discretion is needed by those who reside among strangers, and would make efforts for their good !"

## FRENCH PROTESTANT SERVICE.

" I have not yet described the Protestant ' temple,' which was opened shortly before my arrival in Oran. The government has granted a licence for ' a teaching ' under certain restrictions. In a good part of the town, half-way up the hill on which the fort is built, and at the angle where the beautiful shaded avenue, leading to the Prado (or public walk), joins the main street of Oran, stands a building of no great size or architectural pretensions, raised above the street on a basement of stone, which you ascend by ten or twelve steps. The words ' TEMPLE PROTESTANT' over a rounded doorway, indicate the nature of the edifice. You enter a room, lofty and cool, capable of holding from two to three hundred persons, seated on benches. They stand to pray on entering. There is a pulpit with a railed space in front, seats round this, and a small table on which a large open Bible rests, turned towards the congregation. The schoolmaster says, ' Let us commence this sacred service by reading the Word of God.' He reads a chapter which has before been selected by the minister. A hymn is then sung, the minister ascends the pulpit, reads a hymn, then prays, and a sermon from a text follows. After this a hymn, then prayer, the creed, the Lord's Prayer, and the blessing is pronounced. Being the high festival of the year the administration of the holy communion took place. An address on the sacrament was given, and as each stood at the table, he was addressed extempore, before receiving the elements. These had been consecrated by the minister, who held them while he repeated the words of institution. A hymn was afterwards sung, prayer was offered, and the blessing given. The recipients were few. The words addressed to me I understood to be words of welcome, alluding to my being a stranger, and a missionary, and an exhortation to me to ' persevere unto the end.' "

The following letter, of date January 1859, addressed to his sister, then sojourning as an invalid at Torquay, contains some valuable reflections on the efficacy of prayer, and on the special service which the sick have the power of rendering to others. To some the heaviest part of their affliction often is the thought that they are shut out from benefitting others. Yet no. Their silent ministry is specially efficacious; they instruct by their patience and submission ; they glorify God by their hope in His word, and their joy in tribulation ; and they aid others by the effectual help of their prayers.

" . . . . I have of late years thought much upon the fact that our business is, primarily, to prepare for another world ; that the thought that much labour for others is required of us, may lead us to the neglect of this principal object ; and I have remarked that the greatest good to others results from the undesigned influence of those who are occupied chiefly with their duty to God and to themselves. The sick and the feeble are specially called to this kind of usefulness. All other efforts are precluded to them ; and I throw out this hint that it may, by God's blessing, prove an exhortation seasonable, and also be a comfort to you.

" Prayer for others is a means of doing good which seems to be specially reserved for the sick and suffering Christian. We all know, in theory, the value and efficacy of prayer ; few have not felt occasionally that there is a crisis in all affairs in which the decision for good or otherwise depends not upon ourselves. It is always true, but there are times when we are conscious of the fact. How little is man capable of doing! The elements of material nature are beyond his control; his sphere is confined within narrow limits, and his work is constantly exposed to destruction from causes which remain beyond his reach. When we come to the metaphysical, *i.e.*, to the circumstances in which the agency of beings, having a nature more than merely material, is involved, we see how powerless is man. All political affairs come under this head, indeed all that relates to our dealings with our fellow-men. God rules the hearts of men; we can but guide them occasionally. I need not cite the Scripture to prove this; it is the teaching of experience, and accords with the revelation of God. The whole history of Israel manifests this truth, while, at the same time, the vast importance of individual action is also demonstrated. Man is admitted to be a fellow-worker with God. The greatest simplicity (ἀπλότης—Eph. vii. 5) and self-abnegation then are our duty and our wisdom, while the greatest diligence and self-sacrifice are demanded of us.

" ' Who is sufficient for these things?' He who can say, 'I can do all things through Christ which strengtheneth me.' I feel that I have lived too much negligent of prayer for myself and for others. I ask your prayers that my life may be more conformed to the Divine will. If my position or employments, or my engagements, be contrary to the will of God, then it is that some light, clearer than that of worldly prudence or of intelligence, is needed to say, as it were, 'This is the way, walk ye in it.' " . . . .

The poverty of the Spanish protestants was distressing. They had not lost the Spanish indolence in changing their country and their religion. To remedy this evil, and to give an opportunity of employment to those who would avail themselves of it, Mr Ogle took a small house in the neighbourhood of Oran, with ground attached to it. "I am become a Colonist," we find him saying, writing to the Society in Edinburgh, in March, 1859.

" The Spaniards do not prove to be good husbandmen, and they are extravagant in their demands, asking three francs per day more than the ordinary wages of the country, so I have dismissed them. However, I have now the means of employing men, and I am willing to receive those who are persecuted for conscience' sake. Any honest and humble man will find food, wages, and work with me. I have a large garden and some unoccupied ground near my house in the country, which I shall cultivate. You may write to your agents to send me labourers who are obliged by persecution to leave Spain."

Later we find him writing :—" I have twelve men to-day planting the sweet potatoes (yams) in my garden, and tomatoes, &c. There were a company of soldiers *en route* for the war, in the village. The Major set some to work, so I got seven to assist me. I talked to them (of the all-important matter) of course, and they will not forget in the field of battle the peaceful occupations of Figuier and the English ' colonist' there. The soldiers' correctness of eye enabled them to draw my lines for planting without the cord and reel, and very handsome work we made of our day's labour. The seeds of divine truth must be sown ' without observation,' quietly, and as opportunity offers. This occurs to me every day, thank God. I find myself led on from day to day, and do missionary work, as I find occasion, with all with whom I come in contact. I have little doubt that these conversations will, by God's grace, alter their minds on these important subjects for the rest of their lives.

" The Spaniards often say to me, ' Don't you want to eat ?' I say, ' Presently, when I can find time.'

" There is work here in Oran for a hundred labourers, if you could send me them. There are numbers of people in every street to whom, by judiciously taking your time, tracts may be given, and a few words spoken of a pure Gospel which has never yet been proclaimed to them by any man."

### VISIT TO FIGUIER—AN ADVENTURE.

" The other day I was at Figuier, about four miles distant from Oran. In the evening I took possession for the night of an uninhabited house belonging to a friend, bid my servant look to my horse, while I made the coffee. In came a traveller, a Spaniard, to beg a night's lodging for himself, and for leave to put his mule in the *Quadra* (square court.) He was not well favoured, but said he was 'sick and poor; had come a long journey, and was going to Oran.' I thought, I have often entered a house with a similar request, and found hospitality, and the Scriptures say, 'forget not to show it'; so I bid him welcome to anything I had. A bed I had not for myself, only the good waterproof sheet, and a blanket, and some grass. He helped me to make the fire; gave of his wine; took my coffee; thus we became friendly. ' He had been for three years a slave among the Moors in early life, was now a settler in Algeria.' I found him lamentably ignorant. For instance, he said, ' he knew the country of Jesus Christ; that He was the son of a soldier, and could speak Arabic better than the Arabs of that country.' I read to him in the Bible, and conversed; others came in. At 8 P.M., he brought in his bed, the mattress saddle of his mule, and folding himself in his ample cloak, slept. Next morning he was off before I woke, but I have his address, and I mean to go and see him at home.

" I must return to Oran, as it is post day. It was high day, and very hot (March 3d) before I could leave Figuier. I could ride leisurely along on my white Arab over a plain covered with tufts of grass and low shrubs, a sort of asparagus. Many flowers are pushing through the soil before the leaves are grown, as if Nature here delighted most in giving her beauties and luxuries, and supplied the *useful* as a secondary matter. The trees have not yet put forth even a shoot, but there is so much verdure, that one does not regard the dead trees. In a month's time all Nature will wear a different aspect. The cedar, the palm, and the mantling vine, will beautify the earth. Thus may it be with us in this winter of our existence, pushing flowers out of the cold clogging earth, verdure and buds of promise; and though much seems to remain sterile, yet may we be trees of the Lord's planting, to bloom and fructify anon." . . .

The following letter to his sister relates to his household arrangements, especially his recent purchase of an Arab horse, which he finely describes :—

" I have bought another horse.   He came from far away on the Atlas mountains, and is a *nonsuch;* colour, light-grey, with dark legs, very strong and handsome, but not very tall or light made.   He is very docile, and yet full of fire and spirit.   The hair of his forehead comes down to his nose, and his mane is the most beautiful you can imagine.   He is somewhat too fat now for comfortable use.   .   .   .   I lent him to an Arab one day, and he was in ecstasies with him.   The horse seemed to do just what he desired, prancing, leaping into the air, galloping as if the ground were an elastic cushion, which repelled his feet, and the next moment as quiet as a lamb.   I mounted him immediately after, and though at first he frisked and danced, he soon became quiet.   The horse belonged to an Arab chieftain, and is called the ' Agha of Feudah.'   He is not always easy to ride, but I find it useful to have a stimulus of the kind.   One cannot live in such a country as this without much courage and resolution, and the lessons a noble horse may give to his master, at least until they are well acquainted, are not useless.

" I think *you* would take more pleasure in a poor little Arab horse that I bought in the summer, or in my faithful chestnut, a pretty little horse, that is doing good work at the plough ; or in one of the laborious mules, docile as children ; or in a patient ox, that follows its master wherever he leads the way, with patient steps all through the day ; or with a little donkey, which I could almost carry in my arms, but which would carry you very well if you were but here.   I want nothing to make me always content and happy, but a rest in God, and a conviction that I am doing His gracious will.

" The state of my own country troubles me too ; I fear for her.   But there is a sure reward and a sure refuge too for those ' who fear God,' who ' fear before Him.'   My prayer is, that you and I may both experience the truth of this most gracious promise; and that, if it be His gracious will, we may have together a place of refuge in the coming troublous times; not separated, as now, by seas and by land, nor agitated by painful recollections, and by present dissatisfactions. . . . May you together, with all our dear relatives, receive at this solemn season abundant consolation, and have peace and joy in believing; that peace which no fears assail, and no storms disturb. God will bestow it; He will be all to His people that they can ask or think, according to His riches in glory by Christ Jesus. Amen, dear sister."

## CHAPTER XV.

### THE ATLAS MOUNTAINS.

THE climate of the Algerian plains varies much from that of the mountains, although the latter may be only a few miles distant from the sea. In summer the plains are burnt up; the country becomes like a sandy desert, and then it is that the Algerian fever sets in, and that the European who may have lingered in the lowlands, must cross the straits into Spain, or remove to the more elevated tracts bordering on the great Atlas. Mr Ogle, after the hot weather had continued for some time, found his strength giving way, and he therefore resolved on visiting the Arab tribes who inhabit the Atlas range. He might have returned to England, but he chose in preference to seek out in their own dwellings those sons of the desert for whose souls no man cared, if haply he might bring some of them to the knowledge of the Saviour, and open a way for other missionaries to follow.

But before passing over the French lines, and venturing into the lawless parts beyond, it was essential to obtain a safe conduct from the governor of the province. There were *Dili-*

*gences* plying between Oran and some of the neighbouring towns, and so far the journey was safe ; but travellers who wished to visit the interior always took care to provide themselves with an order for an escort of the volunteers of Algeria, the scarlet-cloaked spahis. These spahis are generally the elder sons of the Arab chiefs. Several squadrons of them have been formed under French officers. They find their own horses and accoutrements, and the service is a popular one. To them are confided the "posts" on the different roads leading into the interior. Mr Ogle made application for the usual "authorisation" for an escort. "I will give it you as a traveller," was the reply of the official, "but do you not intend to take religious books with you ?" "Certainly," replied Mr Ogle, "I intend to use my birthright as a freeman to disseminate, as opportunity offers, the knowledge of the Word of God, which you, Monsieur, since you know something of England, know it is the duty of every man who possesses it to make known." The application was ultimately refused, and Mr Ogle came to the determination to venture alone among the Arab tribes. The details of his visit are given in the letters that follow, written in June and July of 1859. In Oran the expedition was regarded as one attended with great risk, on many accounts, but chiefly from the reputed character of the Arabs ; but by the good hand of God upon him our missionary went and returned, and no evil befell him. He pitched his tent amid the tents of the Arabs ; he partook of their salt ; he received from them acts of kindness, and he rendered them acts of kindness in return ; he spoke to them of the matters of their eternal salvation, and when he departed he left behind him an impression which will be the best passport of any European missionary who may follow him into these regions.

## FIRST VISIT TO THE ATLAS MOUNTAINS.

. . . . " I have been to the mountains. They are the delectable region of my present latitude. Where the torrid ray has consumed every green thing except the dwarf palm, which, with its dark, rounded tufts of evergreen foliage dots the surface of the plain of Oran, wherever culture has not dispossessed it, the mountains which form the boundary line, rising in the blue distance, give promise in their lofty stages of fresher breezes, and of freedom from many ills. . . . . To tell of my journey, however :—I left Oran by diligence, June 22d, having despatched my baggage and horses to Figuier, distant four miles, from whence my real journey was to commence next day. My mule was laden, two large panniers containing my tent and cooking apparatus, and a bag with Bibles, &c., to distribute, if occasion served. I took my Jewish servant with me. Our progress was at first slow. We had started at four A.M. At noon we had reached the farms situate at the foot of the mountains. We stayed till three P.M. at the house of an intelligent colonist to purchase barley and to avoid the midday heat. He asked, ' What do the English newspapers say ? for we like to know what those say who may write what they think, which we cannot do in France.' I gave him my views upon the politics of the day, and introduced my Bibles, *apropos* of liberty. He did not purchase, but was hospitable and kind, and we resumed our route. Hitherto we had passed over a sandy and parched plain. The earth becomes like sand under the sun's rays at this season of the year, and is so hot you can scarcely bear to touch it. Iron too, becomes, if exposed to the sun, too hot to hold. We soon entered the region of the mountains by a narrow gorge, following the windings of a stream, fringed by oleanders in full bloom. The steep and craggy rocks on either side are covered with shrubs, an enticing prospect after our weary march through the parched and sandy plain. We soon found the stream had but little water in it, but it was clear and flowing, and by its leading we reached a valley where an Arab encampment was permanently fixed. We entered it to inquire our route, which could no longer be discovered, by reason of the number of tracks made by the Arabs and their herds. We are to ascend by a very rough road, a mountain ridge, separated from the principal summit by a cleft, as by an earthquake. Our road then winds along the face of declivities, and thus we pass this considerable mountain at about half its altitude. From one of the summits, looking north, I had a fine view over the Sahara-like plain of Oran, in which are the farms now parched and arid, but covered with stubbles of gathered crops. The city itself was visible, and the blue waters of the Mediterranean beyond. To the south was a lofty range of mountains. Here also we found food for the horses. The Arabs cultivate the fruitful spots upon the hills, and thrash out the corn in the field and leave the straw. This forms the food of all horses here.

"Some Jew-merchants with mules came up while I lingered; they filled their sacks with straw and pursued their way.

" From this point the scenery greatly changes and improves, verdure clothes the hills, and fruit-gardens fill the glens. These gardens are the property of nomad tribes. There are no houses visible, the gardens are unprotected by fences. They are little coppices of fruit trees. I noticed the fig, and the apricot, and apple. Melons and maize sometimes cover the ground, and vines festoon the trees. A veritable feast is here formed by the bounty of God's providence ; for first, running streams of fresh water are abundant, while on either side of this narrow belt are desert tracts scorched, and generally water-less. By artificial means alone is water there obtained, and this is often very bad in quality, and salt. Much as I enjoyed the rich appearance of verdure, a gushing fountain of the purest water, issuing from under a face of rock, and falling into a natural basin, and then running over to find its way into a stony ravine, attracted me most. Fruits luscious, and verdure luxuriant ; lowing herds depasturing in natural meadows, gay with flowering plants; patches of cultivated land, gardens or corn-fields, all are inadequate to produce the same sensation of satisfaction and of gratitude which a gurgling rill of pellucid water does. The traveller and his horse bow together to the stream, luxuriating in its freshness and abundance. My animals seem to be insatiable, they drink as though they would exhaust the fountain, but it flows on in undiminished vigour, and will continue to do so—a never-failing source. How well is this emblem selected to make known to us the character of those supplies of grace which the thirsty soul of man needs in this wilderness world. What an argument is the choice of this illustration in favour of the fulness, the freeness, and the loving kindness of our God. Would that our desires were commensurate with our deficiencies, and that we answered the generous supply by an adequate appreciation.

"To resume the thread of my narrative :—We began to descend by a wide ravine. The sun had disappeared behind the western range of mountains, and the sombre valley disclosed but dimly its resources of cultivation ; a few yellow patches of corn were to be seen ; here and there a whitewashed cottage relieved the large breadths of undulating and broken ground, grassy hills, and broad palm-covered mountains all around. I selected a shaded situation, under large holm oak trees, to encamp for the night. Here, however, I might not abide ; an old Arab, who was seated at the foot of one of the trees, warned us off. From another, who offered me some apricots, I learned that he was owner of the property. Alas, poor man ! the good news of the gospel might have come to cheer his aged heart had he opened it in hospitality to the European. He little knew the treasures I carried on my laden mule. How the unwonted possession of property sometimes steels the heart and injures the character ! This old man's race is renowned for hospitality to strangers, but he has changed his nomad habits and has become a proprietor of the soil, and so he sits solitary amidst his possessions, and will not permit the traveller to rest under his trees. Well, we soon found attractions for a bivouac outside his domain, and very soon the preparations were accomplished satisfactorily to all. A recess formed in a thicket of oleanders, which were 8 or 10 feet in height, carpeted with flowers, was just the place for my tent. It could be pitched so as to leave a space of 5 or 6 feet between it and the shrubs, which is always necessary as a caution against serpents and other undesired guests. The pink-coloured line of oleander blossom, which marked the course of the stream through the valley, was in front, and we were soon enjoying our evening meal, after which, with grateful feelings, and in delight at the promise of success, given by so agreeable a commencement to my excursion, I lay down on my mattress to sleep. Very early in the morning we were aroused by the sound of horses neighing·and tramping, and found a troop of Arab horses near. My horse, a fiery animal, had broken loose in attacking one of them, and I beheld him galloping off. It was some little time before we recaptured him, but his tether was gone, which was a great loss to me. My baggage mule required rest—the Arabs said he had been bitten by a serpent, and recommended me to send for a serpent-charmer, who would quickly cure him. I sent him word, therefore, that I would remunerate success."

## An African Vanity Fair.

" Meanwhile, I heard that an Arab market was being held not far off. So I mounted my horse, and taking some Testaments and tracts, in Arabic, from my store, set out to find the ' Vanity fair' among the African hills. It was soon discovered. An elevated space of ground, including several hundred acres, appeared before me, apparently crowded with human beings. From two to three thousand white-robed Arabs, sons of Edom, of Moab, and of Ishmael, formed the singular looking assemblage, evidencing the populousness of this a favourite locality of the tribes.

" There were a few trees on the ground, a stream of water nearly surrounded it, and a solitary building which enclosed a courtyard, was an evident centre of attraction. In front thereof were the places of merchandise—a square formed of tents, pitched at equal distances, in double line ; there might be about 300 in number. Between the lines was a broad space for walking, free to all. There could not be less than 700 horses tethered upon the ground. Each was caparisoned in Arab fashion, with high-peaked saddle, and embroidered blinkers, and other trappings. Their riders, when mounted, wore a straw hat two feet in height, some red, some white; a black or a scarlet burnous, huge spurs, and they generally carried a musket or a pair of highly-ornamented pistols. I entered this strange-looking assembly with my bag of books, and selecting a cool and shaded place for my horse, went into the market, and holding aloft my precious wares, exclaimed alternately in Arabic, Hebrew, French, and Spanish, the words, ' Bible !' ' Law !' ' Prophets !' ' Evangile !' Soon I had a crowd around me, among whom were the French officers in charge of the market. Some Jews seemed to wish to become purchasers, but they were evidently intent only upon getting a cheap bargain, and I would not abate my price. While engaged in this way, a disturbance arose at some little distance from the place where I stood. The market was instantly deserted; the white-robed crowd rushing in the direction of the large building uttering loud cries. They resembled, to my imagination, the leaves of autumn driven by the wind. I followed the crowd, by and by, with some trepidation within, for I feared that my horse had broken loose and done some mischief. I met an Arab, pale with rage, and bleeding; he had a huge stone in his hand. The man had been assailed by one of his own race; he passed on, and, as I afterwards learned, died soon after. My own fears were groundless, but they showed me how much I need more of that strength from above which makes a man, in all circumstances, above fear.

" Alas ! I was obliged to leave that market without having disposed of a single Arabic Bible. I gave a Spanish copy to an honest-looking Spaniard, and he thanked me with tears for the gift. I have good hopes that in his case good seed has fallen into ground prepared.

"It made one's heart ache to witness so large a congregation of many thousand men, whom none make an effort to en-lighten as to the way of salvation. Can it be that Christian England has tens of thousands who are capable of setting on foot this work, and the world still remains in its deep darkness ? Unacquainted with the Arabic language, I could not announce the good tidings of peace to one of all the crowd, and I left

them with a sad heart, and returned to my tent.* To give
my mule a rest, I did not pursue my journey on that day, but
rose early the next morning to do so."

This is a novel and exciting scene. Let us try to realize it.
On a great plateau of the desert, afar from the ways of
European life, the majesty of the Atlas mountains, and the
silence of the sandy wilds all around, there is gathered a great
concourse of the nationalities of the desert. The scene is such,
in dress, in manners, in features, as Arabia, or even this same
Africa, might have presented four thousand years ago. The
multitudes are busy buying and selling ; they are occupied
only with the meat that perisheth ; of that 'Bread' whereof he
that eateth shall never die, they have never been told. Suddenly the hum of business is partially suspended, and all eyes
are turned in one direction. What has happened ? A stranger
from afar ; a man unlike all others in the market, solitary,
tall, well-built, and with face beaming with kindness, has
suddenly appeared among the sons of the desert, and standing
up and holding aloft a Book, announces it as the Word of
God, and able to make wise unto salvation. 'Doth not
wisdom cry ? and understanding put forth her voice ? She
standeth on the top of high places, by the way in the places
of the paths. She crieth at the gates, at the entry of the
city, at the coming in at the doors. Unto you, O men, I
call ; and my voice is to the sons of men. O ye simple, understand wisdom : and ye fools, be ye of an understanding heart.
My fruit is better than gold, yea, than fine gold ; and my revenue than choice silver.' So did wisdom now cry. She
stood before this assembly of the sons of the desert in the
person of her missionary. But, alas ! her voice was little
heeded. There was no one in all that great market that
would buy her wares. They listened a moment, and went
back to their merchandise. And yet not one of all this
multitude was there who had not his own burden of sin and
sorrow, and longed to get rest. Not one was there here who
did not thirst, and yet they made light of the offer of that

* Two years after this a similar opportunity of visiting an Arab market
occurred to Mr Ogle, and many gladly received copies of the Word of Life.

' living water,' whereof he that drinketh shall thirst no more. The kingdom of heaven was come nigh to these Arab tribes, but they knew it not.   The messenger appeared in humble guise, and they estimated the worth of the message by the appearance of the messenger ; had he come with a grand dis- play of authority, had he put on the airs of this world's wisdom, these tribes of the desert might have paid greater deference to his message ; but the great hindrance lay here, that their hearts were engrossed by the love of this present world, and they knew not the nature of that salvation which the missionary offered to them, and could not value it.   What a picture of mankind !   What is the world but a great market, wisdom standing in the midst, but unheeded by the nations, who pursue war, commerce, power, and neglect the ' one thing needful.'   And so will it be till there shall come a great out- pouring of the Spirit of God.

## CHAPTER XVI.

### ARABS AND THEIR ENCAMPMENT.

WE proceed in our narrative of Mr Ogle's sojourn among the Arab tribes of the Atlas, as recorded by himself in letters to his sister.   There is a marked difference between the Arabs of the villages and the nomads of the desert.   There is an approach on the part of the former to the habits and feelings of civilisation.   The latter disdain all restraint, their home is the wilderness, and their habits are predatory.   But they are not cruel, nor bloodthirsty, nor ungenerous, when any one shows that he has confidence in them, or entrusts himself to their protection.   There are said to be about thirteen millions of Arabs and Kabyles in North Africa.

The villages are always placed in some glen or ravine, and generally far up on the mountain-side.   This enables them to

see any visitor who may be approaching long before he reaches
the village.   A steep rugged donkey-path is commonly the
only road to these villages, a circumstance which gives
additional security against any sudden hostile attack.   Before
resuming our extracts from Mr Ogle's letters the following
brief sketches from recent travellers may not be unacceptable.

" The Arabs in Algeria are divided into almost endless
tribes.   There are about ten or twelve principal tribes in the
province of Oran alone, nineteen more are scattered throughout
the province of Algiers.   They are not reconciled to the
French occupation, and they always entertain hopes of regaining
their liberty."

## THE KABYLES.

" The *Kabyles* are said to be the true aborigines.   Their
moral character places them in the foremost rank amongst the
natives of Algeria.   They prefer the house to the tent, and
unlike the Arabs they are fond of labour, and despise idleness.
The Kabyle prides himself on his loyalty and hospitality, and
on the sacredness of his word.   The person of any one, be he
friend or stranger, who takes shelter under his roof is invio-
late.   He is quick and intelligent, though illiterate.   Few of
the Kabyles can read and write.   Their memories, like those
of the bards of yore, are filled with Arab traditions and war
songs.   The Kabyles are chiefly to be found in the Atlas
mountains, where for centuries they held their own against all
invaders.   They live in villages, called *dashkrahs*, consisting
chiefly of huts, *gurbies*, composed of mud and loose stones,
covered with reeds or palm tree branches, and thatched with
straw, or the long fibrous spikes of the aloe.   They were con-
quered by the French in the year 1857, but not until many
fierce and bloody struggles had been passed through by their
invaders."

The Arabs may be rich or poor—inhabitants of the city or
of the country, but the fashion of their costume is unvarying.

The closely-shaven head is always covered, and the flowing burnous is universal.    In material it differs, of course, according to the means of the wearer.

The Bedouins may always be distinguished from the town Arabs by the coarseness of the texture of their garments, the addition of a black burnous, and in the covering used for the head.    When in any of the towns, for the purpose of trade, their delight is to congregate in the Kahona or coffee-house, or under a wide-spreading carob tree to enjoy their pipe in perfect idleness by the hour together.

Mr Ogle was much struck with the gravity and contentedness of the Arab character.    They will remain for hours seated in a circle, apparently thoroughly well entertained by one of their number who, in the centre of the ring, merely makes a most monotonous sound, and this only at intervals, while they continue to sway themselves backwards and forwards in measured time.

Poor Arabs! no effort for their spiritual enlightenment is permitted by the government.    When will another venturesome, yet divinely protected, missionary visit their villages, and hold forth among them the word of life ?    How precious, however, are the few copies which have been distributed !  Shall they not be followed by the prayers of every devout reader of these lines ?    O Lord, fulfil Thy gracious promise :  " My word shall not return unto Me void."


## My Tent in the Arab Encampment, Satavouri Mountains.

" It is sunrise, and the orb of day here, looks upon a scene such as the world scarcely furnishes in more striking characters.  It is an African valley, fertile and beautiful ; in it a company of Arabs are encamped.    There are twenty Arab tents in a circle.    An enclosure around them is made of faggots, and contains also within its circuit about two hundred sheep and goats, one hundred beeves, ten horses, twenty asses, and dogs.

"The world is just astir. The sheep ruminate, and rise by degrees; the young goats are playing at their sham fight; the air is cool and fresh. There is dew upon the ground, and clouds obscure the morning in low thick volume, but these will soon disperse, and the day will be hot and bright. My little tent is pitched in the centre of the Arab circle. J. F. O. is within it, four Arabs are seated at the entrance, one is sewing and J. F. O. has also been putting a button in its place. He is soon called to other occupations,—to tend his sick mule, like to die, but better to-day, thank God; or to catch his runaway steed. Soon the sun is too hot even to write; the ink dries up in the pen; though I have contrived a screen that I may write to you.

"Is it not remarkable that I can write to you from the centre of an Arab Douair? I was not able to obtain the customary protection from the authorities by which travellers are commended to the care of the Arab chiefs, who are thus made responsible for their safe return, and are obliged to supply food for men and horses, guides, and other requisites, at a fixed tariff. At Oran it is thought impossible to travel without this, while with it you may go to the borders of the Great Desert in safety. If any harm happens to you the tribe in which you have suffered loss is made responsible. But as the missionary object of my journey had become known this was refused to me, so I set out, relying on higher aid. At first I rather avoided the Arab encampments, knowing the Arabs to be uncertain folk, and I ignorant of them, and of their language.

"On the evening of the 24th I had again pitched my tent as described before at a distance from an encampment which I descried in the valley, when the Arab sheik, dressed as for a visit of state, accompanied by the elders of his tribe, visited my little camp. He begged me to come to his tent, and to put myself under his protection, assuring me 'it was dangerous to remain solitary and unguarded;' or offered, if I refused this, to send two of his tribe as guards during the night. I assured them I had no fear to remain alone, and preferred my solitary bivouac. Were they not in fact the very persons against whom all had so emphatically warned me? At last, however, I yielded to their pressing and truly courteous entreaties; suffered them to carry my goods into their douair, and pitched my little tent with my own hand, in the place indicated—the centre of their circle. The pitching of a tent is not an easy affair without taking accurate measurements, etc., and the speedy erection of mine on this occasion gave rise to the display of much friendly feeling on their part; I seemed to have been *enabled* to do it with unwonted skill and celerity; not a mistake was made, and all was soon in order within and without. My scarlet-lined waterproof sheet formed the carpet, the mattress my couch, and the blue rug a mat for the sheik.

" It was a beautiful sight, that douair among the mountains of Algeria. The circle of large black tents, around the numerous herds of many-coloured cattle, with sheep and goats; the tall Arabs walking about like sheeted ghosts folded in their burnous, some black, some white.

" My little tent in the midst of their encampment with a bright light shining through its white canvas. I often wished a Landseer's pencil could picture in panorama the scenes I, for the first time, now witnessed; that it was night was much in my favour. By daylight squalor was too apparent; but when night lent a veil of sombre hue, or early morning lighted with grey glimmer of light the motley assemblage, the sight was perfectly beautiful. I can now imagine better the life and the daily surroundings of Abraham, Isaac, and Jacob; the patient solemn camel; the recumbent flock; the ruminating kine; the neighing and impatient steed. Sheep, oxen, asses, camels, and goats, completely covering at night the space enclosed.

" When my little tabernacle was pitched, I gave the chief a little tobacco, with my good wishes and salutations to his tribe. He said ' the English and Arabs are good friends,' &c., &c., and driving off the dogs, departed. Presently he returned, bringing me a can of milk, and asking ' if I wanted anything more?' sending me also straw for my horses.

" I shall never forget that night,—the novelty of my position, a solitary foreigner in a strange land and among a strange race. The sons of Ishmael, unchanged in character or condition from of old, subjugated, but not subdued; masters of the patrimony of their ancestor, though owning the sway of another race. This occupying those parts of the land which the other had never cared to use; the sea-port for commerce, and the plain for cultivation; and leaving them unmolested in their mountain homes. There they live in peace, benefited by commerce, and enriched by many accessories to their personal and domestic comforts, but living in general in the same style in which their sires did twelve centuries at least ago. Their wealth still consists of kine and of horses, of sheep and of camels, their goats' hair tents, and their few cooking utensils —all their goods—living in simple patriarchal style in the midst of abundance, and, till of late, in peace.

" The shadowy outline of the big tents; the numerous herds gathered for security within the Douair or circle; the gaunt form of ruminating camel seen against the sky; the ancient stars with their Arabic appellations, 'Veja,' 'Aldebaran,' 'Rus al gettan,' &c., &c., recall with irresistible force all one's picturings of the patriarchs of our world. It is still the mode of life adopted by a large portion of the family of man.

" I remained happily with my new friends for five days, during which time I gave no presents, simply paying for what I received from them, resisting from the first all encroachment or intrusions, and yet establishing the basis of what I hope will be a lasting friendship."

An incident which occurred during this visit is narrated in the following letter :—

### A JEW MERCHANT.

" I was sitting in an Arab tent when two Jews, merchants, came into the camp, and cried aloud, ' Bring wool, bring barley, bring charcoal; buy sugar, buy oil, buy pepper, buy fruit,' &c., &c. Crowds of ragged children and many women quickly gathered round them, bringing baskets full of wool, barley, and other commodities, and the Jews gave in return apricots, oil, &c. I went up to them; they gave me apricots; and as they refused to take my money in exchange, I offered coffee. This was accepted. Coffee was prepared for them; also a batter of eggs and flour fried in oil. We eat upon the ground under the shadow of their horses in the centre of the camp. Presently came a message from a large tent begging for some coffee, and inviting us to adjourn thither. We did so, and following the messenger found a well-dressed Arab reclining upon a large mat. He was better dressed than any I had yet seen. A bowl of kuss-kuss was brought, my coffee was cooked at their fire, and we all enjoyed this simple fare. When the Jews left, they addressed to me a long salutation, and I felt grateful to have made a favourable impression upon them, hoping to improve the occasion at another opportunity; and even should I not meet these men again, yet other Jews will be the more willing to receive what I shall offer to them."

## THE DEPARTURE.

*June 27th.*

"A change has come over my fair dream! I am suffering from the effects of the heat, and perhaps of anxiety. My baggage mule is dead, some one having cut off his ear in the night, he bled to death. My servant, who was my interpreter, has run away, some trick probably done by the Arabs in fun, having frightened him.[*]

"I am writing by the margin of a stream in a lovely bower, formed by oleanders. The bower is like a chamber, four yards long, and four feet wide. There is no undergrowth now; above are the flowering shrubs, with their attendant brambles, and other creepers. The birds are singing in the branches; one has a note sweet as the English nightingale. No English garden is so rich in flowers as this charming

[*] The Jews are greatly disliked by the Arabs. They were at one time their slaves, but have been emancipated by the French. A Jewish servant would doubtless not have been chosen had the traveller been aware of this national antipathy.

country. Oleanders follow the course of this streamlet for many miles, and cover its water from the sun. They are in fullest bloom. Oh, what a luxury is flowing water in a torrid clime! Last Sunday the heat was overpowering. I never felt it more so when in the Tropics. But the nights are pleasant. At 3 P.M. the day begins to cool; at 5 P.M. the air is warm, but no longer sultry; and at 8 o'clock it is fresh and cool. If duty and prudence did not say 'Depart,' I would stay in the mountains a few days longer. But I must move homewards to-day. My position might be a hazardous one, as I am alone, and have no means of communicating with my friends. My work in Oran also requires my return. At present I am great friends with all here. The caïd (sheik) who brought me milk at first with his own hand, has directed his people to supply me with all I need, so far as they are able, viz., milk, butter, eggs, and honey. He and his marabout come daily, and sit on the right and on the left of my tent door, while I take my evening meal. There is a circle of men, old and young, not far off, on the ground, in Arab fashion, resting on their elbows, each ready to serve me. One lights my fire, another brings water for myself or horse, which is tethered close to my tent. I give a cup of coffee in return for service; and to the caïd and his companion a little tobacco, as also to the aged men when I visit them. *Voilà tout!* The women are not afraid of me now. They have all paid my tent a visit, but only to stand near and look around. The children are sometimes troublesome, but not one has touched anything about my tent; when they crowd around, I keep order with a bough, and beat *the ground* with it vigorously, which is generally sufficient to arrest their progress.

"Do not forget that I am describing life in an Arab Douair, among the Atlas mountains, and that the Arabs are the reputed robbers of the desert. It is true, that when my servant ran off, they began to ask me questions, and evidently expected I should be much annoyed, but I made light of the matter, learnt the Arabic for 'nothing,' and so expressed my estimate of the man I had lost. When the mule died they whispered together. I could see that they began to feel, as more civilised people are apt to do, when they see trouble coming upon a stranger, but it is 'all right" at present. I am, however, somewhat perplexed, being alone, and fearing that my horse will resist the burden of my baggage, for he is a spirited animal, and apt to strike with his fore feet, but he has always been quiet in my hands. However, I go to prepare for the journey back to Oran."

## JOURNEY BACK.

" I have dismounted, and secured my horse for refreshment, to write to you a few more lines, as this must be posted when I arrive at Oran. I wish you could look over my shoulder, you would then be upon the highest part of the mountain, which is seen from Oran, as the southern boundary of its plain. How came I here ? I will narrate.

" While in my bower by the stream, I was aroused by an unknown Arab, who brought my horse all foaming and bloody. He had broken his cord again, and had been fighting with others. Telling him to tie him again to his stake, I went to the encampment, but had to lead my own charger, following Arab customs, coaxing and beating him by turns. To go that night seemed now impossible, or at least, unwise, lest the tribe should be offended, and I should have a ' Laban ' chasing me for damages. However, I will make a parting feast, so I begin to prepare for the same—barley, milk, wheat, prepared like our barley, and a fowl. I make a fire between stones, in front of my tent ; put on my boiler ; kill and dress the chicken, and set on all to boil. The Arabs notice me, and come to sit round my fire. I tell one to attend to it, and go into my tent to make ready for departure. Finally, with the addition of two gourds and coffee, the repast was ready. The caïd had arrived, bringing as usual more milk, also sending for water from his own tent, and all who were invited to partake seemed to enjoy the repast.

" The caïd is a fine fellow, and to the last tenderly solicitous for my comfort, never allowing his people to interfere with my arrangements, and when I left his Douair, he led my horse for at least half a mile, and only left me at my own request. Three of his people wished to attach themselves to me as servants, but I know not their language as yet. We all parted very good friends. I gave my address to the caïd, and I hope to see him again some day. Of course I had a few things stolen from me, such as knives, and other trifles, but these were probably taken by some youths who were the idlers of the company. God's Providence has watched over me, and I rejoice in having had this opportunity of cultivating friendliness with these sons of the desert. The good feeling may be evanescent, but by these things we dispose men to listen to our instructions, and to take our books. My horse has now become impatient, and I must proceed on my journey."

## CHAPTER XVII.

### VISIT TO GIBRALTAR.

Mr Ogle's journey to and from the Arabs' country offered also occasions for seed sowing among Spaniards. These are the cultivators of the plains, but they are also found occupying small farms among the mountains. They and their fathers have possessed this part of the country since the 16th century, when Spain was master of the sea-board, having pursued the Moors in their retreat into Africa. Mr Ogle resumes :—

"On my return to Oran, I found new enemies at work, and I also found a good friend to our cause. The Rev. R. Monsalvage and his family have arrived from New York, and I have had the great pleasure of welcoming them to my comfortable house in Oran. At first sight I knew him to be a simple and happy Christian, a wise but child-like man, a man of God. He arrived with wife and four children from New York, via Carthagena, where he has laboured for some

years with great success. You may remember having read of
the circumstance.

"He left the ship which conveyed him and his family, a
burning wreck. Scarcely had they left it in a boat, when a
terrific explosion of the powder on board destroyed all his
goods, books and writings. He met with friends in Carthagena,
whither he had been thus driven, and founded a church there.
His sermons have power and gospel faithfulness, and his
labours were greatly blessed. He could not support his
family, however, and he is seeking employment. I have
obliged him to come for the present into my house, for I know
he cannot find elsewhere in Oran, so healthy a situation, the
room for his family, or the comforts that I have. For me
(alone as I am), these things are nothing, for him they are
needful.

"But five priests from Spain have also come over to put a
stop to the conversions reported here, and to convert in their
turn. They have made a great excitement. I never witnessed such a scene as I beheld at the concluding sermons
of these men.

"A monk, the very type of monkhood, with black hair and
beard, black gown, white rope, well fed, and stentorian voice,
preached. For some time he appeared to be merely depreca-
ting 'the missionaries of the Spirit of Evil—the Devil.' At
length he rose, and turned towards the altar, all the congregation, numbering fifteen hundred people at least, chiefly women,
turned also. Soon sobs commenced, then cries, then floods of
tears, and a scene of weeping such as I never before witnessed.
Would that they had been looking to Him whom they have
pierced! Alas, I fear this looking at bleeding pictures is but
Rome's counterfeit! Some on this occasion evidently wept
from sympathy; even men were thus affected. The preacher
at first used soft but exciting tones, spoke of the 'blessed
sacrament of penance, and of the purified souls going forth
from the temple cleansed and white!' Then his voice changed
to louder tones, he repeated what appeared to me to be a
'credo,' but as the people responded I could not understand
the words used. Then he cried out, 'Viva, viva,' &c. The

response being deep and general, 'Viva.' Then in Spanish, 'Cast out,' 'Cast out,' several times. He seemed as if he would hurl his crucifix at me, who stood before him silent and unmoved, save with inward grief and indignation at the scene. I held the Bible before my breast, and looked at the preacher. The Spaniards did not attempt to 'Cast me out,' though at times I almost expected it, so great was their state of excitement.

"It was over. As I went home I addressed a Spaniard who with his wife or sister was also returning home. I asked him, 'Why did not the preacher tell you of the gospel of Jesus as the food of the soul rather than the "sacraments?"' and assured him that it contained the true food and true medicine, exhorting him to search the Testament diligently, to see 'if these things are so.'

"He heard me silently and with interest, and at last wished me good night with much fervour. I said, 'The grace of God be with you.'

"The preacher went out into the streets of Oran and continued till midnight, singing and shouting in a very excited manner. I thought he hoped to stir up the people to attack us, but in the Spanish quarter where he went I believe I have acquired a kindly influence; certainly none of the Spaniards would touch a hair of my head, and they have shown themselves still more friendly towards me since this occasion."

It is needful to remark that though these monks were permitted thus to excite the people, and to slander the Protestants, a strict silence was enforced upon the latter. The only way in which Mr Ogle, who feared them not, could shew that he at least was willing to hear them, and to confute them from the Word of God, was by the courageous act described above. But he further resolved to seek for an opportunity of conversing with, and openly refuting these men, which opportunity shortly after occurred. When their term of service was completed at Oran, they proceeded to Gibraltar, where they intended to institute similar proceedings. Mr Ogle no sooner heard of this, than, in dependence on the Divine blessing, he resolved to accompany them thither, and to oppose them, not by mere controversy, still less by personal invective, but by lectures upon great principles of Scripture truth ; to challenge them to prove their statements, and so to refute their assertions. When asked why not have left the Protestant missionaries and others already in Gibraltar to deal with the invaders, he replied, 'A person who stays but a short time in a place may with propriety make more strenuous efforts, and will be likely to be more at leisure to do so than those who are resident, though they may be equally earnest in the cause.' Moreover, had he not, in his own field of Algeria, patiently listened to their arguments, and painfully witnessed their conduct ? He had, therefore, so far an advantage in dealing with them.

## MISSION TO GIBRALTAR.

GIBRALTAR, *August 9th*, 1859.

" I am now rejoicing in English soil and associations. The feeling is very like that of stepping ashore after a long voyage. At sea all is uncertain and treacherous. The sky may be clear and the ocean calm, but the unruffled mirror which has reflected a cloud, may toss into a tempest. We step on shore, and all is stable, firm, and solid. We seem then to breathe a different air. So I feel on England's free and happy territory. Would that no fears for its stability distracted my dreams, but when volcanoes vomit fire, and lava streams desolate the soil, it is impossible not to apprehend an earthquake !

" I find Gibraltar much changed since I visited it fourteen years ago. The 'Rock' seems to have expanded its base, and to have encroached upon the sea. Houses are so built upon its slopes, and gardens formed, that it appears to be much larger than my recollections paint. The fortifications also present an appearance more pretentious. Would that upon the policy of England were inscribed, 'Except the LORD keep the city,' &c.

" All things seemed to favour my journey here, and I resolved,

P

if so, to comply with openings for work. The sea was calm, the weather bright. Many opportunities occurred during the voyage of useful conversation, even with the preaching and declamatory friars, as well as with the sailors, with Arabs, and Moors, and Jews, who were on board.

"The port is full of English vessels. I have spoken of the good news of the gospel to very many in the market-place since my arrival, and have seen Mr Ruet. He seems to be a man of an amiable and ardent Christian spirit, and one who will, I trust, make good his work. He tells me of churches founded in Spain, in three of the principal cities, and that there are good hopes of more. It is on account of this that my companions, the friars, have come to thunder terrors, and to persuade by enticements, by force of voice, if not of argument. We will only take the sword of the Spirit, 'the word of God,' and with the weapon of 'all prayer' we shall convince and convert many.

"You will believe that I have many occupations here, although my challenged antagonists are not to be found. . . . . I go out every day among the Spaniards here, taking the town in order. I meet with much opposition, and with some encouragement also. It is good seed, and though not one in *four* fall into good ground, yet that shall bear fruit 'thirty, sixty, one hundred fold.' I have addressed the different Spanish congregations in several churches here. To-day I was invited to speak at a soldiers' temperance meeting, and have met with success, which will help to fill my place of address on Sunday next (*D. V.*), when I am to preach to soldiers. Next week I give three lectures. I frequently go to the Wesleyan chapel on week days, and take a part in prayer. Whether I shall find the same Christian bond of fellowship among the churchmen here, when I come to know them, as among my brethren, the Nonconformists, remains to be seen. A pious young officer was one of my auditors to-night, who will, I have great hopes, follow the steps of Hammond and H. Vicars.

"Until to-day I have been busy at work, but I have been now to see the 'lions of Gibraltar,' the fortifications, and the 'Rock.' By a somewhat strict regulation, no one is permitted to go beyond the town, so that, I dare say, half the inhabitants never were a mile away on the Spanish side, nor ever ascended the magnificent heights that overhang their habitations.

" You know the Rock ?  Everybody knows it ! lying in the south-west corner of Europe, like a couchant lion, its watchful head towards Spain, the teeth of the monster only shown when it vomits smoke and fire.  They are the ' galleries ' formed on the face of the precipice on the north side, which are pierced only by small apertures for the muzzles of the heavy cannon to look out.  In the rock is also the spacious chamber called ' St George's Hall,' which contains seven guns.

" The Prince of Wales has just been here, and the print of royal feet (they are rare here) is fresh upon the pavement of these corridors.

" The march of progress is noticeable.  On the summit crumbles into decay the feudal stronghold of masonry, pierced, with loop-hole and creuelle for archer's occupancy.  Below, the solid rock itself is constructed into a fortification, and the mightiest works of this century—the mile-long tunnel, and the monster gun, replace the winding-stair and the rude arrow of mediæval times.

" I read from the Scriptures (Isaiah ii.) to the soldier who accompanied me, and again in Spanish to an ancient man, a goat-herd, met with upon the higher ranges of the Rock.

" After leaving ' the galleries,' I pursued my way alone over the Rock, climbing the steep stony face to the loftiest summit, and finding my reward in magnificent prospects over Africa and Spain, and the ocean, east and west.  There are few positions more striking, and none more suggestive than the heights of Gibraltar.  The scene is diversified, and bold and beautiful.  Yesterday's rain had cleared the atmosphere, and the west wind had driven the clouds from all but the very highest summits, where, as in Scotland in autumn, they rested in fleece-like forms floating in pellucid air.  With the excellent glasses of the signal station I could make out the architectural features of all the principal buildings in Ceuta on the African coast.  There is war now between the Spaniards, its masters, and the Moors, their neighbours.  My eye tracked carefully many a league of coast, and peered far into the interior. No trace of occupation by man could I discover, all is precipitous rock and mountain; wooded, and no doubt beautiful, but peopled only by the beasts of the forest.

"Great interest is felt here as to the war in Africa. The Sultan of Morocco lies on his death-bed ; and three of his sons, besides other aspirants, will fight for his throne. The monarchy is elective, subject to the decree of the Sultan of Constantinople. Two of these sons have friendly relations with England. They have travelled much, and have received attentions from us. The French favour one of the aspirants, the English another ; the old father and the army support the claims of the third. . . . .

"I have distributed since my arrival some three hundred tracts, &c., on board Spanish steamers, and to boatmen from Spain. The desire for tracts and Testaments is very great. Each day I am obliged, after having been some little time at work in the streets, to stop, because I am so thronged that obstruction of the thoroughfare takes place. The police know me now and give me a friendly word.

"I have issued a challenge publicly to all Roman Catholic priests, cardinals, Pope, &c., to prove one single word falsified in the version, Spanish or English, published and circulated by the Bible Society, adding that any who shall prove this in writing to the satisfaction of twelve learned men, six Catholic and six Protestants, after my reply has been considered, shall receive £1000, lawful English money. I am casting about for means to advertise this through Spain. Everywhere I meet the accusation, 'Your Bible is false.' E——— writes it from his prison, 'It is in all mouths, and why ? *Because we have never challenged the calumny*, or the results of the old disputes are forgotten.' I add, moreover, that if they of the Romish Church dare to reply by a counter challenge, I will immediately take it up."

## PRIESTS LEAVING ROME.

"How shall I describe the joy and the hopes with which my mind and those of our friends here are now filled. Within these few days of my sojourn there has arrived here from T—— a priest who has been for ten years a missionary of the Roman propaganda, a man much loved and respected by his flock.

"He has come to seek admission into a Protestant church, and says that ten other priests, in various parts of Spain, are only waiting to know the result of his application, and are willing to take any kind of employment in the Protestant cause. We have sifted this man's case with much caution. He bears an excellent character. Many letters arrive by each post from members of his former flock, begging him to return to them and to teach them what Protestant doctrine really is, &c. Is not God working in this land? Five missionary monks go forth to overthrow our work in lands where we are restricted from replying to their assertions, and can but oppose them by our prayers; but ten from their communion come to us for instruction unsought and unknown.

"The priests whom I accompanied from Oran have never preached or appeared in public here. I believe they have gone on into Spain to M——, where the little church formed by S. R——will be the object of their attack, fruitless, by God's grace as at Oran, except to make a stir among their own people. Perhaps inasmuch as they do preach some truth, and denounce sin fiercely, they may break up fallow ground, on which we may sow the seed of the kingdom."

The freedom Mr Ogle enjoyed upon the English territory made him feel the more deeply the enforced restrictions of the French "free colony of Algeria." "In Gibraltar, where I was really free, I went daily with a bag full of Bibles, &c., and stood for hours in the public thoroughfare and in the markets —I would do the same willingly, in Algeria, were it permitted me." To Algeria he now returned. The priests whom he had followed to Gibraltar had passed into Spain, where no free discussion on points of religion could then take place. His journey, however, had not been in vain. He had been occupied in most active evangelistic efforts all the time that he lived on the Rock.   There was nothing more meanwhile to be done, so he returned, as subsequent letters tell us, to his selected field of work in Oran.   The following simile of the life of man, 'a spark in tow,' suggested itself to him one night about this time on a solitary ride home.   He turned it thus :—

> " This Life of man ! 'Twas once a deathless fire,
> Lit in ashes.  By heavenly unguent fed.
> By sin that flame was quenched ; henceforth no more
> Than a frail spark ; couched in frail tow, so frail,
> A breath can put it out, &c., &c."

## The English Fleet.

" The fleet came in from Malta, while I was at Gibraltar, with two Admirals on board.   The Marlborough, 131 guns, with twelve hundred and twenty men, six other ships and two steamers.

" The big ship had a mutiny on board they say a few weeks since.   The state of these ships as to religion appeared to be deplorable—one chaplain for the whole fleet ! one Sabbath service all his appointed work !   Every day boats came ashore with hundreds of men on leave.   Their language was dreadful ; they were constantly swearing, and uttering horrible expressions.   I spoke to many. . . . . At last I wrote a letter to the authorities, begging leave to go on board, as a ship missionary, for six months.   My request could not be granted there, so I left Gibraltar and returned to Oran.

" I find, on my return, all my goods and my late harvest wasted, my horses mere skeletons, starving ; no work done, my head man in Oran dressed very fine, my garden had not even been watered, and was uncropped ; the ground strewed with heads of Indian corn and old melons.   I have had difficulty in knowing what to do—to sue my head man at law ? to refuse him his wages, and turn him off ? . . . .   He may have been negligent through ignorance or forgetfulness.   If there be a hope that he was not intentionally dishonest I would cling to it, . . . but the losses inconvenience me sadly. . . .

Our heavenly Father overlooks my neglect in His vineyard, and in my own, and forgives and has patience with me; even rewards the little I do for Him ; so feeling that I have somewhat attached these poor people to myself, and in the hope to do them good at length, thinking that the loss of this hope would be far greater than that I have suffered from them, I have at length decided ' to forgive.' "

## Return Voyage to Oran.

" I returned to Oran in the ' Felucca,' a small vessel of forty tons, too small, my friends here thought, for this uncertain season, but I had been long enough at Gibraltar, and could save some weeks by taking advantage of the opportunity, besides, the captain is an old Mediterranean ' salt,' and well acquainted with the navigation. With such men there is generally something to be learnt, and a higher good may also come from our intercourse.

" We had a lumbered deck load, and no cabin ; a few feet square of hold immediately under the main hatch appropriated to two female passengers and their children. I laid my carpet upon some baskets which were full of ' Henna,' and with a loose coverlet at night, was as comfortable as ever I have been in ' roughing it.' "

The superstitions of the crew, however, had well nigh endangered his life.

" From the wind being contrary for getting out of the port, which was crowded with vessels, nine men-of-war, steamers and sailing vessels of all nations, we had much trouble. The mate of the ' Felucca ' hearing that I was a heretic, was very angry with the captain ; protested that all would come to grief, and each time a difficulty occurred, which put the men's quickness in handling sail to the test, this man tore his hair, beat his breast, and abused the captain, as if all was over with us. At length, just as we got out of the shelter of the Spanish

coast, into the tide-way of the Straits, passing the point of the
Rock, the vessel came for a moment broadside on to the sea,
which, though not high, was very lively, and agitated by a
stiff breeze.   A toppling wave came on board and drenched
us all.   It seemed to strike the very spot where I was sitting,
sheltered by the weather bulwarks.   The poor man exclaimed,
'It is the devil coming,' and again protested against the captain for shipping a heretic.   For a moment I thought the men
might bring about some mischief to the ship by their panic,
or might become rebellious, and handle me as Jonah's ship-
mates did him.   The old captain stuck to his tiller, and said
neither good nor bad when no orders were necessary.   I prayed
that it might please God to show them that no harm comes of
sheltering such 'heretics' as I am ; and eventually all went
well.   The wind being fair now, our voyage (which is one of
forty hours for a steamer) was concluded in forty-eight.

"I could not accuse myself that in leaving Gibraltar I was
following Jonah's course, though I surely think that I have a
message to deliver to my countrymen in England such as he
had upon his conscience.

"During the voyage to the Falklands, I wrote a letter entitled
'The Voice of Jonah.'   It is among my papers, with much of
the same sort of matter.   Among the sins which are bringing
down judgments upon us, I consider those ambiguous and Rome-
ward-tending expressions of the Church of England, by which
we obscure the truth.   But, alas! corruption extends throughout the land, and, as in Israel of old, 'There is none that
understandeth.' . . . . It is part of our national policy, and
thought to be necessary to our national preservation, to say
nothing of what is due to God and to true religion, and not
to protest against Rome, its blasphemous deceits and tyran-
nical usurpations : yet in an English colony the governor
condemns a Christian minister because he distributes papers
freely announcing—

'A Sermon on the Obligation which lies upon every
    Man to study diligently the Sacred Scriptures.'"

Mr Ogle here refers to a private reprimand given him by the Governor of Gibraltar for distributing an announcement to the above effect.

" I was reprimanded by the Governor (privately) for my forward action towards the Roman Catholics of Gibraltar, and told by him that 'he would not permit one portion of her Majesty's subjects to be preferred to another, or to offer offence to another.'

" How long will it be ere our Rulers learn that they cannot serve two masters ? that the support of two systems necessarily antagonistic is not only suicidal, but unfair to both, *and ruinous to those whose policy is the less aggressive ?* 'They support *equally* the two religious *parties.*' Well, but the word ' party' no more expresses things identical than any other 'general' term. One *party* uses weapons of offence, the other does not. One *party* is political in its machinery and in its objects, the other strictly religious. It is obvious that to support and further the objects of the two equally is far from equal justice ; the *equality* ought to be measured from another point of view. It is a stultification, like many of which this age is the victim ! the acceptation of a logical fallacy of the most palpable sort ! as if words were incapable of deluding— as if ' party,' ' Church,' ' religion,' &c., must mean the same in all men's mouths ! The least examination shows them to signify differences as great as there are between the most diverse of things, when employed by Protestant evangelists, who search the Scriptures for their definitions, and by the hierarchical Papists going to ' decretals' and 'extravaganzas' for theirs.

" *To be consistent, the English Government ought to allow the proper proportion of* AUTO'S DA FÉ, BURNING OF HERETICS, BIBLE DEMOLITION, &c. ! !

" It is possible that an individual looking from the summits of the Atlas, over Catholic Spain, France, Italy, Austria, may be too lynx-eyed, but in my opinion the British Government are *doing* nothing else when they pay to the education of priests and other promoters of the Roman Catholic tyranny £130,000 in Great Britain and Ireland, £12,000 in Australia, in Canada, &c., and give 7000 dol. in a year to a college conducted by priests in Gibraltar itself! The action of their protegés is not seen as yet save in solitary examples, *e.g.,* Escalante; but it will appear and confound the innocent abettors, not the less miserably that it appears not till the remedy is too late." . . . .

The following letter, addressed to the Rev. J. E. D——, with which we close this chapter, gives us a lively, but melancholy, idea of the numerous obstructions that impeded Mr. Ogle's work in Algeria; and shows us how little freedom for the Gospel there was in the "Free Colony of Algeria." Alas that it should be so! How ingenious in devising plausible excuses and planning subtle restraints is tyranny when it dare not openly persecute. The restrictions, however, that were here encountered, were of a different sort from those he experienced at home; they fettered his action, but they did not hurt his conscience.

" Alas that I have not to record a great work doing. We are circumscribed by a system which, while it professes to be liberal and impartial, really retains power over every portion of the social machine, so as to put a check wherever it may be needed to secure their object. We have cruelly experienced this within a short time past. The great means of introducing light is by the press and especially by Bible distribution. We distribute Roman Catholic versions, consequently opposition cannot be with good grace directed against the Book; it is therefore against the distributor. *We are refused permission to colport.* Three applications, one of which I made for myself, have been refused. They pretend,—for it is but a plea, the real motive being hostility to the blessed gospel,—that the state of the population renders religious propagation of dangerous political tendency; again, that our persons would be exposed to danger! Truly considerate they are. When sermons of the most inflammatory kind are permitted to be preached in the chief pulpits by foreign missionaries! when they cry to an excited populace, 'Away! away with these missionaries of the devil!' truly the *care for our persons* is special (?) indeed. No, it is an accomplishment of the prophecy, 'The kings of the earth stood up, the rulers took counsel together against the Lord, and against his Christ.' 'He that dwelleth in heaven shall laugh them to scorn.' Let us only be single-eyed, faithful, zealous, and we shall see it. I have written to the Foreign Office to beg that my reasonable request (reasonable because without permission of Colportage one is liable to fine and prison for *lending* a book!) may be sanctioned by the vice-Consul. The reply is, 'They will not interfere.' Perhaps when they are in need, and ask for aid, they will receive the same reply. What to do it is hard to say. One is afraid of overt action, because it is morally certain that the first case which can be laid hold of will bring about one's expulsion, and so the work will be finished, as far as the individual is concerned. I have been following another course. Establishing myself in the country as a colonist. A landed proprietor in England, I could, without any change of habits, become such in Algeria. The field is open, and I have put my hand to the plough. It is vexatious to feel that one's energies are divided; but perhaps it may be good for one's pride and self-reliance to be thus set aside. Moses was forty years a keeper of sheep on hills barren and rocky as an Atlas range, learning lessons of wisdom and faith, to have an open ear and an obedient heart. Few have been greatly useful in God's way without such a preparatory discipline, and, besides, it seems to be the way of Providence, to send the shower and direct the rill, not with the force and precision of machinery, but in tortuous channels and gentle distillings whither He will.

"Often have I found my best opportunities in the homely path of labour. The necessity of employing and dealing with men is favourable to acquaintance, and so to remove prejudice; and sometimes we may find an opening for the gospel. Only

let us be really desirous and the means will be found sooner
or later. With respect, then, to Bible distribution, I fear
much cannot be done at present. We have had positive
refusals, with intimation that the *minister's* directions are to
refuse permission. This is extraordinary! One would expect
*more* liberty in Algeria than in France; and lo! that which
was never refused in France is so here. What becomes of the
profession so often repeated, 'That all religions are alike treated
in France?' 'The State knows no religion.' The case we
find to be, that Protestantism is persecuted wherever it is safe
to do so. One of the means of doing this is through the operation
of the custom-house. It is incredible what difficulty I have
met with in this respect. In fact, I have not for some months
been able to get a single tract of some hundreds which are at
the custom-house for me. I fear it will be the same with a
box of Bibles, &c., my brother has just sent, having entered
into opposition actively against some Spanish missionaries, who
came hither purposely to overthrow our work. I am so
watched and counteracted that I can scarcely do anything, so
I devote my time to the study of languages, and take farming as
recreation and exercise. My health suffered in England from
too much thought and study, and inaction, here it is, I believe,
by God's blessing, being greatly invigorated, so perhaps my
years will not be lost in the retrospect of a life.

"The question, what we ought to do, is of very hard solution.
'Trust to providential care and go forward. Did not the sea
divide its waves. Did not Jordan's swollen flood open to give
entrance to the hosts of the Lord?' To obey *this* direction
demands faith in it as God's. Now I have not yet this faith;
it is all conjecture. I rather seem to hear, 'Your strength is
to sit still.' 'Enter into the defenced cities, and let us be
silent there, for the Lord of Hosts hath put us to silence, and
given us water of gall to drink.'

"If you have opportunities, I should say, *send Bibles:*
probably *Algiers* is a safer place than Oran. I do not know
that our friends there find much difficulty. The reason we
are so persecuted is (1) we are few; (2) there is a Spanish

mission here.   Our enemies are determined to destroy us in
the outset if possible.   I grieve to see some of my companions
giving way, and saying, ' We can do nothing.   Let us go.'
It seems to me a motive for abiding.   To stand our ground
when our adversaries are numerous is something.   There will
be three or four hundred priests in the Province.   *We* are
five !   ' At the rebuke of five shall they flee.'

   " My hope is to introduce a good quantity of Bibles.   I conceal them in safe hands, hoping the time may arrive for their
distribution.   The world is full of this.   We shall not be
exempt here, and when barriers are overthrown, the host of
the Lord will go up on every side.

   " If we had now hundreds of Jewish books we could distribute them, as there is a large influx of refugees from Tangiers
and Morocco.   I have had interesting conversations with some.
' This is the first step towards Jerusalem.'   'That is our hope,'
they replied.   ' Do not think of returning whence ye came.'
' Onward, eastward, Zionward !'   ' Yes, yes ; good !' they cry,
and ask me impatiently for books.   I distributed in half an
hour all the tracts I had, and there is a great demand for
more.   Being free from special obligation to any society, I do
my work as it comes, sometimes in one way, and sometimes
another.

   " Africa has wild and unfettered freedom in the trackless
regions and the sand bounded expanse of its interior.   It has
all the charms of summer in warmth and luxuriance, when,
with you, winter reigns ; but, lacking Christian truth, with its
corresponding morality, intellectual culture, and social institutions, destitute of liberty in thought, in word, in action, even
under European rule, it remains branded as with a curse.
' The heavens are as brass, the earth as iron.'   The one circumstance that renders a residence in such a land endurable,
is the assurance that beyond the cloud shines the sun ; that
the beneficent protection of the same Providence orders and
controls all things here, as well as with you, and that a common
faith and hope animate to labours of love, and bind together
those whom distance and diverse circumstances divide."

# CHAPTER XVIII.

## A FARM RENTED, AND A BOOK DEPÔT OPENED.

IN Algeria Mr Ogle found himself living on the confines of two worlds. Away in the south, sleeping movelessly in their ancestral deserts, were the Old Times, and on the north was the Modern World in the fringe of European civilisation which extended along the sea-board. At the gate of Oran sat an Arab boy as shoe-black; on the other side toward the wilderness rose the tents of the Bedouins. The eye of Mr Ogle rested on both at the same time. He stood on the line which divided the New and the Old. He was here to lead in the New; to bid the Modern Times march on; to say to them,—Cross the boundary where meanwhile you halt; scale the Atlas, and from their summits pour the light of day upon the tribes beyond, which still dwell beneath the ancient night. But on what instrumentalities did Mr Ogle rely? What power had he to change the opinions and usages of thousands of years; to chase the night from a continent, and "turn the shadow of death into the morning?" He relied on no earth-born forces, which he knew could not lift man higher than the earth out of which they were sprung. He advanced to this great conquest armed with the sword of the Spirit which is the Word of God. It was against the darkness that he was marching, and he carried thither the light, that true light which God has created for the soul, and which alone has power to bring nations out of their sepulchre.

But in Algeria, a French colony, Mr Ogle found himself very differently situated from our missionaries in India, or in any British possession. He was free, and yet he was not free; for his action as a missionary, though not absolutely interdicted, was greatly fettered. He was watched by the Romish Church, which had sent thither her agents to thwart him, and these emissaries often compelled the colonial government to see when, if left to itself, it would have been blind. Many impediments were placed in Mr Ogle's path. He could obtain from the authorities no licence to act as a colporteur : he could erect no missionary institute or school ; he could not openly preach, or meet with converts and hold public worship. The government did not indeed expel him from the country, or cast him into prison ; but these perils hung continually over him, and any act of open propagandism would, he knew, subject him to expulsion or imprisonment. Mr Ogle studied to avoid these risks, not because of the suffering to himself, but because of the injury to his work, which would thereby be stopped. He must be wise as a serpent, and harmless as a dove. He must convey to men perishing through ignorance a knowledge of the truth, but in such a way as would leave to the government no pretext for saying that the public peace had been disturbed, or the law of the country violated.

We have seen how successfully, on the whole, Mr Ogle had managed to do this hitherto. He had dressed as the natives, lived as the natives, talked with them in the street, visited them in their houses, cultivated their acquaintance in every way, and won their respect and love by kind words and kind acts, so that the setting sun closed no day on which he had not reason to believe that good had been done to some soul. Although still refused licence as a colporteur, he was doing the *thing* very effectually ; tracts, bibles, and portions of bibles were by his hands placed in many a Spanish dwelling and Arab tent, whose inmates would peruse them all the more attentively that they remembered the soft accents and beaming face of the man who had brought to them a book so new and strange. Thus here and there 'in that barren land were dropped seeds that could not die. Some of these seeds germinated under the very eye of Mr Ogle; the springing of others was reserved to greet other eyes, and gladden other hearts in days to come.

But much did Mr Ogle long to have a yet wider access to the population. He cast about how he might attain this. It occurred to him that one way, perhaps the most effectual way, of getting at his object was, while remaining the missionary in reality, to become the colonist in guise. This would bring around him numbers of the natives, between whom and himself such relations would be established as would greatly multiply his opportunities of access to them, and vastly strengthen his influence over them. It would change the stranger into the master and the benefactor. It helped to recommend the plan to him that land was abundant, and cheap, and fertile. He decided on this course, and accordingly he rented some thousand acres of African soil. He sowed and planted, he digged wells and erected dwellings in that land; he had sheep and oxen, horses and asses, maid-servants and men-servants; he had Arabs for his shepherds, Moors for his husbandmen, Spaniards and Frenchmen for servants and labourers. He was now at the head of a large household, a numerous body of dependents, going daily out and in before them, with not a little of the authority and reverence of the patriarch or sheikh. With the same stars over him, and a similar state of society around him as another great missionary colonist, and pilgrim, Mr Ogle set up his altar in this land, and " called upon the name of the Lord, the everlasting God."

But our missionary never lost sight of the main business which had brought him into this land. All this rearing of cattle and growing of corn, and paternal supervision of servants and dependents, was in order to open a door for the gospel, and to keep it open. How different the conquests of the

Gospel from those of war! The conqueror comes with a great host, he fights a pitched battle, and a province is added to his dominions. The kingdom of heaven cometh not with observation. It does not aim at conquering a kingdom at a stroke. The process is long and silent, but the victory so gained lasts for ever. Mr Ogle knew that the work he had set on foot in Africa must necessarily be slow, but his patience was great just because his hope was strong. He aimed at enlightening the whole of that dark land, of subjugating it all to Christ, but he was content to win it man by man, and heart by heart. Every Bible he succeeded in placing in the Arab tent, or in the Spanish dwelling, was so much more ground gained. All the great harvests of Truth have in like manner been prepared long before by single sowers. The seed scattered by the hand of Wycliffe lay an hundred and fifty years in the soil before it developed into the Reformation of England. Claude of Turin in the ninth century, Arnold of Brescia in the twelfth, Savonarolo of Florence in the fifteenth, Huss and Jerome in Bohemia, and John Wessel in Germany, were the first pioneers in their respective countries of that great movement which, under Luther and Calvin, changed the face of Christendom in the sixteenth century. Whatever is destined to be great must begin by being small. The conversion of a nation, the evangelisation of a world, must have their commencement in the illumination of a single soul. These were the views which guided and cheered Mr Ogle, and therefore did he exceedingly rejoice at every new instance of the seed of the Divine Word being received, if but into a single heart. A result apparently so insignificant, a man of the world would have derided; he would have asked, "How long shall it be, at this rate, till Africa is converted?" The sower in spring knows well that the sowing of the seed is not the harvest, but he knows that every handful he scatters brings the harvest nearer, and therefore he goes on sowing. And so did Mr Ogle. Every seed

Q

that fell into the earth he accepted as a pledge of harvest ; and
though he knew that he should not tarry till that harvest had
come, he saw it afar off with the eye of his faith.   He beheld
by anticipation the fields ripe, the labourers busy, and heard
the songs wherewith the reapers would carry home their
sheaves.

So far as opportunities for evangelising were concerned, Mr
Ogle's farming arrangements answered their end.   He came
daily into contact with the natives, and on a wide scale—for
Algeria is a sort of meeting-place of nations, eastern and
western—and on a footing which enabled him to appeal to
them with great effect.   The hours of rest from labour afforded
him many openings for conversing with Spaniard, and Moor,
and Arab on divine things, and making known to them the
Saviour.   And when the working-day was ended, it often
happened that many remained with Mr Ogle till far into the
evening to unite with him in prayer, and to receive instruction on the things of the kingdom of heaven.   Thus the farm
became, in fact, a missionary institute ; and its scholars were
none the less in training in the gospel that they had their
several occupations assigned them as gardeners and ploughmen,
as feeders of cattle and keepers of sheep.   The plan was
sagacious and far-seeing, and no better spot could have been
chosen than this colony.   Algeria is a grand centre, and whatever impulse is given here will necessarily and naturally propagate itself away into the deserts on the south, and along
both shores of the Mediterranean on the north.   We venture
to predict that in the age to come this method of evangelising
will be far more generally resorted to than it has yet been.
When the countries of the globe open, and their governments
shall be able to guarantee security to life and property, colonists,
combining missionary with industrial operations, will spread
themselves over these countries, and exhibit to the natives the
attractive spectacle of the religion of Great Britain in union

with the arts and industries of Christian life. Some little might be done in this way, even now, in the countries of Spain and Italy, where soils, that would repay the British colonist an hundred-fold, are much of them lying uncultivated or under a husbandry of the rudest sort. Turkey and central Asia will probably in a few years be opened to a similar enterprise, and its vast plains—formerly a garden, now a wilderness —be redeemed for the plough, and its natives for the gospel; and so the promise made good which foretells a two-fold redemption in the latter day—that of the earth from barrenness, and of man from superstition. "Then shall the earth yield her increase, and God, even our own God, shall bless us."

Mr Ogle's experiment had not a few drawbacks which would have made its success, as a financial scheme, doubtful, and might have deterred him from venturing upon it had he proceeded on the principle of "profit and loss." The rains in Algeria are very uncertain. The husbandman may carry home in autumn an hundred-fold what he has sown in spring, or he may be doomed to see his seed perish according as the shower shall fall in its season and in its due quantity, or be withheld. The natives, moreover, are indolent and indocile, and, like all such, they are inveterately wedded to their old methods. Algerian farming, too, differs from English farming. All these difficulties, and others, Mr Ogle had to contend against. He tried to overcome them, as we shall see, by the introduction of machinery from England, and had time been given him we do not doubt that he would have surmounted all drawbacks, and that his farm would at least have defrayed the charges of working it. More he cared not for. But, as it was, it was a considerable financial loss, over against which, however, Mr Ogle set what really was the all-important thing with him—the spiritual gain. Much of the seed of earth which he sowed came to nought, but he consoled himself with the sure hope that the seed of the Divine Word which he was scattering as opportunities

offered—and they offered largely through this very arrangement—would not die, but bear fruit unto life eternal.

The history of the farm may be gleaned from frequent
references to it in the letters that follow. Meanwhile let us
turn to another and more directly missionary project which
Mr Ogle set on foot for the enlightenment of the dark land in
which he was sojourning. We refer to a book depôt which he
succeeded in opening at Oran. He records the event with all
the joyousness of a soldier who recounts an onward movement.
The letter is characterised by that thoughtful play of fancy
which so strongly distinguished the writer, and nothing could
be happier than the contrast chosen to set off the beneficial
and blessed operation of this armoury of light.

Magazin de Bons Livres, Oran,
*April 2d,* 1860.

"It is with great pleasure, and I trust with lively sentiments
of gratitude to God, that I am able to put the superscription
to this letter. It is an event in the history of mission labour
at Oran, the opening of a shop for the sale of books really and
truly ' good.' I believe, verily, there is not here one which does
not merit the title, and in this mixed world it is a thing very
seldom to be said. The ' Bible Depôt ' at Oran, which after
long waiting and some difficulties we have obtained permission
to open, is situated in the principal street of the town, is
admirably arranged, very simple, and very neat and well furnished with its proper stock,—Holy Scriptures in twelve
languages, French, Arabic, of *three kinds,* Judaic, Berber and
Arab proper, Spanish, also *three dialects,* German, Italian,
English, and Hebrew. The style reminds one of that treasure
of the exhibition of 1851,—the Bible Society's case of Bibles
in 150 languages. Like that well-stocked book-case, our de-
pository is stored with an armour of proof, ranged with the
severe simplicity of stands of arms. I remember well the
reflections and anticipations of a very different character excited
by the sight of the château of Vincennes at Paris, the arsenal of

France, and its vast magazine of weapons for destruction. Stories of spacious apartments, the whole filled with piles of arms, of every description, bristling with bayonets and glittering with sword blades. I think the quantity was for one hundred thousand men. A shudder of horror passed through my mind, as I realised the fact that these weapons had been contrived, forged, and destined for the destruction of the human race! Each one of those myriad sword-blades is intended to find its way to a heart that beats as mine! to put a period to a life precious, in the estimation of its possessor, beyond worlds. nor less precious in the sight of Him who made the universe.

"What diabolic ingenuity has been exercised in the creation of those rifled engines of swift death. Those heaps of murderous bullets will produce a harvest of destruction. What pain, what misery, what bereavement, what desolation, will be let loose like fiends, to ravage the earth when these go forth upon their errand!

"I turn to a happier theme, that which has suggested the above reflections, but how different!

"These piles of arms, 'the sword of the Spirit,' have in them nothing to affright, nothing to cause apprehension, or to suggest melancholy. Their errand is to destroy, to do battle, to break down and sweep away; but it is to destroy superstition, to do battle with error, to break down barriers of prejudice and opposition to God's truth, to level to the dust prison walls, and to set free those who are bound in chains of sin.

"One is too little accustomed to cherish sanguine and hopeful anticipations, but what may we not hope from the establishment, for the first time, of such an arsenal as this Bible shop presents, even in a single city in Algeria.

"I rejoice in the simplicity of the object for which it has been opened. Nothing but the Bible and a few good tracts and books are here. Among six thousand books you shall not find one that is not able to point out clearly the way of salvation.

"The Bibles stand two and three deep upon the shelves. In the window (which is wide and lofty), open Bibles lie, presenting to every passer-by a specimen in his own language of the treasures within, and inviting each, as it were, to come and take of the bread and the water of Life. . . . .

"Already many books have been sold. There has been no clamour nor disturbance ; no crowd, no excitement. Priests and other ecclesiastics have come in to inspect, and some have expressed their astonishment that the government should permit these things to be.

"Jews, Arabs, and others, universally express their approbation, but as yet they do not buy much. The priests have begun to preach against our effort, and employ missionary monks to go to the villages and preach on Sundays and week days, gathering crowds. They intend to excite disturbances no doubt. Our help and hope is in Him whose servants we are, under the shadow of whose protection we desire to remain, whose work we hope to accomplish, 'to open the blind eyes, to turn men from darkness to light, from the power of Satan unto God.' Pray for us.*        J. F. OGLE."

## CHAPTER XIX.

THE following chapter is a somewhat miscellaneous one. It embraces generally the affairs in which Mr Ogle was occupied during the year 1860. The anniversary of his sister's birthday called forth a letter which no one can read without special profit. It is richly fraught with spiritual wisdom and Christian experience. The writer traces with true discrimination the signs of growth in grace, and furnishes tests and evidences by which Christians may know whether they are making progress in the life divine. This leads Mr Ogle into a critique on BUNYAN's world-renowned work, *The Pilgrim's Progress.* It required no little courage, as well as great mental independence to sit in judgment on such a work, and to hint that there

* In this "magazin" fifty pounds worth of books were sold during the first year, a most encouraging commencement.

are defects in it; but we think the majority of our readers will agree in the justice of Mr Ogle's observations. Their admiration of the genius of the book, and their thankfulness for the good it has accomplished and will continue to accomplish till the world's end, will thereby be no ways diminished. The letter, moreover, shows how observant Mr Ogle was of the hand of God, and hence his thankful spirit, and the multitude of mercies of which he finds occasion to speak, and which made his cup to run over, "Whoso is wise and will observe these things, even they shall understand the loving-kindness of the Lord." The death of an aged relative gives the occasion for another letter containing some important reflections on the covenant mercy of God which oft-times is seen beautifully running down in families. From these graver topics the writer passes to speak of the military preparations then going on in Algeria, and also of his own farming operations. His farm, as we have said, was in truth a branch of his missionary scheme. He had embarked in it with no view to profit, but as a means of bringing the natives around him, and of establishing such relations with them as might enable him to take them on a course of instruction in divine things—an end which the farm so far served.

*March 13th*, 1860.

"MY DEAR SISTER,—As this letter will reach England about the 18th inst., I must not forget your birthday. My remembrance of it will, I trust, take the best form—that of prayer for you.

"Were all our years marked by growth in grace, how increasingly happy would birthdays be; new occasions of thankfulness to the Author of our being, on account of that existence, productive of so much real and prospective good, of bright retrospects, and of prospects brighter still, the light 'that shineth more and more till the perfect day.' Ere this can be, we must have a clear evidence that we have given our

hearts to God, have entered upon the pilgrim's progress from the
city of destruction to that of glory, are walking and are pro-
gressing in the narrow road, have attained a certain forward-
ness, passed certain preliminary stages, are able, if not to
mark out with precision the place to which we have arrived,
at least to show that some well ascertained stages have been
passed, and that we have made an appreciable advance during
a definite period.

" What analogy is there between the Christian life and an
earthly *pilgrimage ? i.e., journey.*   There is no map in the
road-book (Bible) which sets forth the progressive stages, and
defines the route for all.   The Christian life is rather like that
of Israel in the desert, a *wandering*, but guided by a heavenly
hand, by tokens of a directing and of a protecting Presence;
Ebenezers erected here and there to notify deliverance, Jehovah-
jireh inscribed on memorials of provision in straits, and of supply in necessities, and the conclusion deduced from multiplied
instances of this kind is, ' If the Lord had not helped us, it had
not failed but our soul had been put to silence ;' or, ' If the
Lord would have destroyed us He had not showed us these
things.'   Thus, comparing our experience with that of the
people of God, we are led to conclude that we also are ' among
the children,' and that we may look forward also to the same
heritage, ' the pleasant land,' and ' the portion of Jacob.'

" I have always thought it a defect in ' Bunyan's Pilgrim's
Progress' that he did not take the Israelitish *wanderings* as
his ruling idea, and the absence of any kind of allegorical
propriety in respect to the stages of progress which are marked
out in that beautiful poem confirms my impression.   Beyond
the first part of the journey—the escape, the struggle, the
passage to the wicket gate—one loses sense of correspondence
in the parallel between the Christian's walk of faith and that
of ' Christian.'

" The burden lost at the Cross, the enlargement of knowledge, chiefly deduced from ordinary incidents spiritually applied, *e.g.*, at the Interpreter's house, the hill Difficulty, the
dark Valley of Conflict, Doubting Castle, Vanity Fair, &c.,
might be inserted and transposed in almost any order without

detriment to the instructiveness or the appropriateness of the allegory as a picture of Christian experience. All these do occur to almost every one, but at different periods of their Christian life. It is only at the conclusion, and in the commencement, that we seem to find ourselves. In the delectable mountains, the dungeon, field of slumber, and the last entry into the land of promise, we have a close and exact correspondence with the reality. Israel's wanderings *were* such, in the absence of way marks. Forty years they passed in traversing a region for which forty days had well sufficed, great part of their journeyings were *retrograde*, back to the wilderness, hither and thither, now near to Sinai's dreadful precincts, now touching Canaan's pleasant borders, mostly in the mere desert—vast, howling, waterless, terrible. Many a Taberah, a Massah, Kibroth-hattaavah, and but one Elim all the way!

"It was a space of *time* that had to be overpassed, and not of *distance;* a period of probation to be endured, sufficient for the experience to be acquired and for the inculcation of the lessons that had to be learned. (Deut. viii.)

"Had Bunyan more markedly pourtrayed progress in his hero's personal character we could have pardoned, or even have admired the absence of incidents which indicate advancing stages, but this I scarcely think he has done. The placing of Doubting-castle so far on in his story seems a defect of position; for surely it is in early and in quite initiatory stages that temptations to distrust the Lord occur, so far as to plunge into that distress of which Giant Despair is the impersonation."

Mr Ogle's own experience is here described. During four or five years in his earlier religious life he passed through great mental agony from this temptation. Few of the letters which were written by him at this period of his life have been preserved, but they are well remembered by some of his friends, as descriptive of a mind under the deepest conviction of backsliding, which vindicated the justice of God, but could not take hold of a single promise as applicable to its own case. Most earnestly did he at that time write to, and personally address, those whom he thought were in danger of falling into the same dungeon of despair, by a careless walk, by negligence of the means of grace, or by the seductive pleasures of clever but sceptical associates and literature. To these sources he attributed his own loss of the sense of God's favour as his reconciled and loving Father, which, during the first part of his religious life, he had enjoyed. We resume the letter.—

"However I am not to decide this point, and to pursue a criticism on the Pilgrim's Progress was not my intention, it ought to be more deliberately done than in the current channel of a familiar letter. My wish is rather to induce you, dear sister, to look for, and to cultivate, that growth in grace, of which St Paul speaks. The marks of which are, perhaps, more love to Christ, more knowledge of Him, more strength against temptations, whether these are to sin and worldliness, or to indolence, or to distrust, and doubt and fear; more knowledge in things of God, experience of divine faithfulness, and felt and enjoyed directness of communion with Him, larger views of the designs of God; brighter anticipations of the future; more assured hopes, more ardent love to our fellow-men, specially to our brethren and sisters in the faith.—2 Peter i. 3.

"There is an ever-growing correspondence between the sympathies and the sentiments of all true Christians. Whenever taught of God they are taught alike, and the most exact accordance is often observable between the scholars of this school, though they may never have interchanged an idea, or been associated by any intermediate and common link of connexion.

"You will notice this most clearly in the babes in Christ. In these there can be no intended derivation of class notions. They follow impulses vigorously urging them from within, while they acquire slowly from without; now in all these the impulses may be perceived to be the very same; the same firm seizure of cardinal truths,—Man's corruption, his need of the Holy Spirit's regenerating power, as well as of the Fountain that cleanses from all sin, the same interest in the conversion of others, Jews and heathens; love for souls, delight in the Scrip-

tures, desire for spiritual refreshments, &c.    The same anti-
pathies, too, may be observed, *e.g.*, Popery in all its principles
—*superstition* and *counterfeits of grace.*    The same spirit and
temper of mind, humility, love, tenderness, conscientiousness,
faith, truthfulness.    Alas! alas! while I write thus, I seem to
condemn myself; for I have very little of these things.    I
should but deceive were I to be judged by my knowledge; this
is derived, by God's special mercy, from the right source, from
Holy Scripture and good books, together with some imparted
inner light, but in attainment, in practice, I am wretchedly
deficient.    May I prove an instructor to myself."

The letter continues;—

"I have written enough to give you suggestions .... to
stir you to increased efforts and more sustained conflicts.
Satan, if he cannot entangle you in sin, or in errors in doctrine,
will seek to draw you aside to vanities, and unprofitable pursuits, that he may diminish your spirituality, undermine your
principles, darken your evidences, lull you in slumber, and prepare the means to assail you in some weak or little guarded
hour with sharp and terrible assaults.    Oh to be aware of his
devices, to be ever leaning upon our Rock, never wandering
from the fold, always looking to our Shepherd, and following
His steps."

## THE SHEPHERD—SCRIPTURE ILLUSTRATION.

"How instructive this Scripture emblem of a shepherd; I
have it often called to my mind.    Here, as in Palestine, the
shepherd goes before his flock, to him they look; when he lifts
his hand they desist from eating the food he thus forbids; a
gentle call brings them to him, 'they know his voice;'
directed by him they pass through luxuriant fields without
feeding; they are forbidden ground, not *his*, therefore not for
them.    He halts in some scant pasture, but sweet and wholesome; by streams at noon he makes them lie down, in safe
circle of the tents by night, where they are guarded from the

beasts of prey.    Such, dear sister, be your path through this world—

'Fed and guided by His hand.'

The last few days has shown how fleeting are human dependencies.    My best friend here, Mrs M——, is gone to her heavenly rest. . . . . She was precisely what I would wish my sister to be—simple, affectionate, charitable to a fault, always occupied in practical usefulness, her children her constant care.    As a wife, obedient, faithful, pious ; all loved her, most of all those whose loss is greatest in her removal.    I have imagined her very like our dear mother: there was in her face a perceptible similarity of expression to that in the portrait which used to be in our drawing-room.    Ah ! would that home influence had never been replaced by a school and college and world-formed life, in which almost all good and simple and humble traits are extinct; if not wholly so, to Grace alone be the praise.    This life in a heathen land does little to encourage ; the stream of evil seems too strong for me, and I can make no head against it.    Seclusion is often my only resource, and it furnishes leisure for such poor proof of my affection as this from your absent brother,                    JOHN."

The estimate of his own character, given in this letter, was not, it may be truly said, that formed .by others.    Many of God's people who have mentioned the impression his visits left upon their minds, have borne witness to the manifestation in him of the work of the Spirit of God, in the particulars mentioned above, in an unusual degree, and have felt in their own spirits a reviving from the warmth of his earnest and self-sacrificing love.    "I could not have believed it, unless I had seen him myself, and conversed with him," was the remark of a devoted minister of Christ, when speaking of his singular simplicity of character, of his ardent love to the Lord, and zeal for His cause.

About this time an event occurred which caused Mr Ogle to fear, that the good understanding which he hoped he had established by many kindly acts between himself and his neighbours, arose only from a temporary cessation of those acts of hostility, which marked his earlier residence in the country. One evening, after dark, as he was returning to his house at Figuier, from his labours in Oran, a bullet whistled past his ear. It did not harm him, and he records respecting it. " From many perils, and amid many difficulties the Lord has mercifully preserved me." When the occurrence became known in the village where he resided, so much unexpected sympathy and regret were expressed by his neighbours, and so much kind feeling was elicited generally, that Mr Ogle very willingly believed the explanation universally suggested to him, that he had been mistaken for another individual, against whom ill-will existed. The circumstance, however, illustrates forcibly the state of the country, of which he writes : " the demoralised state of the people is such, that robberies and other crimes are of frequent occurrence, and the sufferers have little hope of redress when those in authority are often of notoriously bad character."

## TO HIS BROTHER ON THE DEATH OF AN AGED RELATIVE.

ORAN, *April.*

. . . . "I had not realised the probability. your previous letter announced. On reading your last, my feeling was 'glory be to God for his abundant mercy, through Jesus Christ.' We have now, for the sixth time, in the case of our deceased relatives witnessed the truth of the Word, 'the end of the just is blessed : they shall enter into peace.' Death has been deprived of all its terror in each case ; it seems to be an earnest for us, that when the circle is completed there shall be perfected harmony and likeness, for, though various in some points of character, in the close of their earthly career they were alike. 'A life hid with Christ in God' was hers whom we now mourn. 'They also serve who only stand and wait.' 'Who best do His mild will may serve Him best.'

Perhaps the service of heaven may be for the most part 'rest' and ecstatic enjoyment, of relief from every trouble, relaxation of every toil, tranquillity and peace.   Such a state, I think, those Scriptures which speak of heaven indicate.   Honour and pleasure are there, but toil is not.   Praise is the occupation of those sweet societies whose bliss no discord mars, no sorrow qualifies, sickness enfeebles them not, nor age nor labour wastes the constant vigour of their renovated constitution. Youth is renewed without its fluctuating and transient frames, that like the days of spring are bright only at times—oftener clouded and overcast.   'There everlasting spring abides, and never withering flowers.'   But there is a gulf between us and them—a separation ; the land is very far off, the shore seems distant, for the strait which lies between is too wide for human vision, and though report speaks of it as narrow, and the passage as short, our eye cannot discern the opposite shore, and we think the river terrible and the land remote.   It is very sweet to think of death in the connection in which you have brought it to my mind.   My anticipations as to the future on earth which is for those who remain are certainly sombre and dark, but it is a darkness in which gleams are visible, it is a *last* tribulation, a *final* struggle, the end.   It needed not the earthquake which last Sunday shook all our dwellings here, nor the warlike preparations which parade our streets, and manifest themselves from morn to midnight among the (from 50,000 to 100,000) soldiers; nor the rumours that come to us from without—rumours that make war appear to me inevitable.   The French officers here have their appointments ready named in ' the army of Italy:' the last sight to be seen at night is soldiers going home burdened with military equipments; the first in the morning, soldiers taking into the camp their daily provision.   The rappel or the clarion's shrill notes disturb the night, the day is busy with marshalling hosts, preparatory armaments, and the parade of mimic war.

  " The emperor speaks fair, but his acts are not as his words. The slumbering nations that surround him, cajoled by his flatteries, are still.   But we cannot predict the future, and if we could, it is not given perhaps to such as me to modify the character of our times. Still it is miserable to view the stately ship, running on to the rocks, and to anticipate the time when thousands now slumbering in security shall awake to ruin. A great tribulation is foretold in the last days. We are not, as a nation, to expect exemption; the Christian may, however, hope to be carried through it without having more laid upon him than he can bear—to have a little sanctuary provided for him—and to find, as our dear relative has found, an entrance into peace without excess of trouble. In the sorest earthly calamities there is abundant room for the exercise of God's tender mercy, and we have the promise given, 'As thy day, so shall thy strength be.' Even when at last the earth is rent, and the heavens pass away, 'they that are alive and remain shall be caught up in the clouds to meet the Lord in the air, and so shall we be ever with the Lord.' Let us prepare for this; doing our Lord's work; be found watching, feeding his sheep; spreading the knowledge of His gospel. Alas! when I look at my own life, I feel my own deficiency. I am perhaps more occupied with the secular part of my work than is good for me; but Joseph was sent down into Egypt to save life. I am in a very similar country, but in a happier condition than he; nothing would be more agreeable to my pen than to recount my mercies; how my anticipations have been changed, joy has come out of sorrow, and in many ways I have received a hundred-fold more than I have resigned for the cause of Christ. I could tell of many interesting things about my work among the people, but there is nothing new for you, all goes on well. As to the farm, we are planting yams, and there is a promise of an abundant harvest. Easter approaches. I have a Jew as my servant, and from him I shall learn the customs of the Jews, which are peculiar to this country. I have a charming house here in the 'garden' of Oran. There is a large camp of Arabs just now near my place at Senia, which I hope to visit as soon as I can find time to do so."

To his sister F——.

## A Bivouac on the Bed of the Great Salt Lake.

"The most interesting of my letters will probably be those written, as this will be, in places and in circumstances where the simplicity and nature of the locality contrast with my love of an inartificial life. . . . . I have journeyed with a Spanish servant for three days in the desert. We have only seen Arab tents. This is a picturesque locality in which we have halted, but it is surrounded by a dreary waste. A group of tamarisk bushes, in a green dell, where we have grass for our horses, plenty of fuel, in fact everything that a wayfarer may wish, except water, and that we have brought with us. We deemed ourselves alone, but were surprised by a brown Arab looking over the bank, and then he came to watch our proceedings. His sheep (which follow the shepherd in this country) came also; their brown faces and long curled horns, *three* in number sometimes, peep over the bank, and then rush away in great alarm. The shepherd's voice reassures them, and arrests their flight. The Arab is now close to me. I have given him the usual Arabic tokens of friendship, and with the admirable Arabic expression of confidential amity, accompanied with many gestures, he welcomes me, and seems to say, you appear to be enjoying Arab life, come and live amongst us. He is dressed in a long white burnous, and has a necklace of black beads which I believe reminds him to say his prayers, and to count how many. Such is the brother-man who is just now my companion. I offered him coffee, he accepted it, but before I had given it he went for milk, and brought me a delicious cup of milk, foaming new—poor man, I wished I could do more for him than conciliate by a few words and signs his good opinion, but he could not read, and I know little Arabic. But I count it something gained to have shown him that there are Europeans who do not treat poor Arabs with contempt, who own that all men are of one great family, and all have one Father."

Soon after his return from Gibraltar in 1859 Mr Ogle gave up his house in Oran, finding it too expensive, and retired to his farm-house in the country. There he was in the midst of his dependents, and in habits of daily intercourse with them, ready to avail himself of missionary opportunities as they offered. His more immediate domestic arrangements may be learned from the following extract-letter, addressed to Mrs Peddie, Edinburgh, and dated March 5th, 1860 :—

"I have been living in the country, at the farm cottage at Senia, a village of three or four hundred inhabitants, six kilometres, i.e, four miles from Oran; I found my house at Oran somewhat a drain on my resources, and having a favourable opportunity to transfer my lease just at the expiration of Mr M. Salvage's three months' occupation, I did so. I have been living (rent free) in the house of an English proprietor, part of whose property I rent.

"Some systematic attempts were made by me to visit the neighbours, but discontinued as quickly, for I found ill-will to result. I was threatened both by good and bad, 'that if I went about to disturb the religion of my neighbours I should not be permitted to live among them.' It seemed, therefore, that I must either risk the breaking off of my work and life here, or adopt another plan. My resolve was to settle down into a quiet residence, occupying the place of a colonist, having as much to attend to as would take my spare time and wait for favourable gales. In this I have persevered, have got both my smaller holdings in good hands, and in tolerable condition. These are of the nature very common here ; a combination of gardening on the great scale, with farming on the small.

"The property at Senia is part of a purchase I made last year, but have not retained. I occupy as tenant. There is a small house, a garden of two acres, and about six or seven acres of ploughing land, one acre of vineyard and tobacco ground; the three acres require constant labour and are arable by a machine worked by horse. This ground, then, is all under culture. There is a Spanish Protestant, his wife, and three children in the house. I am well satisfied with him, he is a thoroughly honest, industrious, sober, simple-minded man and attached to me. There is no such a man in Oran besides, I fear.

"At *Figuier*, a village on the same road, at the distance of six kilometres to the south, I have a garden of two acres, and ploughland of eight acres. The soil is different, and better than here. My garden is planted in potatoes, beans, onions, and culinary vegetables, garlic, &c. There is a machine for irrigation requiring a horse or two in constant employment. This is managed by a Spaniard, a Catholic, who is a very hardworking and skilful man. His wife is sickly, he has two nice children. I do not know that I have much influence religiously with him, but from his open character and industrious habits, I have hopes that the Bible I have given him, and conversations from time to time will, by God's blessing, be useful. I have a farm at Figuier of **150** acres purchased recently. This is let for the year. I am looking for a man to manage it for me next year. The land is so good that if I were successful in finding an honest, industrious, and capable person, it would pay the whole cost of the purchase and expenses in one year.

"While it may be somewhat satisfactory to contemplate Christian settlements in an almost heathen country, and to acquiesce in, what appears desirable, the extension to the world of the advantages protestant England and Scotland possess in *resident* proprietors, who will exercise Christian influence, still more direct and active operation on the heathenism around us is to be desired. This is too much neglected at home, and therefore, will be less expected where prohibition, and risks, and penalties exist, where an organized institution (the Church of Rome), vigilantly watches such aggressions on its usurpations and wields power to prevent and punish. In such circumstances, perhaps, my inaction, for generally I am wholly inactive in Missionary work, may be excused though lamented, and were it not that I cherish an urgent and impatient longing for the time when doors may open and opportunities present, I should deem myself unworthy to subscribe myself your faithful fellow-worker,

JOHN FURNISS OGLE."

Mr. Ogle had now a little Spanish congregation to which he occasionally ministered. In his letter, June 19th, 1860, he gives an outline of a sermon he one day delivered to them on Prayer; and the observations addressed to these neophytes will be found not unneeded by, nor unprofitable to more advanced Christians.

" Remember the *efficacy* of Prayer. It was my subject last Sabbath in preaching to a congregation of Spaniards. ' Whatsoever ye ask, ye receive.' Oh I urged my hearers. Examine your faith, lay afresh the foundations, for the inefficacy of prayer exhibits the feebleness of faith. It is attainable, pray, 'Lord help my unbelief.' He is willing, we fail : vain desires, unapproved petitions, an unsubjected will, these hinder the uprising of supplication and divert the channel of blessing, dim the evidence of Sonship, and the assurance which would be ours, were all our petitions accepted. Oh for the will conformed to God's will, then we should be disposed to ask only what God is disposed to grant, and the largeness of his favour far exceeding the limits of our petition, we should acknowledge Him to be a God giving ' abundantly above all we can ask or think, hearing and answering prayer.'"

Mr. Ogle continues :—

" I am surrounded by idolaters and the ignorant and can do little to instruct them. I marvel at the inertness of others, but my own is more astonishing, the few bold efforts I make condemn me, and I long to trust my wings, instead of clinging, fluttering, to the rocky ledge of prescribed limits. Impious restrictions ! when God has commanded universal liberty, ' Go ye into *all* the world, and preach the gospel to every creature.'"

" I made an effort on Sabbath last among the lowest of the Spaniards, and was graciously protected, where I might well have been stoned. God's evident providences directed me, and influenced my hearers ; raised me up friends, and silenced adversaries. I have since heard that these people to whom I then preached an acceptable gospel, now declare they will stone me if I go again. Such is our life, a little rising, and then a falling : again a lifting up ; each time, I trust, mounting higher ; but ever uncertain whether like the lark soaring and singing it may not seek the next moment a nest on earth ; or, whether its angel flight shall know no fall, but that of adoration at the footstool of the Throne."

Africa has its days of high festival. Then the sons of the desert gather from far and near to display the fleetness of their steeds, and their own dexterity and delight in mimic martial exercises. Their features, their dress, the barbaric splendour of their accoutrements and ensigns, give a picturesque magnificence to these assemblages. The following scene, described by Mr Ogle, and which seems to blend the amusements of the English race-course with the fiercer excitements of the tournament, is such as is not now to be seen in Europe :—

### THE CORRIDAS.

ORAN, *October* 17, 1860.

" The scene I am about to describe is the great Algerian festival, 'the Corridas.' It took place yesterday at Oran : something similar to it had formed a chief feature in the programme of the Emperor's late visit to Algiers. Imagine a vast open space, two miles long and one wide, 'the central portion a quarter of a mile in diameter, is staked round, and fenced by ropes in a double line, forming a road or course. This course passes in front of a range of tasteful constructions containing covered seats for a distinguished company of visitors. The general who commands this province, occupying the central pavilion. Around the course, and outside of the ropes, are ranged those who are to take part in the 'Corridas.' They are Arab horsemen, distinguished by the boldness of their bearing, the richness of their costume, the gay embroidered caparisons of their war steeds ; curious oriental arms, and horse furniture. They are 2000 in number, one half being men of distinction—kaids or chiefs of tribes ;

Aghas, Kaliphs, etc.; officers of the wandering hordes who inhabit northern Africa. They come from far—from beyond the Atlas mountains, from the borders of the Great Sahara, from the plains of the Zell and of the Sucliff. It is an imposing spectacle. A vast circle of warriors, their dark, fierce looking features, their prancing horses, their banners, green and scarlet and gold, inscribed with Arabic sentences, their glittering arms profusely ornamented with silver, saddle and bridles also covered with gold and silver embroidery.

"It is mid-day. Presently the martial sound of the trumpet and other instruments proclaims the festival begun. A dozen horsemen, in white, enter the course and ride slowly past the pavilion. The trumpet again sounds, and they start forward at full speed round the course, the central space of which is occupied by French officers, ladies in carriages and on horseback, etc. Shouts of applause, of encouragement, or the contrary, excite the riders to madness. A more strange or wilder spectacle is seldom displayed. The horses seem to participate in the enthusiasm, and strain every nerve to overtake or to retain the place of honour. The horseman stands bending over the neck of his steed; he seldom plies the whip, but flourishes it aloft, or stretches it out at arm's length, his face is fixed, and he looks stedfastly before him. Huge spurs, six or seven inches long, inflict wounds if the horse flags; thus they compass the circle, and arrive at the pavilion; there ends the strife.

" Again the trumpet gives a signal, again a troop of Arab horsemen issues forth, and holds a friendly rivalry for speed. This is repeated twenty or thirty times; each race occupies two minutes, the distance is one mile.

" The most characteristic part of the display was, however, to come next. This is the ' Fantasia.' The ropes are removed, and the circle of horsemen ride in military rank from all sides towards the pavilion, and pass the general in review; they then form into squadrons and companies to the left of the ground; their aspect, when thus collected, with banners flying, was very beautiful. The contrast of the white and the scarlet burnous, the glittering of their arms and gilded trap-

pings, their erect and noble bearing presented a scene not
soon to be forgotten. At the trumpet's blast the chiefs in
scarlet from the front rank, form the phalanx, and rush at full
speed, a troop of horsemen. Their arms held aloft, brandishing
their firelocks, they come ! they come ! The speed is terrible,
and the gestures of the warriors how animated and fierce !
Each presents his musket, takes aim, and, at the moment of
passing the general, discharges it into the air ; another troop
follows, and another, quickly the volleys succeed each other ;
the air is darkened with smoke and dust, no longer are the
forms of steeds or features of men visible, flying columns and
flashing fire form a dense and lurid cloud, from which thunders
are heard. Just discernible in the distance, on either side are
the motionless masses of French cavalry and the Arab horsemen.

"The growing night lends enchantment to the scene ; the
enthusiasm of the vast assemblage of spectators, the fierce
rage of the riders, perhaps not quite simulated, now recalling
their once lofty ascendency and the fierce carnage which has
as yet scarcely ceased to destroy ; the pressure of their con-
querors, and their own vast numbers and martial aspect ; at
such a moment what breast will not glow with hope revived !
The presence of ancient chieftains, the recollection of successes
not twenty years ago, fresh in the memory of many, still kept
alive by prophecies of restoration ; all these and more influences and sympathies invest the Corridas of north Africa with
an interest belonging to no European spectacle ; an interest
closely akin to that which belongs to the field of battle alone,
or to those semi-barbaric displays of chivalry familiar to past
centuries of the (old) world, or to the regions remote from
civilization of South America or of the East.

" My description does but feebly present the reality. The
scene of yesterday was to *me* but as a theatrical performance
in which the heart takes no share, for all was unreal ; a costly
pageant, the mimickry of action and of life. I could, however,
with difficulty say this of the part the Arabs took. To this
scarcely civilised people, the sentiments of simple ages are preserved with the manners, customs, dress, and habitations,
religion and traditions of their fathers. There is no question

that the Arab of the present hour is the Arab of the seventh
century, his dress unchanged since Mahomet's hordes subjugated fallen and corrupted Christendom; his tent and its
antiquated furniture, the few and rude implements of
manufacture, and of agriculture, material wealth in flocks
and herds, his domestic institutions, political administration, all carry us back to the earlier centuries of the Christian era, nay, from all we can gather from the most reliable
history, and from all that observation and analogy seem
to teach—to the very patriarchal ages, the earliest period of
history of the human race. Strange it seems to me, and not
less sad than strange, that extremes so wide apart should thus
so closely approximate ; that the march of progress has reached
no further onward, that civilisation is arrested by the feeble
barrier of an almost extinguished nationality. That the
Gospel, that only effectual regenerator of nations, stays its
course of bloodless victory, and leaves the Mahometan on the
confines of Christendom. The walls of Jericho have fallen
before the blast of its trumpet, but the feeble hosts of our
Israel hesitate to go up to take possession !

" It will show you something of my position here, to relate
what has occurred while writing to you this letter. My servant called me. I went to the door, and saw approaching the
house an Arab mounted on the back of a mule, attended by
three others in white dresses. They were coming up the
avenue of mulberry trees to my house. I immediately recognised an Arab chief, who lives in the mountains, about forty
miles off, whom I visited last year in his camp. I went forward to greet him, he alighted from his mule, and walked with
me to the house. I ordered his mule to the stable, and racked
my brain how to entertain my guest. Arabs are hospitable,
and expect hospitality. I had little in the house, having just
dined, and was intending to go to Oran with my letters ; however, I found half a loaf, and some melons. Coffee was put on
the fire, and my guests were well contented, the melons being
very good, and a great treat to them. I sent to the village
for more melons, some bread, &c. ; till these arrived I amused
the simple folk by displaying treasures from England. The

bright polished barrels of the gun you gave me were much admired, also a small pistol of six barrels, a hearthrug with a lion pourtayed upon it, some prints, books, Arabic bible, &c.

" The sun had now set, and my guest commenced to take off his burnous; I thought he was going to sleep after his hearty meal, as he soon appeared clad in white, his turban replaced by a sort of nightcap.    He asked for water, and then turned to the west, then to the east, and bowed himself to the ground, repeating words which I understood not.    It was the hour of prayer !

" His companions, however, took no notice of this, they continued talking and laughing, and eating their melons and bread.    I waited very silently and seriously till he had finished, lamenting sorrowfully the absence of that true devotion through the Mediator, which alone is well pleasing to God, and I looked out in the Arabic bible such passages as John iii. 3, &c. &c., to show to my friend.    Coffee, and more melons, and bread loaves were brought in, to which he did full justice.    I then expressed my intention of going to Oran—it being the day for despatch of the mails, and offered to leave him to keep house for me, sleeping upon my Turkey carpet and lion rug.    He lay down and expressed his satisfaction, but soon said that his wife was in Oran, and that " where the wife was the husband ought to be," so we prepared to travel together.    I intended to walk to the town, but no, he would have me ' nearer to him,' so I mounted his mule.

"The chief, a very stout old man, the broad pack saddle, a sack of provender, and myself,—we concealed every portion of the poor animal but his tail and the tips of his ears !!"

## CHAPTER XX.

### THE FARM.

IN the working of his farm Mr Ogle had his full share of the perplexities and disappointments which beset every colonist in Algeria.    These arise from a great variety of causes.    Seed, implements, and other things have to be imported from Britain, but the shipping arrangements are such as to occasion many and most vexatious delays. The regulations of the custom-house, in many instances unnecessarily strict and annoying, are rendered doubly so not unfrequently by the caprice and imperi-ousness of the officials to whom the display of their own authority is often a matter of more consequence than the protection of the interests of commerce or of revenue. Another great draw-back is the insecurity of property in Algeria. To guard it in the presence of reputed thieves, which swarm on every side, is both troublesome and expensive. The processes of law are tedious; and even when one has gained his plea, one is as far as ever from his object. The party has fled, it may be, into the desert, or into the mountains, where one cannot follow him. The climate, too, is uncertain. Were the shower to come in its season the land would yield an hundred-fold, but month may pass after month, and still a burning sun is blazing in a cloudless sky, and the hopes of the husbandman perish. The earth is turned into cinders and the crops die. A system of irrigation, such as the Moors employed in the southern provinces of Spain, would remedy the evil, and make the farmer independent of the rainfall; but in Algeria there is no irrigation; no one thinks of conducting the streams of the Atlas over the plain of Oran, as those of the Sierra Nevada were made to flow over the Vega of Granada, and so the sun is left to do his work upon the unprotected soil, and the farmer is left to look and long for the shower which never falls at all, or falls only after his crop has been destroyed. And besides all this, not the least of the difficulties which attend farming in Algeria is the indolence and indocility of the natives. Reared in utter idleness and ignorance, you cannot make them industrious and skilful labourers. They are inveterately set upon their own methods, those which have been handed down from their fathers, and you cannot break them into yours; they either will not do what you wish, or they do it at the wrong time, and as well they had not done it at all. They are moreover improvident and wasteful, and often destroy the property which it is their duty to care for and preserve. Such are the uncertainties and perplexities amid which farming is carried on in Algeria. Mr Ogle's object, as we have already said, in the extensive agricultural operations in which he embarked, was in no degree gain, but he not unreasonably hoped that the farm would be self-supporting. He set the low price paid to the French government for the land, and its naturally fertile character, over against the uncertainties and drawbacks which he foresaw, believing that the one would be found a counterbalancing compensation for the other. But it did not so turn out. The difficulties, as will appear in the sequel, were found insurmountable, though at first the prospect was promising.

"I find my farm," writes Mr Ogle, "answer in the one particular for which I have undertaken it—the evangelistic opportunities it affords to me. All my work-people (who are Spaniards) come of their own free will to listen to me while I read to them the New Testament, (a book, till then, never seen by any of them), and they stay with me for conversation and prayer till quite late on in the night.

"I do not try to proselytise men, but to make them Bible Christians, and to fortify their minds by the knowledge of the truth, &c., that they may follow the more excellent way."

In *June* 1860 he speaks of a marvellous opening and means of enlargement, help, favour, and blessing, though with trials, of patience and failure intermixed, and thinks he ought not to allow minor considerations to prevent his continuance in the country.

"*October* 29.—I cannot think it right to give all my time and energies to make the farm answer; that were to neglect the opportunities of usefulness which I seek wherever I find a door open — and yet I cannot afford to neglect the farm altogether. I desire to benefit temporally the Spaniards as well as to seek their eternal good, but I cannot afford to lose all I have expended in this matter, and yet alas, alas, I do lose, and very vexatious are the difficulties I encounter. V— spends my money unnecessarily, destroys my property, wastes the provender, allows my horses to be injured, and is most insolent and abusive on the occasion of quite a gentle rebuke. I am silent in return, for I know he is put up by others, and if I relinquish the opportunity of doing him good, I miss the object for which I undertook the work. After all, I know not a more honest man. He has been led by others, and if I turn him off, he will fall with his family into the wretched state in which he was before I took him—starving, sick, and miserable. It is a perplexity in which I am tempted greatly to be angry. I could enlarge further, but have said enough to enable you to comprehend my position."

In November, however, the accounts were more cheering, his forbearance had been rewarded by a return to duty on the part of his servant, and on taking a retrospective view, he says :—

" *November* 12*th.*—I am very full of business. I have now a farm of nearly one thousand acres. I am endeavouring to arrange all things so prudently, that I hope to show my books some day against the Moravian and Patagonian missions, to compare expenses and results ! I believe a large undertaking will be found to be less expensive in the end, because more generally remunerative than a very small one. I have among the persons employed upon my land, Arabs as shepherds ; Moors as reapers of the crops ; Spaniards and French as labourers. Thus I am brought into close contact with many people, and I thank God it has not been without result, though from my own failings and deficiencies these are but small as yet."

Mr Ogle did not deem his family circle broken, though one

part of it was in England and the other in Africa. Thoughts and associations are the links which bind mind to mind and heart to heart. These disdain material boundaries, and bring together, in sympathy and communion, those whom space divides. There is no doubt a more sacred bond which unites all Christians, and a more glorious centre, where they all meet, but this did not hinder Mr Ogle bringing into requisition the ties of old festivities and customs to effect, as it were, a family re-union—to join Africa with England, at the time of Christmas. This he made subservient, as he did everything else, to the great missionary object which he had in view. Thus we find him writing, December 24th.

" To-day I have been preparing for a Christmas dinner to-morrow, to be given at the farm. All my labourers and their wives will be there. My head is rather confused, for I have to execute impossibilities; to be profuse without affluence and without prodigality; to unite discordant natures and jarring interests; to influence aright an assembly of persons little used to Christian sentiments. I hope to make a profitable as well as pleasurable use of the occasion. Turkeys, geese, calf, ox, gazelle, contribute their quota. I shall do my best in the spirit of David. It is my duty in my present circumstances to share the joys, and to contribute to the pleasures of those I seek to influence. I have before experienced the beneficial result of such efforts, and must sacrifice my taste to theirs. I remember that David, on entering upon his apparently desperate struggle—the shepherd boy against the envious monarch —with no other comfort than the promise of his anointing, and with confidence in the Divine protection and blessing, invited to his company the outcast, the bankrupt, and the distressed. 1 Sam. xxii. 2. Four hundred men! Oh the faith, the courage, the reliance upon God, requisite for such an enterprise! David's son now struggles with Saul's master for ascendency. His men on earth must share the fortunes of their predecessors, and imitate their example of constancy. Pray for this grace for your brother John."

## 1861.

He determined during this year to give the farm a fair trial, by devoting more time and thought to its management, and by adopting a better system of husbandry than the Algerian. He accordingly sent to England for thrashing and reaping machines. The expenses of the undertaking made some decisive change necessary.

"ORAN, *January* 1861.—I cannot but hope that God's providence follows my steps. This week I have sown a good breadth of land with wheat. Now in this country it often happens that the seed lies for months without rain (because of the uncertainty of the seasons), but we have had abundant showers. I notice this the more because the most fertile portion of my land was not sown last week. I perceived signs of rain, and sent express to say, 'Sow such a field, rain is coming,' the field was sown, and now the harvest may be said to be in great measure secure. The hope may be disappointed, but I do not so distrust 'Ebenezer.' I will cherish that frame, and though my sins deserve all affliction, I will trust in the mercies of the Lord, which are greater than our sins.. . . . . To-day I have placed a Bible and a Pilgrim's Progress (Spanish) in a hitherto Godless family, with good hope that they are valued, and that they will be useful. Your schedule of subjects for the week of prayer is very encouraging. I received it in time to direct my thoughts to it on Monday. The subject of Christian union on an evangelical basis had been on that day already occupying my mind.

"*January* 1861.—My sowing is concluded, so I am going with Mr M—— into the interior for a few days, *D.V.* I anticipate much enjoyment. The weather is beautiful, hot sun, cool air, bright sky, verdure, flowers. I hope to have some interesting accounts to give on my return. Shall try to do some good. Oh may grace and wisdom be given! Yesterday and to-day have been days, I hope, of much usefulness, indeed, I cannot remember one day last week which was not. My own heart alone is a cause of humiliation."

To his brother :—

"I went with my guests to the mountains. They shot a gazelle, hares, and partridges. I the meanwhile did, as I hope, some work for my Master, so that, though I carried my gun, I did not fire it. . . . my work is like yours, the healing of the diseased. Oh what a lazar-house is here. Thank God, the sick do not reject the visits of their physician though they have not confidence in him as yet. I could fill twenty sheets with details of interesting conversations I have held. To me, the fact of having to speak in foreign languages makes these an intellectual effort, but I have always found that the more serious the subject, the more ready I am, and the better understood. I do hope I seldom fail to make my hearers comprehend what I feel to be really of importance to their soul's health."

As to the state of the clergy, he writes :—

"The clergy (Romanist) are just now so embroiled one with another, and propagate respecting each other such serious scandal, founded it must be confessed upon facts known to all men, that we may consider the power of the Church of Rome over the people's mind to be, for the time, almost gone, and its interdicts against the Scriptures are consequently being called in question. The Spanish 'Cura' (priest) has replied to the reproofs of his superiors in letters ably written, breathing, not much of the Christian spirit, but repudiating the kind of authority claimed over him, quoting Holy Scripture and the Fathers to prove his point. This priest was sent here, we believe, specially on account of our little mission to Spaniards, and to defeat it. The Spaniards are very much changed of late in their behaviour. I have received the most friendly treatment, and had my books welcomed, even in a place where of late I abstained to visit, because they threatened to stone me the last time I was there. This threat I know from a former experience was not intended to be a vain one. Shall I give up my efforts then, when such facts are before me ? No : losses are not a ground for concluding that we ought not go forward,—they are a token that we must not rely on material or temporal aid."

BEN SABBIA, *February* 1861.—"It is from the summit of an African mountain I write. All around is in primitive wildness, I alone a civilized creature. I have just read that verse in Psalm cxix., 'I am a stranger upon earth, hide not thy commandments from me.' While I use the prayer, I feel how truly I deserve to have the will of God hidden from me ; as it is from the land in which I am a stranger, and am thankful that it is not as I deserve.

"I have a beautiful Spanish hymn lying on my paper which I have translated thus :

'From scenes of strife and tumult far to flee
From the vain world, O Lord, I seek to Thee ;
Those haunts my soul abhors where Satan raves,
Spreads his vile snares and makes mankind his slaves.

'The lone retreat, the tranquilizing shade,
For praise, for prayer, for lamentation made,
By thy kind hand disposed, I seem to see,
For those who through this world will follow Thee.
Here if thy Spirit breathes upon my soul,
If grace divine my bosom's storms control,
In peace and love with joy I may aspire
To offer up to heaven the sacred fire,
The sacrifice of praise and love I owe
For mercies multiplied. Thus here below,
Unseen as those above, commence the song,
To be perfected there, 'mid yon celestial throng.'

"I look over from here to the snowy Sierras of old Spain, and long for the time when they shall be still more beautiful with the beauty of the 'feet upon the mountains of the heralds of the gospel of peace,' when the kingdom of Jesus shall be exalted above these hills of earth. Let Christians unite in destroying the snares of Satan, and the mysterious entanglements of iniquity and of falsehood, by which he holds that beautiful land in slavery."

## THOUGHTS ON USEFULNESS.

. . . "Enlarge your schemes for usefulness;" says he, writing to his sister, February 11, 1861, "try to do and to

spend in the cause of God more—more than your share—
plenty of persons will do and spend less than theirs.    But the
most useful and the most blessed are those *personal* efforts in
which money takes but a small part.    It is the heart of love
with the hand of liberality which does most good and with
least materials.    I have a longing to stir you up to what I
imagined would be a higher usefulness than you have at present attained to, and to the acquisition of a loftier character.
We must both seek these at the same source, viz., the Mount
of Calvary, and the village of Bethany.    To be ' risen with
Christ—to come to the Mount Zion, the heavenly Jerusalem,
the innumerable company of angels'—Heb. xii., the realization
of the blessed privileges of which I was speaking yesterday to a
sick Christian lady ; the glorious common hopes of all Christians, of whatever land, distinguished though they be by many
different names on earth."

## DISAPPOINTMENT.

The time of sowing for the Algerian harvest is dependent
upon the fall of rain in January.    This sowing accomplished,
if heavy rains again fall the seed springs up quickly, and an
abundant harvest is ready in the month of May, or even in
April.    This year the February rains were withheld, the
ground remained arid and dry, and the fair prospect of a good
harvest, mentioned in a previous letter, was in a few weeks
rendered hopeless.    Nothing but desolation, disappointment,
and loss, could be reported to his anxious friends as far as
the farm was concerned.    But, though not insensible to the
disappointment, he took comfort in other considerations.
In the hope of promoting the spiritual interests of his neighbours, he found a relief from his own disappointments.

    " My loss will be small in comparison with that of a
neighbouring colonist, a Dane, a very industrious and deserving
man.    I must do all I can to help him, that he may not
just now be ruined.    God grant that the broken-hearted

W. —— and his wife may find a blessing come after their reverses and disappointments. I have great hopes to be able to introduce religion into this house. Affliction has, I trust, prepared the way.

" This man had seventy-five acres of flax a month ago in the most flourishing condition, and worth 15,000 francs; it was a beautiful sight; now not a blade of grass is to be seen, and the fields of corn are yellow as a stubble field in England."

## The Drought.

*April*, 1861.—" It is indeed sad to see the crops one after another turn yellow and wither. The grain not being yet formed, and the leaf being still tender, it curls up and shrivels. If you pull up a stalk, the roots are found to be perfectly dry and mossy. In fact, the grain which was sown dies in the earth, and perishes from the root upwards. The sight of my blighted hopes for a good harvest so disconcerts me, that I long to leave the desolate neighbourhood; but the arrival of the reaping and the threshing machines will keep me at my post. . . . . Whether I can say that I have the consolation of firm confidence in God, I can hardly tell. I have a dread of saying too much on this head. Alas, I feel that I need and merit chastisement from Him, and I regard my trouble in that light. . . . . My earnest prayer is, that our All-merciful and gracious Father in heaven may renew daily my fallen nature; make me single-eyed, simply and solely devoted to His service, and to do all things to His glory for Jesus' sake."

## Landing the Threshing and Reaping Machines.

The Farm, Figuier, near Oran, *May* 14, 1861.

" My dear Brother,—It is long since I wrote from the Farm, the fact is, I have not often been there, and so what was bad has perhaps, if possible, become worse. However, I am going to try to write in a more cheerful strain. It may be that even when we speak of real misfortunes, we are complaining, murmuring, unless we are careful to acknowledge that all is

infinitely less than we deserve.    Jacob says, 'Few and evil
have been the days of the years of my life,' and yet his spirit
was not complaining, for we find him acknowledging himself
'less than the least of all the mercies' which he had received.

"I have had this day occasion to acknowledge mercies.    *The
Reaper has been at work*, and I have made my 'wave sheaf.'
It was literally such.    I will give you the history a little *in
extenso*.

"A week has been spent in getting the machines: there was
a host of difficulties, as is always the case in French affairs.
Everything is under *administration*, and nothing proves so
great a source of satisfaction as 'something to do' for the
1000 officials, who mend their pens, and write their names, or
draw caricatures from sheer inanity.    When *something to do*
comes, then their wits are to seek, and their books of regulations,
and their inferior authorities to be consulted.    You wait two
or three hours, and then 'must come to-morrow,' when the
Sub-inspector will have seen the *chef de Bureau*, and the latter
have decided the knotty point.    I had my share of these annoyances.    First I brought ashore and took to the custom-house a
part of the goods.    This was 'contrary to law.'    I ought to have
had a permit to disembark, and the consequence was a 'proces
verbal,' which means a 'summons,' fine, forfeiture of goods, &c.
&c.    So I was glad to get the matter overlooked, and to be
allowed to re-embark the affairs, but I was to make a 'declaration' to state precisely what I had to import.    I pleaded
inability, not having received any particulars from England.
'Twas but an excuse for a considerable fee.    Then there was
a 'company having monopoly of the quay,' the use of crane,
boats, &c.    These gentlemen engaged to put on shore my
machines in the course of *three or four days*.    'On shore' is
not 'chez vous,' and the Ports of Avernus, the Douane, were
not passed.    The company that debarked expected to be paid
extravagantly to carry them to the custom-house, so I resolved
to do this myself, but how? you know what a threshing-
machine is.    Two pieces of furniture, weighing one and a half
ton each, have to be set on wheels, and then transported.    I
was in some difficulty, for, though the machine in general is

familiar, yet when it is in pieces, and you have no directions, or plan, the reconstruction is not so simple a matter, as at first sight it looks. However I made no confidants of my perplexity, and knowing there would be no one here who had ever seen a threshing machine, I resolved to work out the problem for myself; I took particular note of each piece, and after a little study made out the greater part of them, and fixed a day on which to perform the operation. I had eight Moors or Arabs and two Spaniards, with my man from the farm, and succeeded in sorting the pieces, placing them, and in directing the whole reconstruction, without a halt. When I came to lifting the large piece, a lucky observation did me immense service. I remarked the place of the wheels, and from thence deduced the centre of gravity, so that the crane should work easily. ' Here,' said I, ' is the centre of the weight, put the rope here.' There was a little dispute because it looked wrong, however some one said, ' the master says it is here, so it must be put here ; ' the crane was hoisted, and the piece entire swung in air, poised as on a pivot, to the admiration of all. Next I mounted my machine ; it was found to be so very manageable, notwithstanding the weight and the awkward length, that they all said, ' The English were no fools, and that the machine must have cost a mint of money, and that I was a magician, that the colony would march now that the Anglais sent their machinery to help it, &c.' A Spaniard remarked ' What a pity that all I knew and all I had, would be of no use to me, for I did not believe in God above.' This gave occasion to a discussion between my Protestant Spaniard and the speaker, at the close of which the bystander said that he wished they would tie all the priests by the neck and consign them to —, so the matter went on. It would be too long to describe all the trouble we had, to weigh the pieces of the machine, for this was *sine quâ non* at the douane, and I was told that I must after all send to England to have a certificate of ' origin and weight,' and deposit a plan with the proper authorities, &c., &c., and that, perhaps, in two or three months I should have the use of my machines ! At last I was allowed to carry them to a weighing machine, the use of which was with difficulty obtained, but we had now to construct a platform to allow the wheels to pass on the weighing frame. Then back to the Douane where, as 550 francs were demanded, I was stopped, not having the money. This was Saturday night. Monday morning I got the money, and paid it in hard cash, received my permission to carry off the goods and chattels, brought cart, horses, and men, and entered upon the last stage of the operation. Now another species of difficulty occurred, viz., to satisfy the various demands,—extra-official. We started at length in good order. A villanous ascent brought one of the three vehicles to a stop. A mule unaccustomed to such work refused it, and we were nearly backing down the hill, into a heap of barrels and merchandise among men and animals, if not into the *port* at the bottom of the descent. However all ended well. I was to be seen rushing about : putting stones under, and spokes into, the wheels, &c. The result is here we are, and to-day the ' wave sheaf' has been lifted with a silent prayer, and a vociferated ' Hurrah.'"

The arrival of this agricultural machinery was the occasion of the manifestation of an increase of good feeling, and Mr Ogle sought to turn it to good account. The principal and other inhabitants of the district were invited to the farm, to witness its working, now, for the first time, introduced into this colony. Practical men at home heard with no less surprise than was experienced by the uninitiated witnesses abroad, of the successful landing and setting up and working of these advanced instruments of English husbandry, by one who had never either superintended their use at home, or had the opportunity of closely observing them in action. The occurrence is interesting as showing the vigour with which he addressed himself to whatever lay before him, and the ability he possessed, quickly to make himself master of a subject, and to bring his knowledge into practical use. " My Cambridge studies in mathematics enabled me to poise, and to put together that unknown and ponderous machinery."

But it was the constraining power of the ardent desire to prove himself a real benefactor to those whom he longed to make willing to listen to the elevating doctrines and saving knowledge of the gospel of God, which actuated him in this as in the daily efforts of disinterested self-denial to which he submitted.

He records with the greatest pleasure, not the satisfaction which it were natural to every man to feel at the accomplishment of a difficult project, but " that I have had useful conversations with my neighbours. I am now acknowledged to be a public benefactor. If I go on humbly and diligently, there is, I believe, good ground for the hope that my highest expectations will be fulfilled." . . . .

## The Greater Freedom.

" The reaping machines have created quite a sensation here, though they will not now be of any use to me this year. I have lent one to a neighbouring colonist, and he has used it successfully for a late crop which has not suffered so much from the drought as my own has done.

" I have many opportunities now for conversation upon religious subjects. I have been able boldly to declare the truth and to preach the gospel in a long and very interesting conversation, at which both —— and ——, persons of civil and ecclesiastical importance were present and took a part. I can now more freely distribute books, and enquirers will come more freely. The state of feeling among the people is so much better in times of adversity like this, that I prefer suffering with them. During prosperous years wickedness of every kind is so rife that I cannot but hail adversity, and they are now quite willing to be instructed and talked to by me."

In a letter in which he mentions a robbery which had taken place on his property, he says :—

" It is, however, only wonderful that I have not lost more

T

of my property here, considering the state of society, and that Algeria is the safety-valve for redundant criminality in Spain, France, Italy, and Morocco—the Botany Bay of Europe. The poor Arabs are always blamed when losses occur, but I believe them to be the most honest of all the inhabitants. Some of my things, I hear, are at the police office, having been found in the house of the thief."

The following extracts do more than show us the obstacles Mr Ogle encountered, and the efforts he made to overcome them. They present us with a deplorable picture of the moral state of the inhabitants, and they teach us that nothing but the most patient and persevering Christian efforts can ever rescue them from the abyss in which they are sunk. Nothing but the gospel need be tried in a case like this ; nor will even the gospel gain its end in the thorough eradication of such evils, save in the slow course of successive generations.

### HARVEST—A SPANISH SERVANT.

"On coming to my farm to-day I found one Spaniard (the overlooker) mending an old door, my horses standing still, and the threshing-machine in consequence stopped, the other men variously employed contrary to my orders, the corn wasting in the fields; that brought home had been thrown into heaps on the ground, instead of (as when I am present) being properly stacked. I set to work with the man to put things in order, but he soon tired, saying, he had 'a bad foot,' took his chattels and *walked off* to a place six miles distant, where, after two days, I found him smoking a cigar in one of my houses, with his wife and family, who had taken possession also of one of my private rooms. He had the effrontery to ask me to give him a certificate of good service, and to lend him a cart and a horse that he might go to the mountains and earn his living without servitude. This gipsey sort of life is what the poorest and most degraded of the population lead. I wrote out for him a sketch of his past history before I gave

him employment, of the poverty, sickness, and destitution in
which I found him, the comfort in which he at present lived,
and the ruin which he would bring upon himself and family.
I reminded him that I had, at some trouble, got for him comfortable furniture, had enabled him to pay his debts, and that
he now had about 100 francs of his own.   This sketch I then
read to him, and told him I should not let him go.   The fact
is, I do not think him a bad man.   No.   He is a Spaniard.
He has in many things proved himself to be an honest man,
and is really attached to me, and to my religion.   His faults
are those of a nation long abandoned to luxury, idleness, im-
providence, and pride.   I ought, therefore, to bear with him,
and not to chase him from me.   May He, who pardons so
many far more grievous offences in me, give me grace, by His
spirit of wisdom and of love, to act as His steward in this
matter.   The social state here is bad—from head to foot
corrupt.   In the dearth of a benign and wholesome influence,
the moral condition of most men is far below the most
ordinary standard in England, and this seems to impose upon
me a course of action towards offenders against my property,
different and more lenient than I should adopt under a better
state of things.   There are some from whom I have suffered
far more seriously than from the one in question."


### TRIAL AND APPROBATION OF REAPING-MACHINE.

"Now I must give an account of my successes to counterbalance the impression I may have so far produced on your
mind respecting 'the farm,' and my feelings respecting it.   I
was sent for express to meet the Inspector of Colonisation for
the province of Oran, that the threshing and reaping-machines
might be inspected.   With two soldiers instructed by my
neighbour Mons. ——, I reaped at the rate of seven or eight
acres a-day.   We have a little altered the reaping-machine so
as to leave the crop slit in 'winlows' of considerable bulk, so
that a cart may at once follow the machine.   Two men can
thus both reap and gather up the corn, and this we did with
very little loss of grain.   The Inspector expressed himself well

satisfied with the machine and with the work done; of the reaper he said, 'it is precisely what is wanted for this colony.' I shall send you his report when it appears in the 'Official Journal.' Thus far I am satisfied that, if God blesses, I can make my farm self-supporting. This year is, I am told, an exceptional one. The Major of the commune tells me that he has not seen the like in twenty years. He has a large field of arable land—one half is level, the rest slightly inclined—all has been cultivated and sown with wheat. What do we now behold? On one half the crop is heavy, on the other, which is sloping ground like mine, all is withered and burnt up, and will not be worth cutting. Is not this disappointment sent to me for some other end than merely to exercise my patience and to correct my faults? I know it is the Christian's duty to use every effort within his power to spread abroad the knowledge of the gospel of Christ, and as far as I know myself, I do not allow any inferior object to rule my actions. The establishment of Christ's kingdom of peace and righteousness on earth is what I long and labour for. Perhaps I have given to the secular element a disproportionate share in my personal service. There are two methods of working, one by the special employment of material aids, such as our position, money, talents, &c., the making friends of the mammon of unrighteousness, the putting out to usury the talents entrusted; the other, the more spiritual method, simply trying to spread the gospel. I think I am not as yet called to the exclusive employment of the spiritual method in this land. Obstacles to my future progress may arise—failure of health, political disturbances, providential visitations, human counteraction. These risks belong to every enterprise. To listen to such apprehensions would be to cease from all labour. The world would become a desert, and mankind sink into a savage state! Ebenezer is the word I would rather inscribe as the waymark of my journey.

"The great safeguard we possess against mistakes in respect to our course in life, is that we are guided by the will of God. He alone knows 'our frame,' our capacities, our talents, our opportunities. He alone knows what will result from the complications which will arise, partly from ourselves, partly from others, above all from His own providence. That providence, I mean, which seems to *allow* rather than to *direct*; that providence which yet restrains, as He pleases, the erring ways of well-intentioned ignorance, as well as the perverse ways of wicked men."

## CONTROVERSY.

" A Spanish priest has been writing to one of our Spanish Protestants, ' What is the difference between Protestantism and Catholicism? tell me, oh ignorant and blind, and I will convince and confound thee.' In reply, I have written for the latter a long letter, and have read it for the instruction of others. Have also invited our Curè to meet me in a public or a private manner, that we may discuss the great points whereupon we differ, but he has declined the challenge. He does not dare defend his own creed, nor attack mine.

" The mayor of the commune has now given me permission to give books and to instruct privately (*i.e.* quietly) all who come to me. My way is slowly opening, and very few opponents now present themselves; while persons who are really inclined to Protestantism do very often. Since I can say this, it is not much if I am a pecuniary loser by my farm. . . . . There is a crook in every lot, and if I had not the oppressive burden of the knowledge that government prohibits my work for Christ, I should find all others easy to bear." . . . .

### INTERVIEW BETWEEN THE GOVERNOR AND FRENCH PASTEURS.

The following interview between His Excellency the Governor of Algeria and the French pasteurs has its interest. We do not know that the evils complained of were ever remedied, or the hope of better arrangements which the words of the Duke appeared to hold out ever realized, but the conversation which passed between them shows very affectingly the exceedingly feeble and depressed condition of French Protestantism in the colony of Algeria. The interview is recorded in a letter of date November 12th, 1861 :——

"The Governor (the Duc de Malakoff) has given great pleasure to the worthy French pasteurs by calling for them at the audience, and talking to them some time, hearing patiently, and entering into their difficulties in a remarkable manner.

"The following conversation took place :—

"'How many Protestants are in Oran?'

"'About three hundred.'

"'How many temples, and what provision for those at a distance?'

"Here the pasteur complained that there were not any pasteurs in the provinces, and stated that he and his colleague are obliged to make long journeys, thereby causing great neglect of home claims, and of spiritual instruction generally.

"*Governor*—'In case of death, how are the last offices performed (in those cases)?'

"*Pasteur*—'One of the members of the Church reads a portion of Holy Scripture, and a prayer is offered.'

"*Governor*—'Ah! and in baptism of infants?'

"*Pasteur*—'This is a cause of much sorrow to us. Many parents call the Curè (the priest) to baptise our infants. Thus the children of Protestant parents are claimed as Catholics.'

"With some surprise His Excellency remarked : 'Since baptism implies the duty of bringing up the child in the tenets of the community baptising, I would for my part prefer to baptise my child myself rather than give it to the minister of a creed which I did not approve.'

"*Pasteur*—'I entirely agree with you, but, unfortunately, many parents attach much importance to a black coat and white cravat.'

"*Governor*—'Aye, aye : that is true. Well, I will try to arrange your affairs better for you.'"

## THE BIBLE DEPÔT.

. . . . "Every day brings as usual its average amount of purely missionary work. I do not, however, record these details, they would have little variety for you. Pray for me.

. . . . " The Bible depôt has been very successful ; twenty-two Bibles were sold during the first month, and these sales continue. The priestly party are very irate ; but have not been able to overthrow the work. I have before me an evidence of its usefulness. It is a printed letter from one of the most intelligent French citizens of Oran (who bought a Bible at the depôt some weeks ago). In this letter he gives his views upon ' The right and duty of reading the Bible,' arguing very well, from the Scriptures, and quoting all the well-known passages upon the subject. He asks conclusively, ' How can the Scriptures be ' searched,' be meditated upon, be in the heart, how can they make us wise unto salvation, if they are locked up and prohibited ? ' etc.

"There are, I verily believe, quite a considerable number of Protestants at heart, among those to whom I have the opportunity of speaking of these things; but if I were to say anything of conversions to God, I should speak more hesitatingly. The time for a shaking among the dry bones may yet come."

In answer to a letter containing queries respecting the customs of Algeria, Mr. Ogle sent the following notes :—

"The grain is kept in places like cellars under ground. I have one thirty feet deep which has never been used, because the crops have been so poor ; but in an ordinary year it would be used. In a good year the wheat is often five or six feet high, but this year, although a little rain fell late, the best stalks were but a foot in length, and the ears almost all gaping, only three or four grains in each, and many were quite empty. These cellars are lined with masonry in towns, and can be fastened up by a trap door, chambers are often made at the sides of the original hole. If I had a good year, and wanted more room, I should send men down to excavate a chamber. No barns nor granaries above ground are ever built; these pits protect against rats and insects. As the ground si perfectly dry, and no rain falls except at certain times of the year, there is no trouble with them. The Arabs use the same plan ; are careless about their ' holes,' often have them open, and they are dangerous in the night time. When I was sleeping among the Arabs, my dog was lost, he had fallen into one of these. The wells for water are a source of danger too, sometimes, for they are unfenced. Four pigs fell down my well (which is a hundred and twenty feet deep) the other day, in their eagerness to get at the water, which is drawn for them. When the herd is too large to drink all at once at the troughs provided, they rush wildly about, and these four scrambled up the slight fence which I had erected round my well, and fell in ; two of them were taken out alive.

"This, I think, explains how necessary it was found in the East to have the well's mouth guarded by a stone, and how useful Jacob's help would be to Rachel. In this country, a man generally goes an hour before the time of watering the flocks to draw the water which is necessary."

## A Day's Work.

"*December.*—To-day has been like a fine day of April or May in England ; and it is the time of flowers and of verdure. It is the rainy season, but most days are fine. I have not had a wholly rainy day. My farm occupies me very much, but I find occasious to pursue the great work every day. You will, for instance, take the record of to-day. In the morning at the plough, (it is necessary to superintend all things), I talked with my ploughman respecting the ' mass' which he told me he was going to attend to-morrow, and showed him from Holy Scripture that it is not an *eating* in which the mouth takes part that is meant by the expression, ' Except ye eat the flesh of the Son of man,' &c. ; and he seemed to perceive that the soul must be benefitted by a *spiritual* exercise, and that we must receive our Lord Jesus Christ by faith in the heart. After this, others who came for worldly advice and temporal help received, with this, words of higher comfort and importance. On returning from work at the farm in the evening, I had a long and amicable conversation with several of my workmen upon religion, and concluded by reading the word of God and prayer with my Spanish servant. . . . . I find every day too short to finish the work I find to do, and all my powers too feeble. The season, so far, has been favourable for agriculture, and I have hopes that I shall (*D.V.*) next harvest realise my expectations. All my labourers seem to be attached to me, and all desire to continue in my service. Instead of finding it difficult to procure workmen, as is not unusual here, the only difficulty I foresee will be their dismissal when so many are no longer required. Had I not lost so large a sum last year, partly from the failure of my crops, and partly from frauds, I would find work for them till the coming harvest, but I cannot afford this, as I am paying wages at the rate of twenty pounds per month, and have other heavy expenses connected with the farm.

"Still I go on sowing in hope to receive the fruits of the earth in their season. May Jacob's lot be mine. I am, like him, in a far off land, and surrounded by those who act oftentimes unjustly; but if Jacob's God bless me, I need not fear. He will, I know, give me the portion that seemeth to Him good, and will keep me from evil. That prayer is often mine respecting my affairs here :—'Give me neither poverty nor riches; feed me with food convenient for me. . . . . That thine hand might be near me, and that thou wouldst keep me from evil, that it might not grieve me.'" . . . .

## A Zouave of the Garde.

"My Dear Sister,—It is at the close of a day of work I take up my pen to write my weekly letter. The wide house is still, and its busy world absorbed in sleep. As often happens, the master wakes. It is eight P.M., a brilliant moonlight recompenses the short day. Sunset is at 4.45 P.M., rather later than with you. It is the same moon which looks in at your window, and reminds us *both* that the Hand which made all these things 'is Divine.' It will fill my paper, and perhaps serve you for an hour's amusement, to describe *this day*. According to the prognostics of yesterday's cloudy sky, thermometer 57-61° in house, 61° at night, this has been a day of *rain*—a great and joyful event with us. The country was suffering, as it is the rainy season, and we have had a month without rain. I was beginning to fear for my year's work, and all were holding back. I am almost the only one in this commune who has done much ploughing. My neighbours are not inclined, and many are not able to sow much land. I have got from two to three hundred acres ploughed, and have sown some twenty, and had I not been led by the example of others, I should have sowed much more. Last year I had more sown than I have ploughed at this time, and I think I shall regret the different plan; but in culture very much depends on the particular season, which one cannot provide for, being in the Rule of One who declareth not His purposes. This thought I like very much. In agriculture one is so constantly led to think, all is just as God wills; for, though it is true *always*, it is more *evidently* so in this occupation. I grieve and am ashamed to think how little these thoughts are practical with me.

"The expectation of rain brought me to the farm on Monday. I had eight men at work, two of them new hands. I felt that if not there nothing would be done, and perhaps mischief might arise. So, though a little poorly, I got off to Oran early to receive my letters, and returned to the farm, fourteen miles, at mid-day. There is a coach at that hour which, as my riding horse is ploughing, is very convenient. A fellow passenger was a remarkable person—the bizarre half-oriental dress of a Zouave, or French African soldier, surmounted by a *white* turban, showed me it was not one of our Zouaves, for they wear *green* turbans.

"I asked, 'You are from Paris?' 'Yes.' 'Of the Emperor's Garde?' 'Yes.' 'You are going to Balbec?' &c. It was *no ordinary man*, as I saw at a glance. He spoke Arabic, and very few Zouaves are real Arabs, for it being the crack corps *de l'armée Française*, most of the Zouaves are cockney Frenchmen, and wild lads, '*mauvais sujets*.' When I had ten of them working harvest work, I thought myself well quit of them without loss or disturbance, and I got very little work out of them. The other day I met some of them on the road,

I stopped. 'Where are you off for now?' 'We are going to Mexico.' 'Oh! in company with the English? You will have something to tell of when you come back. May you always fight in a just warfare, and may God go with you and protect you.' 'Thank you, thank you. Good day.'

"One of these, perhaps these very men, at least a comrade, one who had been at the farm on that day, or the next, went into the house, no one but a little boy and girl being there at the time, took my best gun and went off. The little boy (nine years old), followed him crying. The country is wild, and there are no neighbours but Arabs. The girl ran to call her father, working a mile of, but the Zouave, alarmed by the child's importunity, gave him the gun! (they are *mauvais sujets* those Zouaves!) Well, to my Zouave of the *Garde*. Imagine a deeply chiselled wrinkled face, the forehead round and good, the head shaven high up, in African style, eyes dark, long fine eyelashes, a Roman nose, slight moustache and Imperial, and weather-beaten complexion. It might be a Turk by the eye and the general expression; but intelligence is written in the countenance, and self-respect, and there is a wide-awake and active air that does not befit a declining nationality. The Zouave takes advantage of a minute's delay to call a little Arab (such a one as Miss Whateley describes, who 'wished he were a girl'), saying in Arabic, 'Fetch bread for four sous, run, run, quick, quick.' The order was obeyed, though unrewarded, the Zouave remarking, he had had no time to eat. I offered some apples I had bought for two-pence half-penny a pound; but he declined, saying in Spanish, 'I prefer dry bread.'

"You have often had worse fare, I dare say, for I see you have seen service.' Medals of the *Crimea*, the beautiful Queen Victoria, with four clasps—'Alma,' 'Balaclava,' 'Inkerman,' 'Sebastopol,' showed a soldier comrade of England, who had gone through the Russian campaign. The Napoleon medal of the war in Italy, the good conduct medal, and the Croix, the medal of Honour,—each and all told their tale. I asked, 'Is the *Alma* anything like the *Sta Crux?*' (the mountain of Oran). I had an impression that our country

is just like the Crimea, and it is of the same geological
formation. 'Precisely.'

"Pointing to a part of the hill, I said, 'The Russian posi-
tion would be, as it were, on those lower hills, and you
Zouaves climbed up the steeps behind, and took them in rear?'
'Yes' (with a significant gesture.)

"'The river would be at the foot, and the English went over
it straight up to the enemy?' (How I wished I had got a
tract, one of the beautiful ones in French, written expressly
for the war, but I had none, and could not introduce the subject of religion). 'You are an African?' observing a blue
mark on his hand. 'Yes.'

"'How long in French service?' 'Fifteen years.' Ah!
thought I, what have not these fifteen years done for France,
and for the world. This Mahomedan instructed, disciplined,
civilised, but not Christianised, is one of the evidences.

"His pocket book contained letters of certificate and recom-
mendation, officers' cards, his service papers, and an 'Alphabet
des Enfants.' France, at least, has known what use can be
made of her annexed and usurped conquests. If France had
had India instead of Africa! India! vast, fertile, rich, popu-
lous, instead of a barren strip of coast, peopled by miserable
nomads, and destitute almost of the barest possibilities of
existence! France *has fought her way to be the first of
nations by means of these very Zouaves.* It was African
blood she shed so profusely in Italy, and it is by these very
baubles this man displays with such pride on his breast, these
four bits of metal (of which the English is the only one worth
a shilling!)—by these *bits* she rules this fierce and untame-
able Oriental nature—the representative of the Janisary of
Bajazet, or the follower of Islam! Well, at length I reached
the farm, one P.M. Not a man at work! Out they came,
and prepared to go to work. I scarcely said, 'Good morning,'
but looked at my watch, and soon found myself quarrelling
with Vicente. Is this the day to make festival? for it will
rain to-morrow, and then no work will be possible. They
were soon at work, and in less than an hour a heavy shower
soaked them to the skin."

The following ode, which would appear to have been written on the Taking of Sebastopol, may here not inappropriately find a place :—

## ODE TO PEACE.

Peace, lovely peace! how manifold thy charms;
Thy voice how grateful to a world opprest;
Thy gentle presence dissipates alarms,
To the vex'd nations thou restorest rest.

War's horrid features thou transformest all,
Changing destruction to fertility;
Widows shall bless thee, and the orphans call (wail)
Thou soothest with the tend'rest sympathy.

Great science with her sister industry
To bless the nations all in vain have striven,
Till thou return'st, and in blest company
Religion comes with charity from heaven.

The olive and the palm, the clust'ring vine,
The river, and the rock, resemble thee;
T' enrich, to cheer, to shelter, to refine,
To beautify, to spread felicity.

Then haste thee Peace, why tarry now thy flight?
Forth from thy lustrous pinions shake the dew;
War's night is o'er, the eastern skies are bright,
Rise lovely Peace, and the sad world renew.

J. F. O.

## CHAPTER XXI.

### TRIALS AND ENCOURAGEMENTS.

A VARIETY of matters does the following chapter bring under our notice. It shows us difficulties thickening round the path of our missionary-colonist, nevertheless the great object which brought him to Algeria is being steadily prosecuted, and we can mark advance in the midst of many outward discouragements and temporal failures; nor are we at a loss to discover, in Mr.

Ogle's own growing spirituality the secret springs which feed the strength of his heart, and keep his soul joyful in the midst of troubles. "In the world ye shall have tribulation, but in me ye shall have peace."

ORAN, *December.*—"Oh for that light of the Holy Spirit," says he, writing to his brother, "which is a word saying clearly, 'This is the way, walk ye in it.' For a heart wholly for Christ,—a fervent, ardent, constant, longing for His coming again to reign for ever! That time is not, I trust, far off. The state of the world accords with such a conclusion. I do not say the state of Africa; but of England, of America, of Europe. Oh day of joy and triumph, that which will make an end of sin and will bring in everlasting righteousness! the kingdom of our Lord and Saviour Jesus Christ. Purified, justified, sanctified, the elect shall enter upon a new condition, in which all shall harmonize, and nothing shall offend. Then no unprofitable toil, no violated engagements, no selfish and dishonest proceedings, creating confusion in society, and frustrating honest and benevolent endeavours.

"'We, according to His promise, look for new heavens and a new earth wherein dwelleth righteousness.' Fain would I have done something to renew this present world, to originate a little community that, Christian in profession, might reflect the Christian character, and, though in the world not be of it, but from day to day, I have seen my own christianity compromised, 'Peace and love and joy,' the fruits of the spirit do not exist here, but much that is selfish and much absolutely dishonest and wrong. Whether I have been able to effect any change in others I am not sure, the outward aspect of things is not in favour of the supposition, rather would it appear as if I had yielded to the current and am being borne along thereby."

The allusion here is to work which Mr Ogle had contracted for, and to be paid by a mutual benefit from the crops. This arrangement, customary in those parts, he made with a view to relieve himself from the secular work of his undertaking, and to lessen the risk in case of failure in the harvest. " I have been involved," he writes, " in Sabbath breaking. Yesterday five men at least and eight horses were in full work on my farm." To explain this it is necessary to bear in mind that in Algeria the principal market is held upon the Sabbath. It is the only day on which public auctions take place; ordinary employments, therefore, are attended to on that day by all who are not immediately under the control of a master who respects the Sabbath. In many letters the fact is mentioned that his expenses were often much increased by his determination neither to buy nor to sell, nor to permit farm work to be done upon the Sabbath day. His inadvertence in not inserting in the terms of his bargain that Sundays should be respected led to work being done on his farm on Sabbath, by the person with whom the contract was made, to Mr Ogle's great grief.

The weekly letters at this period are full of multiplied cares and anxieties; but they show that the most painful of his trials came from those for whose good he was labouring. How often has it been seen that the most difficult part of the work of reclaiming the sunken lies in their own unwillingness to be reclaimed. The slaves of spiritual tyranny are ever the greatest foes to their own emancipation. Where is the Reformer and Deliverer from Moses downward, who has not experienced to his poignant sorrow, the truth of this ? Governments and priesthoods may be powerful opponents, but the greatest opposition will ever be found to arise from the blindness, ingratitude, and perversity of their victims. The men to whom Mr Ogle was giving food and raiment, and whom he was labouring to instruct, were the men from whom his bitterest disappointments came. May we not apply the lesson to ourselves ? From whom come the great hindrances in the way of our salvation ? Do they not come from ourselves ? The opposition of Satan and of the world, our Divine Deliverer looks for and has overcome : but the blindness, thanklessness, wilfulness, and lusts of Christians themselves are to Christ more offensive than all. These "grieve" the Holy Spirit. But how amazing his love! He does not cast us off.

We cannot quote a tithe of the evidence to this effect with which Mr Ogle's letters abound : let the following extracts suffice. They are selected on the principle of exhibiting the peculiarities of the country and usages of its people at the same time.

*January* 20, 1862.—"The great advantage of my farm *was* that it was so situated as to have a right to the *free* pasturage of a 'Communal' on its borders; this advantage has just been taken from me by the *commune*. They have offered by auction the pasturage, on the plea that 'all are poor and have no flocks,' thus I am compelled to hire the necessary pasture ground, to save my cattle, for they cannot now be sold without great loss.

"Whole villages in this neighbourhood are depopulated in consequence of the failure of last year's harvest. This year promises well, and when we remember that North Africa was once a granary for Europe, it is easy to believe what is said, 'that last year was an exceptional year.' But I leave all in God's hand, He knows what is best.

"I hoped that the poor Spanish Protestants whom I employed, would have been honest and industrious; but this was not their character, and being in the midst of a population who are hostile to one's establishment among them, the difficulties I have had to encounter have been, and still are, very great; but I believe I am doing a good work. The Protestants are oppressed and very poor, and I am putting them in a way by which they can gain support for themselves and their families."

In another letter he says :—. . . . "I had a good flock of three hundred sheep;" many of these had been fraudulently sold by his shepherd. "It is the dishonesty of these things that troubles me."

## Arab Horse and Arab Woman.

"My horse, which was somewhat too gay for me, is now nearly quiet and carries me beautifully. He is a true Arab, comes into my parlour and eats soup out of a plate like a Christian; in fact, when he is pleased, he is as quiet as a lamb, but let his fiery nature be roused and he is wild as his native hills. I have adopted Rarey's plan, and have attached him to myself; but I fear we must part, and for the same reason that induced 'Hassan,' to part with his faithful steed—poverty. One does not wonder here at the value and importance attached to the Arab horse and the affection he inspires, he is the peculiar treasure of the country. The poor women are but miserable slaves, objects of any sentiment rather than of admiration. Prematurely aged by hardships, and generally ugly, the poor creatures have a miserable lot.

"I encourage a cheerful hope that I may be enabled to do some good among the poor Arabs. I see glimpses of such a day. My agricultural work is the ground-work of the picture. Green fields growing golden, and green hills white with sheep; free and happy Arabs careering on noble steeds and living their nomadic life under a Christian chief! laborious Spaniards singing blithe songs in well-cultivated fields and gardens gay! giving and receiving mutual benedictions with your loving brother John."

Sanguine hopes like these were necessary to sustain his perseverance in the work.

*April 22.*—"I am now happy in respect of the order and fidelity of my household, and when you are told that it includes thirty persons; members of different families and nations; viz., ten Mahommedan Arabs, eleven Spaniards (one a Protestant), the rest French, with occasional Jews, Italians, and Morocco Moors or Negroes, you will form some idea of the care and observation of character requisite to maintain peace and security.

"Work, hard work, is the secret of rule. When there is plenty to do all goes on well; a bad servant is quickly dis-

U

covered and discharged. The care for the good of the souls of my people is often in my thought; but I fear I do not desire it as I ought. I have been obliged to dismiss some whom I most esteem owing to the afflictive season. It has pleased Him who maketh poor and maketh rich, that I should lose all I have laid out here, by another drought, so that the number of labourers must be diminished. A famine eats up all. I am sometimes perplexed; however I reflect that this is not the ordinary state of things (as I am assured), and I trust that God will make the earth again to give its fruits in their season. Some of my largest crops, however, have just been destroyed by continued drought and by insects. A gracious rain has fallen at last, and thus some of the late sown crops are saved for the present; but the hot season has commenced, and there is much anxiety for the harvest. Still, there is room for hope.

"Affliction is sent to kill all evil within us, and to give a greater conformity of mind and will to that of our heavenly Father. I am much cheered by the greater readiness exhibited by the people to hear the Gospel; but there is a thick darkness as to spiritual things over the land.

"The world is full of woes. Poland suffering oppression and struggling for liberty, but not desirous of Gospel freedom. Italy also casting off its ancient yoke, but in danger of falling under a worse. France full of sounds and sights of war. All nations busy in forging weapons of offence and for defence; and this in Christendom—kingdoms professing to serve the King of Peace.

"Happily for us, His own word leads us to expect such things on earth before His coming again. Let us hasten unto that joyful day."

Six days of sirocco completed the destruction of the harvest for this year, and made it necessary to dismiss most of the people. During this time his own work in Oran itself was not neglected, frequent notices of days spent there occur in different letters. The progress of the Bible shop also was watched over by him with much interest.

## THE BIBLE SHOP.

To Rev. J. E. D——.—"I have always been very anxious for the maintenance of our 'Bible Shop' at Oran; but it is now closed owing to the illness of the director. I have therefore hired a smaller place that we may not lose our 'license,' and hope to have a grant of books to sell, for I have a Spanish Protestant ready to take the business. . . . . Would you believe it, the French government have made a special exemption of the Arabs in the permission granted to *Colport.* I have been recently told that the present prefect is ready to grant me a permission of Colporterage, but with this exception. I shall not in that case ask for the permission, lest I should compromise myself."

Mr. Ogle found it better to lend copies of the Arabic Bible to those chiefs who could read. The friendly communications which he had been able to establish with many of these personages, induced them to come to his house from time to time, to give a report of their progress in knowledge, and to receive such instruction as his limited knowledge of the language enabled him to give them. "Very few Arabs can read, and some of the tribes, for instance the Kabyles, do not understand Arabic."

"*February* 11; occultation of Venus about half-past six o'clock P.M. It occurred when the moon was three or four days old, and the smaller planet crescent-formed, so that the spectacle was one of special beauty. The tiny crescent of the planet descended gradually on the dark orb of the moon, like a silver diadem in the cushion of a coronet. It appeared to rest a moment on the faintly golden sphere before disappearing behind it. In about an hour it reappeared below, having passed nearly in the vertical diameter of the moon. The slowly diminished light of the planet was very observable; in the case of a star it would have been instantaneous extinction or reappearance.

"Ask H—— his opinion as to the expediency of combining secular and religious enterprise. Whether missionaries should enter somewhat into the pursuits of the inhabitants, or had better confine themselves to evangelistic work ? By the former plan, may they not hope to become acquainted more quickly, to gain influence more easily and in a larger sphere ? St. Paul seems to take a sort of credit to himself for a purely disinterested, laborious (in secular labour also), and self-denying course, when he deemed the occasion required it. Yet he acknowledges that ' he who preaches the Gospel should live of the Gospel' and all this by Divine direction ; this, however, may be taken to apply to those who are stated ministers to a Christian Church, more than to those who are evangelists to the heathen."

### CHRISTMAS FESTIVITIES.

Among the efforts which he made to make himself understood among his neighbours as their well-wisher, was the annual feast he gave about Christmas time.

FIGUIER FARM, *January*, 1862.
(à l'Anglais).

" I have not yet described my New Year's Feast given to my neighbours and dependents.

" My entertainment was very successful, for it contented, and, I trust, profited all the participants, and has conciliated several who were not of that number. It was somewhat costly to me, but it has left a good impression in the village, and I am thankful for this result gained. A well-covered table, a little good wine (champagne at 3s. 4d. per bottle), and a series of country sports, in which ' bullet pudding' played a great and much approved part, have excited quite a sensation and filled Fame's trumpet. Nobody knows what to make of the ' Anglais.' He is most commonly abused for his economy, which means that many who think to make unfair gain out of him are foiled, though they sometimes hear of a foolish bargain which he has made, or of some piece of extravagance, and so they oscillate in their opinions and must give up the solution of a problem too hard for them. The fact is, I am so full of thoughts as to the best way of working, of calculations as to possibilities and probabilities, that my motives are too various for their ken. The only thing you will deem remarkable about my feast was the expedition with which it was provided, considering the adverse circumstances in which I suddenly found myself. I had made arrangements long before, had furnished my store and issued my directions; but when, on January the first at twelve o'clock, I came to my farm, I found that the coach from Oran, which was to have brought me a sack of meat, with flour, apples, oranges, pomegranates, raisins, figs, almonds, chestnuts, sweetmeats, etc., had brought nothing! The driver, not recognising the address upon my parcels, declined to bring them. I went to my farm-house, in which my feast was to be given, in very low spirits, to find the house empty and desolate.

" To sacrifice a duck, two geese, two fowls, was the first, but smallest matter. My embarrassment was speedily exaggerated by the arrival of two families from Oran, ignorant of my intentions, come to make me a call. One of these—two ladies and a gentleman—stayed in my house all the afternoon, to whom I gave as many polite attentions as active co-operation in *making* the table and furnishing the same allowed. At six o'clock P.M. (the hour appointed), nothing was deficient, save that I had forgotten that candles imply candlesticks; and we had to make bottles serve that purpose, all else was well appointed and attractive, even to the silver knives and forks, and champagne glasses. My table was in the form of a cross. At the upper and transverse end were placed the guests of high degree, my work people sat below.

" The host was tired, felt dull, and as if he could not get through two whole hours with his foreign guests, but he resolved to try. To transform the busy ordinary work of a farm—such as was going on that morning, in spite of my orders to the contrary, into a scene of festivities, and be in the same day purveyor, cook, carpenter, butler and host, requires more flexibility of nature than I possess; and I believe a good many hosts would have found the placid countenance and successful conversational power the most difficult part of such a day's duty. Peace is not like patience, a virtue one can take up when wanted. Nevertheless, by the help of God, my guests were pleased and satisfied, and I do hope they were benefitted too by what occurred."

## VISIT TO A COTTON MILL.

This journey was to pay a visit, long delayed, to ——, whose wife is a Swiss Protestant, who has a cotton mill and farm at the " Sig."

" On January the 6th I set out. Having, with a farmer's economy, secured half a day's labour for my horse on my farm at Figuier, I walked with a friend the first stage. We arrived, after a delightful drive through a country new to me, at dusk. Nothing is more unlike one's idea of a cotton mill than this establishment, a large and handsome-looking house, approached through an avenue of trees, surrounded by gardens and corn-fields, stables near, and good horses, a straw-yard with horned cattle beyond ; not a sound of machinery, no smoke, no crowd, no prison-like construction, its mill wheel (the only mechanism) turned by a stream of water in a land of desert and of drought. You can imagine my first impressions were favourable, and the subsequent experience was in harmony therewith.

" The next morning we went to some marshes for shooting, a country where thousands of ducks and other wild fowl make their home. They are much chased and are very wild. My first shot at a snipe made the whole marsh alive, and my companions' bang, bang, were of no avail but to increase the tumult : one snipe was all my bag. M—— had a duck and a woodcock, and a third sportsman one duck. It is fine sport, nevertheless, but the game rises just out of shot; again and again I saw my shot fall thickly around the victims, but no sign of damage. The birds were teal, widgeon, mallard, black duck, plovers, grey and common, stilts, snipes, flamingoes, storks, pelicans, and a variety of other ' waders.' Many birds of prey also abound; eagles, vultures, buzzards,—in fact, it is a menagerie of the feathered tribe.   I saw a king-fisher among the rest.   Such a swamp I never before saw, one foot of mud and one of water, a thick herbage covers all.   In spring, I am told, there is grass and flowers.   I am now too bad a shot to enjoy much such expeditions, for I almost never shoot.   During the five months of partridge-shooting I have never touched a feather."

## Conversation with a Sceptic.

" We returned in the evening to our hospitable host. I fear we had not a profitable time, for the conversation turned upon the evidences of Christianity, a gentleman present talking long and loudly against Christianity, and the inspiration of the Bible.   The miracles and the divinity of our Lord he rejected: the account of the 'creation' he deemed a fable. M—— replied to him well; but he was not convinced.   I am not master of the language of this controversy, but I gave him at the close of our acquaintanceship a tract which, if he will read it patiently, can conduct him to the truth.

" Is not the Christian religion proved best by its appeals to the conscience, not to the intellect of man ?   By which I mean that there are evidences which every man can feel, but which any man may deny.   If he excuse his unbelief by saying that his intellectual faculties find difficulties, and do not find con-clusive evidences, he is left in the dilemma.   I cannot but think that had it been God's will that Christianity should approve itself to the *natural* intellect of man, He would have left in it fewer difficulties, and have given us more of direct evidence.   I very much doubt whether the ' evidences ' addressed to the intellect are so convincing as the advocates of ' external evidence ' maintain.   They boast that there is ' evidence ' sufficient to convince all opposers ;  these take them at their word, and show that there is not evidence to convince them, and I am inclined to think that they are, so far, right. . . . I believe that God, to whom all men owe the obedience of faith, presents His claim in quite another way than that of intellectual evidence, and has taken little pains to supply such. Intellectual evidences have ever been eagerly sought for by intellectual men, and important contributions to the evidences for Christianity have been elicited, but these do no more, in my opinion, than to show that the *intellectual attacks are futile*; that the religion is not subject to be overthrown by such means.

"The lucubrations of our modern sciolists on questions of deepest concern to our spiritual life may appear to some to be dangerous and deadly. I count them to be nought! Come students of theology and lend your powers of intellect, while yet no preconception has sophisticated, and no claims of interest have entrammelled them,—while yet free to form your unbiassed opinion of what is and what is not to be believed,—to the solution of these enigmas. God has given to man power of mind and faculties of discernment. Employ them fearlessly, diligently, determined to abide by the decision to which they shall conduct you, in prosecuting the great inquiry, 'What is Truth?' From my professional position,— builded, as I know well, not upon an uncertain foundation of unconnected verities, but placed upon a solid and a consistent scheme of scriptural doctrine, constructed by wise master builders into a lucid and harmonious system,—I call to you, as did the founders of my school. 'Prove all things, hold fast that which is good.' The faith I have embraced is not an indiscriminate reception of theories that time's broad current has floated down and cast upon our shores. It is rather—to pursue the metaphor—the freight of many an argosy from far off lands; jewels extracted from deep mines, and pearls from unfathomable depths, gathered by skill and toil, tested a thousand times by incorruptible assayers, and placed in your hands to be purchased at a corresponding price of toil and patience. I fear not to submit them to your scrutiny; to teach to you the use of the crucial test, and to assure you that the *more keen and critical that scrutiny*, the greater labour and assiduity you sincerely use, the higher the power you invoke to your aid, the better will you appreciate your riches. The more solid and stedfast will be your assurance that the faith you inherit from the martyrs, the confessors, the founders of the Reformed Church of Scotland (he had been perusing a copy of the *Witness* sent by a friend), is no cunningly devised fable, no adulterated extract, no impure admixture of traditional assumption with primitive purity, but a draught, clear, limpid, and sincere, from the fountain of celestial truth. . . . . . . . .

"We left the 'Mill' next morning early, and on my way home I composed my varied thoughts in a poetic form which you shall some day see if you wish it—'On Finding a Christian Home in the African Desert'—I describe the region around as it appeared, deserted, dark, and desolate.

"E'en so on desert moorland
 Stands the snug shepherd's cot,
E'en so on Alpine summit
 Blooms the forget-me-not.

What principle benignant
 With love and genius rife,
Broods o'er the chaos stagnant,
 And quickens all to life?

Each heart responds, 'tis Woman,
 Earth's universal queen;
Unmarked her work, and common,
 An influence felt, not seen.

Where her sweet face is absent
 Rude savageness appals,
But peace abides complacent
 Where her soft shadow falls.

Incense of adulation
 Shy modesty disdains,
Benevolence thy passion,
 Thy recompence, thy pains.

Yet scorn not thou the tribute
 To thy just merit due,
No other eye beholds it,
 None other hears but you.

"The property I have bought I have not time now to mention, it was a neighbouring and a very necessary acquisition, giving me pasturage near to my farm. In these things Providence appears to favour me. I have another journey at hand. . . .—Your loving brother, J. F. OGLE."

## PERMISSION TO COLPORT.

" *February* 18*th.*—The Vice-Consul has announced to me that through the influence of the Director-General of Civil Affairs in Algeria, the opposition to my having permission to colport or distribute Bibles will be withdrawn ; and that I have only a few days to wait before receiving authorisation. I have rented, for six months, a shop in a principal street of Oran for a Bible depôt, which I hope to establish on a self-sustaining basis ; a few pounds more than I can spare will be wanted at first, and for this I have written to the Spanish Evangelization Society."

## PREACHING TO SPANIARDS.

" I have frequent opportunities of prosecuting missionary objects, sometimes with freedom and success. On Sunday I was twice enabled to preach to Spaniards, who collected in some numbers, and was, by God's help, carried through all the opposition.

" A company of Spaniards had gathered round me, about twenty in number, for conversation. We were in one of the public squares in Oran. I sat down upon a big stone, and read the Scriptures to them. At first many reviled me, and blasphemed the name of God, but His Word prevailed, and those around me soon exclaimed, with that warm manifestation of feeling which is natural to Spaniards when deeply moved, addressing themselves to those who opposed and interrupted me, ' Calle,' &c., ' Calle,' &c., (Be silent, be silent, this man can speak ; yes, indeed, he can speak). This sentence they repeated in concert until they had procured their desire.

" This was the more remarkable since they were reminded of the persecutions now going on in Spain against some who have been detected by their priests in reading the Bible.

" It is a surprising, but also a very encouraging circumstance, that these persecutions are widely known throughout Spain, and even here ; and this not by our means. The priests make it known ; they denounce Protestants vehemently, and to add the force of fear to the weight of their authority, tell the people ' that two Spaniards have just been condemned to the galleys for seven years for having the Protestant Bible in their possession ! '

"After I had concluded my address my auditors dispersed quietly, their adversaries, however, still jeering them, ' You are going to be a Protestant.' "

## ARAB MOURNING.

"On returning to his farm one day he found one of the wives of his Arab labourers seated upon the ground, her face besmeared with black ashes, uttering piteous cries. Her infant had been burnt to death, while she was absent to draw water. She refused for some time to have any fire in the house. The Arabs think houses so much less secure than their tents. Probably the habit of making fires in a particular manner in their tents makes them awkward with our greater conveniences. Could you see their fires you would wonder that the tents are not burnt down constantly. A few stones or a wall of earth (generally surrounded *outside* by dry thorns) in a corner of the tent forms the fireplace, and they crowd round it in cold weather so closely, it is really surprising that the children are not often burnt."

## CHAPTER XXII.

### VISIT TO FRANCE, SWITZERLAND, AND ITALY.

WE, in Great Britain, are accustomed to associate only sun and warmth with such countries as Spain and Algeria. True, the raw air of England, and the mists and cloud which often embarrass its sky are there unknown ; but these countrie

have other and greater drawbacks. The cold is there often
intense—intense to a degree never experienced in Britain.
At night there is frost, at mid-day a burning sun. Nor are
the dwellings at all adapted to protect one against the extreme
and sudden variations of temperature and the bitter winds
which often blow. Walls of red earth plastered, tiled floors,
chinky windows, unceiled rooms, no fireplace, and scarce any
fuel to feed the stove which in the better class of houses is its
substitute, are not promotive of the health, and still less of the
comfort of the sojourner from Britain. During the summer
months the climate of Algeria is specially trying to Europeans.
Northern visitors are liable to the fever of the country, the
recurring attacks of which weaken their constitution. It is
the third summer, ordinarily, that these climatic effects are
the most severely felt, having by that time accumulated and
culminated.

Mr Ogle had now been three years in Algeria; the ener-
vating influences of the country, with the anxieties and toils of
his work, had told upon him, and he found it needful to leave
his work for a while, and to recruit his health and strength
by a visit to Europe. Italy had just come under the sceptre
of Victor Emmanuel. From the Alps to Sicily there was not
a city or hamlet in it all (the diminutive portion reserved to
the Pope excepted) in which the Bible might not be circulated
and the gospel preached. Here was the fall of the tyranny
of ages, the dawn of a new day to that most interesting land.
These auspicious changes drew to it the eyes and the heart of
Mr Ogle, and he resolved to take Switzerland on his way to
London, and while benefiting from its reinvigorating air, he
would visit a French pasteur living in one of its high valleys,
and learn upon the spot the probabilities of missionary openings
in the neighbouring land. He hoped, if health and other
circumstances permitted, to "have some share in the evangelization of Italy." "Too much," he said, "cannot be attempted

just now," and he set out, hoping that his strength would, by the cooler air of Europe, be so far restored as to enable him to visit the newly emancipated nation.

Our missionary is now to traverse some of the most interesting scenes in Europe. He goes on his way now philosophizing, now describing, in the former case with so much wisdom, and in the latter with so much truth and vividness, that we, who are permitted to be his companions, are alike instructed and delighted, and regret only that the journey should so soon come to an end.

"LYONS, *July.*—I visited here a family of weavers whom I had seen on a former journey, and found them in the same house and condition as then. They were interested to renew my acquaintance, and I left them some tracts, and preached the gospel to them. They complained much of the state of the silk trade, but their dwelling, though much encumbered with silk-looms, looked cheerful—the more so that the father and all the family were clean and well dressed, though the looms were silent. One is apt to disregard the opportunities which daily occur for speaking a word in season, but it should not be so. During a very casual visit one may be enabled to leave impressions favourable to true religion, to the increase of contentment, and a feeling of the universal brotherhood of man.

We English, who know the truth, or who are at least free to learn it, live too much for ourselves. It is God's will that we should impart to others what we have from Him received. Is it not for this cause that we are so much dispersed abroad over the wide world? Some weary of home, some seeking occupation or remunerative employment, some health, some riches; all are being dispersed abroad. The Christian traveller should, like the rivers of fair and fickle France, bring and leave behind him blessings. As he pursues his course he should promote happiness and refresh languid life.

"Some travellers do, no doubt, fulfil this mission, they are the lights of the world, the salt of the earth. It will be sad

if war should come upon us and generalize this lot by a dispersion of our nation upon a gigantic scale! A compulsory
exile from England will be a very different thing from these
voluntary ones. But even that would be much alleviated if
we had the conviction that a gracious God orders it for the
greater good of the world, and intends to produce thereby a
glorious result such as that described in Isaiah lxvi. You see
I cannot forget the old theme. It is not that there is the
flaming hand in the sky, but there are signs among the
nations. The language of every journalist, the tone of our
statesmen, the state of the nations, the aspect of every city,
declares war unmistakeably. Though delayed longer than I
used to anticipate, I see more and more the same indications of the coming end. I thank God that we have wonderful proofs in Italy how a war may be overruled for good.
I long to be there, that I may do something towards this end.
Then when the days of darkness come, which I anticipate will
succeed this hour of Italy's light, I might have the satisfaction
to think that I have wrought my 'one hour.'"

ORSIERES—CANTON VALOIS.

"*July* 24*th.*—I am particularly happy to-day," writing to
his sister, "and so hope to cheer you by a few lines, descriptive of the circumstances which contribute to my felicity.
You see *where* I am, and I am pleased to think you have been
here, and almost wonder you have not said more about this
beautiful excursion to the great St Bernard. But you travelled
easily, perhaps, and when one has little trouble to attain an
object, one lacks that which gives the keen edge to enjoyment
which is necessary to produce a strong impression. There is
another reason, Switzerland brings so many successive scenes,
novel and enchanting, before us, that we lose the distinct
image of any one in the general pleasure resulting from all.

"But I must not philosophize or analyze, but describe.
We, that is, I and my pack, left Geneva at half-past six in the
morning, by steamer, following the south bank of the lake.
The morning was fine, but heavy clouds and fog are on the
higher mountains. On the south side the mountains of Savoy

crowd up against the lake, and their pine forests climb and cling to the precipitous steeps with difficulty; cascades come tumbling down at intervals; a rich verdure prevails oftentimes. Trees of stately growth, chesnut, oak, elm, plane, &c., seem to have been planted on a rich sward rather than to have been sown by nature; beautiful villas are not rare, though the greater proportion of the numerous habitations one sees are simple Swiss cottages, châlets, and farms. There are many pretty villages with their broad dark-looking roofs, their church spires, and ample auberges.

"We had a curé on board the steamer, the priest of Chablais, a benevolent-looking old man, quite a picture. Alas, that he is no shepherd of souls, in the best sense; but some of these rural priests are good men, and I could believe this one to be such.

"I could not converse with him, for I wanted to assail his errors, and as he was so much my senior, it was hard to do so without excuse. Ought such considerations to prevent the only opportunity I had from being embraced? Alas! there are heavy responsibilities for neglect of duty upon all. I should not burden my conscience, for every occasion of meeting with those who are in error is not an opportunity for usefulness to them; but still I cannot but feel that if all who possess the truth sought grace earnestly, they might lovingly and prayerfully turn most occasional meetings into opportunities for good, and thus our steps as travellers would be traceable by results.

"At half-past ten A.M., we were at the head of the Lake. The clouds now allowed us to have occasional glimpses of the Diablerets, &c. The rain of yesterday has made the cascades very fine. We could trace their silver lines from the very summits of the mountains. I noticed one of these shining streams crossed almost a hundred times by a zig-zag road; a succession of bridges enabled this, as in childhood's play, to skip backward and forward over the stream from rock to rock. At the foot of the mountain it tumbles into a gorge by a fall known as the Pissvache."

## The Drance and Ascent of St Bernard.

"At Martigny I procured a porter, and set out for the pass into Piedmont. There is a charm in footing one's way which no conveyance can give. Oh how much one loses in those close prisons called first class carriages; they have need to be cushioned. How different the sensation when all one's limbs and senses are unfettered, one treads the firm earth and feels one's own littleness and nature's sublimity, where one has leisure for reflection ; to pick up a stone, or cull a flower, to sketch or to scribble at one's will. I traced the course of the furious Drance, roaring, tumbling, surging, rushing, realizing all Southey's epithets, and defying description, whether from pen or pencil. How many times I stopped to admire it, to wonder as I thought, that for a thousand years it had done so, now day, now night, now summer, now winter; no rest, no change, save for a larger and more tumultuous torrent. If I did not hope to be able to recall its image to your memory by a few words, I should bid you read Southey's poem, realize each of the ten thousand expressions, give them ten miles in length and six thousand years in duration, and you have the Drance as it was, is, and will be, till the heavens are no more. I became lighthearted and joyous, as if by sympathy. Such we ought to be.

"Coming from an icy home, or from out the rock, hard its lot and rough its experience ; oppositions and obstacles everywhere, and yet it holds on, ever increasing in impetus, smoothing everything, fertilizing everything in its way, till at length it merges quietly and unobtrusively into a broader and less beautiful river, content to have done its work. What a lesson for man ! ambitious, blind, impotent ; like the river only in his impetuosity, he would arrogate to himself a name, a separate existence, an individuality, or else refuse all action, all utility ! Again, I thought, how does the human aggregate resemble this river. When actuated by a purpose, borne along by an impulse, launched into a downward current, how mighty then its force, how uncontrollable ! A monarch who should aspire to control its onward movement would resemble a log on yonder torrent, and be borne along, helplessly tossed and driven till shivered to pieces, or stranded, left behind. Such were Francis I., Ferdinand of Austria, &c. The wise man will, like Napoleon III., cut a channel, divert a portion of the water, if not the whole volume, direct and utilize : then what marvels ! what motive power ! what impulses to man's industries ! what aids are given to his efforts !

"What mighty forces exist in this disordered world, which only demand a skilful direction. Alas ! one must be content to see them like the Drance, unused for good. The channel assigned to them is their destiny, and all that such as we can do, is to divert an inconsiderable streamlet to turn our wayside mill !

"There is in the world, however, much that each man may do, though 'twere as vain to try to divert the direction in which nations tend as to attempt a mill to utilize the furious Drance. But when it becomes a river, it is more tranquil, the imagery which is employed in Scripture is often this ; 'Thy peace shall flow as a river.' 'The blessings of the Gentiles as an overflowing stream.' 'The swelling of Jordan.' &c., &c.

"Oh when shall the gospel roll on as an impetuous current, and bear away all opposing things; make crooked straight, and rough places plain ? When shall the *united* energies of Christians do for this morally sterile world what rivers do for the barren soil ? When? but when Christians shall be like them, nourished from heaven, and sustained by constantly recurring fresh supplies; when they, simply obedient to the will of Him who directs and controls all things, shall exhibit no unwillingness, but a freedom and liberty, heaven-born in their obedience ; then, and not till then.

"I was made glad by the bright and cheerful, and prosperous appearance of the country through which I passed. The peasantry healthy, robust, and active, busy with harvest. Broad-brimmed hats and jackets of various colours gave a neat comeliness to the women. I stopped to rest, and to talk to some mowers. They cheerfully left their work, and I had all who were in the field around me in a moment. We understood each other perfectly. The peasantry take me for a Frenchman, till I discover by my sentiments that I am very different.

"You will remember the route to the St. Bernard, closed in by dark pine-clad mountains for some distance ; opening out as you ascend, and giving peeps of snowy crests here and there. The pretty villages, at intervals, with their cumbrous wooden dwellings, that are more picturesque than convenient. 'Il est defendu de trotter' (It is forbidden to gallop), was a notice which amused me much. I thought the prudent town's folk fear their houses would fall if but a John Gilpin made the pavement rattle. The narrow street, without a footpath, explains, no doubt, the restriction. I am now in a clean and wainscotted chamber, in the little town of Orsières, it is eleven P.M., the moonbeams silver the snow and the mountains ; and the Drance roars below."

## THE HOSPICE OF ST. BERNARD.

"Next morning I rose with the dawn, and set out for the hospice of the St. Bernard. Had to get a mule at Liddes, as I found I could not accomplish the journey without this help. After passing the hamlet of St. Pierre, you reach the wild valley where the *Cantine* is the sole object, save rock and glacier and stony steep pasturage. The desolation of the upper portion of the pass seemed like an entrance to a new world ; from fertility, all was changed to waste and barrenness. I made, however, quite a collection of flowers, from above the snow line, as I walked over the rocks. Turning a point of the rock in the narrowing defile, the gloomy Hospice came into view. It reminded me of the Falklands, as did the whole of that desolate region. A spongy soil, rocks strewn on the surface or cropping out, a trackless waste, the sun scarcely having power to warm you, your narrow horizon bounded by barriers of scarped rocks. The rocks are identical as are the mosses and many of the plants. If you remember the pass of St. Bernard, you have an idea of the country in the Falkland isles.

"Within the Hospice itself, was everything to suggest a first rate house of hospitality; a well-proportioned room, with parquetry floor and pannelled ceiling, handsome fire place, vases of Sèvres china made expressly for the Hospice; a piano, an harmonium, &c., &c., all presents from grateful guests. No gloom, no austerity, no images, no pictures of saints or virgins, nothing visible to remind you that it is a convent, except the monks and the travellers' book. I engaged one of the servants to conduct me, and, accompanied by two or three of the dogs, we ascended the mountain.

"No one who has merely passed along the beaten tracks of Switzerland can form any idea what a view from a summit is like, where Mount Blanc stares you in the face, and the great peaks rise sheer up from sudden depths, like black spectral forms of old world-wreck—splinters from Chaos—ridge behind ridge, all rock, no verdure, only ice and rock—a stormy ocean petrified—one cannot describe it; so dread, so dark, so savage, so sublime; all around the same prospect, save where the valleys into Switzerland and into Italy descend, and these drop down so suddenly that you scarce can see where the black pines begin.

"We stayed half-an-hour to read 2 Pet. i. 7, to sketch an outline, and to enjoy the whole.

"The sun was warm, not a breath of air seemed to disturb the calm. There were flowers; the daisy, the gentian, the forget-me-not, the heart's ease; even at the summit, the 'chenalethe.'"

## ITALY.

. . . . "I long to spend, if only a week, in active evangelization work in Italy. It is a most important time. Now is *the day*, 'the night cometh when no man can work;' there are so many signs which indicate that even now the midday of Italy's day of grace may be passed, and that the shadows of the evening lengthen, that I dare not put off till another year what may be done to-day. I would that all English Christians, who can spare the time and the money, should go to Italy this year to distribute Bibles, tracts, &c., &c., and by their conversations and their example, help to enlighten the still dark inhabitants; the night will, else, overtake these and they have no star to guide, no lamp to direct. The Bible in every house, even if in every village, would be such a lamp; and if I could, I would organise and secure that every single hamlet of this land be visited by some evangelist. If I can afford it, after consultation with Mr. C——, I shall set out and make excursions from places to which books can be sent for me, from Turin or from Nice. If this should delay the time of my return to you for a month or more, I believe you will be gainers, for I feel even now, after a week's sojourn in the more bracing air of Europe, to have twofold more of activity and cheerfulness; and I may hope, if this plan prosper, to get health and vigour, and to have Christian love and other graces strengthened."

## A Scorpion Collector.

" Started at five o'clock A.M., for Val D'Aosta, on Thursday; overtook a pedlar and his wife—a man of the country, who carried on the singular trade of collecting scorpions. He goes for them into the plains of Italy, purchases them at twenty francs the thousand, and retails them at three sous a-piece. I conversed much with him, and I hope to have gained him for the work of colporterage; he promised to meet me at Courmayeur, to inquire if he could be so employed. I often notice how correct is the judgment of many quite unlettered men, and had an instance during our conversation to-day; the pedlar was telling of cases in which poor persons were hired to go on crutches to a certain altar and there to declare a miracle of healing. I said, ' What appears to me most astonishing is that God suffers such blasphemy and falsehood to continue.' He replied, ' God is full of mercy, He does not punish immediately, He has all eternity to do that in, if men persist in refusing His mercy.' A justification of God's dealings, worthy of a divine, profound and true, and not by any means what one would expect from an ordinary mind. I could fill pages with the conversation held with this man only.

## Wayside Conversations.

" I had a conversation with a Curè and with many peasants, which will, I hope, be remembered by them. I read the fourth chapter of St. John. The appropriateness of the narration—Christ's conversation by the wayside—seemed to strike my companions forcibly; the lesson taught, ' God is a spirit, and they who worship Him must worship Him in spirit and in truth,' which I illustrated by contrasting the little chapel by the road side with the magnificent temple, the universe, in which it is an unheeded toy. My companions talked faster than I about Rome's religion being one of *money*, and said, ' the priests ought to *give* us the Gospel, but they *sell* their religion.' I have heard the same sentiment respecting the mercenary character of Rome's religion from so many persons in different countries, where it is known, that I am persuaded it is a very general impression."

We may well ask the question, Would the Romanists be so anxious to get hold of England were she not reputed to be a wealthy nation ? Let those who have gone over to their Church say—if they can do so,—that they do not pay a good price for their privileges. The demands of the Church of Rome, for the maintenance of her costly machinery, are insatiable, and few, whether individuals or nations, can prosper if her *claims* are allowed.

## Val D'Aosta.

" The day was fine, but clouds were frequently on the summits around. As we descended, a storm of thunder, with heavy rain, passed over us. We had shelter among some vast walnut trees. In the east, a beautiful rainbow spanned from mountain to mountain the lovely valley, and Mount Blanc in the west, attired in his robe of clouds, loomed grandly through a curtain of rain.

" Nothing enhances scenery like these accessories of storm ; the thunder cloud, the rainbow, and the rain sweeping down an Alpine valley in well defined lines of vapour, or veiling it like a transparent shroud. A shower is one of the finest elements in the sublime, as the masters of landscape painting well know ; thus, though I have not *seen* the panorama of the Val d'Aosta which lay before me, I count myself particularly favoured in the fact of its having been *thus* obscured."

COURMAYEUR, *August* 1.

. . . . "Courmayeur, as you may see by the map, is a village of Italy. It occupies the northern extremity of a valley coming down from Mount Blanc, a cul-de-sac. Curiously enough, Mount Blanc is not visible, a lofty rock intervening, as is often the case.

"To see the summit of a high mountain, you must be either far off or at a great elevation, so that I contend you obtain ideas of vast size nearly as well in Scotland, where you see the mountains from near at hand as in Switzerland among the Alps. Courmayeur consists of a cluster of houses with broad brimmed roofs and balconies, like Swiss châlets; the streets are narrow, ill-paved, and tortuous. There may be in all about 200 houses, the people are poor and industrious, living by agricultural employments.

"Their cows, goats, and mules, are their chief treasures. Milk is abundant, meat scarce, hotels expensive. I am in lodgings, and they are so pleasantly situated and so comfortable that I hope you will see them some day. . . . .

" On Sunday there was a French Protestant service at nine o'clock A.M. Pasteur C—— preached a good evangelical sermon from the text, " My son, give me thy heart." He announced a controversial sermon for the evening. At eleven o'clock came the English Church service, and at three P.M. The patience of English people is admirable, for though the Church service is so beautiful, the way in which it is often performed demands patience. It was a fête day in the village, so that music and dancing and firing of guns desecrated the day. At night a few persons came to the controversy, which was well conducted.

## Mount Blanc.

"On Monday I set out for a solitary walk up the valley; the day was bright and cloudless, meadows green, hay being cut, and corn ripe. I entered the valley on the Italian side. Mount Blanc with a precipitous face of rock forms its northern wall, a steep wooded hill, that would be esteemed a mountain elsewhere, its southern boundary. Glaciers come down like streams into the valley, and look like rocks of a greenish grey out of which rivers issue in impetuous torrents; huge piers and pinnacles of black rock shoot upward destitute of vegetation. A peasant pointed to Mount Blanc. 'That black rock?' said I. 'Yes.' So Mont Blanc, like other celebrities, loses immensely by a close acquaintance!

"On ascending the hill, I stopped at a pretty châlet, but sought a drink of milk in vain; however, I soon found water sweet and cold, purling in a grassy channel through the mead. Beyond and above me is the pine forest, rocky and difficult of ascent.

"My thoughts turned to liberty and to America :—

"Don't you hear the volunteers,
   Now we shall be free,
No more chains, and no more tears,
   No more slavery."

Thus I sang to the ancient rocks, witnesses, once, to a slavery more cruel; and now the chief barriers against a new and terrible kind of domination. I do believe Mont Blanc is less a mountain now that the tricolor floats from its summit.

"Soon I obtained a beautiful view over the black rock, and found that this is indeed a part of Mont Blanc, but only one of its lower buttresses. On this side one is so immediately under the mountain that you can see but little of its height. The summit is fifteen miles from Chamounix, but from this elevated valley it can scarcely be five miles distant. Like all of the monarch class, it cannot be seen to advantage unless you occupy a lofty station, or are at a great distance. I climbed a grassy hill till I had a full view of the majestic mountain, which well repaid me. The sun was hot though the snow lay

in the hollows of the rock at my feet.   Rich grass, spangled
with a multitude of flowers, carpeted the hill-top—a beautiful
Alpine meadow.    I made the descent to Courmayeur, on the
opposite side, in two hours.

"*Tuesday*, I rested.    On *Wednesday* I ascended Mont
Cramont, which is celebrated for the fine view—the finest of
Mont Blanc, and of the Italian Alps—Monte Rosa, and Mont
Cervin, and Mont Velan ; some of the Oberland snow-peaks
are also visible.    The ascent is easy but fatiguing, it took us
six hours.    In descending, I extemporised a sledge, placing
my hands on the grass, and extending one leg, I slid down on
my heel, and found great relief, being very foot-sore ; but the
guide said it was not a safe method.    However, I never allowed
myself to go beyond control.

"I am much disappointed to find but little doing for the
evangelization of Italy.    Bibles and Testaments have been
distributed, and have been burnt, and now I cannot get one
here, which is much to be regretted.    I am learning Italian,
but cannot speak it yet.    If I were not so anxious to see my
sick sister I would not come home; a few weeks spent in Italy
in Bible distribution might do great good."


### VALLEY OF COURMAYEUR.

"Sending my baggage by diligence, I decided to walk.    A
splendid day.    Fancy a close valley, twenty miles in length,
and nearly straight, coming down, as it were, from Mont Blanc.
The 'monarch,' grand, and more grand still as you descend
the valley.    A roaring torrent, his mighty messenger, by your
side, beautifully situated villages, forests, cornfields, vineyards,
rocks, new mountains, &c., coming into view, and you have
the picture, but without its infinite variety, its superb climate
and colouring, its accessories of sensation and of incident.    I
had conversations with some ten or twelve persons during the
day.    One was with a man of about forty years of age.    He
had come out from Rome, but not to a belief in the gospel of
Jesus.    He said he had been a student in —— College,
'when going through the course of Humanity and Rhetoric

my eyes were opened. They wanted me to be a priest. I could not shut my eyes. I left the college..' I expressed my sympathy, and said, ' I too have left for conscience sake my home,' &c. His reply was very just. ' It is easy for you who have money, but for a man who depends upon his work for his bread it is very painful (*penible*).' However, he did not complain of poverty, but seemed to rejoice in his freedom, and told with great pleasure how different the influence of the priests throughout the country since the year 1848.

"This man did not know the New Testament, and is a specimen of one in ten thousand in whom the light of science has sufficed to shatter the prison-walls by which Rome holds her slaves. All say the same upon one point. ' It is a shop, a trade—we *pay* for masses, baptisms, burials, marriages, and for the forgiveness of our sins.'

" I have heard this repeated fifty times in different Roman Catholic countries.

" I gave my companion the promise of a New Testament, and I trust good will follow from our conversation."

### VILLA NUOVA.

" I visited an iron foundry. The motive power is water, and the solvent charcoal. The machinery appeared to be simple and effective. Villa Nuova has a lovely situation, formed by a transverse valley which breaks into isolated peaks the lines of the valley of Courmayeur, and brings into view glacier mountains to the right and left, with a variety of picturesque scenery, cascades, gorges, rocks, ravines. Here the valley of Aosta begins. It is wide and very fertile. The Doire meanders along in a broad stream ; the mountains are, for the most part, without snow, except in patches; but in traversing its length, Monte Rosa, Mont Cervin, and the Gracian, and the Pennine Alps are here and there occasionally visible. I do not think of its scenery as superior to that of the Oberland, from Thun to Interlaken and Grindelwald. Arrived at Aosta about 6 P.M."

## TURIN.

"Next morning to Ivrea by diligence. I had a pleasant companion in the brother of the poet Longfellow. We talked of America. He expressed a hope that the war would result in the destruction of slavery. If he had heard of the defeat of the Federals he did not mention it. The Federalists have an Irish, and the Secessionists a French general in command.

"Arrived at Ivrea, the iron road puts me once more in communication with all the world—Turin, Milan, Rome, Naples, Paris, London.

"Next morning early, left for Turin. We are now on the plains of Lombardy. The Alps form a northern barrier, vast and imposing; icy summits along the upper line, vapours from the plain, or the great distance, allow you to see little of the form of the lower elevations, so that the view appears to be bounded by a black cloud-ascending barrier, not very unequal in height, except where Monte Viso in the west rises a superb pyramid of ice and rock above the level of the chain.

"Turin is beautiful; its buildings of stone, with deep red roofs, are relieved by noble park-like scenery standing out grandly against the verdurous hills of Italy to the south, or the majestic chain of snow-capped mountains to the north. It contains finer streets and squares than perhaps any other city in Europe, and fewer of a meaner order. The houses are built together in blocks, each of which forms a square. These have from some points of view a palatial appearance.

"The Po is a fine river, but is here in an early stage of its course. I find I noted it down as '*domestic*,' that is to say, occupied in supplying individual rather than general wants. Its banks were clothed in linen, its waters occupied by baths and stationary machinery. It is spanned by a noble bridge of five arches, built on the widest part of the river.

TURIN, *August 7th.*

"Turin has the appearance of being a deserted capital, the streets in the court quarter being empty. The palace stands with its doors and windows open. There are no signs of royalty visible. Priests there are everywhere it is true. A busy political fervour seems to prevail; would that the Italians were more in earnest upon the really important point—to cultivate their minds, to form new habits as well as to found corresponding free institutions. My lodging is in the Italian street. There is a continual crowd of foot passengers, for it is one of the great thoroughfares. I watched them this morning for an hour, and was struck with their respectable appearance—the domestic look; no black hair and eyes, no fiery Italian expression, no dark complexion, rather a north-Europe population seem to be here. Many English equipages passed along. I wish Victor Emmanuel may not have made a mistake in going to Naples—better to have remained here till king at Rome. The papers are full of the insurrection in the Neapolitan territory, it is said that Francis and his party sustain it. I don't like what I hear about Italy, and have my fears lest the result be a disappointment."

## Passage of the Alps.

"*August 9th.*—Set out for Paris. Diligence across Mont Cenis, ten hours, which will be exchanged for *minutes* in a few years, when the tunnel is completed. The ascent of the mountain was imposing, and on the Italian side we had distant and beautiful prospects—a long valley opening into the 'blue plain,' so celebrated in Italian landscape—you fancy Rome must be at the end of that long vista, and so, in fact, it is. The French boundary is marked by a desolate Douane on the very summit of the pass. Of the descent I can write but little, it was rapidly made in three hours, through cloud and night, black with forest and precipitous chasms. When morning broke, I found myself in the valley of Chambery. It looked cold and pale after the warm tints of Italy, but is rich in corn and wine, and is clothed in some parts by forests, and made beautiful by its rushing river and its boundary of Alp.

" Finally, after a journey of forty hours, I arrived in Paris at 4 o'clock A.M., my purse and my progress having been so nicely adjusted that I had just two sous in my pocket; these I gave to a person poorer than myself, and walked through the deserted streets with my luggage and with a light heart. During the few days in Italy I have put into circulation several hundreds of excellent tracts, and during the journeys have had most interesting conversations with fellow travellers and others by which I trust Jesus has been made known to many."

---

# CHAPTER XXIII.

## CHURCH OF ENGLAND—THE BAPTISMAL AND BURIAL SERVICES —THE ACT OF UNIFORMITY—SACRAMENTALISM.

Mr Ogle arrived in England in greatly renovated health. If his journey had recruited his physical powers, not less refreshing to his spirit did he now find the Christian society to which his return to his native land admitted him.    But he did not rest.    The " International Exhibition," then being held, had attracted crowds of foreigners to London, and the opportunity of usefulness thus offered was too inviting not to be eagerly taken advantage of.    The Spaniards, as usual, especially interested him.    He preached to them in their own tongue, distributed tracts and Bibles among them, and these and similar labours, which occupied him from morning to night, so engrossed him, that he had not time to set foot within the exhibition, and two weeks passed away, before he permitted himself the gratification of going down to Lincoln-shire and visiting the members of his own family.    During his stay in the country he preached several times, and experienced the fulfilment of the promise that " He that watereth shall be watered also himself."

At home Mr Ogle's attention was naturally turned very closely to the state of the Church of England.    He had

given up his living in that church, being constrained thereto
by the conscientious objections he felt to the burial and
baptismal services.   It appeared to him that these portions of
the liturgy had in them Popish principles and tendencies, and
he could not give his " assent and consent" as then required of
ministers of the Church of England.   But although he had
gone out from her, it was with sorrow—a sorrow mingled with
a hope that he would yet be able to return.   He carried with
him the loving heart of a son : from the distant sphere of his
labour he watched every indication of returning purity and
life on the part of that church, and ever as he knelt in prayer,
it was, like Daniel, with face turned toward the "Holy and
Beautiful House" in which his fathers had praised God, and
in which he himself had faithfully ministered to a loving
flock till his growing doubts compelled him to part from
them.

The views and feelings of Mr Ogle on this important subject will be best understood from his own statement of them.
Of the extracts that follow, some of them were written at a
date prior to that at which we are now arrived, but we deem
it best to give them here, along with others of later production, as affording thus a more complete and connected exhibition of his views, which appear to have strengthened
as he advanced in life, and the sincerity of which was
attested both by the modest firmness with which he held them
and the lifelong sacrifices to which he submitted in carrying
them out.

The first extract-letter we insert is dated " Oran, Jan. 3d,
1860," and is addressed to the Reverend J. E. D——.

" Will you permit me, dear Sir, to mention the Liturgical
Revision movement to you, and to express a hope that you
will not concur with those who will let *ill* alone, while they
acknowledge and feel the extreme inconsistency between
Evangelical teaching and the baptismal service, and confess

that the burial office is extremely unsuited to the present condition of the mass in England, yet are content to let things be. Here surely faith is imperatively demanded. There is sin in sitting still. We ought to trust God for consequences; duty is plain. Archbishop Usher said, 'The root of Romish superstition is still in the soil of the Church of England. We (the Reformers) have cut down the tree. If those who come after us do not complete the work we, by God's help, have begun, it will be a just judgment that will permit all the growth of superstition to re-appear.' I do not quote, but give the sense of a page that struck me most forcibly, as *the very history of the disorders we are now lamenting.* I have been invited to be a member of Lord Ebury's Committee; however I do not see it my duty to leave my post here, the more as I have no hope that *Parliamentary agency* will, except a national repentance precede, bring any relief to those whose consciences are truly aggrieved by the present state of our Liturgy. I therefore sit still and wait, hoping, at least, for enlarged spheres of usefulness. Had the Liturgy been free from Romish doctrine, I, for one, should have rested in my country parsonage among people I loved. But it was not to be so. 'Go ye into all the world and preach the gospel;' and I can give my testimony that I never found peace, or freedom, or pleasure in my work till I obeyed."

The next letter, which treats the question historically, is addressed to his sister, and was written from Cambridge, whither he had gone to visit the scene of his University years, and where he says, "All seems the same, and I could fancy I am not changed myself; but it cannot be so: I am changed." The letter is dated Oct. 7, 1862.

## ACT OF UNIFORMITY.

" The Church of England I must not think of. Whatever be other men's duty, mine seems clear, whatever be the sacrifice, to make it cheerfully for conscience' sake.

"There is no ordinary difficulty in the question, What a man ought to do? but surely the difficulty has been much lessened by the circumstances. We are brought to a point. We have the Prayerbook to study and compare with the Bible. Then we are called upon to declare, "I do assent and consent to all therein contained," and if a man has any scruples he is bound by the plainest duty not to make that declaration. How is it that any man has ever done so? This is really the strangest thing in the whole; but historically it is intelligible. The above declaration was demanded for the first time of the whole body of clergy who were habituated to use the Prayerbook without being obliged to fully approve of it. On a certain day they were called upon to make the declaration or to forfeit their livings. Two thousand out of five or six thousand acted on their conscience, and resigned their preferments, which to many of them was their all—old men with families and affections and interests. It was indeed a noble testimony to faithfulness and to right and truth. But how came this noble example not to be followed by all conscientious men? This is intelligible. First they were not required to say so much except when inducted to livings. The deacon only promised to conform to the usage as by law established. The priest did no more; and by the time he became beneficed he had accepted some of the many ingenious apologies for the services as they stand, or of the modified interpretations put by bishops on the meaning of Subscription. If any scruple remained, a sense of the important good to be expected from compliance, and the mischief of separation and resistance satisfied these. Men of humble minds did what others they esteemed better than themselves had done without too curious inquiry. Some in one and some in another way bridged over the gulf; and for a century at least it seems never to have been agitated in the Church. Many bishops declared that they understood the words as only implying a willingness to use the Prayerbook on ordinary occasions; and when informed of scruples, sympathized with them themselves, and said they constituted no bar to entering Holy Orders.

" The people never troubled themselves with the question, though it was their matter quite as much, though not so interestedly, as that of their pastors.

" Thus things went on, and thus they go on now, although in these times of enquiry and advanced religious as well as other knowledge, probably there is a far greater proportion of men excluded by these objections, as well as of persons of defective views who are encouraged to enter by the state of things.  The poor church loses both ways : her faithful ministers are diminished, her unfaithful ones increased.

" What will be the end ?  I cannot doubt that it will be sooner or later a depravation of doctrine and a general corruption.  One feels very anxious to check such a consequence, if it were possible ; and as this becomes worse while the evil of subscription or tacit consent does not but remains the same, I can conceive a man from conscience submitting when all seems desperate to what he could not when there was some good left.

" The whole subject is full of enormous practical difficulties and perplexities, and to balance the matter wisely and decide so as that all shall approve the decision, is almost too hard for human nature.

" Baptist Noel, as a strong man was likely to do, cut the knot, and boldly took his position among declared and determined Dissenters.  Canon Wodehouse timidly, and after long deliberation and discussion, withdrew into the negative or disapproving rank, and there quietly remains.

" I have followed, or rather preceded him, in the same course ; and probably there are hundreds of others who could say as I, that but for these conscientious objections we would have lived and died, as far as we could be, faithful, laborious, humble ministers of the Established Church of our native land.  It seems to me a layman and woman's question.  The laity imposed the yoke ; they do practically now impose it.  Alter the Act of Uniformity, and release the clergyman from his ' assent and consent ;' leave the Prayerbook open to such comment and correction as all *human* laws and ordinances ever must be subject to : bind him by Articles to certain grand doctrines, and leave him liberty as to non-essentials. What judge would accept the Statute-book as we are forced to accept the Prayer-book ? Not one. Each thinks himself at liberty to seek alterations and to remove the faults of the Law which rules him, and why fetter the poor clergyman with a special yoke ? I can see nothing in it but a wicked determination that the church shall be deprived of its best and most faithful and perhaps, too, of its most able men. This object was avowed by those who introduced the obnoxious law to get rid of Baxter, Howe, Owen, and the rest styled Puritans, and they succeeded ; and worse, they drove into the less advantageous and influential as well as in some respects dangerous position of Dissent, not only these, but almost all who had received the pure gospel and the uncorrupted faith of the apostles from that time to the present.

"Would that I could call myself one of these. In doctrine I am, but in practice not. But the more nearly I approach to them in spirituality of mind and in unblemished conduct, the more firmly I shall, I believe, adhere to the course they set before me.

"I should like you to feel satisfied, and to approve ; but more, because I think doing so a test of sound discriminating and independent judgment, than from any desire to have many more of the same way of thinking with myself."

The next extract is from a letter also to his sister giving a brief account of a sermon which he preached in one of the parishes of England ; where and when it is not said, but most probably during his short sojourn at home in 1862. It indicates a painful apprehension on the part of Mr Ogle that "Sacramentalism" was spreading among the people of England.

## ON SACRAMENTALISM.

. "Hearing that some among my hearers were beginning to think the sacraments the main part of the Christian religion, I showed that as such they have no part in the economy of redemption as regards its execution or purchase. They are signs of completed acts, occasions of exercising faith, and so of securing the benefits they commemorate. In the age before the Westminster Confession and our own Articles were drawn up, almost the whole of Christendom had come to believe in the sacraments as the only channels of grace. It was putting things into the right track to show that if the sacraments be channels of grace, it is only because the spiritual acts of faith to which the blessings are promised are therein performed. I believe we have a fiery trial before us, in which all who will not again bow before the Sacramental Idol will have to pass through the "burning fiery furnace" of persecution. May God grant to you and to me the faith which supported the martyrs and confessors of the Old and of the New Testament." . . . .

The next is addressed to a relative, an aunt, after his return to Algeria in 1862, and expresses his stedfast adherence to his views despite they subjected him to perpetual 'exile.'

"I regret increasingly the cause which induces me to live abroad, while there is so much more freedom and field for greater usefulness at home. But as long as my objections to the Church of England Liturgy (founded on the baptismal service principally, and also extending to the use of the burial service, in all cases, irrespective of the life and character of the person for whom it is employed) shall continue, I do not see any prospect how I could act as a minister otherwise than as a dissenter; and I see so great dangers and objections to that, as to make me prefer, if God will, to suffer exile rather than to take a position at home so full of grave and serious difficulty. The course pursued by Baptist Noel, by Dr. Winslow, and other eminent Christian dissenters, does not make my way clear, and for this reason, I think I ought to be content to remain deprived of the position and influence and comfort of my profession as a clergyman, till it shall seem fit to the Almighty to open the door for my return. I do not take credit for superior conscientiousness, but having the views of truth and duty which I have, I can, for my part, do no other. I condemn no one because they differ from me."

## CHAPTER XXIV.

### Resumes Work in Algeria—The Famine.

Mr Ogle was greatly refreshed by his visit to England. It restored him for a while to those privileges of Christian intercourse and intellectual interchanges which are the distinguishing and invaluable peculiarity of free and Christian Britain. But this season of, to him, exquisite spiritual enjoyment, was brief. Tidings from Algeria, that things were not going well in his absence, recalled him to that land. The agent left in charge, had made contracts which he was not able to fulfil; a law-suit was imminent; a forced sale of the stock of the farm was threatened, and Mr. Ogle had no alternative, save to hasten back to Oran. We resume the extracts.

*October* 21.—"By the good providence of God, I write again from Oran in good health and safety. I have many mercies to record, and a better state of things than I feared. I have arrived just in time to save my property from dispersion. . . . .

"It is pitiable to see the effect of the last year's drought; the herds and flocks have had to be taken from place to place, throughout the province, to seek for pasture; there is no store of food for man or beast.

"The village near my farm is more desolate than you can conceive; more than half the inhabitants are gone, the rest, for the most part, in deep poverty; but there are some few left, and all seem to welcome me back with satisfaction. I hope that affliction here, as elsewhere, is preparing the way for that ready reception of the truth which I have so long desired to see, though I cannot say that I have laboured and prayed for it as I ought to have done.

"All God's dealings with His children are to wean them from the love of this present world, to teach them to 'Cease from man,' and to make them long for, and prepare for, the coming of the Lord Jesus.

"The voyage from Marseilles was stormy, torrents of rain with lightning. My water-bed did me good service; and a short run into Spain (as usual), with the opportunity of distributing a good number of books on the third day, which was fine, made me all right again, and I had a good night's rest, and was quite vigorous on arriving in Oran.

"I hear very good accounts respecting Senor R——, that he is still following the good way. He left his rags of priest-craft at —— (this refers to a young priest who came from Spain, and was for some time under his instruction, the year before). A tradesman from Oran has been with me for some time, he tells me of the blessed result which has followed the reading of two of the tracts which I gave away in Oran on my way here."

## AN ALGERIAN RUSE.

*November* 4. "In my absence in England my agent had a general direction to use my horses and implements in any way that would be remunerative. He had therefore undertaken a contract to carry merchandise from a place distant from Oran about 100 kilometres (60 miles). He purchased also a quantity of barley at this town, that he might have a return cargo, and arranged to pay £20 in advance, on condition that a load should always be ready for him on arrival. This continued for three months. He sold the barley at Oran immediately. I found that on the whole I was a loser by £16 for repairs of waggon and the loss of one of my horses; still the contract must be completed.

"On Wednesday last, the agent brings me a legal document, 'Voilà une affaire!'

"The purport of this was, 'Seeing that A. has not completed his contract within the time specified, B. summons A.

immediately to take the whole remaining portion of grain off B.'s hands, and to pay down £120 plus expenses.

"A. thought it was an expedient to get rid of the bargain made with B., by imposing upon him conditions which he knew he could not fulfil ; or it might be only the preliminary to an action against him, supposing that B. had not been able to get rid of his barley as quickly as by contract agreed to. . . . .

"My decision was soon made ; happily, I expected a remittance from England in a few days. Barley is what I must purchase to sow my land in a few weeks, and though the quantity will be much more than I shall require, I organised a scheme to help all the inhabitants of my commune who are in the last extremity for want of money to buy grain to sow their land.

"I asked God's guidance, and felt grateful for a prospect of so satisfactory a conclusion to my difficulty. At once I went with my agent to hire a magazin in Oran where it might be necessary to sell some of the grain at once. The money I had to borrow *at twenty-five per cent.* (the usual interest in times of scarcity), but the thought of the scheme by which, like Joseph, I might relieve my poor neighbours, made me happy ; so, writing a letter to the inhabitants of my commune, offering to give them barley in exchange for labour, I set out with the agent on my journey. The first night we slept at the house of a friend, and rose at one o'clock A.M. to pursue our journey. It was a night of fine weather after heavy rain. The road lay through a bold and mountainous country, without inhabitants save the nomade Arabs. Of these we saw few ; now a tall white sheeted, dark visaged figure standing against a telegraph post by the roadside, looking like a giant with a spear of Goliath ; now a group in advance of us upon the road, looking like a band of Bedouin robbers, waiting to fall upon us. As the morning broke, the scene was visible in all its grandeur, mountains on mountains ; ' Alps on Alps arise,' all savage and desert. At nine o'clock A.M. we arrived at Mascara.

"It was market day. Some two or three thousand Arabs thronged the place, and with their wonted vivacity and volu-

bility, gave life to the scene. Jewish merchants, in little
shops, displayed attractive and costly ware. Spaniards and
Italians, retailing fruit and vegetables. A regular fair of
horses, cattle, and of sheep ; and one would-be missionary
looking anxiously for a customer—one who would be willing to
receive and to value treasures more precious than the wealth
of worlds, without money and without price. With one or
two exceptions, none were of the Pilgrim's mind, 'We buy the
truth.'

" Meanwhile, my agent went to see the vendor of grain.
He returned, saying that the latter had written the letter to
get rid of his bargain, and that he had not a handful of barley
to dispose of. He had acted under the advice of his legal
adviser."

Mr. Ogle's letters narrate numerous occurrences of a similar
kind. It was these, rather than the uncertainty of the
seasons, which formed the most distressing part of the
Algerian experiment, and which induced him to make arrangements to relinquish the idea of a " self-supporting mission
establishment." " I wish I were well rid of these affairs," we
find him writing, " for I cannot feel satisfied that it is God's
will that I should pursue them ; but if I were to relinquish
the conflict *because* it is a difficult one, I should feel that I was
procuring ease at the expense of duty."

" Having made arrangements and given promises of seed
for sowing the land of the commune, I purchased barley from
another merchant.

" Rain continued to fall, and my return journey was imperilled thereby. A bridge on the road was carried away by
the rising torrent, and a village had been inundated since I
passed it a few days before. I telegraphed to Mascara, therefore, to delay the transport of my barley until the road should
be safe for traffic."

We thus behold difficulties of various kinds thickening
around the path of our missionary colonist. All his available

resources he was obliged to expend in meeting the engagements made in his name in his absence, and in relieving to
the utmost of his power a community smitten down by famine.
In the midst of these manifold trials and losses, his zeal in
the prosecution of his work remained unabated.   He writes :—

Oran, *November.*—" I am ill with fever, and have obscure
poverty also before me ; but I would endure anything to secure
the objects I had at heart in coming here—to support the
Christian, the Protestant cause in Algeria.   May it be said of
me, ' he hath done what he could.'   My heart is sick when I
think of giving up the work I have attempted.

" I know how poor, how very poor, the cause of Christ is
here ; and cannot bear to see a poor unprotected family looking to me for aid in vain.   I have indeed—by spending so
much on the undertaking—accepted poverty for their sakes,
but I can do no more.   Oh, would that my heart were right
with God.   He sees me unworthy of so glorious an office as
an ambassador for Him."

---

# CHAPTER XXV.

## Work in Spain—The Church of England.

In tracing the course of our missionary traveller we are
now brought to the year 1863.   Matters went on this year
much as in previous ones.   Anxious not to press more
heavily than necessary upon his home resources, Mr Ogle
still retained his farm, and with it a large establishment of
herdsmen, ploughmen, and miscellaneous workers, forming
quite a little colony, in the hope of making the country he
sought to evangelise bear its due part in the expense, and of
providing a home for Spanish converts.   " I wish to use
Algerian resources," we find him saying, " and not to rob my

own land, from which I am an exile, until, by relaxing the terms of subscription imposed upon her clergy, she permit me to preach and to minister with a free conscience as a parish priest." But as yet he had not succeeded in making the Algerian mission self-sustaining, nor even nearly so. His farming operations did not prosper. The seasons were uncertain and unpropitious. His work-people were unskilful, indolent, and in too many instances unfaithful; and the consequence was that his financial difficulties, already great, became this year still more formidable. Something must be done. Proceeding as he had been doing hitherto, his home resources would be speedily drained, and the whole work brought abruptly to a close. He now began, though unwillingly, to entertain the belief that duty called on him to yield to the wishes of his friends at home and give up the prospect of forming a colonial home for enquirers and Spanish Protestants, with all the labour, anxiety, and pecuniary loss which it was now seen to involve, and to confine his attention to less onerous and more purely evangelistic labours.

What helped to bring him to this resolution was the state of his health. The climate had begun to tell with decisive effect on his constitution. The fierce heats of summer brought fever and dysentery in their train, and not only did the physical exhaustion thereby induced unfit him for that oversight and unceasing attention which such a multiplicity of affairs demanded, and which never went well save when his own eye was on them, but he was compelled to leave Algeria for several months every year, and seek the restorative influences of Europe. From these excursions he returned improved in health, but fated to experience the mortification and annoyance of finding that his goods had been wasted by mismanagement, or purloined by dishonesty, during his absence.

As regards the year on which we now enter it will not be

necessary to go so much into detail as we have done when speaking of the events of those going before it. Our readers can now sufficiently realize Mr Ogle's position in Algeria, and his mode of evangelising. What is new or characteristic only need be now given. The state of the Church of England, the growth of Romanism in Great Britain, and the dangers which he foresaw accruing from thence to his native land, occasioned him more uneasiness, and weighed more upon his spirit, than did even his own embarrassments. In the greater evils which he believed to be impending he forgot his own personal afflictions. He preferred Jerusalem above his chief joy. It was the good of the church and of the world which was the first object of his labours and prayers, and however it might fare with himself, he rejoiced when he could see even the smallest tokens of revival in the work of God. Though difficulties thickened, his ardour increased, and he but the more perseveringly prosecuted his work among the heathen in proportion as he felt, which he now began more and more to do, that the time was short during which he would be permitted to labour. His hopes and fears, his views of public matters, and his cravings after the higher life, will be best seen from the extracts that follow.

The year 1863 opened auspiciously. Hopes long cherished, but often disappointed, seemed at last on the eve of being realized. How amazingly fertile is the soil of Algeria when other things conspire !

"ORAN, *May* 28, 1863.

" Were this year the type of our climate, this would be one of the richest countries in the world, and there is reason to think, in the Roman times, it was such. I never expected to see it as now. While I write my hat is wreathed with ears of corn ten inches long and eighty grains each. We found one root, the produce of a single grain, with fifty-seven ears. Of course it is not all such. I have had £500 offered

for my crop—a small one. We are very busy with hay
making. All the country is covered with hay. The cattle
have not been able to spoil the pastures for the scythe; a
horse tied with a short cord finds enough to eat for a whole
day. The sheep are in danger of being lost, for you cannot
see them in the fields, and this in a land where last year at
this time there was not a blade of grass, a few withered herbs
black and scrubby alone remained, the crops were about four
inches high, and withered as they came into ear, now fields
of waving corn breast high, and in full ear, cover the same
ground. One year of abundant rain leaves the earth in · a
very favourable state for the succeeding.

"The fertility of Chaldæa in ancient times, as described in
Rawlinson's *Ancient Monarchies*, was not unlike. 'Of all
countries that we know,' says Herodotus, 'there is none that
is so fruitful in grain. It yields commonly two hundredfold,
and when the production is at the greatest, even three
hundredfold. The blade of the wheat plant and of the
barley plant is often four fingers in breadth.'

"Theophrastus, the disciple of Aristotle, remarks in
Babylon, the wheat fields are regularly mown twice, and
then fed off with beasts to keep down the luxuriance of the
leaf, otherwise the plant does not run to ear. When this is
done the return on lands that are badly cultivated is fifty-
fold, while on those that are well farmed it is an hundred-
fold.'

"'Instead of the luxuriant fields, the groves and gardens
of former times,' writes Chesney, *Euphrates Expedition*,
'nothing now meets the eye but an arid waste. Many parts
of Chaldæa, naturally as productive as others, are at present
pictures of desolation. Unwholesome marshes, with gigantic
reeds, occupy large tracts. Other large tracts lie waste and
bare, parched up by the fierce heat of the sun. In some
places sand-drifts accumulate and threaten to make of the
whole region a mere portion of the desert. The great cause
of this difference between ancient and modern Chaldæa is the
neglect of the water courses. The modern Oriental is content, even in the case of a rich soil, with a tenfold return.'"

This enables us to understand the years of plenty with which another part of this same continent was favoured four thousand years before. Then the earth brought forth in handfuls such as those which Mr Ogle now gathered. And yet nowhere are seen more frequent or more terrible spectacles of famine than in this land. By way of contrast we may extract the following from the *Times* of January 1st, 1868, which, along with the paragraph that follows it from an Algerian print, gives us a vivid picture of the destitution and misery with which Algeria is at times scourged. " He turneth a fruitful land into barrenness for the wickedness of them that dwell therein."

" A frightful famine, reminding one of that which devastated Orissa last year, is at present ravaging Algeria."

The *Echo* of Oran says:—" On the 3d December last, the bodies of ten natives who died of hunger were found at Mascara. On the following day fourteen perished in like manner; and on the 5th, twenty-three of these poor creatures were carried to the cemetery by their co-religionaries, who only submitted to this duty under blows. The total number in three days was forty-seven."

Mr Ogle's state of mind at this time, as regards the indications of Providence, and his own line of duty, was desponding.

" By the good hand of a gracious and merciful Father I have to record many alleviations in my trials. I pray to be preserved from slothfully shrinking from what is laborious and difficult, but that I may see my way to get rid of affairs which are too cumbrous; which entangle the spirit in secular concerns and anxieties; and engage time and powers which ought to be entirely devoted to the service of GOD.

" Yet I am full of grief as I think of giving up the work I have attempted for the temporal benefit of the poor families around me. I know how poor; how very poor, the Protestants are here. I have indeed accepted poverty for their sakes. I am as economical as to my own expenditure as pos-

sible; but I can do more, I would endure any privation to
secure the cause I have at heart.    I fear that God sees in my
heart motives less sincere, less unselfish than I had hoped, and
judges me unworthy of success in so great and glorious an
office as I aspire to fill to support the cause of Christ in
Algeria—May it be said of me 'he hath done what he
could.'

"Remember that I shall have to give 20 per cent for
money, and that delay in my payments exposes me to forced
sales and ruinous exactions.    I hope to be able to transfer
the lease of my farm; meanwhile it is sowing time, which must
not be neglected."

"Ought I not to trust that He who has very graciously, and
to my mind, wonderfully, led and preserved me hitherto in
Algeria, gives me these occasional trials lest I should be injured
by the prosperity which on the whole has marked my course
there.    How many openings for the gospel work have I had;
how many obstacles have been removed, how many dangers
avoided, how much has the state of things in my own neighbourhood changed for the better!    It is only the cares and
distresses from pecuniary losses which hinder me from rejoicing in my work and praising God for success.    I do not think
that these indicate His will that I should retire from my
experiment.    If I give it up all past labour will be lost.    Let
us be earnest in prayer for an outpouring of the Spirit."

To diversify his pursuits, and relieve his mind from these
cares and anxieties, Mr Ogle took occasional excursions into
the country.    Besides tending to recruit his health, these
short journeys brought him opportunities of proclaiming the
message of salvation, it might be to some tribe of wandering
Arabs, or to some equally benighted colonist.    Take as a
sample an excursion made somewhat earlier in the season
than the period at which we are now arrived.

"Having the letter of *le Maire* of Valmy, I set out at 8
o'clock a.m. with two horses and my cabriolet, my servant and
provisions for two days.    A lovely May morning, the thermo-

meter at 66° at 10 a.m., a frosty dew still visible, the earth carpeted with butter-cups, daisies, and pink crocuses. A fortnight ago, not a blade of grass was to be seen; now the whole land is verdant; the singing of birds, chirruping of grasshoppers, with frogs and other such fry chanting chorus made a very atmosphere of song. Young lambs sport in the pastures, flocks and herds revel in exuberance of forage.

"We drive to the village of Valmy, where lies the farm, to see about the hay, to speak to *le Maire*, and to hire some one to bring home the flock—find that at 12 o'clock the said pasturage is to be let by auction; now, if I do not again rent the communal land as in 1861, and 62, I shall be surrounded by unenclosed lands, and shall be obliged to incur great expense in fencing to protect my fields. I decided, therefore, to be present at the letting, and drove to the town, hired some of the land, and sending on the servant and horses took my gun. After shooting a few partridges and two quails I went to see an old colonist; he gave me dinner, and with his family listened very attentively, while I read to him and conversed upon the leading doctrines of true Christianity as differing from Romanism."

The summer of 1863 was passed in the discharge of such duties as the management of his farm and the superintendence of his numerous establishment imposed upon him, and also in such occasional evangelistic efforts as the state of the country and the openings in Providence made possible to him. The heats of the season left him exhausted, so that it was again necessary for his health to leave Algeria for a while and return to England. His journey was as usual made subservient to his great work as a missionary.

"SARAGOSSA, *September 19th*, 1863.

"MY DEAR BROTHER,—What, wandering still! Yes, and I trust not out of the way, though literally led by a way which I knew not. I left Oran, as my last led you to expect, on Wednesday the 16th inst.—the earliest opportunity which presented. In hope of shortening the journey—for I had in-

formation from one who professed to know—I took the route
across Spain, being also told it was not more expensive.
Arriving at Valencia at noon on Thursday, I expected a train
to Madrid. . . . Owing to not having Spanish money, my
French being refused at the station, I had to stay at Valencia
till Thursday, and then take express to Madrid and Bayonne
by way of Pampeluna.   On my way, as I shall narrate, I fell
asleep from exhaustion, for I had never been without work,
and had most encouraging conversations with fellow-travellers,
and was carried against my will to Saragossa.

" The afternoon of Thursday was spent in Valencia ; several
books were given away, and in the most public places, and
with conversations—all well received.   Called on a relative of
Don Felix, a very nice woman, apparently a Christian ; had a
conversation with her, in presence of a priest, on the evil of
misunderstanding one another—Protestant view of the Church,
as invisible, and its bond of union—apostolic doctrine and
communion of saints with their common Head, Christ Jesus.
I fear Don Felix is gone back to his ecclesiastical office, but I
hope he is growing, though not strong enough yet to give up
Spain and friends and emoluments for Christ.   I am pained for
him, but hope predominates.

" During the long journey of seventeen hours from Valencia,
I threw broadcast the seeds of spiritual life in the shape of
small tracts, and at length books, whenever a knot of
labourers, or a face of peculiar intelligence, or other circumstance, invited.   Thus scarcely a village on the route has
been omitted, for I had packed quite a large assortment of
books and tracts in my luggage—a little afraid of the custom-
house, but the examination had been cursory.   I threw all my
packages open, and said nothing, and all passed.

" Yesterday one man insulted me very much in the train.
At last I heard him say, ' What patience that man has ; any-
body else would have told me to hold my tongue in a moment.'
I had been at first good-humoured ; refused to take seriously
his abuse, and thus disarmed it entirely ; but I was afterwards
very silent, and this provoked him, and he tapped me rather
roughly on the head more than once, and said he would mur-

der me when we arrived, &c., so I thought it time to be angry, and, with few words, threatening him with police, he was silenced. . . .

"This day has been remarkable for answers to prayer. I rose very sad, owing to the deep oppression produced by a heathen country, where one has no opening for the gospel. I had but one resource—prayer—that, feeble and blind as must be all *my* efforts, Christ would still order them for the furtherance of His kingdom. At six A.M. I set out with a good store of gospels and Scripture extracts, also Mr Dalton's ' Collar of Pearls'—a compendium of the New Testament in Scripture words, without additions. Not one person during the day has been unfavourable, though I must have distributed one hundred nearly. My usual address on presenting one was, ' This is a work of faithfulness and truth.' ' Yes, yes,' was the almost universal reply. Some followed me. Seeing others take the books, a blind man, who was selling songs, &c., took three to put on his stall, after I had read part to him. *In the Queen's Palace* I left two ; the door-keeper received one gladly, and a second I put into a confession-box in the Royal chapel. Who knows whether I may not now (at Saragossa) be baffling, conducted by my Master's hand, a pursuit ! A rich man, travelling with his family in the same carriage with me, took two books, and read others, expressing himself delighted, and asked, ' Can the Government forbid these excellent books ?' He bid me go on and give them freely. He was of Segovia.

"To-night I find at the hotel a school-fellow of Trigo's, from Granada, with whom I have had a friendly discussion.

"This Trigo is one of the Spanish prisoners, a converted Spaniard, an advocate, and of a good family in Spain. I have left him at Oran to take charge of my affairs during my absence.

"The tracts left in the Palace at Madrid were on ' The only way of Salvation.' In the train I put books into the hands of all the readers in four compartments, and gave also to others. The excitement of continued conversation on these topics in a foreign tongue is quite exhausting, and while wishing in a quiet moment I had taken my ticket further than Bayonne, I

fell asleep and was carried on to Saragossa, from whence Don
Trigo comes, and I have hope of a work for God here."

What is narrated above is a beautiful illustration of the
way in which Spain was being prepared for the opening which
soon thereafter followed.   At that hour scarce were there any
signs of that opening, and no one could have believed that it
was near.   A dominant priesthood possessed the land :
masters of the country, they had grasped the power of the
government, and they wielded it for the object of keeping the
Gospel out of Spain.   The priest and the *gens-d'arme* were
in league to prevent a single copy of the Word of God entering the country.   It was at his peril for any one to distribute
a tract or a Bible, and the certain fate of any Spaniard
found reading or possessing the Word of God was to be
sent to the galleys or condemned to a scaffold.   Such was the
condition of Spain no later than 1863 : the land was all dark ;
the country was shut in and guarded : at every one of its
gates sat a sentinel : on all its towers were posted watchmen
to sound the alarm should danger approach, or signs of day
appear in the sky.   And yet despite all this vigilance, and in
defiance of all these perils, there were men who knew how to
enter Spain, and to scatter over its fields that good seed which
they were well assured would one day spring up and bear
plenteous fruit.   Among these was Mr Ogle.   He never passed
from Algeria to England, or back again from England to
Algeria without taking Spain in his way : or halting at one
or more of its ports, and during his stay of perhaps a couple
of hours distributing a hundred or so of tracts and Gospels.   In
his present rapid journey through Spain we see him acting the
part eminently of a light-bearer.   He scatters from his car-
riage-window the seed of life.   Not a village along his whole
track at which God's message to men has not been introduced.   It may have been but a few words or a single sentence,

but every ray of light is saving. Before the *gens-d'-arme* had time to be informed and to set out in pursuit, Mr Ogle was hundreds of miles away. Like the Parthian, but in a nobler war, he discharges his arrows as he flees. How many eyes may have been opened as the result of this journey who can tell, or how much the tracts and Testaments distributed in this and other such visits to Spain may have contributed to the awakening which has since taken place in that land, will never be known till the great day.

The case of Spain admirably shows the co-operation of God with the efforts of man in the work of evangelisation. When we do our part we may rest assured God will do his. " Knock and it shall be opened unto you." This precept applies to the case of nations as of individuals. The gates of Spain were closed : a double tyranny held them shut ; but the command to Christians was to " knock," and when they began to knock, God's providence in a short while opened. " He that observeth the wind shall not sow," says Solomon. Verily the winds were contrary in Spain at the time of Mr Ogle's journey : and had he permitted this consideration to rule his conduct he would not have sowed. He would have said—There is no use in scattering seed at this hour : it will be but thrown away : a sacerdotal and political tyranny will tread it under foot, and extinguish it : let me wait till the winds shall have changed, and the country has been opened. He did not so reason : he withheld not his hand, but scattered the good seed as widely as he could, leaving it with God to change the winds and make the shower to fall in His own good time. It was a sign that the morning was near to Spain when "the feet of them that bring good tidings, that publish peace," began to be seen upon her sierras.

And so it turned out. While these devoted men were distributing the Word of Life in that dark land, God was guiding political events so as to open the country at the very first

z

moment that Spain was ready to profit by it. There
is nothing in our times that more strikingly reveals the hand
of God, and the co-operation of Providence with the missionaries of the Cross, than the opening of the Iberian Peninsula.
First a little band of sowers went forth : as the fruit of their
labours a few Spaniards were converted, and, taught by the
Bible, they formed themselves into a little society or church.
They were arrested and thrown into the prison of Grenada: their
sufferings attracted the notice of their countrymen. " There
must be truth in Protestantism," said the Spaniards, "when
men are willing to go to prison, and to endure the galleys for
it. We should like to possess that wonderful book which has
so fortified these men : we too should like to read the Bible,
and judge for ourselves." Thus the confessors of Grenada became preachers to their countrymen, and the story of their
punishment, proclaimed over all Spain, only awakened a desire
among all classes of Spaniards to possess the Bible. The good
work of Bible distribution went on more prosperously than
ever : the converts were multiplied : and the priests finding
their vigilance eluded, and their efforts baffled, began to persecute the professors of the truth with yet greater violence.
The new converts, among whom were several priests, fled to
the Rock of Gibraltar, and found protection under the flag of
England. Thither had the hand of God led them as to a school.
The Protestant ministers on the Rock took them under training, and taught them the way of the Lord more perfectly.
When their instructions in the Gospel had been finished, this
little band of Spanish converts came, one day, to the resolution
of forming themselves into a church—the Evangelical Church
of Spain—and of devoting themselves as a body to the
evangelisation of their native land. From that hour they
held themselves in readiness to enter Spain and begin the
work of Reformation the first moment the political restrictions
should be relaxed. They had not long to wait. Their sacred

bond of union and operation was formed in April 1868, and only five months thereafter, September 1868, a revolution drove Isabella II. from the throne, the power of the priesthood was broken, and the doors of Spain stood open to the entrance of the missionary. General Prim now took possession of the government, and one of his first acts was to assure the representatives of the "Evangelical Church of Spain," that civil and religious liberty was now the law of the country, and that they might enter Spain "with the Bible under both arms." In this marvellous way did God hear the prayers and second the efforts of his servants. Scarce had they begun to sow when the rain fell. Scarce had they knocked when the "bars of iron" were broken, and the "gates of brass" fell back. In that same country in which, in 1863, Mr Ogle, as we have seen, could but drop a few tracts and Testaments as he fled before the *gens-d'-arme*, the missionary in 1868 could distribute the Word of Life and preach the Gospel without let or hindrance.

The evangelisation has taken root in Spain: Protestant congregations now exist in almost all the principal towns of that country: especially is it so in Madrid and Seville, where the evangelicals are numerous and their assemblies flourishing. The religious liberty granted in 1868 has ever since been maintained: even in those times when threats of insurrection rendered it necessary to suspend the political constitution. In that unhappy land the violence of faction is still rife, and the strife of parties sometimes issues in civil war; nor is it likely that Spain will be an orderly and peaceful country for some time to come, but there is ground to believe that the Gospel will not again be driven thence; the Hand of God will guard the young plant which it has set there, till it has grown a tree whose boughs will touch the Pyrenees on the one side and extend to the Straits of Gibraltar on the other. And at that day the names of those who laboured for

this result : who sowed the seed in peril and tears, will be
mentioned with honour : and among the brightest of these
must ever be placed the name of Ogle.

In due time he reached England, but after a short sojourn
at home found it necessary again to return to Algeria. The
delight experienced from the Christian fellowship of his own
country was saddened by what he saw in Britain. This gave
him a deeper pang than the evils he witnessed abroad, being
more unexpected. Abroad he had continually before his eye
and upon his heart the great systems of idolatry which
flourish there, with all the demoralisation and vice which they
engender, and all the misery, temporal and eternal, which
they draw after them, but at home he was even more grieved
by the coldness, the formality, the selfishness which he saw
prevailing amongst professing Christians, and the apathy with
which they viewed the spread of a system which he had ever
found as inimical to the gospel as heathenism itself, and as
much the enemy of the blessed Saviour. He disburdens his
heart on this head in terms which attest the depth and
sincerity of his grief, in the following letter to the Rev.
J. D——, written just on the eve of his departure for
Algeria :——

"Ripon, *Nov.* 6, 1863.

" My Dear Sir,—Thank you much for your pressing invi-
tation. I should very much like to avail myself of it. The
deep oppression which rests on my heart would lead me to
pour into a sympathizing ear many troubles. The world is
nominally Christian, but really it has succeeded in dethroning
Jesus from his rule in the earth, and setting up his enemy.
Nothing save ancient heathenism can be more contrary to
Christianity than what we see and meet with everywhere.
Where is Christ as the Saviour loved and sought ? Where is
His gracious Spirit cherished ? Where are the Evangelical,
the Apostolical, the true Christians ? The heart is sick to see
that called Christianity which is unchanged worldliness or gross

superstition, and we have this less than the first Apostles had. That they were clear and decided in their resistance to authority when putting restrictions, as the Sanhedrim : or compromising the truth as Peter himself.   Now there is so little *light* that none dare to act but with the leading string of the *multitude* (albeit of *believers* as they suppose).   I do fear that the days of darkness are on us, otherwise (dear sir), would not there be clearness of view and accord between the Christians on these points ? Should we not, instead of having abandoned Romanists to their superstition without attempting to evangelize them, and often softening down their abominations, be as earnest and as self-sacrificing in their conversion as of *any other heathens.*   I fully believe myself, after many years in Roman Catholic countries, that *there is no religion on earth so decidedly hostile to the Gospel and so exclusive of it as Romanism.*   I allow that presenting in some sort as truths the vicarious sufferings and the glorious ascension and intercession of our Lord, &c., the Roman Church does bear testimony *to facts*, and that these facts are not unfrequently received by her nominal adherents, who, I hope, know little of and reject all her other teaching.   But no thanks for this to the Church of Rome, if in spite of her effort to overthrow the Church of Christ, and to destroy the Gospel, its life-giving influence prevails to the snatching of some souls from perdition.   The Church of Rome has only afforded an evidence of our Lord's prediction, 'the *gates of Hell* shall not prevail against it,' like the heathens who ' having not the law were a law unto themselves,' &c., and therefore there is a duty on us, and this duty we do not as a Christian nation perform.   Can I say that any individual does ?   I never heard of one who did to my apprehension, and I am sure my own conscience accuses me, and I am abased and miserable to a painful and humiliating extent on this account.   ' What,' it may be said, ' have you not exposed your liberty and life, ruined your prospects, and damaged your property, spent years of toil and privation and exile fighting against Rome with unmitigated and uncompromising ardour, and for many years ?' No, I reply, I have desired to do this, but I have not as yet gone further than a few occasional and spasmodic efforts, timid chiefly on account of the impression that all the judgment of Evangelical men and their example is against doing more than I am. It is for this that I have taken a farm as an outpost, as it were, not venturing to attack the fortress itself, and by the indirect influence I thus obtain hope to do some little. Oh, how have I been disappointed and chastised. Now I should like to consult with you prayerfully to see if I could obtain one Christian to agree with me on a definite course of action, and also to have his wise and divinely directed counsel, and after much prayer and self-examination to go forth, if need be, to prison and to death. My dear sir, these are my sentiments. I must say I have little of the martyr, and love ease in Zion and long for a quiet dwelling-place and a smooth course, but I trust God, for Christ's sake, will make me willing to do all the good pleasure of His will."

He had made an arrangement, before quitting La Serria, by which a distressed neighbouring colonist, a protestant, would be enabled to retain his own farm ; and, in return, superintend Mr Ogle's affairs during his absence. He knew him to be an industrious and skilful agriculturalist, and he hoped he had left his work-people, his flocks, and herds, under good care, while he was also saving a neighbour, by timely aid, from impending ruin. But the accounts he received were unsatisfactory, and he hastened back to prevent a failure as the conclusion of his own enterprise. In the journey back, he again used the opportunity it afforded of a few hours work in Spain.

"Arrived at Marseilles 1.30. The steamer for Oran was a smaller one than usual and much crowded, hundreds of soldiers besides colonists and their families—no room to move. The wind was fresh, and on the second day we had a thunderstorm with torrents of rain and a dashing sea . . . The coast of Spain in sight ; but the sea was too rough to allow us to enter the port as usual. We therefore anchored about half-a-mile from the mole. My fondly cherished visit to Spain was, however, accomplished. I am sorry to confess that when I saw the difficulty, for a moment I was tempted to excuse myself; the recollection of the Spanish dungeons came before me. But it was only a moment, a dark Spanish priest got into the boat for the shore and I instantly dropped down into it and arrived with him. I was disappointed in not finding a friend at home, and again the joint conviction of danger to those to whom I should give books as well as to myself arrested me—God graciously encouraged me however. I spoke to a stranger, and he received my tract with joy, also other books, and I walked on, giving away more than fifty of the Scripture selections, and many Gospels. The people quite crowded about me after I had distributed a few. Knowing that I had but one hour I gave to those who were anxious to have. Had I had ten times as many books and papers I could have distributed them. I told the assembled crowd plainly, ' these books are Protestant.' They only cried more loudly, ' give, give.' I opened the Testament and read a few verses from St Matt. v. ; they were silent. I ceased ; they cried again, ' give me, give me,' and so I gave till all I had with me were gone. A Spaniard followed me for some distance while I talked with him. He said, ' *The priests teach us what they please. Their's is a religion of money.*' On deck was a poor woman, scantily clothed, with an infant; she was ill, a storm of rain came down, she fell helpless. No one noticed her. I raised her up and put her under shelter, and by moistening spunge-cake with water and warming it upon the engine, procured a nutriment which satisfied and quieted the infant. Before the voyage was over I had the pleasure to see it *smile.*"

Such simple acts of Christ-like kindness have an effect which words sometimes fail to produce. It was so here :—

" Hard-featured men pressed forward to receive tracts after this, and the hearty farewell which was given me by many of the soldiers and passengers persuaded me ' that it is not for nought that one is led to take distant voyages ; all our steps are ordered of the Lord.' Let us, dear sister, unite in earnest

supplications that we may be employed largely in the service
of that blessed Master, who went about doing good and
gave Himself to die for us—His acts had no alloy of self.
Pure, simple, love and pity for rebels and enemies."

"We touched at a Spanish port, and there left about three
hundred copies of the different Gospels. I believe they will
be valued as they ought to be in a country where the true
light is rarely permitted to shine.

"How sad that it should be true of our day as of the
times of old, 'Darkness hath covered the earth and gross darkness the people.' Oh may the prophecy, which follows that sad
description, speedily be accomplished, 'The Lord shall arise
upon thee.'"

"As I entered the city, at its gate sat an old man by a
little booth. He looked intelligent, and I asked, 'if he could
read.' 'Yes.' He took one of my books and began to read the
Gospel of St John.

"'It is a ray from heaven,' he said, pointing upward. I
said a few words to him respecting the book and the need of
prayer to God for the Spirit's teaching, and my time being
short, hastened on my errand into the town greatly encouraged
to see the barriers which superstition and tyranny have placed
to keep out the truth, being broken down."

"I have news from America that Mr Salvage has been sent
on the mission to P——. It seems that my offer of £40 has
encouraged the Society to employ him. He will spend part
of the year in S. America, where he has been so largely blessed
in time past. We must make America the subject of our
prayers. It seems to me that the position of Christians in
England has this great advantage—the largeness of the sphere
to which not only their sympathies and prayers, but a direct
usefulness extends. A very small contribution, nay your
prayers alone, may make you fellow helpers with many
labourers in the vineyard, no matter how distant their habitation or how various their circumstances."

On his arrival in Algeria his worst fears were realized.

"I am so hedged in," he writes, "with my engagements, I

cannot honourably quit them. I could bear losses cheerfully, but when trusted, benefited persons ill-use us, one is apt to lose patience. On this account I have passed a week of more vexation and irritation than I ever remember to have felt. My harness and farming implements are lost or destroyed ; my animals are in so poor a condition from neglect and abuse that they cannot work ; my threshing floor testifies to the waste and extravagance which has prevailed. I have received back but a sorry remnant of the flocks and herds which I left behind—about fifty left out of the flock of two hundred. Enough of this, my heart is sadly rebellious, but I do strive and pray, that I may not ' be overcome of evil.' Oh how difficult it is to love and to do good to those who have injured us !

" I have had encouragement in my true work. Do not be disheartened about me. May wisdom, and grace ; faith, patience, and power be given to me, and may God's truth be honoured and His cause advanced.

" I met with Bishop Gell in France on my journey. He was on his way to India. He was very cordial. He is now upon the Indian ocean. *O si sic omnes* !"

Notwithstanding the state of matters at his farm, the things of the kingdom of God were ever first in his heart. It is necessary to notice this ; because his own consciousness of how much was yet to be attained, caused him constantly to lament in his letters over his remaining love of the world and want of constant and fervent love towards God ; even at times when the impression produced upon others was, that an unusual fervour of love, both to God and to man, burned in his heart and shone in his life.

" I arrived at home on Sunday last, and during the day had many Spaniards who came to see me ; to whom I read the Scriptures. At night, just as I was going to prayer with my servant, a knock at my door, and the old shepherd of the village and his wife came in. I bid them sit down, and read John x., speaking to them of the love of Jesus, and they then were willing to kneel with us in prayer. They seemed to be deeply impressed. The old man afterwards repeated most of what I had said, to show that he understood it. Thus, you see, how much I have to be thankful for and to rejoice my heart, though absent from you all and with many trials awaiting me. I wish to remind you of the poor prisoners in Spain, they need constant supplies to alleviate the hardships they suffer."

## CHAPTER XXVI.

### 1 8 6 4.

IT does not appear that the abundant harvest of 1863 was repeated. The rains were again withheld, and the consequence was an earth parched with drought and a harvest so scanty as to leave the natives liable to the visitations of famine. Mr Ogle was now convinced that his scheme of joining extensive farming operations with the mission must be abandoned, and this year we see him working his way gradually out of these engagements. We find him intimating his change of plan in the following letter to the Rev. J. D—— :—

ORAN, *Aug.* 9, 1864.

" Since I partially retired from the too secularising employment I had taken up though with a higher than secular object, I have been moving about more than usual, and have run over nearly the whole province in various journeys of five to eight days each. I take a spring cart and two horses with tent and cooking utensils, and thus am quite independent.

" Trigo the Spanish refugee was my companion in one journey, he did not like the tenting, being afraid of the Arabs at this unquiet season, and being a father of a family it was reasonable that his wife exacted this condition. I don't intend my wife to dictate to me in anything. I hope I shall some day find one who will not object to share my journeys and perils. We have met with a good reception from Spaniards generally, and the stock of 'Collares de Perlos,' 'Extractors,' &c., is nearly out. I have sent many to Mexico and some few to Spain. Alas, the papers inform us that the new Government has inaugurated its accession to power by publishing a new code against foreign books and interference with Catholic religion—they make a crime punishable by imprisonment the distribution of any book printed out of Spain, impose a fine for offences against the Catholic religion of 100 to 500 piastres with imprisonment. . . . . . I was myself taken prisoner in Africa a few weeks ago. I was distributing in the market at Mostayaneur tracts and gospels, an agent of the police accosted me and conducted me to the station after examination by the Commissary and delivering to him examples of the books I was circulating. I was dismissed with orders to attend the decision of the Sous Préfet. This was to let the matter pass, but I was straightly charged to distribute no more. I went out and recommenced my work, only avoiding to do so in sight of the police. I long to see some sense of responsibility towards these neighbour nations, falsely called Christian, awakened in English Christians. Next to our own blind and culpable encouragement of Popery, it is the saddest and strongest sign of decay of religion amongst us."

## Spanish Hymn Books.

" There are however some who sigh for and labour for the advancement of Christ's kingdom, and I am glad to hail your Spanish Hymn Book as an instalment of this feeling. I agree with you that Füster's hymns are not of much value ; a few of them are good in spirit and more bad. But we want an evangelical poetry for Spain, specially that kind adapted for congregational singing. Surely England is specially rich in this species of literature. Newton, Cowper, Toplady, Watts, Wesley, and many more have given us store of hymns devotional and animating, but they do not bear translating. I am inclined to think that we need not be very anxious about *music* for Spanish hymns. The exception in Spanish metrical composition is the stanza—the rule a sort of irregular metre ; this they sing to airs of a simple kind, and blank verse can be readily used. Impromptu song is common, and though I never heard a company unite in singing, I dare say that it would be easy to bring a congregation to sing in unison. Let us choose good hymns and the music will follow. The Spaniards are a musical people and their language poetical and sonorous ; few understand or use *notation*—the ear is trained to certain cadences, and habit leads them to adopt one or other of these in all singing with every variety of length of line and arrangement of verse. I have no doubt Carvajals' Psalms would be sung by any guitarist to measures that most of his audience would join immediately on knowing the words."

## VISIT TO ARAB CHIEFS IN PRISON.

" To return to our own work. You will be glad to hear that one of your St Matthew's Gospel has gone to the Arab Chiefs in the late insurrection. I obtained permission to visit them in prison, and though I had only one left it was thus bestowed and very thankfully received. I urged on them to make use of their imprisonment, to apply their minds to those subjects which are of general interest to all men. The sermon on the Mount in illustration of this advice seemed to interest them, and strike them with great force, and I left the Gospel with them. I did not see a single countenance like that of a warrior.

" There is an important change of government here ; the civil authority is subordinated to the military, I hope we shall now obtain the liberty we have been seeking ; if so, I shall want many more books. It is doubtful if I shall return to England this year. I have nothing to do here, ' all men are afraid of me.' The Bible Society refused to employ me on the mission to South America which I applied for. My own resources are narrow for accomplishing any considerable work. ' Not by might nor by power' must be my watchword."

The following letter to his brother brings into view a variety of subjects :—

"La Serria, *August 30th* 1864.

"I do not find my journeys to present any thing new. It is the same thing over again. The good is confined always within the same narrow limit of a tract given to a villager or to a passenger and a few words in commendation of it, and perhaps a longer conversation. The country is such as I have often described, the hills retain a brushwood verdure which is very grateful now that all is parched, the flush of a partridge or the rustle of a rabbit serve to sustain the effort of exertion necessary in climbing rocks and supporting 90° Fahrenheit. I am not much a sportsman. It is seldom I go shooting, and when I do it is not often that I hit. During three days last week, part of each spent on the hill, I never touched a feather, I am generally occupied with some subject of thought, very often a text, and when a partridge startles me, I have to drop my thread of discourse and take sight, and before this is accomplished, the poor bird is generally safe. It would seem strange to preface a sermon ' As I was following the chase on the mountains of Jebel-oilia, my thoughts were directed to the text,' &c. But so it has often been with me, and sometimes I sit down under a Tamarisk or a Terebinth and pencil my thoughts. It is thus that you often get 'an expression of opinion instead of a description of scenery! I daresay you will not be displeased with this, as concluding that it is more wholesome for the body to be occupied in active exertion, and if the pursuit of those subjects which form the higher object and occupation of life can be continued contemporaneously, it is well to prepare thus for future usefulness and no loss for present occupation. I have not yet obtained any liberty of evangelising. Our pastors here are very reluctant to stir the volcano which may one day burst and overwhelm them and us. I am not so prudent."

## PREACHING IN PUBLIC.

" On Sunday week, I preached for the first time in this village. It was arranged beforehand that Vicente, my old Spaniard, who is working for himself now, should allow me his house, and on Sunday I wrote one note to one of the principal inhabitants, inviting him and his family, and another of general invitation to seven families of Spaniards. At the appointed time, 7 p.m., I went. The Spaniard Vicente and his wife were murmuring and not prepared; they complained 'that I should make them an object of hatred in the village, they could not live there, &c., and that I could not preach there.' I said, 'very well, I will preach outside then, leave me to my Bible.' The murmur stopped. I waited; presently some persons came. I had sent a carpet from my own house, which I took into the court of Vicente's, and spread under two great trees, and so, taken by storm, and having a little crowd with me, I had no further opposition. At first I thought to stand, the company being seated, but finding them unwilling to sit down, I took a lamp, and sitting on the carpet, opened my Bible, and began with some solemn words. Immediately Vicente and some others were desirous to show me attention—one brought a table, another a chair, &c., and I had some difficulty not to be perched up inconveniently. However, I went on, and soon found opportunity to read Acts xvi., then discoursed on man's sin and peril and misery, and Christ's salvation, and the only way— 'Believe and thou shalt be saved.' All was profound attention within the enclosure ; without it a great uproar—men singing, first in accord and then in discord, shouting, &c. ; in fact all the village was at the door. Still no disturbance took place amongst us. The whole circumstances were so similar to those described in the Acts of the Apostles, that I could not help feeling hope that there might be a Lydia amongst us, or, at least, some one disposed to inquire, 'What must I do to be saved ?' After having spoken for about an hour, there was nearly silence outside, and some had come in to listen. One of these, however, came with no good intent. Suddenly the table at my side was overturned, and we were left in darkness. I did not stop, or change the tone of my voice, but continued what I was saying, and thus no one was alarmed, but presently some of the women, saying it was too late, rose to go home, and so the preaching came to an end. Those, however, who remained were very favourably impressed, and I had great satisfaction in the remarks made to me. One young man accompanied me home. When we came out into the square it was still filled with knots of men and boys. They made exclamations I did not understand. My companion was irritated, and said, 'If you throw stones I will shoot you.' Hearing this, I returned to them and said, 'If there is any one who wishes to throw stones, here I am—stone me.' They denied the intention, but said it was 'very wrong of me to come and preach there.' My companion on the way home showed much sympathy, and said he should like to go to a Protestant place of worship. He is one I had long had an eye upon, and whom I think I saved from consumption, and helped to a good position in life. May God bless the feeblest effort to make known His saving truth !

" As Vicente did not wish his house to be used any more, I have not again had a service. My own house, being a quarter of a mile from the village, would not be suitable. However, to have preached once is a satisfaction for which I thank God.

" Process of law was threatened, but I hear no more of the matter, and perhaps it is as well to wait for another opportunity. I feel on these occasions a sad want of love and devotion to my Master, and how feeble is my faith, but always experience the good to my own soul from the effort, and the exercise of such measure of faith as I have.

" This is the vintage season with us. I am now eating grapes (I should prefer gooseberries), both purple and white—the former have the finer flavour, and resemble those of English hot-houses, though yours are better, and you have more varieties."

In the following letter he reverts to the subject which was weighing more heavily every day upon his mind—the state of the Church of England, and more especially the war within her, between Popery, under the form of Ritualism, and the Gospel. His views, even then, at that early stage of the controversy, were sufficiently gloomy, nor would he have been able to have taken a more hopeful view had he lived till now. The anticipations and fears expressed in his letters have since been but too sadly realised. The issue it is impossible to foresee.

" I have to thank you for a box filled with *Collares de Perlos* and *Extracts*. . . . The changes of government have brought no relief. . . . The new Préfet is known to be still more opposed than was the former to Protestant efforts. . . . . . Still I am very glad to have my supply of books replenished. I was nearly out of ' Collares,' and as Trigo obtains occasionally opportunities to send to Spain, and I am always looking for larger openings, they may any day be called for. . . . . My great disappointment is not from the world, from whom I expect nothing, but that Christians are so lukewarm ; so exclusive, so divided. I am myself unable to see with any body or denomination, still I can agree to differ and concur cordially with all who seek to advance the Gospel of Christ. The church I love and cherish is tainted with sacramentalism and clings to ancient abuses, though the case against her is as clear as argument can make it, viz. : that while the faithful portion of her ministers reject baptismal regeneration, her services support this heresy and her ablest men (Dean Goode, &c.), expend their ingenuity and employ their learning to apologise and explain away this anomaly. ' England,' says a correspondent from Constantinople, ' has deserted *truth*, righteousness, and judgment.' My own view is, that baptism *confers* no grace and has no promise annexed. It is as circumcision was, ' a seal of the righteousness of the faith' in possession before baptism, a rite of introduction into the church visible ; and I see no passage from Scripture which teaches more—to quote John iii., ' born of water,' for baptism is to assume a right to attach an interpretation which early fathers and modern Divines repudiate. . . . . How then can I accept the complicated teaching of Dean Goode, and as I must think the only possible apology for the Church of England service ? Why not acknowledge at once, that the Church of England, like all other churches, has erred and needs reformation ? If this be allowed, and we have a relaxed subscription which allows us freedom of conscience, we can adhere to it and work with it and in its ranks while seeking its purification ; if this is not permitted, whatever be the sacrifice of influence and position and opportunity for doing good (comfort, social happiness, and emolument do not deserve to be mentioned), the sacrifice must be borne. Those who agree with me must 'come out of it and be separate.' .... The evangelical clergy accept the expressions objected to *in the sense put upon them by the whole nation,* both in the *popular acceptation* and in *the judicial definition* of the passages, and however removed from a natural interpretation we may deem it, it is at least both *honest* and *avowed. The nation, not the evangelical clergy, are to blame.*"

Notwithstanding his sense of the growing declensions of the Church of England, or of an active party within her, from the pure faith of the Scriptures and the confession of her Reformers, Mr Ogle did not see his way to take up the position of a Dissenter.

" So long as the Church of England remains as now almost wholly closed against me (though the report of the late meeting of the Liturgical Revision Society gives me more hope of relief than I have ever yet before entertained), I must not think of England as a fitting residence for me. The position of a dissenter, however few be the points of dissent and how many soever be those on which I can cordially adhere to our Established Church, is too painful to a loyal and patriotic and obedient mind to be endured if escape be possible.

" Though exile, expatriation, rather aggravates some of the privations of the dissentient, it relieves others, and is, I judge, best upon the whole,—at least so long as conscience does not demand that he who disapproves, declare publicly, and agitate respecting the matter of his disapproval ; and I pray that I may never be called upon to do this."

And again, writing August 1864 :

" There is but one obstacle to work at home. The conviction that the Church of England, in which alone I wish to work, is culpable before God and man in her reservation of

Popish tenets and tendencies which have so recently shown themselves in their true character as germs and roots of popery. As 'subscription' seems to me to oblige us ministers to endorse all these, and to declare our consent and assent — or assent only, if you will — I felt it right to leave my incumbency; and, having done so, I see no reason to change except for some positive action, instead of this painful negative and unprofitable state. I have before quoted Calvin, who seems to have hit the nail on the head. In his reply to one George Whittingham, who asked his opinion of the English liturgy, he said, ' There are in it many *tolerabiles ineptiæ*—endurable follies! There is not such purity and perfection as is to be desired—imperfections to be borne for a time in regard that no manifold impiety is retained; and it was therefore lawful to begin with such beggarly rudiments that the learned, grave, and godly ministers of Christ might be encouraged to proceed further in setting out what was more pure and perfect.'

" This expresses exactly my feeling in respect to the English liturgy, especially the Offices. And as I see no limit to the time we are to bear with the imperfections, and observe the mischiefs growing out of them, I have thought it my duty to protest even by resignation."

## CHAPTER XXVII.

### DEATH OF HIS SISTER—THE EMPEROR NAPOLEON'S VISIT TO ALGERIA.

THE opening of the year 1865—the last that Mr Ogle was to see on earth—was clouded by tidings of the death of his youngest sister. Her illness he attributed to a residence during a cold spring-time in Flamborough, and her care for a sick servant in his house. Her death touched him all the more deeply on that account. To one so affectionate in disposition, and so thoughtful for the comfort of others, the parting from his sick sister on his return to Algeria was no light trial. He received tidings of her state from time to time, but only to learn that her condition did not improve, and that her dissolution was evidently drawing nigh. The sorrow this caused him was gilded by the joy arising from the faith of her who was about to depart. She "knew in Whom she had believed, and that He would keep what she had committed to Him." The separation would be short, how short Mr Ogle then little thought, and it was sweetened by the assured hope of meeting in a world where sorrow and sighing, tears and death, are for ever unknown. The dispensation drew from him the following touching letter.

*" December 13th,* 1864.

"From what I learn of my dear sister's state, though in extreme weakness, she is supported in perfect peace, trusting in her Saviour. This almost forbids me to desire her restoration, so much and so long prayed for while there was room to hope that her life might be prolonged in comfort to herself and in usefulness to others.

" You know well my views respecting the times in which our lot is cast; they have undergone no change. On the contrary, I see clearer signs and a nearer approach of apostacy and of consequent judgment.

" As to personal duty I am in some uncertainty, and therefore follow the only safe course for seasons of darkness, waiting 'the Lord's leisure,' abiding in my lot until it shall please God to set me at liberty," by the disposal of his property in Algeria, "and to assign me another and a more promising sphere of labour.

" It is true that this land is a wilderness, religiously as well as physically speaking, and it is one of the last places I should of my own accord have fixed upon for a residence, but I think God has chosen it for me and I am the more confirmed in this view, because though I have, in deference to the wishes of my friends, consented to give up my farming project, and have been able to get quit of the large farm which I occupied, still I am unable, in any lawful way, to dispose of the remainder of my property here, and to abandon it does not appear to me to be lawful.

"I hope you constantly pray for me that I may be disposed and enabled to do God's will in all things. I feel how far I am from perfect submission to that will.

"Of her who is most in our thoughts at this time, she is perhaps even now 'laid on sleep,' folded in the true shepherd's fold; joined to the blessed company of those gone before, entered into the joy of her Lord. Oh what blessedness to exchange a life of suffering and weakness for pleasure and peace in the society of those of whom she unceasingly thought and longed to see again. She is perhaps even now absent from the body for a little while, whom we may hope soon to see where no clouds intervene, no doubts arise, nor sin disturbs. It is lawful to shed a tear for society interrupted, and intercourse broken off, but it is for ourselves we weep. The bright bow of promise appears in the clouds and tells of reconciliation complete.

"As a family we have indeed cause for a grateful and implicit trust in God. He has, we have reason to believe, been 'our fathers' God' for many generations. Some of our departed relatives have been burning and shining lights, useful and influential, and as salt in the circle with which they were connected. Shall this be said of the present generation? I trust it shall."

The following was written in anticipation of the news which speedily followed of his sister's death :—

"*December 30th*, 1864.

"Your trial is too severe for me to touch much upon that, and I need not offer you the consolations which you know where to seek better than from even a brother's heart. There is a Friend 'closer than a brother'—better than all earthly ties whatever. I shall not be surprized to hear that our beloved one is yet spared, but if not, we can yield her up, knowing in Whom she has believed, and trusting His love.

" ' Be ye steadfast, immoveable, always abounding in *the work of the Lord.*' Perhaps you feel a painful doubt whether *mine* is such. Do not doubt it, dear sister. It is not so secular as it looks. It calls forth constant prayer, and exercises patience, faith, love, humility, long-suffering, hope, charity. Paul and our blessed Lord Himself at least, if not all the rest of the apostles, exercised secular callings, and herein were made like unto their brethren, and fulfilled the task of fallen humanity. ' In the sweat of thy face thou shalt eat bread.' I well remember among the proud thoughts of my early life, that any handiwork or labour other than intellectual, was regarded as beneath my supposed talent. How sadly those fancies of superior ability have as yet been disappointed. And I am like a Nebuchadnezzar driven out to the fields, and deprived of almost every kind of usefulness such as I destined for myself. I pray that I may not be blind nor disobedient, that I may be restored to some humble but useful sphere here or elsewhere, and made a blessing to my generation and a comfort to you all.

" I thank God for the peace and mercy bestowed on our suffering sister. What a pledge of better things to come !

' Why should we mourn departing friends ? '

" I ask you, dearest, to treasure for me as much as possible of dear F.'s words. If she lives still ask her to forgive John all that he has caused her of pain, and assure her that her words are treasured and attended to by me, and that she has been a chief means of keeping me from going far astray, and I trust of bringing me back to God. Perhaps for this she lives, and I trust her hours of suffering are cheered with the thought that she did not so live in vain.—Accept my most affectionate love and gratitude, your brother,     JOHN."

On the 10th of January he learned that his sister was no more. He writes in reply as follows:—

" ORAN, *January* 10*th*, 1865.

" MY DEAR BROTHER,—Though I have only received Jane's letter of December 31st, I think I know all. Your former of the 24-5th, left me very little expectation of hearing again of our dear Fanny in life. It was very consolatory to me to observe the calm with which her last hours were attended. It is a thought which may well impress *us*, that of the family to which we belong by nature more than half is now, we trust, in heaven, *i.e.*, 'entered into rest,' and shall not we long to join father, mother, infant and adult sister, in that blest society, where no chillness of love or difference of view is admitted to disturb a full communion ? Oh may our dear parents stand in their lot with all their family united, no member absent, saying, Here am I and the children God hath given me. Oh may they rejoice in a larger company than that of kindred, in their own and our spiritual children, and if natural descendants be vouchsafed and human generations yet succeed, may these be added too."

## Nursing Institutions.

The intelligence that such an institution had been formed in Derby called forth the following letters to his brother, in which he expresses his views of the necessity of such institutions, and the wisdom of employing the *use* as a remedy for the *abuse*. We are at this hour in danger of being brought into the bondage in our hospitals, of which we have an illustration in the following letter. The public are apt to be caught by the bait of "such good nursing," and hood-winked by the promise — a promise which is not, which cannot be kept — "they do not meddle with religion." Let alone the suspicious incongruity of a "religious" nurse being enjoined, and promising not to speak about religion, actions speak louder than words. The fact, moreover, is notorious that *ecclesiastical* nurses are of a school which is zealous above all others to make proselytes ; and more than this, their ecclesiastical bias is found to be antagonistic to good nursing. In one hospital in London a whole regiment of "sisters" were obliged to leave because they not only interfered with the

chaplain, but because they enjoined one of their practices
upon the patients (fasting so many hours before and after
communion) which, to say the least of it, was very bad nursing.
Again, in another, a country hospital, where the governors
were caught napping, and a certain Sister Mary was allowed
to be the lady-superintendent (offering to do so " for nothing")
notwithstanding her well-known antecedents, and that she had
been trained in a Sisterhood, the last moments of a godly
Wesleyan girl were embittered, and therefore surely the nursing of the patient was wholly in abeyance, by the said sister
placing at the bed-foot a cross, and putting before the poor
girl's face a picture of the crucifixion, in spite of her remonstrance, hindering also the Wesleyan pastor from visiting her.
With such facts as these before us at home, it is sadly
opportune to record the opinions of one who had witnessed
the unrestrained working of this agency :—

" I truly rejoice in your recently announced work, the
Nursing Institution. I see that such institutions are among
the demands of our time. I observe what mischief the perversion of them does, and I agree with you that the true
remedy is in keeping them within their proper sphere, and to
do their own work. I have, I believe, no more dangerous and
bitter enemies, and none more difficult to combat, than the
so-called Sisters of Mercy ; they are the terrible hand of
an apostate church, gloved in woman's exterior of tenderness, laid upon the lambs and the weaker of the flock. Oh
what I felt and saw of this in the case of the poor Mexican
colonel. Had he consented to let me nurse him, I believe he
would have lived, and perhaps too, rejoiced in a new life to
God. I will not give up the hope, but it was terrible to see
the minister to his earthly sufferings, keeping the door against
spiritual consolations, and succeeding in shutting it against his
sincere and sympathizing friends. It seems as if the craft of
Satan could have no subtler exhibition than this—nursing
Institutions for infancy and decline, in schools and hospitals,
and both under the control and almost exclusive conduct of

Sisters of Charity ! We ought to fight against such a system with all our might."

Again we repeat it, let the people of England look well and speedily to this matter, for it concerns some of their dearest interests. Whilst men slept the enemy sowed tares. Nursing has been too long neglected. It is a work specially worthy of the attention of Christians. It is a shame to them that the field has been so long neglected. Let them even now go up and take possession of the land that lies fallow, " redeeming the time because the days are evil." Derbyshire, in the person of Miss Nightingale, and more recently as a county, has set an example which ought to be followed all over the kingdom. Not that the work is complete in Derbyshire, nor half complete, except in the sense that it is well begun. Not until every town in a county has its branch, and every town and village its " district" nurse or nurses, and every hospital is a school for nurse-training, and is put under such administration as that the training shall be a reality ; not until nurses thoroughly instructed in their profession can be at command ; not for nothing, which in the long run is a fiction, but at reasonable and remunerative wages; not until this is accomplished can the work be considered in any way complete. In order to this every county ought to have its own association for the improvement of hospital, district, and private nursing, and the different county associations should work together and help each other through a metropolitan centre. There is a great future yet open to a British nursing association of this kind, and if Christian people would only be foremost in the campaign, and be true to their principles—not talking but acting their Christianity and their Protestantism—doing the work thoroughly well, and avoiding every device (however specious) that is not primarily and necessarily connected with the undertaking—in a word, with a single eye, they would beat Romanists and Romanisers out of the field. We would speak with all kindness of deaconess nurses such as Pasteur Fliedner's at Kaiserworth, and of their congeners at Totenham, but these are from their very distinctiveness exceptional. An agency that requires the tact and organising power and self-devotion of a Pasteur Fliedner or the purse of a Mr Morley, to say nothing of the qualifications in the subordinates—including submission to a great deal of unnecessary drudgery, and the exhibition of that fictitious, semi-romantic, and more than half Roman requisite of self-negation (a very different thing from self-denial) which is required from the agents employed, is obviously exceptional, and not suited for the general public service. Derbyshire has happily shown that all ecclesiastical machinery whatsoever may be discarded, and that Christian men and women, church people and nonconformists, may, without compromise, cordially co-operate with each other on a simple practical plan of operation. It was in contemplation of this proposal, before it was in being, that Mr Ogle wrote as above, and again, January 31, 1865, to the same effect, he says these weighty words :—

"The peril is great, greater than even you imagine, I fear. The preparatory provisions have been long making, and now *the Institutions of Romanism are being introduced*, in the same stealthy, disingenuous, un-English manner by hole-and-corner meetings, packed quasi-public gatherings, '*banded Unions persecuting opinion*,' and such methods of overruling a passive and somnolent majority. The sisterhoods at Salisbury and elsewhere show plainly to what issue the Derby Tractarians look forward. The cloven foot has peeped sufficiently at Ashbourne—thank God for a Mr Wright.

"*Female Agency* in former times was shut up in convents, and as instructors of youth and fomentors of spurious devotedness in what is called a life of piety, exercised a remote and silent but powerful influence on society. The genius of our times is different. Now the female clergy must be seen. You meet them in every street, you find them in every con-

*voi;* scarcely can you travel twenty miles but you have two or more as your companions.    By sea and by land they are ever 'going about doing'—(the searcher of hearts is their judge.) The feeble classes of society, every individual in the weaker moment of his life, infancy, and disease, and death, is (wherever they are fully in possession of the place they arrogate to themselves) *in their power.*    I have seen many instances, and never failed to note a sort of dread of offending ' the sister,' and a sort of tyrant look and manner she discovered, and the implicit obedience she exacted in the household.    In France this is aided by many regulations.    A medical certificate of cause of death is imperative, consequently the physician has *a right* in the sick chamber which it is at the peril of the sick or his friends to oppose.    If rich he may choose his physician, if poor the government chooses for him, and at the will of the latter he is consigned to the hospital, *i.e.,* to an Institute where the sisters swarm and rule ; to resist the sister *there* is to be exposed to neglect and cruelty.    The Protestants have generally such a dread of the hospital on this account, they had rather die than go.    Once there, the chamber and the bed is guarded by these attendants, the Bible must not be read, the priest must be admitted and his ceremonies performed, religious conversation prohibited.    If attempted, the friend will find the door closed against him, as was the case with Trigo and myself in Colonel Gutierye's case.    My own feeling you know.    I can only say, I should prefer infinitely the state of social desolation of the Nomads and savages of the remotest regions of the earth, to the awful tyranny of a dominant sisterhood in the midst of organization, and all the appliances of advanced civilization.    The stamp of tyranny is on all.    The physician is but a creature, he can be advanced or deposed at the will of the Sisterhood.    The priest directs the whole machinery, even the Government is subject to this control, *fastening itself on the* HEART *of humanity.*    Well, said Solomon, ' Oppression maketh a wise man mad.'    While I write I trust I feel for you in your noble and Christian attempt, ' *obstare principiis,*' and pray that I may be useful to you even though absent.    It is reliance on Him who is mightier than the mightiest, that can and will preserve you from falling, either into power of the enemy or giving place to him by subjection even for a moment, though invested with the sanctity of a Peter or the authority supposed to attach to an apostle."

## THE FARM TO BE SOLD.

Mr Ogle, at this time, was a good deal occupied in winding up his affairs. Two of his three farms were taken off his hand : his flocks he was able to dispose of, and then the burden which had pressed so heavily upon him for some time past, was lightened. His letters show that now he breathes more freely. He rejoices in the sight of nature, just bursting into spring. But he was not without annoyances. The fraud- ulencies of certain with whom he had money transactions drew him into a law plea ; touches of deep sadness for his sister's death, and the course things were taking in England, visit him at times ; but his less entangled position now enables him to make excursions into the country, and to give himself more exclusively to his strict missionary work. On these we do not further dwell. The event of the summer was the visit which the Emperor of the French paid to Algeria. Of that visit Mr Ogle has given us some graphic details. He exerted himself to give a fitting reception to Napoleon, when he entered Valmy, the village where he was then residing. Banners and flags were displayed from the mulberry trees, and so arranged as to form a sort of triumphal arch, and quite an ovation awaited the emperor on his approach. Farther, avail- ing himself of the permission given to all, Mr Ogle presented two documents to the Emperor : the first a formal address of welcome ; the second of a more practical nature, giving a view of Algeria from an Englishman's standpoint, and specifying certain grievances in the administration, the correction of which was indispensable to the substantial prosperity of the colony. We present the reader with these documents, and other details of interest.

## The Emperor Napoleon's Visit.

The Emperor's visit was made early in May—harvest-time in Algeria. The season had been exceptionally good, and the country looked lovely. Writing to a friend, Mr Ogle thus describes Napoleon's reception at Oran :—

" I printed an address, beginning ' Un Anglais, colon a Valmy depuis 1858, &c.,' and gave it into the imperial hand on his visit to the village. It had an object beyond doing what one can to contribute to show respect and gratitude on the occasion rare in all history, of great monarchs condescending to visit little villages in a secondary portion of their dominions. Certainly Napoleon III. would not regret having done so, if it do not occupy his thoughts in a disproportionate degree to its importance dynastically, which is his affair, for the demonstrations were most liberal ; and Africa never looked so radiant, or never was so fertile and flourishing before. Oran was really very beautifully ornamented. The Rue Napoleon was an avenue of tricolours—above, aloft, athwart. There were three handsome Arcs de Triomphe, and a banner at the Marine, of novel and elegant design. It represented a woolsack of silk, with gold embroidery, hung 40 or 50 feet high, from elegant white poles. The photographs taken in shadow, give little idea of its lofty and elegant appearance. Every evening all the principal buildings and shops were illuminated."

Writing to his brother, May 16th, Mr Ogle says, " this day ought to be marked with a white stone, for this day the Emperor of the French visited my village of Valmy." He thus describes the Emperor's reception and appearance :—

" The Emperor passed five times, and ought to know my chateau at La Senia by heart. Once we gave him a regular ovation. It was the last day. I had arranged a tricolor banderalles on a cord, with the English ensign in the centre.

My address emblazoned on one, with the rising sun above it, and on the blue ground of the tricolor, which looked very well. These I suspended with two flags on poles from the mulberry trees at the road. A crowd collected, Pegie and Riente and family, Marles, Reys, and the children brought bunches of poppies, and made a great circle on the ground. I stood in the centre, holding Pegie's child, with a bouquet of roses, &c., and we all cheered lustily as the great man passed. He smiled and bowed very graciously. There was an expression on the Emperor's countenance at Valmy, when I had opportunity of remarking him, which surprised me. It was that of a man under powerful and kindly emotion. All his acts showed that he deeply felt the reception given to him, and he acknowledged it in words as strongly as possible."

The following is the address presented by Mr Ogle to the Emperor. After touching briefly on the historic and physical interest of the region, the document refers to the years of suffering which had just passed over the colony; Mr Ogle's intention being to correct the wrong impression which it was natural for the Emperor to form of the condition of the people, from the exceedingly fertile but exceptional aspect the country then wore—

"A SA MAJESTÉ NAPOLÉON III., EMPEREUR DES FRANÇAIS.

    "Sire,

"Un Anglais, colon à Valmy depuis 1858, est heureux en cette occasion de se porter au devant de Votre Majesté pour lui offrir avec ses concitoyens Français, l'hommage de ses plus respectueux sentiments.

"Et puisque Votre Majesté daigne visiter notre village, nous userons de cette insigne faveur pour lui rappeler quelques faits de notre histoire.

"La commune de Valmy a été un des premiers lieux d'occupation militaire après la prise d'Oran en 1831.

"Sous l' ancien Figuier, à l'entrée du village, les traités de soumission des Arabes étaient signés.

" Si l'extension projetée pour son territoire avait lieu, ses limites s'étendraient jusqu'au pied des montagnes pittoresques qui bornent l'horizon au sud, une chaîne secondaire de l'Atlas. De ces terres cultivées on arrive sur un sol vierge, et on peut voyager sans obstacles jusque dans l'intérieur inconnu du continent de l'Afrique méridionale.

" Or, la commune de Valmy se trouve sur la limite extrême des terrains soumis à la culture européenne, et sur le bord même du monde civilisé.

" En passant de la France en Algérie, on a traversé la distance qui sépare la civilisation la plus avancée de la plus primitive.   On est retourné cinq siècles en arrière.

" Si les colons, installés sur le sol Africain, jouissent de quelques-uns des avantages de la Mère-Patrie, ils se trouvent ici entourés par des difficultés qui affligent l'*enfance* de tout effort civilisateur.   Les indigènes sont encore à cette époque de leur histoire.

" Ils auront donc le droit de réclamer une considération bienveillante de la part de Sa Majesté.   Leurs méthodes de culture, leur condition sociale et matérielle, ne peuvent être mis en comparaison avec ceux d'aucun pays de l'Europe.

" Ils luttent sur un sol assez fertile en nature, mais exposé à des changements capricieux, à des conditions atmosphériques qui rendent impossible tout calcul de résultat.

" Les huit dernières années en ont fourni l'exemple le plus frappant.   Pendant les cinq premières années de cette période, les récoltes étaient absolument nulles ; tout signe de prospérité avait disparu.   Les colons propriétaires ne subsistaient que de leur travail journalier ou chargeaient sur leurs terres ou leurs habitations les avances nécessaires pour le maintien de leurs familles ; ils doivent à une subvention opportune et paternelle de l'Autorité civile les semences pour leurs terrains.

" Enfants de la France, de l'Espagne, de l'Allemagne et de l'Angleterre, ils supportaient avec un courage obstiné leur dure épreuve, fiers d'être dignes du nom historique de leur village qui rappelle un des plus glorieux faits d'armes pendant les guerres de la Révolution française, en 1792.   Ni la miséricorde de la Providence Divine, ni la sympathie du Gouvernement de la Métropole ne leur faisait pas défaut. Trois années successives d'une abondante récolte leur ont fait presqu'oublier leurs misères et les aident à réaliser l'ancienne ressource de l'Afrique, le grenier de Rome, et de comprendre

' Quicquid de Libycis verritur areis.'—HORACE.

"Ce jour de joie, d'exaltation, de reconnaissance, leur rappelle le souvenir étrange du passé pour aiguiser leur satisfaction et pour s'inspirer de nouvelles espérances.

"Ils osent espérer que le récit de ces faits ne pourra déplaire à Sa Majesté, car il lui fera comprendre l'enthousiasme reconnaissant de son accueil et les espérances reposées sur son appui à l'avenir.

"Restants sous la protection de la Providence omnipotente, gardés par la puissance de Sa Majesté l'Empereur, veillés par sa continuelle bienveillance et dirigés par sa juste et impartiale administration, ils ne peuvent manquer d'arriver à un haut degré de prospérité matérielle.

"Aujourd'hui, ils se relèvent de leur abaissement ; demain, ils se mettront en marche vers leur but.

"Suivant l'étendard glorieux du Successeur des Romains, le sol leur rappelle les victoires remportées par leurs prédécesseurs il y a vingt siècles.

"Depuis lors, le progrès de la civilisation vers le Sud est resté stationnaire, ou plutôt est allé en reculant. Les ruines qui encombrent cette terre ne servent que de matériaux pour renouveler les anciennes entreprises. Les instruments perfectionnés par la science, et les travaux déjà commencés, les aideront à rebâtir l'édifice sur des bases inébranlables.

"Ils ne forment qu'un vœu, Sire, c'est d'être trouvés dignes de contribuer à étendre l'empire de la civilisation sur l'ancien sol de Jugurtha, en suivant les traces victorieuses de Sa Majesté l'Empereur Napoléon III.

"Vive l'Empereur !

"Vive l'Impératrice !

"Vive le Prince Impérial !

'Te salvere jubemus.
    Fulgentem imperio fertilis Africæ.'—HORACE.

"VALMY, le 15th Mai 1865."

*[Translation.]*

" To His Majesty Napoleon III., Emperor of the French.

" Sire,

" An Englishman, a colonist at Valmy since 1858, is happy on this occasion to present himself before your Majesty, along with his French fellow-citizens, to offer the homage of his most respectful sentiments.

" We embrace the opportunity afforded by the signal honour done our village in your Majesty's gracious visit, to recall to your memory several facts in our history.

" The commune of Valmy was one of the first places to be militarily occupied after the taking of Oran in 1831.

" Under the old fig-tree at the entrance of the village was the treaty of submission signed by the Arabs.

" If the projected extension of the territory had taken place, its limits would have reached the foot of the picturesque mountains which bound the horizon on the south, one of the lower chains of the Atlas. Beyond these cultivated lands one sets foot on virgin soil, and can pursue his way without obstruction into the unknown interior of southern Africa.

" The commune of Valmy lies on what, for the time being, is the extreme limit of lands subjected to European cultivation, and on the farthest verge of the civilized world.

" In passing from France to Algeria one traverses the distance that divides the most extreme from the most primitive civilization. He goes back five centuries.

" If the colonists established upon African soil enjoy some of the advantages of the mother country, they here find themselves surrounded by difficulties incident to the beginnings of all efforts at civilization. The natives are only as yet at this stage of their history. This gives them a right to the benevolent consideration of His Majesty. Their methods of culture, their social and material condition, cannot be brought into comparison with those of any European country.

" They have to do with a soil by nature sufficiently fertile, but exposed to capricious changes, and to atmospheric conditions, which render all calculation of results impossible.

" Of this the last eight years have furnished a most striking example. During the first five years of this period the
crops were absolutely nothing; all sign of prosperity had disappeared : the colonist proprietors could subsist only on their
daily labour, or get advances on their lands and habitations
for the necessary maintenance of their families. They are
indebted to an opportune and paternal supply from the civil
authority of the seed to sow their lands.

" Natives of France, Spain, Germany, and England, they
support with an obstinate courage the trials of their lot,
proud to be worthy of the historic name of their village,
which recalls one of the most brilliant exploits of the war of
the French Revolution of 1792. Neither the pity of
Divine Providence, nor the sympathy of the Metropolitan
government, has been wanting to them. Three successive
years of an abundant harvest have made them almost forget
their miseries, and help them to realize the ancient riches of
Africa, the granary of Rome, and to understand, as Horace
says,

' The abundance that may be gathered from the fields of Lybia.'

" This day of joy, of exultation, of thankful remembrance,
recalls the unusual memory of the past in order to augment
their satisfaction and inspire with new hopes. They dare to
hope that the recital of these facts will not be displeasing to
His Majesty, because they will enable him to understand the
grateful enthusiasm of his reception, and the hopes cherished
of his support in the future.

" Reposing under the protection of an omnipotent Providence, guarded by the power of His Majesty the Emperor,
watched over by his unceasing kindness, and guided by his
just and impartial administration, they cannot fail to reach a
high degree of material prosperity. To-day they recover
themselves from their fall, to-morrow they begin their march
towards their object.

" Following the glorious standard of the successor of the
Romans, the territory reminds them of the victories won by
their predecessors twenty centuries ago. Since then the pro-

2 B

gress of civilization southward has remained stationary, or rather has gone back : the ruins which encumber this land only serve as materials for renewing the ancient enterprises. Instruments perfected by science, and the works already inaugurated, will aid them in rebuilding the edifice upon immoveable foundations.

"They have but one wish, Sire, even to be found worthy to contribute toward extending the empire of civilization upon the ancient soil of Jugurtha, in following the victorious footsteps of His Majesty the Emperor Napoleon III.

"Vive, &c."

The second document we also subjoin. It touches on two points : the state of the law-courts, which permit the dishonest to escape, and the honest to suffer ; and the want of religious liberty, which forbids the Bible and cringes to the priest :—

"To His Majesty the Emperor Napoleon III.

"Sir,—As an Englishman, nearly seven years resident in Algeria, and during six, an occupier and cultivator of land, I beg most respectfully to avail myself of the permission given to all colonists to approach your Majesty, and to state their views on those great and important matters which concern alike ourselves and our rulers. I will as briefly as possible allude to such as appear to me the most to need your Majesty's attention.

"I. The complicated nature of legal remedies. legal processes, acts of notary, notifications by Huissier, &c., are a great burden and impediment to justice. Defendants are generally without property, and commit breaches of contract, and frauds coming under the category of civil actions, with impunity ; while the greatest facility exists for such powers to employ the law as a means of injury from the complicity of inferior agents of the courts. Huissiers and even advocates are known to promote litigation for a share of results, as remuneration in case of success. I can suggest no remedy other than penalties for conspiracy for the latter case ; and the diminishing of fees for the former. A judiciary power in the hand of local magistrates, with an inexpensive appeal to tribunals, would avoid much of the expense which operates as a check to seeking legal remedies, and which the *mileage increase of huissiers' fees,* an *extraordinary* source of expenses, augments to a ruinous extent. The judicial system in civil actions, appears to me exceedingly defective ; and I have reason to know that law *expenses* are a burden so grievous, that the property of the colony will be transferred into the hands of the legal profession in the course of a very few years. Property changes owners, on an average, every five years at least. In thirty years the whole value of land will have been paid to the legal profession in fees of transfer. Hence the number and wealth of the legal profession in Algeria.

"II. The absence of religious liberty. The vast majority being Catholics, a Protestant finds it very difficult to discharge any part of the duty he feels incumbent on him, to make known the truth to others. It is a precept of universal obligation, ' Let your light shine before men,' and according to a Protestant's creed, the command ' Go ye into *all the world* and preach the Gospel to every creature,' was addressed to all the disciples or adherents of the faith of Jesus Christ, and not exclusively to an order or Ecclesiastical hierarchy. When therefore he finds a restriction put upon his performance of this great duty, he must feel that his liberty of conscience is infringed in the most important of its exercises.

"I have felt this to the full in Algeria. In 1859 I applied to the Préfet for permission to distribute by gift or sale religious books and tracts, chiefly the Bible or portions in the received versions—all these not only permitted to be printed in France, but enjoying a large liberty of circulation there. This permission was absolutely refused without cause assigned. I have the honour to enclose the letter of refusal. I have not repeated the application, as no change has taken place in the circumstances under which it was refused, and I have received from both France and from England large quantities of Scriptures and religious tracts, of which

very few are controversial, and the great majority may be
fully defended, as consistent entirely with the teaching of the
Holy Scriptures, and of the most eminent of the Fathers of the
Church.

" That any restriction should exist as to the circulation of
these books, which are permitted to be printed, seems to me
anomalous and contrary to the fundamental principles of that
liberty which is an inalienable right of mankind.

" The other evils to be complained of in this colony, and
they are neither few nor unimportant, are to me *nothing in
comparison of this.* I can compensate by economy and calculation the inequalities of climate. I can subsidise the
deficiency of manual labour and its cost by machinery. I can
protect myself by prudence and by aid of the law against injustice. I can uncomplainingly endure such events as arise in
a semi-civilized state of society. But when authority interferes to deprive me of my liberty to minister to the spiritual
necessities of millions around me, ' perishing for lack of
knowledge,' or forbids me to diffuse instruction in what concerns the salvation of the immortal souls of men, I feel myself oppressed by a burden for which there is no relief, of
which any words of mine are incapable of conveying even an
impression.

" Touched by the sympathy your Majesty has manifested
for all classes of your dependents and subjects, I cannot believe that you will refuse to listen to my earnest representation
of a great injustice, nor to withhold the only remedy possible,
the entire removal of power from any individual acting under
your authority, to restrict the free circulation of the word and
truth of God.—I am, your Majesty's, &c."

The state of things which drew forth these remonstrances
and protests may be learned from the letters we have already
given, and from the one that follows, in which Mr Ogle,
writing to an official of one of the evangelical societies of
England, gives a most startling account of that whole deplorable array of impediments and restrictions by which the

French government fettered the circulation of the Word of God among its subjects. We cannot but regard Mr Ogle's letters as a voice from the grave against that tyranny. The student of Providence cannot fail to mark that the dynasty that imposed these obstructions, and heard unheeded the request to relax or remove them has itself been swept away. " I will overturn—overturn."

" But, I believe it is not realized as it were well it should be, what is *the peculiar action of the French system on Christian enterprize.* Allow me before entering on the reply to your inquiries to explain this as I find it.

" The French have placed every social institution under a strict and absolute *régime.* There are provisions of Government for regulating all the departments of social science. Not only is the military, the financial, the administrative organization subjected to the supreme authority; but the action of Government extends to the municipal and almost to the domestic circle. Nothing can be done without Government interference. It takes account of all you possess, and subjects all to its own direction. This is equally the case in religious as in moral respects. Every sect or denomination has its limit of liberty prescribed; no individual freedom exists. Nothing can be sold or bought or given but as authority sees fit,—where it pleases it places a barrier. Generally this power is not exercised to the impediment of the individual action in respect to secular matters ; a well-disposed and civilized community is tolerably free, the regulations of the Government are so adapted to the popular sense of convenience and propriety that no collision takes place. But let a sentiment exist in contravention to the idea of the ruling power, and immediately the absence of all freedom of action is felt. *This is the abstract view* of the state of things in the French empire at present.

" Now, in respect of religion. You are aware that this difference of sentiment does exist,—a difference radical and irreconcilable between the section of the population, Protestant and Evangelical, and the ruling authority, which with the majority is Popish, and consequently inimical to the Gospel of Christ. The consequence is that every effort to which our principle of duty impels meets an absolute prohibition. The Gospel may not be publicly proclaimed. Discussions in public are prohibited. The distribution of books, &c., is under restriction. Assemblies are permitted only under certain conditions.

"The individual Christian then finds himself met on every side by hindrance. Beyond his individual intercourse with men he can do nothing. He sees heathen around him perishing under the delusions of a false creed, and he may neither strive nor cry. He may not even publish a word of affectionate remonstrance. He is assailed by opponents in the most public manner—stigmatized and maligned; but he has no liberty to reply, no possible vindication or explanation. He invites his adversary to dispute; the invitation (private of course, he has no public channel open) is contemptuously declined; and the next Sunday, in full congregation, a bishop or priest challenges and defies him, and combats in empty air an imaginary opponent. He complains to authority. The reply is the authority cannot permit interruption of the peace between sects equally tolerated. That the religion of Rome is that of the Government and people of France. He writes and demands permission to print. No! absolutely no! Let me at least circulate the Bible: the truth must and will prevail. Still no!—not without authorization; and if an independent and an earnest—a zealous and active character, the authority is sure to be refused on one or other pretext. If you wish further illustration of this state of things, read 'Brittany and the Bible,' a short but lively and truthful picture of French administration as it was and *is*.

"What I desire to put before you is this serious question. Ought not and can not something be done to put an end to this iniquitous binding of the Word of God and hindering of the work of His ministers? For three years I have looked in vain for some opening, some lawful way to acquit myself of the duty my Bible and my conscience alike impose. *I find none.* Silent, though burning to make known the truth I

have received and love, I am forced to be silent still. The first
overt act or effort would bring on me all the weight of a fully
organized system, in repression, and probably in expulsion
from the soil of France.   I know this, and therefore as I would
not leap upon an array of bayonets, I wait and wish in vain.

"I need not dilate on the cruelty, the severity of such a
restriction any more than point out to *you* its *iniquity*.
When a barbarous people, whose whole character is in opposition and contrast to your own, infringes what you deem a
right and a duty, you confidently assume the attitude of independent action, supported by a sense of justice and backed
by the common sentiment of the enlightened and civilized
world.   But when a nation advanced in philosophical and
practical science and in social order, accustomed to rank
among the enlightened and the just and liberal portion of
mankind, opposes the whole force of the institutions on which
its moral and social organization is founded against what your
conscience dictates to you as the first of duties, the most
sacred of rights, you are confounded, appalled, oppressed,
involved in a conflict between what is religiously your duty
and what is politically expedient and right.   A conflict than
which I can scarcely conceive one more cruel, more painful or
more unjust.   Yet, dear sir, in this our nineteenth century
such is the exact situation of many a Christian,—not in
arbitrary Austria or bigoted Spain, but in liberal and
enlightened France!

"I am aware that you will start at such a description, and refer
to your reports and communications to prove the great liberty
enjoyed by your agents and others in the French territory.
Yes, dear sir, but do you hear also *of the restrictions imposed
in other portions* of that territory, and have you deduced the
real fact from these two conflicting sources of evidence : that
*all the liberty is merely* PERMISSIVE ; that it may at any
moment be withdrawn,—nay, that it is now at this moment
refused wherever the authority sees-fit?   Duplicity and de-
ception added to systematic cruelty and injustice!"

What response did the above representations meet? asks

the reader. Mr Ogle never heard more of them : he scarcely expected that he would. Since that day, brief as the period is, much has come and gone. The fatality that haunts the throne of France has overtaken Napoleon III. His kingdom is departed. In the leisure and silence of exile he may now recall the truths which were pressed on his attention by the missionary, and which, had he given heed to them then, might have been a lengthening of his reign. It was no great matter that was asked of him—only that he would give leave to the message of the King of Heaven to circulate freely in his dominions. To have done so would have been to open a new fountain of blessing to his people, and to rear a new defence around his own power. But he feared the priest. Perhaps he inwardly resolved to give his consent at a more convenient season. Such, however, never came, nor will it now ever come to Napoleon. " Be wise ye kings : be instructed ye judges of the earth." What a folly in monarch or statesman to believe that he can set himself in opposition to God's righteous and omnipotent government, and not be broken in pieces. But we return to Mr Ogle's narrative :—

" I was personally much impressed by the Emperor. I had seen him before, but only at a distance, and conceived the idea of a man whose sensibilities and sympathies were wholly subordinate to ambition—a hard man, whose features never relaxed—one who played a game (of chess) with the nations of the world for pieces—who believed in destiny and disregarded duty. I saw him near at hand when he visited our village, and remarked a sensibility which surprised me ; the notice he took of everything and everybody ; his kindness to a child who was brought to offer him flowers ; and his whole manner was that of a sovereign, taking a paternal interest in the people, because to see and to encourage the feeling was reciprocal. Everybody did all in their power to show grateful sense of his notice. I had an address for him. The mayor refused to present it. I stood in the crowd before him, and did not stir, holding my letter visibly but not obtrusively. He did not look at me directly, and I thought I should not find opportunity to offer my address. The deputation was heard and the Emperor replied : he gave the sign to move forward. The priest came up, and with much fuss and almost rudeness, pushed the crowd aside with his hat in hand, making, as if he were sweeping, a road through. I was very near and in his way. I did not stir and others took little notice. His object was to induce the Emperor to visit the Eglise, which was close by behind me. The Emperor smiled and waved a refusal ; then lifting his eye as if for the first time on me, he partly rose in his seat, and stretched out his hand over the heads of the people. I gave him my address with a low respect. I am confident that if he will always do so—let the priest alone and listen to the Protestant—he will have a throne secure and prosperous.

"The same scenes were repeated, village after village. Everywhere a most enthusiastic reception. At the next village a curious circumstance occurred. The Emperor's carriage stopped beneath the Arc de Triomphe, whereas the Maire and the inhabitants expected him at the place where the horses were to be changed, some hundred yards further. This village is on the limit of the Arab territory, and has vast grounds cultivated and occupied by Arabs. Its market presents scarcely a European, while two to three thousand Arabs throng it ; doubtless there would be four to five thousand present on the Emperor's visit, which took place on the market day. This explains what passed. The Arabs, numerous already at the Arc de Triomphe, surrounded the carriage, pressed upon the Emperor, and made it impossible to approach or to move. Throng on throng succeeded with gestures and vociferations. The soldiers even could not restrain them ; they pushed forward petitions ; they uttered, exclaimed, and manifested all the impetuosity of their natural character; in fact, he was fairly taken possession of for some time. At length the carriage was enabled to advance. Of course the demonstration was perfectly undesigned, and harmless, and good humoured ; but in the unexpectedness of the occasion, it may well have caused a doubt and excited a fear. They say that the Emperor on his journey frequently threw money to the Arabs. I do not know it for truth, but he gave large sums at Oran and elsewhere, for the poor, both Mussulmen and Christian."

The summer was passed in missionary labours as opportunity offered. Mr Ogle saw more and more that the work would be a long struggle and a patient waiting. The ground was to be prepared; the seed to be sown; and the watching and weeding would have to be continued unintermittingly for a long time. It helped to sustain our faithful missionary, that he could mark progress in the exterior of social life, since his arrival in Oran. Morality, he believed, was raised, and honesty was more common; in short, the tone of society approximated more nearly to that of Europe, and even of England; and if the Gospel could have been preached, it would, he believed, not have wanted hearers. We trust this is what is in store for Algeria, at no distant day. What has since happened in Spain bids us hope. The seed sown in Algeria will yet spring up, even as that scattered on Iberian soil is now doing.

## CHAPTER XXVIII.

### VISIT TO ENGLAND— SHIPWRECK AND DEATH.

THE summer of 1865, was trying to the health. After harvest, the great heats set in, and the sirocco began at times to blow. Algeria is bounded, on the south, by the Atlas mountains, which run parallel to the line of the Mediterranean, and are a screen to the country from the hot winds which are bred in the fiery atmosphere of the great African deserts in the south. These unwelcome visitors break in at times nevertheless; and this summer they did so more frequently than was pleasant.

These winds feel like the air from the mouth of a furnace : they come loaded with a fine dust, so thick that one mistakes it for a fog. The Arabs, when they see the sirocco approaching, envelope themselves in their bournouses to shut out the dust. Blight marks the track over which it blows. A few minutes suffocating calm, succeeded by squalls of stinging wind; the leaves wither on the tree; the sand-cloud hides the sun, and darkens his light; and the covers of books are shrivelled as if they had been exposed to a strong fire, and if one touches a stone lying on the ground, the skin is taken from the fingers. The sirocco has a most irritating effect upon the nerves : it is remarked, that after a sirocco there is always an increase of quarrels, murders, and suicides. This awful wind acts as a moral as well as a physical poison. In such a climate, it is not surprising that Mr Ogle should have had an attack of Algerian fever, almost every summer, necessitating an all but yearly journey to England. This fever sometimes proves fatal in a few hours, and when happily recovery takes place, it always brings after it, a long and painful weakness. Mr Ogle, this summer, did not escape his usual attack of fever. Repeated doses of quinine brought him round, but the consequent debility made a journey home advisable for him. In the last days of July, he started off for England. He meant his absence to be a short one, and purposed soon to resume his work in the Algerian colony. But our times are wholly in God's hand. His labours in Algeria were ended, and he was to see it no more.

Crossing the Mediterranean, he disembarked at the port of Valencia, intending to pass as usual through Spain, scattering the good seed on his way, for which he had brought with him the requisite supply. But his books were seized in the douane, and he himself was ordered to appear before the police next morning. Not caring to lose both books and his

liberty, he immediately continued his journey and arrived at
the inland town of Segorbé, where we now find him.

" MY DEAR BROTHER,—It is Sabbath, and by the mercy of
God, I find some rest in a strange land.   My chamber is
clean, and airy, and comfortable, the wind rustles through a
grated iron window, which a luxuriant vine curtains.   There is a
beautiful view through the leaves.   Hills of various form which
" stand about " the city at a few miles distant on every side,
recall Jerusalem ;  indeed, Spain and Palestine must be in most
respects identical in climate and productions.   The implements
of agriculture are much the same, and the practice has
so little varied, that in coming here one seems to have gone
twenty centuries backward.   Alas !  Christianity has been so
discarded that it has produced little effect.   I suppose these
countries socially are what the nominal Christian is spiritually.
They have name and form but no power.   The bells are ringing
for service, but it is the mass they unite to celebrate, a
veritable abomination.   There are congregations, but of fanatics
or slaves, no worship of the head, the intelligence, the spirit.
I passed through the busy market this morning, all was active
trade ;  presently a flute and other instruments little in
harmony were heard, then a procession of about thirty old
men in long black cloaks, each with a lighted taper or wax
torch, then followed one bearing a banner with a gilded cross,
ill stuck on and tottering above.   The banner had figures on
it, which I was not near enough to see.   I halted, not to
come in contact with a ceremony, which, in demanding
homage of the hat, offends my feeling.   A woman close by
exclaimed, " Saints of stone."   I took off my hat to her and
her companions, saying, " excuse me, madam, I am your
humble servant, you have the very best of reasons to say
that."   Nothing further passed, I had not opportunity to give
her *light.*   But the remark showed that it is begun, or at
least, that darkness is breaking up.   El Alba, the dawn, just
expresses it.   Oh, what a loss to Spain is the change since

George Borrow could go about with mule loads of Bibles and sell them in the villages. I could dispose of many to advantage, but how to get the copies. You see, I was stopped and nearly caught at Valencia for having 50 copies, a dozen that remain I am seeking to place out to good interest. May Jesus the ruler of this revolted realm, graciously deal with them as with the five barley loaves and fishes of Philip. Oh, how feeble is my faith, this is the grand lack. Alone, among the ten thousands of professing Christians at home who might be at work, I seem to be the only one, and I am so sinful, so weak, so timid, so cold in love and zeal, so deficient in wisdom! My consolation is this, it is God's way to choose the weak things of this world to confound the wise, and things that are not to bring to nought things that are. Of the latter description seem these cities of old Spain, a cathedral, eight churches, two colleges, priests, professors, canons, &c., &c., a whole population, if attached to any religion, to the Catholic Roman. There appears a tangible barrier to the gospel in all this array of enemies, and I confess I am not strong enough to attack it, to go into churches and protest, to give books to priests and ecclesiastics, to declare openly my faith. No, I wander about streets and lanes, and if I see some humble, industrious, intelligent-looking individuals, enter into conversation and leave them a gospel, or perhaps only read a few verses and say a word, when they cannot read.

"I have made acquaintance with a gipsy, not one of Borrow's gipsies. A young man, rather dandy in style, and engaged in jockeying two horses he has with him. We were at the same village-inn on Friday; as I left, I gave him extracts. He came here, and we put up at the same house. At supper he came to my table and seemed curious. I told him a little, but not enough for him, and his conjecture was that I was a Moro. He seemed to have no sort of objection, and when I quickly undeceived him, said, why not? He told me he was Gitano: that the gipsies of Valencia are not the wild people of the old race, but assimilated to Spaniards. I had noticed his gipsy complexion, hair and eyes and occupation, but supposed him a Spaniard whose race is far from pure. In

this place, I have met with a pure Celtic type of men, the very
Irishman over again, the high-crowned hat of coarse manufacture, the jacket and dress of the Irishman of Cork, his
look and stature. The truth of descent locally indicated by
a street close by, Calle de los Celtiberos, (street of the Celts).
How curious to come to Spain to study Irish characteristics, and
yet it would be no bad school in which the true elements of
national character, the habits, inclinations, tastes, modes of
thought, and motives of action, the way to deal with and
influence this impracticable class, identical in Hispania and in
Hibernia, might be learned. One great obstacle with me, is
fear of compromise. I seem not to be able to approach them
on those terms of concession to their state, religiously speaking,
for fear of flattering false notions, or concealing or degrading
the truth. Among the accidental indications of what is going
on, I may mention a half leaf in which my dose of quinine
was wrapped. It runs thus : " We are all fighting for the same
cause, but our enemies are different. The Catholics of
Belgium have no contest but with rationalists or hypocrites.
You (of Germany) contend at once against heresy and impiety.
But very soon you will arrive at the same point in which we
are ourselves. The day of heresies and of sects is past.
Protestantism is in a state of dissolution everywhere, as well
in Germany as in England. There are observable two
opposite currents, one which returning to the fountain, restores
the purity of the Christian faith, and opens the way anew,"
to the true Church from whence they came, is no doubt the
context defective. But what volumes such a leaflet speaks,
volumes for the activity and subtlety of error and of the
supine indifference of the advocates of the pure and true
religion. True, that religion, had it the same encouragement,
the same open doors, would also have its voice and make it
heard, but what infatuation to suppose as we are doing in
England, that the best way to treat Catholics is to let them
alone, that the way to win the battle is to be silent, to yield
when they resist, to hold our peace when they propagate their
falsehoods respecting our very selves. Well may they conclude,
the days of the opponents of the Church of Rome are

numbered ; the Church will soon prevail over her enemies, all will enter her fold, &c. And for the ignorant and unreflecting mass who have no religion, there is a real danger. When they see the progress Rome makes and the helpless and inactive state of Protestant Churches, they will judge the right to the victorious side. To me this appears a probable issue, and I have no confidence in any check being now put to the downward course, but a *most serious and prayerful revival of spiritual religion*, faithful and powerful enough to shake off the weak dependence many of the best Christians in England retain to the deeply corrupted and essentially erroneous Established Church. All seems to me to say she will not reform—abandon her, her lukewarmness, her mixed doctrine, her widely corrupt practice, all indicate that not in her is safety to be found. *It is a defenceless stronghold which will fall at the first stroke into the enemy's power.* Far better be out of Jerusalem in Pella an unarmed village, than in the devoted city. Such are some of my Sabbath thoughts at Segorbé.—Your affectionate Brother,

JOHN F. OGLE."

Continuing his route by Saragossa, Bayonne, and Paris, he reached England in about a week's time. How much the love of his own family circle, and the fellowship of Christian friends refreshed him, we need not say. At home he was not idle. He preached almost every Sabbath at Muston, thus closing his public labours in the proximity of the spot where he had opened them. The annual Conference of the members of the Evangelical Alliance, was this year held at Hull, and being in the neighbourhood, Mr Ogle gladly availed himself of the privilege of attending its meetings, and taking part in its business. He saw in the Alliance a means for healing the breaches among the Protestant Churches of Christendom, which he so greatly deplored. He believed it possible for Protestants to meet on a great common ground, cemented by great common principles, and agreed in great essential truths

without minor differences occasioning the least collision.
The Evangelical Alliance had proved that this is possible.
And being possible, this intercommunion ought to be cultivated
as a means of establishing among Christians a course of
united action against the common foe, and of abating those
dissensions by which the Spirit of God is grieved and provoked to withhold His blessing. With such views, the
meeting of the Alliance in a town in his own county, was
hailed by Mr Ogle with joy, and he prepared to cast into the
great cause his mite of help by contributing a paper on a
subject which had been proposed for treatment, but which had
not been appropriated by any other. This paper, Mr Ogle
read at one of the meetings of the Alliance, and it was much
appreciated as a philosophical yet spiritual discussion of an
important subject—the spirit and manner in which to conduct
missions.

It was here, at Hull, at the Conference of the Evangelical
Alliance, that the present writer had the privilege of making the
acquaintance of Mr Ogle. We were the guests of Dr Sandwith
of that town, and under this hospitable and truly christian roof,
Mr Ogle and myself passed a week together. I was drawn to
him by a resemblance which I thought I perceived in him to
another friend, since deceased, the late Dr John Duncan, of the
New College, Edinburgh. Mr Ogle seemed to possess the same
metaphysical talent which characterised Dr. Duncan ; less
profound it might be, but united with a greater practical
capability. We met every morning and evening at the table of
our kind host, Mr Ogle largely mingling in the conversation,
but with an unobtrusiveness and kindliness, which, united to
his fulness of knowledge, his piety, and his manifest unselfish-
ness of character, won the esteem of all. The hours when
the Alliance was not sitting Mr Ogle generally devoted to
walks in the suburbs, in which he made me accompany him,
and on these occasions he would run on in a vein of philoso-

phical rumination, exactly as Dr Duncan used to do in similar circumstances. I listened to the wisdom Mr Ogle poured out on whatever subject the conversation chanced to turn, whether the business of the Alliance, the questions of the day, or the great enterprise of missions. There was no mistaking the kindliness of his dispositions, the transparency of his character, the depth of his piety, and the catholicity of his sentiments : but above all, towered the one wish of his soul, the conversion of the world to Christ. I have never met any one who won upon me so much in so short a time, and when we parted, I cherished the hope that we had formed a friendship which would be life-long, and from which one of us, myself, was sure to reap no ordinary profit : and so I feel it would have been but for the catastrophe which so suddenly cut it short. Soon after my return to Edinburgh, I had the happiness of receiving a letter from Mr Ogle, and we continued to correspond at short intervals, till he again set out for Algeria. Mr Ogle's letters to me, I find copied out in his sister's hand-writing for insertion in the biography, and I simply fulfil her wishes in giving them a place. They relate to topics of public interest.

"FILEY, *October* 18*th*, 1865.

" MY DEAR DR WYLIE,—I am quite glad of a pretext to renew acquaintance with you. . . . . We may perhaps never meet again on earth, but I trust we shall, through a Saviour's atonement, unite to sing the praise of ' Him that hath loved us.'

" I have been much interested with your book (' Rome and Civil Liberty'). It is clear, and presents so agreeable a contrast to the sophisms which are current, especially in political circles, respecting Popery. You unmask the treason, and if the world will not see and deal with it, the fault lies not at your door. . . . I have an offer to become the editor of the *Church of England Quarterly Review.* It appears to me too great a responsibility to undertake both the editorial and the responsible charge of such a serial ; and I fear there would

not be a good demand for the exponent of those Church of
England views which were the views held by the martyred
Hooper, and of the ejected Puritans, which, alone, I would
advocate.   I do not like *compromise*, and I fear there is
nothing better desired in the Church of England at present.
Still she has had most excellent ministers, very laborious
students, and most learned and most sound theologians—of
the post-Reformation period.   Oh ! that she might be truly
reformed ; reject sacerdotalism and sacramentalism root and
branch ; and hold to her scriptural principles, her creeds, and
her articles.   Evangelical doctrine is a vital point,—' the faith
once delivered to the saints.'—Believe me, my dear Dr, yours
very faithfully and affectionately,          JOHN F. OGLE."

"To the Same.                              "FILEY, *October* 26, 1865.

" . . . I cannot suppose men are not warned.   Some refuse to believe the danger ; others are paralysed with uncertainty ; the most wait, hoping some one will move in the
matter.

" I, for my part, rejoice that the writer of the ' Durham
Letter' is rewarded with the Premiership.   If Lord Russell
had sufficient courage to act as his heart dictates, he would
generally act right, I think.

" No one has ventured to speak so plainly as he, of our
continual dependence on Divine Providence, from his place in
Parliament.

" I have not taken any steps with reference to the *Church
of England Quarterly*.   It seems to me that another serial,
even on the right side, is not wanted.   I shrink both from
the trouble and expense.   Accustomed to read and to express
myself freely on all subjects, religious and political, I have
never had that severe discipline which is requisite for eminence
in literature, and have not sufficient information for editorship
of a Review.   Fred. Myers (of Keswick) says, in one of his
sermons, ' As far as Christianity is concerned, I believe that
learning has done its work, or nearly so.   A deeper reception
of the spirit of the Gospel by the soul, not a more complete comprehension of its significance by the understanding, is wanted.'

" This was a word in season to me fifteen years ago. I was strongly disposed to the intellectual pursuit of truth,—to evidences and controversy,—to the employment of the under-standing in religion. This passage met my eye when I was deeply feeling the distance between heart-reception and head-comprehension, and I gave up prosecuting the second, hoping that the first would profit more.

" Both, I do not doubt, are necessary; and in my late essay for the Evangelical Alliance I urge the use of the intellect as a handmaiden and aid to faith. It is appalling to observe how powerless is a mere intellectual reception of the truth. ' Write thy law upon my heart' is the prayer we need most to offer. I am deeply interested in the discussions respecting inspiration and the limitations thereof, and think that much might yet be written on that topic. The defects in the Scriptures (as we have received them) are parallel to the spots on the sun. ' Thy word is a light,' ' The law of the Lord is perfect.' ' If any man will do his will, he shall know of the doctrine, whether it be of God.' With affection, J. F. O.

" To the Same. " *November.*

" A party, influential and numerous, is trying to turn Hull from its old Protestant spirit. They have got several churches where the truth was once fully preached, and have just opened a new institute, I am told, with a lecture on ' Church Vest-ments.' There is a daily newspaper (the same in which that letter appeared against the Evangelical Alliance) conducted by a reputed Romanist; and I have received, by accident, a copy of the *D— C—* from Liverpool, which has the same leading observations as this Hull paper of the same date. In this paper ' prayers for the dead' and other Romanising practices are openly encouraged; the arrival of Dr Manning was an-nounced with much pomp as ' Welcome to the Archbishop of Westminster ;' and many other signs of the bias of the editor are noticeable, though occasional letters from Protestants (three of my own among others) have been published. I shrink, however, from a tribunal where the judge can carve the evidence and silence the pleaders. For example, a letter

appeared last week from a Hull clergyman, in which he writes
of 'the authority of the Church and *six* general councils,'—
of the Apocrypha as inspired,—of marriage as a sacrament,—
of the 'real presence in the Eucharist,'—of regeneration in
baptism,—that they are set forth by authority by Cranmer,
Ridley, Latimer, and Jewel!    I replied to this, giving *quotations* from Cranmer, and promising similar from all the other
writers named; but my letter is not printed.    A letter, which
is very well expressed, and shows the matter in a true light,
has been admitted, but without *quotations.*

"I have thought of writing a pamphlet, as matter for it is
not lacking, but want my money for other things.    'We must
work while it is day, the night cometh.'    Letters from Algeria
show me that I am wanted there.

"I hear from a friend at Madrid, who has been working
there during the time of the cholera, both for the bodies and
souls of men.    He says, 'By God's mercy every one to
whom I gave the remedy recovered.'    Deo gratias.

"There is an indifference in England respecting the spread
of Popery, and as to evangelical effort that is appalling.    I
have projected an article for a higher class Review,—'The
Judgment of the Universities *re* Gladstone and Disraeli,'—in
support of Lord Russell; showing that the talent, which the
universities can fully appreciate, does not outweigh, even with
those learned bodies, high principle and sound political conduct.    I instance the cession of the Ionian islands as a signal
mistake, and the beginning of a policy of cession which would
strip us of our foreign strategic outposts,—and intend also to
lay heavily on the THEISM of Gladstone's speech at Edinbro.
Greek, and Roman, and mediæval Christianity have nothing
in common but this theistic element.    Carlyle I do not trust
at all, but he has more practical sense than Gladstone, though
it is strangely shrouded in a verbose and Allemanic jargon.
I hope you Scotchmen will teach him to pipe a more homely
tune.

"I preach frequently against Popery and Ritualism, but,
alas!  I am so little spiritual that I fear I may not be accepted
as a combatant.    Pray for me, that I may be one of those

' that overcometh.' In the grace of Christ and the love of the brotherhood, dear Dr W., yours faithfully, J. F. O."

"FOLKESTONE, *December 9th.*

" MY DEAR DR WYLIE,—The post-mark will show you how very near I am to the limits of English soil, and prepare you to hear that the state of my affairs in Algeria obliges me to return thither. I hope it will be only for a short stay, and that I may soon return.

" But to be at home without doing something to check evil is misery, and I can do very little. . . . . Out of my professional sphere here, in England, you can conceive how like a bird without place for the sole of her foot to rest one feels. A deep plot against our reformed religion is clear to me. I do not find Protestants disposed to combine and co-operate cordially against such an aggression. For myself, I could be anything in such a confederacy, but there are many Diotrephes.

" After all, is not our work the preaching of the Gospel ? and our weapon spiritual prayer ? The Gospel of Christ strikes at the root ; we can but lop off the branches of error.

" I want to feel more spirituality and to see it in others.

" A pamphlet has been published by Mr Dick, of Hull, about ' vestments.' He says they are *illegal* as well as undesirable, and I think he proves his point. But as the proof is necessarily negative,—from contrary custom and the absence of legal sanction,—it is not quite so clear as one would wish for the sake of the people. His quotations are very excellent and valuable. There is one—an inventory—which quite sets aside the ' discovery at Wyoming.'

" I am sorry he did not take up the question raised respecting the testimony of the Homilies. My letter was refused, and thus Mr H—'s assertion, that the Homilies teach his five errors, remains without a reply, though it is a most unfair and unfounded statement. The more I study the subject the more I feel the importance of your *exposé* ' of the aggression being made upon our liberties in England by the Papal priesthood.'

" I hope not to be absent long, and to do some work while

absent.—Believe me, dear Dr, yours with respect and affection,        " JOHN F. OGLE."

So far as appear, this and the one that immediately follows, were the last letters that he wrote. We could not have selected one more truly characteristic of the man than this letter of

## A LANDLORD TO HIS TENANT.

FOLKESTONE, near DOVER,
*Dec. 9, 1865.*

" MY DEAR MR KINGSTON,—As I did not get over to Flambrough again to see you, I will write *farewell*, and wish you the compliments of the season with the experience of those spiritual blessings which a due improvement of these anniversaries brings.

Many think the second advent of Christ to reign is near. I would not say a syllable to the contrary; I regret, however, extremely that I come and go without appearing to help forward the preparation for His glorious appearing.

" It is on our knees, with our Bible, very humbly petitioning for light and grace, for more of the Holy Spirit's teaching, and more Christian tempers and dispositions that we shall attain the most in this way.

" The time is a serious one—the cattle plague appears only to increase, and man's efforts are vain. Surely this is a scourge for our national sins.

" ' Seek righteousness, seek meekness, it may be ye may be hid in the day of the Lord's anger.' This text, and that, ' The blood of Jesus Christ cleanseth us from all sin,' I would leave with you. I feel increasingly that if my relation to you be only for this world, we shall both look on it as a miserable mistake at the last. No, my dear friend, I desire to seek first the kingdom of God and His righteousness and our secular duties afterwards. We cannot live without these, and I have no other source of income than my rents. I wish it were otherwise, for then I could do more than I now can for others. I hoped that I would not spend abroad money taken from

England, but earn my living there where I reside. It seems doubtful now whether I can do this unless I live wholly for that object, and I ought not to do that. So if I see no better prospect, I shall wind up my affairs and return home. This is now very probable, and I hope to be in England shortly, whether to stay there or not is doubtful.

"I find no satisfaction either in the church or out of it as a minister, and fear I can never settle so long as things remain as now. But we can both worship God and do much good.

·"My earnest prayer is, that you may be increasingly useful and happy and holy, and your family advance in the best of all senses. Give my special regards to your son Richard, and say I hope he will settle at Flambrough for good. It is my earnest wish that he should regard 'Ocean View' as his *home*. He will never find me lacking in all I can do as a landlord to help and to encourage him.

"I have to request that you will inform my brother when anything is about to be done in the Church, and from time to time what is done. I hope to return within a month if I can settle my affairs so as to leave them. With kind regards to Mrs K. and to Mrs. R., yours very truly,

"JOHN F. OGLE."

The melancholy sequel we extract and translate from *L'Echo d'Oran*, as given in a Marseilles paper of 29th December :—

"*Account of the Wreck of the Borysthène, extracted from L'Echo d'Oran, December 19th, 1865.*

"The report of a frightful catastrophe was brought last Saturday, which has cast desolation amid the population of our city. The steamer Borysthène, carrying the mails between Marseilles and Oran, was lost in the night before, upon the island of Plane, just opposite the Andalusian plain, 20 kilometres west of Oran, about ten o'clock P.M. This news . . . was brought to Oran at two o'clock P.M., by an officer from the steamer, who was taken by a bark belonging to some 'corailleurs' (who were by chance upon the scene of the accident), and was put on shore at Cape Falcon. The report of this officer was but vague, so much was he overcome by what he had suffered. The number of sufferers is computed to be forty persons."

There is a painful absence of particulars, at least so far as to explain how it was that our beloved brother was among the forty who were lost. There were about three hundred on board. It is just possible that this volume may come into the hands of some one who is able to supply * some incidents of his last acts and words. Faint echoes of them have reached us. How "the man of God stood with his Bible in his hand, calm in the midst of confusion." How his cry from the waves to a poor Spaniard whom he had promised to befriend was heard but . . . . . ! Enough to awaken an intense desire to know more.

Pasteur Laune of Oran in writing to announce the afflictive intelligence, concludes with these touching words :—

"What I know is, that your brother was not of this world; he had neither the spirit, nor the heart, nor the tastes, nor the manners of this world. He was a man of heaven, a brother—a Christian of whom we were not worthy, and whom God has called, to give him, near to Himself, a good and a high place. He possessed the affection and esteem of all who knew him in Oran. He was a fruit ripe for heaven ! Do not weep, he rests from his labours and his works follow him."

---

## CHAPTER XXIX.

### CHARACTER OF REV. J. F. OGLE.

In the foregoing pages we have adopted the plan of permitting the subject of our memoir to be his own biographer. If the story of Mr Ogle's life is before the reader it is from the pen of Mr Ogle himself. Not that he intended to produce an

---

* Communications will be thankfully received by "Dr Ogle, Derby."

autobiography : nothing was further from his thoughts : but he did it, we may say, unwittingly in the letters which he was every week sending home.   These letters were penned in every variety of situation, on board ship at sea, in some auberge of the Alps, under an oleander bush in the Algerian desert, or at night as he rested after the day's toil, while the bright African moon shone in at the open casement.   They were written too in every variety of circumstance.   Did he rejoice ? he seized his pen and permitted his friends in England to share his gladness : was he in sorrow ? he sought relief by unbosoming his sadness to the loved circle at home.   But beyond that circle the writer did not once dream that these letters would have interest to any one, or that they would ever be scanned by other eyes than those of the members of his own family. He wrote, therefore, as he felt ; he put off all reserve : he unbosomed himself entirely ; he unveiled faithfully his motives and wishes, his strength and his weakness ; and thus his letters eminently excel in the quality of transparency ; showing us to the very bottom of the writer's soul, and permitting us, without the least difficulty, to judge of what manner of man he was.

And, unless we greatly mistake, there will be but one opinion on that head.   He was a true man, to use a modern phrase, which never was more applicable than in the case of Mr Ogle.   In all positions, and tried by every test, he was true.   He was true in his parsonage in England ; and not less so in the wilds of the Falklands ; and in the heat and weariness and hunger of Algeria.   Whether solicited by home comforts or subjected to loss, or wronged by mis-construction, or persecuted by power, or stoned by savages—and we have seen him in all these conditions—he was true—true to duty, —true to the great object, to which, at the call of God, he had devoted his life.   We, therefore, make no superfluous addition to the already long roll of christian biographies when we bring this new name to swell the list. A more unselfish and heroic course of life it were hardly possible to imagine than that which passes before us in the foregoing pages. Moreover, neither the character nor the incidents amid which that character was developed are at all of the common type, and its contemplation is fitted to excite to greater devotion, self-denial, and activity, those who are still on earth amid the trials, the pleasures, and the labours through which their brethren whose race is run have more or less successfully passed.

The nobility and self-denial of Mr Ogle's character mainly grew out of his conversion. That heavenly graft is necessary in order to the attainment of the highest style of man. Grace sometimes effects a radical change of the natural dispositions : it makes the churl liberal and the cowardly brave. But Mr Ogle was by nature generous and magnanimous ; and what his conversion to God did for him was to develope these qualities into greater robustness and to sanctify them to nobler ends. At what time this great change was accomplished upon the subject of our memoir we do not know : but the *reality* of it is well attested. His whole life, so profitable to man, so honouring to God, was the proof of it. From his childhood his memory had been stored with Scripture truth, as the result of careful parental instruction, and it is not improbable that it was then by the quiet action of the truth, in the hand of the Spirit, that he was translated from darkness into light. But he was called at a subsequent period of his life to wage a great conflict. The darkness returned : he was exercised with terrible doubts, assailed by strong temptations, and he sunk into almost despair. These sufferings befell him, he tells us, as the result of his slothfulness and pride of intellect. He ceased to seek God by appointed means : he became self-indulgent, and permitted himself to be entangled in the oppositions of science, falsely so called, and, turning his face away from God, God withdrew from him the light of His countenance. In the season of misery that followed he was made to feel how void his own understanding was of light, and how barren his own heart was of happiness, and that, would he enjoy either, he must keep near to God. It may be that he had come too easily at first into the possession of peace: and needed to have his convictions of sin deepened, and his hold of a Saviour strengthened by this storm. At any rate it had this blessed effect upon him. He emerged from the fiery trial with a deeper perception than he ever had before of the fallen nature of man, of the strength of the foundations of Christianity, and the sovereignty and freeness of the grace of God in the matter of man's salvation. Thus was he fortified for the great trials that were before him in his public life, and qualified to sympathise with those whom he met with passing through the same terrible temptations. He could now say, " I know in whom I have believed."

Conscientiousness was another prominent quality in this character. This cardinal virtue shone conspicuously in every transaction of his life. All his dealings with his fellowmen were marked by sincerity, by candour, and a most scrupulous integrity. But especially did this attest itself in the part he acted in the matter of his public religious profession. At an early stage of his ministerial career he detected the inroads which Popish doctrine was making in the Church of England, and he lamented that a pretext should be furnished by certain expressions in the Baptismal service to those whose natural dispositions or whose concealed purposes lead them Romeward. He gave himself with assiduity to the study of the Fathers and the Reformers, and the more he read, the more convinced he became that the doctrines taught in the articles of the Church of England were in harmony with the Word of God. Indeed, he felt that it had been given to the Reformers of England to carry their scheme of reformation to a wondrous perfectability. But there was one defect in their execution which deformed the beauty and marred the success of their noble work : they had erred in leaving one of Rome's seminal doctrines in their system ; they had used expressions in the liturgy which fairly interpreted imply that an inward grace is indissolubly united with an outward form. He thought that the generation which succeeded the first reformers ought to have remedied this defect, and completed their work. This, however, had never been done : the leaven was still in the lump, it was doing its deadly work of corruption ; and the melancholy traces of this were but too visible. So far as his influence extended, Mr Ogle exerted himself for the adoption of measures for purging the liturgy and stemming the declension which had set in so strongly, and which, if allowed to go on, would issue, he foretold, in a universal corruption of doctrine. But as year passed after year and nothing was done his hopes of reformation became less sanguine, and his fears increased in the same proportion for the future ot his church and country. He waited five years deeply exercised in mind on this subject, at last the matter so pressed upon his conscience that he could no longer minister with comfort as a beneficed clergyman of the Church of England, and he resigned his living.

The step was evidently a very painful one to Mr Ogle ; but not the slightest tincture of spiritual pride, or of opinionativeness, or love of singularity entered into this act : he did it in all sincerity and single-mindedness at the call of conscience. He had many ties binding him to the Church of England. His fathers had ministered in that church : he might reasonably have looked for preferment in it, he had the prospect of large usefulness in it ; but all these considerations he subordinated to his sense of duty. He would not eat the bread of a church the liturgy of which he could not *ex animo* subscribe. He did not wish that his conduct should be viewed as reflecting in the slightest on others, he admitted that others, though like himself, condemning the popish tendencies of the baptismal service, might conscientiously come to a different conclusion as to duty. He judged himself only ; and that he felt constrained by the highest considerations to the step which he now took, is evident from what it cost him.

But he never repented of the step. He had frequent occasions, in after life, to review this decision, but it was always to express his growing convictions that he could not have acted otherwise than he did. His only regret was that he had not done it sooner. So far from the course of deformation being checked, it seemed to him to be flowing with a continually growing tide, and though his love for his church never suffered abatement, and though once and again, the question was brought before him whether he would re-enter the service of the Church of England, his reply uniformly was, this was not to be thought of, and that the impediments were greater than ever. He writes (October 1862), " Were the Church of England open to me, I should, though with a deep sense of unworthiness, desire to be one of the Lord's hired servants therein, but *it is not;* and I cannot now afford to spend money to try and make it so ; " (alluding perhaps to pecuniary aid which he desired to give to such agencies as the Liturgical Revision Society) " the way which seems clear for me is Algeria." Did he therefore bemoan his hard lot, banished far from the land and church of his fathers, shut out from the dignified positions and honoured labours for which he was so eminently qualified, and compelled to work in obscurity and comparative poverty abroad ? No. He forgot his own sorrows entirely in the prospect of the greater sorrows which he saw impending over his country. What a noble patriotism breathes in the following words, written in January 1863. " I have spent so much that I am now poor, but the troubles hanging over my country press upon my mind far more than any of my own. Were her prospects bright for peace and truth I would be poor and happy, but if I foresee the ruin of my native land, the destruction of her religion, and of her ascendancy as a Protestant country among the nations, the growth of Popery, the want of wisdom in councils, and no sense of the perils impending, then I must be sad and look forward to troublous times!" These words remind us of another patriot, who, when asked by his royal master, "Why is thy countenance sad, seeing thou art not sick?" made answer, "Why should not my countenance be sad, when the city, the place of my fathers' sepulchres, lieth waste, and the gates thereof are consumed with fire?"

Another conspicuous trait in Mr Ogle's character was his heroism and independence of mind. We refer not now to oceans crossed and barbarous lands traversed; that is a daring of a not unfrequent type in our day. We speak here of heroism of soul. Without the slightest conceit, or wish to stand apart from others or above others, he cherished a noble independence of the world's judgment, and formed his own opinion on the most various subjects. With an originality and perseverance, as remarkable as his transparent simplicity, he worked out for himself many of the problems of life. He never could take things for granted, or yield to the authority of mere custom where he saw an important principle involved. Not only did he refuse to bow the knee to the modern idol of liberalism—a goddess who has so many servants ready, whether to sing the praises of all who will but throw a grain of incense upon her altar, or launch anathemas at those who refuse their homage—not only in this regard did Mr Ogle stand nobly upright; but he displayed a single-eyed adherence to what he accounted duty, even when visited with the misconstruction of men whose good opinion he valued. Another remarkable feature in Mr Ogle's character was his marvellous power of sympathy. He seemed able to understand the heart and enter into the feelings of every one he came in contact with, be his class, his character, his nation what it might.   His genuine, loving, all-embracing humanity was a special gift.   It was by this influence that he acted on men, and drew them to himself.   It was impossible to be in his company for only a few minutes without feeling its attraction.   The Spaniard, the Moor, men of every nation and of every creed, felt it and responded to it.   They felt that this man was laying his heart alongside theirs, that he was making their joys his joys, their griefs his griefs ; that he was sinking every point of difference and contrariety between himself and them, and approaching them simply in his character of a brother-man, and they, in like manner, drew to him on the same footing.   Thus it was that he was perfectly at home amid their encampments in the wilderness, and never did he present himself at the door of an Arab's tent but it was to meet a cordial welcome as a friend, or rather as a brother.

He was also endowed to an uncommon degree with self-denial, which amounted to self-forgetfulness.   In a remarkable degree he lived for others.   In small as in great matters this beautiful trait is seen.   Not only did he embrace opportunities of doing good to others when they offered, but he sought for such opportunities, and when he found them, he manifested a delight which shewed that he had no higher joy than to minister to the distressed.   As a boy he was always generous, and ready to help the weak, the defenceless, and the oppressed. As he grew to manhood this characteristic grew, so that wherever he went, to be in want, danger, or distress of any kind was sure to call forth from him both pity and the most self-sacrificing efforts.   The story of Captain Gardiner's love for the poor Patagonians, moved him to give £500 (though he had to borrow it at the time) to the S. A. Society when in difficulty, and then to offer himself : and the same spirit actuated him on lesser occasions.   In the winter of the Falklands we find him sharing his warm clothing with a shipwrecked mariner, and he tells with thankfulness, as an evidence of the providential care of his Heavenly Father, that on opening a box which arrived there soon after he found a coat ready, not for himself, but for his poor neighbour. In Algeria we find him in like manner hastening to supplement the lack of comforts experienced at their hotel by some English travellers who were not so used to rough it as he was. So again, at Oran, he gives up his apartments to the American missionary and his family, on their arrival, thinking it naught that he himself must live for weeks in what was little better than a cellar. Of a like merciful character were his visits to the Morocco chief in prison, to whom he tenderly and affectionately ministered so long as he was permitted access to him. He never sought great things for himself, but his affectionate nature, upheld by genuine courage, ever prompted him to take the place of greatest difficulty and risk. In the path of duty he was destitute of fear. On recovering from a succession of attacks of Algerian fever, he went, contrary to the advice of some French friends, to visit the camp of French soldiers assembled according to the Emperor's custom in Algeria, previous to their embarkation for Mexico. He distributed to them Testaments and Bibles, and wrote home, "Tell the British and Foreign Bible Society, that if they want a man for Mexico, I can find them two; for I am sure dear Don F—— (the Spanish ex-priest) would go with me. I have no fear either of the French or of the Mexican forces. With a single guide I would set out alone, and go to Mexico itself if I were only landed on the coast, and furnished with what is barely necessary for my expenses." In England, in like manner, we find him going freely into the fever-haunted cottages at N——, in one of which lay a family of seven, sick of the fever, and with his own hand administered the restoratives to the patients. This probably was the secret of the devotion toward himself with which he never failed to inspire even those who needed not his help.

They saw in Mr Ogle a man who loved others, and strove to bless them from no mere sense of duty, but from a spontaneous ever-welling sympathy within him ; and all that he himself endured of pain and distress and sorrow, did but the more re-fine and enlarge a disposition which in the case of too many evaporates in mere sentiment, but in this case ever developed into manly effort. His sympathy did not flow off by the eye in tears, nor by the tongue in good words, but by the hand in solid deeds. He had drank deep into the Spirit of Him who "although He was rich, yet for our sakes He became poor, that we through His poverty might be rich."

Again, we have in these pages an example of a true mis-sionary spirit. If conscience forbade Mr Ogle to continue in the ministry of the Church of England, other walks of honour-able and lucrative labour were nevertheless open, these he refrained from entering, and chose to go afar off and "preach among the gentiles the unsearchable riches of Christ." He did not care to build on another man's foundation, he sought out new ground. Leaving the loves of home, the comforts of British society, he went first to the distant and uninviting Falklands, and next to the nearer but more barbarous Algeria. And God, who had given him this loving missionary spirit kept it alive by His grace throughout all his life in foreign lands ; and how much that grace is needed to maintain the christian tone and temper of one's spirit in a heathen country, those only who have passed some considerable part of their lives abroad can understand. There may be a difference of opinion among our readers as to the plan pursued—combining to so large an extent, agricultural with missionary operations in Algeria. It entangled him in cares, it subjected him to losses, it exposed him to worldliness of mind, and in the issue it failed. But as he himself always said it was "a secular expedient to gain a missionary end." Candidly judged the idea was radically sound and practical. As a colonist his

access to the population, and his influence over them was a
hundred times greater than as a simple missionary.   He wished
besides to provide an asylum and livelihood for persecuted
Spanish converts.   Nobly did he plan and work and wait to
make his philanthropic scheme a success.   He mortgaged part
of his patrimony, he incurred heavy responsibilities, he made
himself poor, and it was not till he saw that the host of evils
—the drought of the seasons, the unfaithfulness of workmen, and
the unfriendliness of government—were too many to be overcome, that he resolved to relinquish his generous idea.   The
point, however, which most concerns us to record, is that in
the midst of these avocations he never lost sight of his missionary purpose.   In the fields, at meal hours, and in the
evenings he laboured for the spiritual good of his dependents.
He distributed tracts and Bibles in the towns, and sought
opportunities of conversing with the population—French,
Spanish, and Moorish—that he might kindle some rays of light
in that dark land, and convey to its inhabitants, perishing for
lack of knowledge, the tidings of the life eternal.   Nor was
he neglectful the while of his own mental culture.   His
labours a-field, manual and missionary, occupied him till
dinner time.   At 7 p.m. he made his frugal repast.   So frugal
that it always seemed to his friends, when he returned to
England, as if, remembering everything else, he completely
forgot to eat.   Bread and coffee was often his sole provision
for the day.   The meal finished, works on theology, or the
classics, or the periodicals of the day were then brought forth,
and he continued to read and study till, often-times, it was far
into the morning.   Thus, despite all the draw-backs of his
position, Mr Ogle was able to cultivate his theological and
literary tastes, and keep abreast of his age.

Hence, no doubt, it was that he possessed more than ordinary conversational powers.   He was full and ready.   He owed
the former to his much reading and thinking, the latter to his

mingling with men. Without monopolising the talk he could converse on all subjects because he took interest in all—art, poetry, politics, the topics of the day. In argument he was fair and patient, seeking not to triumph but to persuade, and in no danger, from his never failing gentleness and courtesy of spirit, to be drawn into heat or asperity. But whatever might be the occasion or the theme of converse, it might always be seen that the ruling sentiment of his heart was the fear of God. His piety ever discovered itself in the most natural way. He had a hatred of conventionality, an abhorrence of cant, a love of simplicity, a longing to escape from what is artificial in life, and to emerge into the ease of nature and truthfulness. With all this freedom he was not neglectful of the rules and proprieties of civilized society ; on the contrary, he put a high value on these, and was studious to observe them ; knowing that if at times these conventionalities contract the flow and check the expression of what is good and generous, they oftener repress the manifestation of what is unkind and evil.

He had a most firm faith in the gospel which he preached. In his youth, we have seen, he was tried as by fire : these terrible siftings led him to examine "the foundations" anew ; the result was a deeper conviction than ever, and from that time not a shade of doubt respecting the truth of Christianity appears to have passed across his mind. We find him at times despondent, but the doubts he expresses on these occasions respect not the truth of the Gospel but his own personal interest in its blessings. In the Gospel he had a firm impregnable faith : it was "no cunningly devised fable," no system of man's device, like those which have, from time to time, received the world's homage and passed away ; as Platonism in early days, and mysticism and illumination in modern times ; but a system dating from the dawn of history and destined to last to its close, and to furnish new proofs with each new age, that it comes from God, that it exerts on man and on society a divine influence, and is to be preached unto all nations as the only instrumentality for conquering the vice of civilized lands, and the barbarism of heathen regions, and blessing man both now and hereafter. Mr Ogle therefore was not one of those who feel alarm when, in the words of Dr Chalmers, "the torch of science, or the torch of history is held up to the Bible." He believed with Sir David Brewster, "that truths physical have an origin as divine as truths religious," and could say with Dr Pye Smith, "the Bible faithfully interpreted erects no barrier against the most free and extensive investigation, the most comprehensive and searching induction. Let but the investigation be sufficient, and the induction honest, let observation take its furthest flight, let experiment penetrate into all the recesses of nature, let the veil of ages be lifted up from all that has been hitherto unknown, religion need not fear. True science will always pay homage to the Divine Creator, and to the Divine revelation of His Word."

Nor can we close without adverting to the humility of Mr Ogle. Humble must all be whom the Spirit has taught that lost by sin they must be "saved by grace," but some possess this fruit of the Spirit in larger measure than others. Over all that he was and did Mr Ogle was ever studious to draw a veil. Even in his letters to his sister he maintains great reserve as to his professional labours, and the good by which they were followed, so that it is not very easy to discover the actual amount of work which he did in the mission field.

Though abundant in labours, he is always lamenting that he does so little. Accountable to no society, and therefore at liberty to form his own plans, and to go to an expenditure in carrying them out, which might not have been prudent in the case of those who are accountable for the funds of others, he did his work as under the eye of the Great Task-master, and was therefore as assiduous as if he had to send in his monthly or quarterly report to a committee, but unfortunately not so explicit in his narrative. This spiritual modesty increased as he advanced in life. We trace it in his growing submission to the will of God, and his deepening sense of personal unworthiness, shown in touching confessions of his shortcomings, and ardent breathings for greater holiness. These feelings send him anew to the fountain of grace and strength, and thus he renews his age. He looks steadily upward, having thus continually in his eye the heights he has yet to climb, and which he pants to gain. Till these shall have been gained he will not glory. And in so far as they are gained, he glories not, for then his humility is perfected, and he casts his crown at the feet of Him who gave it, and who alone is worthy to receive praise, and blessing and honour.

That a man of his stamp, endowed with these powers and graces—many of them not common, and some of them possessed in very uncommon measure—should have been led to work in such obscurity, and that he should have been so suddenly taken away, may seem mysterious. But is it not rather to be regarded on the one hand as an explicit declaration of the most High that he doeth as it pleaseth Him with His own, and needs not the assistance of any of us, and on the other hand is there not here an incidental and striking proof that there are other chief workers in the Lord's vineyard than those who are ordinarily accounted such, men, aye, and women too, who receive their orders from on high, and execute them without the intervention of any other authority or sanction? Faith in cut and dried organisation is one of the great snares of the present day, especially ensnaring to Christian Churches. An example therefore of the power of an individual, and of the advantages of independent action, subordinated only to Christian principle is as opportune as it is suggestive—and not the less suggestive that it is found in the ranks of an ordained minister of the Church of England.

If we may venture to commend this memoir to one class of readers more than to another, it will be to those true and faithful members of the Church of England who can see and who mourn and pray over her Romish tendencies. They may learn here that their fears are not groundless, that their suspicions of 'sacramental' teaching and symbolic formalities are not one whit too lively, and hence they may perceive in what direction their best energies may be spent; and last, not of least importance to themselves, they may be encouraged to hope that if they proceed only in the spirit of humble prayer they may not only *protest* to some purpose, but also act in accordance with their own strong convictions without producing a *schism*.

Never was there greater reason for Christians of all churches to pray:—

Grant to us Lord we beseech Thee, the spirit to think and do always such things as be rightful; that we who cannot do anything that is good without Thee, may by Thee be enabled to live according to Thy will, through Jesus Christ our Lord. Amen.

IN MEMORY OF

## THE REV. JOHN FURNISS OGLE, M.A.,

ELDEST SON OF THE REV. J. F. OGLE, M.A., VICAR OF BOSTON, LINCOLNSHIRE, WHO WAS BORN A.D., 1823, AND WAS LOST AT SEA, DEC. 15, 1865, OFF THE COAST OF ORAN, IN ALGERIA, WHERE HE HAD FOR SOME YEARS BEEN ENGAGED IN A MISSIONARY ENTERPRISE. HE WAS FOR FIVE YEARS THE BELOVED MINISTER OF THIS PARISH, TO WHICH HIS ANCESTORS CAME FROM NORTHUMBERLAND, ABOUT THE MIDDLE OF THE 16TH CENTURY. HE ENDEARED HIMSELF TO ALL BY HIS GENEROSITY AND BY HIS AFFECTIONATE ANXIETY FOR THEIR SPIRITUAL AND TEMPORAL GOOD, BY THE GRACE OF GOD HE WAS ONE WHO COUNTED NOT HIS LIFE DEAR UNTO HIMSELF, SO THAT HE MIGHT MAKE KNOWN UNTO SINNERS THE GOOD TIDINGS OF THE GOSPEL OF OUR LORD JESUS CHRIST.

"THEY THAT SAY SUCH THINGS DECLARE PLAINLY THAT THEY SEEK A COUNTRY : A BETTER COUNTRY, THAT IS, AN HEAVENLY." Heb. xi. 14. 16.

"BE YE ALSO READY : FOR IN SUCH AN HOUR AS YE THINK NOT, THE SON OF MAN COMETH." Matt. xxiv. 44.

TABLET IN SOUTH AISLE OF FLAMBOROUGH CHURCH.

THOSE who have familiarized themselves with the history of that mission, which the subject of this Memoir so earnestly endeavoured to promote, will be well aware of the difficulties with which it has at all times been beset. And yet, when we look back on the Keppel Island Station, we cannot but feel that God was with that initiatory work. The first fruits were reaped when Mr Stirling brought the four Fuegian boys to England in 1865. One of them, baptized by the name of John Allan Gardiner, gave evidence before his death of the deepest love to Christ.

Another great step was taken when Mr Stirling was led, in 1869, to reside alone, for seven months, at Ushuwia, in Tierra del Fuego. This paved the way for a regular mission settlement there, under the Rev. Thomas Bridges, who, after thirteen years' residence at Keppel Island, was ordained in London, and has now, with the assistance of a catechist, been working for more than two years among the very Indians for whose salvation Captain Gardiner and Mr Ogle had yearned.

The most recent tidings announce the baptism of thirty-six natives,* the marriage of seven couples, and still more cheering is it to be informed that prayer meetings are being held and conducted by the Fuegians themselves.

But the salvation of the Indians is not the only end which our dear brother had in view, and which has been in some measure realized.

Mr Ogle, in more than one letter, mentions the destitute condition of the many thousands of our own countrymen living in that

* " *South American Missionary Society,*
11, *Sergeants' Inn, Fleet Street,*
*London, 31st May* 1872.

" MY DEAR SIR,—I have the gratification of informing you that a most suitable lad, son of one of the youths brought to England by Bishop Stirling, has been baptised in your late esteemed brother's name—one of thirty-six Fuegian natives (adult and young) baptized at the recent visit of Bishop Stirling to Ushuwia, where there is a deep religious awakening, through the blessing of the Holy Spirit, amongst the natives, they meeting together for earnest prayer in their own tongue. To the Lord we must give all praise and glory.

" Believe me, my dear sir, yours most truly,
C. R. DE HAVILLAND."

Dr. Ogle.

vast continent ; and this thought weighed heavily on the heart of his beloved companion, Allan Gardiner, the younger, so that in 1861, he commenced his work among the Lota Miners—a work which he continued with great success for seven years.

This was the beginning of an entirely new branch of operations, and stations were rapidly formed at various places.   On the west coast, among the miners and traders ; and, on the east, among the farmers and planters.   Within ten years the following places have been occupied :—Lota, Santiago, Coquimbo, Arica and Tacna, the Chincha Island, Callao, Panama, Patagones, Rosario, Barracas, Colonia, Fray Bentos and Paysandu, Salto, San Paulo and Santos.   A Pioneering expedition has also been undertaken on the river Amazon and its tributaries, to carry the gospel to the Aborigines and the English settlers in that vast river-basin.   The appointment of Dr Stirling as Bishop of the Falklands is a further step in the progress of the mission.

It was Mr Ogle's cherished hope to see the Patagonian Missionary Society burst the narrow limits of Keppel island, and embrace in the sphere of its evangelizing labours the South American Continent. In labouring for this end, it may be truly said that he sowed in tears ; and now in the good providence of God others have followed who are more than fulfilling his most sanguine expectations.

The word of God is fulfilled to this South American mission, "THEY THAT SOW IN TEARS SHALL REAP IN JOY."

TURNBULL AND SPEARS, PRINTERS, EDINBURGH.